DARK MATTER PRESENTS:

THE OFF-SEASON

AN ANTHOLOGY OF COASTAL NEW WEIRD

CONTENT WARNING

This anthology contains content that may be unsuitable for certain audiences.

Reader discretion is advised.

Edited by Marissa van Uden
Book Design and Layout by Rob Carroll
Cover Art by Sylvia Strijk
Cover Design by Rob Carroll

ISBN 978-1-958598-24-5 (paperback)
ISBN 978-1-958598-67-2 (eBook)

darkmatter-ink.com

DARK MATTER PRESENTS:

THE OFF-SEASON

AN ANTHOLOGY OF COASTAL NEW WEIRD

EDITED BY

MARISSA VAN UDEN

DARK MATTER PRESENTS

THE OFF-SEASON

AN ANTHOLOGY OF COASTAL NEW WEIRD

EDITED BY

MARISSA VAN UDEN

DARK
MATTER
INK

For the coasts, the coastal wildlife, and all the humans who protect them.

CONTENTS

THUMBS UP
Anna Lewis

EACH-UISGE
Dave V. Riser

DUALHAVEN
C. H. Pearce

INTRODUCTION

Marissa van Uden

THE COAST IS a weird place. It's the margin between the familiar world we know and the unknown deep, where the ordinary drops away into a world of alien physics, beautiful grotesque creatures, and mysterious minds. On the coast, the real becomes unreal. The wind warps trees into strange shapes. Sounds carry differently. Eerie mists roll in, enveloping entire towns and cutting off the senses we rely on. What better place to set stories of the New Weird?

Within, you will find secondary-world fantasies in the classic New Weird style of China Mieville's *Bas-Lag* universe (is the genre old enough to have classics yet?), eco-horror and boiling hot cli-fi, cosmic-resort horror, colonial-capitalist horror, and a range of literary styles from maximalist and experimental to the kind of minimalist prose that unsettles with its calm, direct delivery. The stories feature characters and perspectives that have been rare in more traditional genres, and explore themes such as identity, climate and ecological degradation, tourism gentrification, exploitation, loss and longing, and our relationships with other species and each other. Every piece was exhilarating to find and read.

The New Weird genre has been growing in popularity recently, reaching new readers who might not have heard of it before, and with that new interest the genre is gently flexing and reshaping itself. For this anthology, it was important to me to honor the roots of the New Weird, not to dilute it with such loose interpretations that it becomes indistinguishable from its neighboring genres; but also to explore its full range, to see how newer writers are interpreting this space and exploring what it can do. My goal was to put together a mosaic of diverse voices and imaginations that show all the facets of the genre as it is today.

For those still discovering the New Weird, definitions may be in order. I want to say up front that I don't buy into the popular but narrow-minded idea that genres are mere marketing tools or gate-keeping labels. Sure, there are people with agendas who use genres that way, but that doesn't describe what genres actually are, which is so much more expansive and interesting.

To me, genres are like ecosystems with identifiable features and inhabitants we can point to. As in nature, these ecosystems are linked together through a flow of energy (our culture's current fears, dreams, politics, and challenges) and nutrient cycles (the types of stories told and retold within them, all in timeless conversation with each other). Like in nature, the boundaries are permeable, and ideas from other genres can cross over and migrate through the landscape, changing what's there.

If the New Weird is an ecosystem, it's a small and specialized niche where the edges of three genres overlap: science fiction, horror, and fantasy. It is definitely not a blending of the whole of those genres, but a strange intertidal zone where a few particular elements of each one overlap and infiltrate each other.

From fantasy, it is the urban, secondary-world fantasy. From science fiction, it is the New Wave (a 1960s British-influenced blending of SF and fantasy that subverted mainstream tropes and focused more on outsider characters and the inner worlds of the mind) mixed with eco-fiction or clifi, which focuses on the natural world and environment. And from horror, it is the grotesque (body horror and distortions of so-called "normal") and of course, Weird fiction.

Weird fiction is the corner of horror that rejects traditional monsters, slasher/shock scares, and known terrors in favor of the inexplicable, the unsettling, and a terrible, sublime awe. As Mark Fisher says in *The Weird and the Eerie*, "In many ways, a natural phenomenon such as a black hole is more weird than a vampire...the very generic recognizability of creatures such as vampires and werewolves disqualifies them from provoking any sensation of weirdness." The strangeness of supernatural entities belongs to a realm beyond nature. "Compare this to a black hole: the bizarre ways in which it bends space and time are completely outside our common experience, and yet a black hole belongs to the natural-material cosmos—a cosmos which must therefore be much stranger than our ordinary experience can comprehend."

In the genre-defining anthology *The New Weird*, edited by Jeff and Anne Vandermeer, Jeff describes the New Weird as having a "visceral, in-the-moment quality that often uses elements of surreal or transgressive horror for its tone, style, and affects" and notes that the stories are "acutely aware of the modern world, even if in disguise, but not always overtly political. As part of this awareness of the modern world, New Weird relies for its visionary power on a 'surrender to the weird.'" This surrender to the weird is another of the key things my reading team and I looked for when putting together this anthology.

All the elements mentioned above make New Weird the perfect genre to explore what it means to be human as part of the natural world, and the horror, weirdness, and beauty of that. It's a space to reject the idea that we are separate from nature, as many like to pretend, and embrace the truth that we are an inextricable part of it.

Anyone who loves a coastal area knows it's one of those places we can feel this connection the strongest. There's an alchemic mystery to this wild boundary, where something in our DNA calls to us. It's also now a place of grief, because our coasts are under such threat. We're living in a profound time for our planet's species, standing witness to a massive global destruction of natural ecosystems and therefore of ourselves—and it's all caused by a very small group of profiteering, short-sighted leaders and corporations who have way too much power. They want us to feel hopeless and blame each other, but we should never forget the reason they want that: it's to paralyze us with infighting and helplessness, because they know that together we have so much more power than them.

The way to save our coasts, and the natural world, is to gather our friends, neighbors, and communities together to force change. We must demand investigations and harsh consequences for climate corruption while physically protecting every tiny scrap of nature within our personal reach. Because altruistic humanity, which is the vast majority of us, is nowhere near as helpless as that tiny group of parasitic billionaires wants us to believe.

I hope you get to stand on a beautiful coast soon and feel that power. And I hope you feel that same energy and power running like a strong undercurrent through the extraordinary stories in this collection.

May your local coasts always teem with life, your forests always know rain, and your reading stay weird.

⚓

ALL THE TRUTH THE OCEAN HOLDS

J. P. Oakes

THE JÄÄTYNYT OCEAN lapped blackly at a seaweed-slick dock. Felix Keller shivered.

"So, you're the man they sent from the city?" Bruno Braun, the manager of the newly constructed *vodnyy uzhas* processing plant here in far-flung Ouluskylä, looked at Felix as if he had ordered steak and received minced liver.

"Why don't you show me where it happened?" Felix said.

Bruno Braun kept squinting at Felix. The man had skin like bark, all whorls and knots. He stumped away, leading Felix into the plant. "They're all savages up here, of course," he said without turning. "Not men of culture like you and I."

Scents of brine and offal assaulted Felix's nostrils. Locals hunched over benches all around them, butchering the vodnyy uzhas. Blood shimmered like oil. Discarded tentacles and strange hand-like protrusions were scattered around their feet. None of them looked up.

"You suspect Selazzi worshipers?" Felix asked.

Bruno Braun stopped and turned. His lip curled. Felix wondered if the man was about to strike him. "This is very far from home," he said, as if Felix was unaware that he had spent three days traveling by rail through increasingly small member nations of the Concord until he arrived here in Ouluskylä on the northern coast, only two miles from an unprotected border with the Selazzi regime.

The Selazzi had landed almost fifty years ago—vast aliens who had traveled untold eons before making landfall. Now, half the world worshiped them as gods, while the other half tried to keep their sanity intact. Up in Ouluskylä, Felix knew, the border with the regime was permeable. Things slipped through: monsters, horrors, creatures like the vodnyy uzhas. But recently, someone in some lab back home had discovered that the vodnyy uzhas contained oils worth more than gold. So, a processing plant had been built—an industrial jewel—and Bruno Braun had been sent to manage it. And now, Felix had arrived to help him solve a problem.

Braun took him to that problem: a twisted ruin of black metal.

"Dynamite," Felix said, examining the damaged oil press. "In a barrel."

"I don't care *how* they did it," Braun said. "Just *who* did it."

"Selazzi wor—"

"They're all fucking Selazzi worshipers up here," Braun growled. "I told you: savages."

Felix nodded. "I'll get to work shortly." He checked his wrist, grimaced. "Is there watchmaker up here? My watch was damaged during my journey up."

Braun's only reply was a sneer.

AS FELIX WANDERED Ouluskylä's streets, he discovered the town held a stark beauty. The buildings were picturesque piles of slate. Ferns, moss, and yellow grass softened the rocky outcroppings.

Trawlers dredging up shoals of vodnyy uzhas looked tranquil from this distance. The people were round-faced and pink-cheeked, and quick with a nod of greeting.

The processing plant was a jarring addition to a town that seemed to have accreted from the ocean. Its sharp edges and towering smokestacks stood in contrast to the tumbledown landscape. Gulls gathered over it, diving into the slick of blood that leached from its courtyard down into the water.

He took his lunch in a small restaurant where two other men bent over bowls of steaming broth. When his waiter brought him his herring, he said, "It's an impressive thing, the plant, isn't it?"

"Aye," said the waiter. "Good jobs. Good money. We'll see if it lasts."

Felix kept his face entirely neutral. "You think the plant is in danger?"

His waiter laughed so hard he had to lean on the table. "The plant?" he said finally. "No. Sorry. No. I meant Ouluskylä."

Felix encountered the same sentiment later, talking to a mail carrier. "You must be happy the plant is here," he said. "A lot of new life in the town."

"Aye. And a lot of death."

"Whose?"

"The vodnyy uzhas," she said, as if he were a fool.

Speaking to workers in the plant, he said, "You must be glad the Concord Nations finally turned their attention here."

"Why?" said one.

"All the jobs," Felix said. "All the money coming in."

"You know they charge five hundred shek for a fishing license now," said one woman.

"Used to be twenty-five," said another.

AFTER TWO DAYS with no progress on his investigation, Felix went walking along the cliffs to clear his head. A mile from town, he saw a small domed structure that gave him pause. The architecture was...ugly. There was a sense of mass swarming. Things bulged where they shouldn't. Gravity seemed to misbehave.

He felt in his pocket for his small snub-nosed pistol.

Closer, he saw a sigil of a man with three heads on the dome's door. This place was dedicated to Zejura, the Selazzi of remaking: a bastion of the enemy here in the Concord Nations. He drew the pistol and kicked open the door.

In the small, cavern-like space beyond, seven faces looked up at him, startled. One woman stood behind a makeshift table of rock and wood, ladling a stew into bowls held by the other six. There was a basin nearby, with water and a washcloth.

After a moment the woman with the ladle said, "Do you seek aid?"

Felix hesitated. "What is this place?"

"You know what it is," she said.

"You worship Zejura."

"We seek help where we can find it."

"Is his help worth risking your sanity?" Felix said.

"He offers to break things down and rebuild them. Your processing plant does the same thing, doesn't it?"

Felix licked his lips and holstered his gun. There was no immediate threat here.

"What are you doing?" he said.

"Charity," said the woman. "These people can no longer afford fishing licenses."

"They could work in the plant," said Felix.

"They spoke out against the increased license fee. Braun turns them away." She nodded her head to Felix. "Neither I nor Zejura reject anyone."

"You invite them to their own ruin."

The woman rolled her eyes. "They're already ruined. I offer them food and a little kindness."

Felix pointed at the broth. "What's in that?"

But the woman looked at his exposed wrist. "Oh, no," she said. "Your watch is broken. Let me take you to someone who can fix it."

THE WOMAN'S NAME was Kirsi, and she had lived in Ouluskylä all her life. The watchmaker she took him to was called Tappio. He turned Felix's watch over with nimble fingers and promised to return it in twenty minutes or less.

"You have to understand," Kirsi said while they waited on the cobbled street outside, "that for a long time, the divisions between Concord and Selazzi have not meant much here. There is no border wall. The vodnyy uzhas have swum in our waters for decades."

"But now that can change."

"Change can be good or bad. Some people are sad to see old ways die."

"Like you?"

"Of course. For some things. But not others."

"Who would be the most sad?"

She shrugged. "Who loses the most and gains the least?"

Tappio returned with Felix's watch. It was as good as new.

AT NIGHT, FELIX dreamed of swimming. He dove into electric blue waters, floated above an endless black void punctuated by glittering stars. His skin became a sheen of twisting scales, constantly shedding into the water, the water entering him, becoming fresh skin for him. He reveled in blubber, and mucous, and the way his legs trailed as a forest of tendrils sensitive to the slightest change in current. He thrilled in the freedom of new self, new motion, new being. When he woke up, he could taste brine upon his tongue.

"HOW CAN YOU still have no leads?" Bruno Braun's face was a bruise of mottled purple.

"A close-knit community like this, everyone covering for each other. It takes time to pull apart the threads." Felix was bluffing. He was getting nowhere.

"The last incident cost us a two thousand shek a day. And you're trying to make friends?"

Felix had no idea the plant was making that sort of money. He wondered what the men below, hacking apart the vodnyy uzhas, were making.

"Banging heads will only cause them to close ranks," Felix said.

Bruno Braun was already stalking away.

FELIX HAD ROOMS above the local inn. Sometimes, as he passed through, he would see Kirsi there having a drink. "How's it going?" she would ask sometimes.

"Slowly."

"Out here, there's always tomorrow." And there always was, and she would always be at the bar again to ask him how things were going.

"What about you?" he asked her one night, and her face fell a little.

"There's a lot of people need help these days."

"How so?" The factory still stood. The smokestacks still churned out the scents of rotten fish and burning chemicals. More and more people seemed to work there.

"They've cut wages again," she said.

His brow furrowed. The factory seemed to export more and more oil every day. "Why?"

"Because they can. No one works anywhere else anymore."

"That can't be right."

"Braun wasn't sent here to do what's right."

FELIX WASN'T ENTIRELY sure how Kirsi ended up in his bed.

He had been in Ouluskylä almost two months. At some point, she'd stopped being a suspect and become a friend. And then one night he told her about his dreams, about the water closing over his head. How sometimes he was scared of sleeping.

"A sensitive man." She stroked his hair. "We are close to the border here. For some people, more than just creatures come across. Ideas. Memories." She ran a finger down his chest. "Maybe you'll learn to love it."

How had they gotten from there to here, he wondered. To this moment of sweaty, satiated bliss, her cheek on his chest, her hair caressing his skin.

He closed his eyes and dreamed of swimming, a flashing flickering body of mucous strands and scaly protrusions cutting through the water beside him.

"YOU IGNORANT, USELESS sack of shit!"

Bruno Braun stood outside his processing plant, rubbing his rough-hewn forehead with one hand. His eyes were bloodshot, snot streamed from his nose. Smoke in all the colors of a bruise billowed from the plant's doors.

It had been a psychic bomb: a Selazzi invention—an abomination. It connected the minds of those inside the plant with the nerves of the unconscious vodnyy uzhas splayed out on the work benches. When the workers brought down their knives, they experienced the cutting as the sea beasts did. They dropped to the floor, howling.

"Do you have any idea how long a cleansing will take?" Bruno Braun growled. "Do you understand how much this will *cost*?"

"The guilty will be punished," Felix said with as much conviction as he could fake.

"And it's fucking obvious who that is!" Bruno Braun howled. "Arrest the bitch who runs the Selazzi temple."

"She has an alibi," Felix said. *She was tangled in sheets with me, and we were drowning in each other.*

Bruno Braun frothed in apoplexy.

THE PLANT WAS closed for weeks. Each day the train disgorged more and more officials from the heart of the Concord Nations. Bruno Braun set up a temporary headquarters in the mayor's offices. The mayor decamped to a bar. Men and women wearing large metal helmets that thrummed with electricity and emitted the scent of burning sage moved through the plant carrying great hoses and wire brushes. Men with gray uniforms and unfriendly faces patrolled the perimeter of the plant and the streets of Ouluskylä.

Felix sat up at night, writing empty reports to his supervisors, while Kirsi massaged the knots from his shoulders. Afterward, they would go to the inn's kitchen and cook stew for the people whose savings could not tide them through this fallow period. Kirsi muttered prayers to her alien god as they cooked, and Felix pretended not to hear them.

When the factory reopened, the men in gray uniforms did not leave, but the mayor did. Bruno Braun stayed in his offices. And when the locals returned to their positions at the work benches and found the hourly wage had been cut again, no one said a word.

FELIX WAS GIVEN a gray uniform, and set to patrolling the factory, searching for signs of sabotage. He was not welcomed by the others who reported to Bruno Braun. On breaks, he sat with the locals. Everything he ate tasted of brine and blood.

Sometimes he and Kirsi would walk along the coastline. The heather, ferns, and grasses on the shoreline had all turned gray, lying in lackluster clumps over rocks stained black by smoke. If they got high enough above the town, they could see there were still patches of sea untouched by the film of oil and offal seeping from the factory. A few bedraggled trawlers plowed through the scum, trailing choking gray clouds from overburdened engines.

"If I find the saboteurs, I can go home," he said.

"Then I hope you never find them."

"You could come with me."

"I can't leave these people behind."

He closed his eyes. He tried to shut out all of reality. He could feel the ocean lapping behind his eyelids. "The Concord Government will fix this," he said.

"The Concord Government is doing this."

"No! Bruno Braun is the one doing this." He was more insistent than he'd meant to be, but perhaps he needed to be. To keep his faith. To keep his feet planted on the slippery shoreline.

"If the saboteurs shut down the plant once and for all," she said, "then you could also go home."

DREAMS OF THE ocean continued to plague Felix. He sank below his sheets into neon plankton rushing up on thermal streams, rushing from vents buried where no human eyes had ever seen, where great, white-bodied giants moved like somnambulists, all fins and tails and arms and blind staring eyes. He felt the great towering gods of the surface world, their psychic effluvia washing down and around him, swirling in with the water, changing him, remaking him over, and over. He was a thousand new creations every night. His body contorted and contracted, expanded and exploded. He was a creature with its guts trailing in the water like bait. He was a translucent scrap of protoplasm. He was a colony hive mind of water mites, a vast network of ropy tendrils, a tiny speck storm-tossed and out of control.

Now, everyone complained about the dreams. Some people refused to work in the plant. It was too near the water, they said. Bruno Braun had to make a second entrance away from the docks. He also issued an edict offering a reward for the killing of any creature that crossed from the Selazzi side of the border.

A frenzy of hunting began, with families desperate to supplement their anemic incomes. Strange, elongated worms with human teeth were pulled from the ground. Eight-legged beasts that resembled a cross between a hare and a tarantula were pursued across rough tundra. Kirsi tended to the broken ankles of the hunters who fell chasing them. Bite wounds were common, limbs turning puffy and black. The fumes from septic lacerations made her and Felix weep over sorrows they'd believed long forgotten.

To escape Ouluskylä's growing atmosphere of desperation and despair, Felix started going to the shore at night, sitting upon the rocks and rough pebbles. He thought about slipping into the waters below, descending beneath the scum of offal into the cool black depths, and of being rinsed clean—of being broken down and remade.

It was because of these nightly wanderings that he was among the first to know of the morskoy slizen'.

He didn't understand what he was seeing at first. It was like some geologic act of childbirth, like an island trying to force its way up above the surface. He thought perhaps a shoal of vodnyy uzhas were being chased to the surface by a predator. Then he thought perhaps he was asleep or losing his mind. And then he saw it for what it was: the long silver-white body, somehow simultaneously rotund and sinuous; the great iridescent frills trembling and shuddering, churning the water white. It was almost fifty feet in length, a blunt, blind tube of aquatic flesh, a monstrous sea slug, the terror of submarines during the Hierophantic Wars. It came crashing at the shoreline, bleating psychic waves of panic and distress that chased him into the dark recesses of his own fears, pursuing him into polluted black clouds of water, casting him into foreign currents, poisoning his body, breaking him down and down until he was nothing he recognized...

HE CAME TO, gasping. Day had come. He had bitten his tongue. People were on the beach, gathered around the gasping, deflating body of the dying morskoy slizen'. It still let out little gasps of psychic distress, memories of his parents screaming at him, ripping through his frontal lobes.

He slowly made his way down toward it. A cordon of gray-uniformed men was arranged between the body and the crowd. Bruno Braun stood on a pile of wooden pallets. "This," he cried, "is what you people worship. This decaying, useless flesh that is dying here, impotent and alone."

The crowd stared in horror. And it was not their god, Felix knew. Because he had been with it, had been in its head as it tried to escape the poison that caged it on every side, the black clouds of pollution that ensnared and sickened it. It was just a poor beast, alone and afraid.

"You people put dynamite in our plant," said Bruno Braun. "We'll return the favor."

He made a gesture with his hand. Men in gray uniforms brought forth barrels and fuses. The crowd scattered.

When the detonation came, chunks of white flesh rained down for almost a quarter mile. Part of the factory was damaged. Several homes were destroyed. One woman was crushed. The fumes made people sick. The whole thing made Felix sick. He wanted to go home, but he had stopped hunting for the saboteurs. He knew no one was reading his reports. He spent the day curled up with Kirsi, finding all the comfort Ouluskylä still held now fit within the circle of her arms.

FELIX WAS RELEGATED to the night shift. He walked the plant when its only inhabitants were the other night watchmen, moving stoic and silent. He liked to stand outside by the docks and listen to the ocean. Sometimes he would pick up leftover scraps of the vodnyy uzhas—scales and limbs and fins—and think about his dreams, about what it was like to be these creatures swimming in endless depths. He thought about what it would be like to swim down there forever, Kirsi by his side.

At some point each night, he would be discovered and sent on his rounds again. He'd wander, flicking his flashlight over hulking machines and between table legs.

And then, finally, he found it: the thing that shouldn't be there.

He knelt down, peered beneath the workbench. It was an iron sphere the size of his fist. It was ticking.

Sweat trickled into his eyes as he slowly unscrewed the front plate of the bomb. He peeled the plate away, exposing its guts— an intricate world of cogs and gears, all churning toward one inevitable ending.

And then it detonated in his face.

A LIFETIME OF lifetimes. Of deaths. Felix was born and killed a thousand times over. His body was snared, was hooked, was clubbed, was asphyxiated. His body that was never his body, that was always another, made and remade, made and remade. He was lifted from his home, from his waters, from his freedom, and he died over and over, in foreign flesh, in unfamiliar skin. And it didn't stop there. His corpse was desecrated a thousand times. He was dissected and flensed and macerated and pulped. He was reduced to his essences, his most essential oils. And then it happened again, and again. He swam away, he plunged deeper. But there was no way out. Walls of poison blocked him in at every turn, at every depth. And he was snared again, killed again, decimated again, reborn again. Again. Again. An endless loop of horror playing out inside his skull.

HE CAME TO, screaming. It had been almost a month, they told him. He'd taken the full brunt of the blast, shielding the whole plant with his body. Even Bruno Braun came to see him, gave him a grudging handshake.

"I don't suppose," he said, "you know who set it?"

"Actually," Felix said. "I do."

TAPPIO SAT TIED in a chair in the center of a bare concrete room. The little watchmaker was stark naked.

"It was when I opened the bomb up," Felix said, almost apologetically. "I knew you were the only person in Ouluskylä who could have made it."

Tappio simply spat defiance and obscenities.

"Please," Felix said. The endpoint of this interrogation felt as inevitable as the fate of a vodnyy uzhas caught in a fisherman's nets. "If you just tell us who you're working with now, this will be so much quicker."

But the watchmaker resisted, and it took Braun three hours to break him. Felix was horrified by how little of the man was left when he finally gave in.

"Two men," Tappio said, his breathing swift and shallow, "planted the bombs. Emil Nieminen and Olavi Salo." He took a long shuddering breath, fell silent.

Felix was startled to feel relief sluicing through him.

Tappio let out a small cough. Then one last name dribbled from his lips. "And Kirsi Hakala," he said. "She organized everything. It was all her idea."

THEY SHOT KIRSI and her co-conspirators at dawn. And they made Felix watch. There was no chance to save her, no time for heroics. He didn't even get to see her until she was led out, blindfolded and in chains. He called out her name once, and then the guns fired, and she fell to earth, utterly broken, never to be remade again.

"There," Bruno Braun said to him. "Your work is done. Now, you can go home."

They left him there with the bodies, and overhead the gulls began to wheel.

HE SAT ON the beach late into the night. He had tried to get drunk, but he just threw everything up. He felt more sober than he ever had before. He had a train ticket in his pocket, and he thought about home, about the gleaming government buildings, about the training he'd gone through, and the pride that had coursed through his body when he swore to uphold the principles of the Concord, to hold back the madness that lurked in the dark unseen half of the world. He thought about everything he'd learned here about what was truly alien to him, about what he could never understand. And he thought about what had really felt like home, and what really felt like warmth, and love, and a promise that could be kept.

Slowly he peeled off his clothes, layer by layer, exposing himself to the freezing air. It was, he felt, an unmaking of his own doing, a breaking down that he had chosen for himself. He closed his eyes. He could still see the ocean behind his eyelids. The black waves going on forever. An ocean of endless depths and possibilities.

As the first of the bombs he had set in the processing plant turned the sky orange, he stepped forward and felt the waves close around his ankles. And the seaweed felt to him like Kirsi's hair caressing his skin. And the currents felt like her fingers pulling him to her chest. And when the boom of the second bomb faded, the waves sounded like her whispering his name across the pillow. So, he kept on walking, and walking, and as the rest of the detonations rippled out across the night like an alien god's laughter, he smiled to himself and let the waves close above his head.

WHAT WASHES UP IN ARIZONA

Zachary Olson

USED TO BE this joke. Stop me if you've heard it. "If you believe that, I've got some beachfront property in Arizona to sell you." I've been dredging off the Grand Canyon Coast for quite a while now, and folks still find it in themselves to laugh.

Ain't no one owns property out here.

I'd just renewed my mooring lease, that June she came to call. Not quite the height of summer, but deep enough into it that the asphalt they still used on Grand Avenue was almost to its melting point. Your foot kind of sunk where you stepped, like walking on springy moss. It was eggs-flash-fried-on-sidewalks hot, but not quite dead-leaves-catching-fire hot.

It was the perfect weather to get on a boat.

I was preparing to shove off when she rapped against the gangplank. She was built sturdy, though the sundress and wide-brimmed hat did their best to imply daintiness. She had a beat-up old guitar slung across her back and a briefcase the color of over-boiled yolk in one hand.

I'm looking for Pedro Escondido, she said. I heard that you were him.

I asked her who was looking.

Lorelei, she said.

I don't know any Loreleis.

I'm a friend of Matt's, she said, smile wide and cryptic. He wanted me to check on you.

Now that gave me pause. You see, Matt had been dead for two years at that point. I told her as much.

She just laughed and climbed aboard. Keep doing what you're doing, she said. You'll barely know I'm here.

Thought about sending her off right then. Truth was, it'd been more than a minute since I went out with anyone else aboard. And then there was the way she smiled. Inviting and guarded all at once. It reminded me of Matt.

I nodded at the guitar, asked if she played. She told me she didn't carry it just for looks. Asked if I had any requests.

None that she could grant, I said.

Just wait, she said. I might surprise you.

DIDN'T MATTER WHAT she said about acting like she wasn't there. Didn't matter that I was already pretty deep in my ration tab. Mama Escondido didn't raise no selfish host.

Gunther at the cantina tried to act tough when I came to pick up extra freeze-dried meal kits, but he's a pussycat when it comes to vintage electronics. A couple Zunes and an iPhone 12 I'd fished out of the bay the week before set my tab back into black.

Why's he even want those, wondered Lorelei at my heels. It's not like they'd ever work. They've been waterlogged for decades.

I didn't bother explaining. How Gunther got the quartermaster gig because it got him extra rice. How he had a hundred little plastic tubs back at his place, a hundred mausoleums to the digital age. The way he'd told me once, with rum on his breath and stars in his eyes, that he swore he'd plugged his duct-taped headphones into one and heard some actual *music*—not a guitar by the fire, not a half-remembered shanty, but honest songs with robot drums and auto-tune. The kind of thing humanity could make when they had the time and money to do something more than feed themselves and keep the lights on. The kind of thing they used to have so much of that folks even got sick of some.

I didn't explain. She didn't pry. We got back on the boat.

SUN WAS A bit higher than I'd've liked when we finally sailed from Port Arroyo. The horizon had its shimmer on, but it wasn't as bad yet as it would be later. Even in the best of times, you never wanted to get more than a mile and a half from the coast, but that safe range shrunk the closer you got to noon. All the best junk washes close to shore anyways.

The water frothed around the *Treasure's* prow as we took her out. First couple hours of the day were quiet. I dragged a low-power magnet behind us just in case anything special caught, but the canyons 'round the port were mostly empty. I ran the *Treasure* parallel to shore, angled ninety-five degrees. Maybe ninety-six. Kept the red rock in my sightline, and the shimmer at my back. You didn't want to watch the haze too long.

Matt had loved to watch it.

Lorelei stowed her egg-yolk suitcase in the wheelhouse and stretched out on the deck, picking at her guitar. Had to hand it to her, she was good. Didn't seem to mind the heat.

How long you been doing this, she asked.

Fifteen years, I told her.

Ever get old?

Why would it? I'm a goddamn modern treasure hunter.

Oh, she said, a smile in her voice. You find a lot of treasure, then?

Enough to live on, I said.

She was quiet for a time after that. Her fingerpicking got real contemplative. And then:

But is it really?

The smile in her voice was gone. She sat cross-legged, facing me, clutching her guitar like it meant to fly away. What do you mean, I asked.

She stared into the haze. I mean, can you really call this living?

'BOUT NINE-THIRTY, WE heard creaking metal. People shouting. Up ahead along the coast, a trawler's net-winch screamed. A dozen fishers swarmed the deck, yanking at the dripping mesh. If they didn't get it up there soon—

That rope's about to snap, said Lorelei.

Son of a bitch, I said. Hold onto the wheel for me.

The water met me like my oldest friend. A splash. A shock. Then the beauty of friction and momentum, of buoyancy and weight, of cool blue cradling and carrying you like a bullet. Half a minute later I was on the trawler's deck.

One sailor among many, I grabbed the net and heaved. This close up, without the shimmer's haze, I recognized the crew. Trawler's name was *Breadwinner*. Captain's name was Cass. Good folk from out Colorado-way. The Rockies didn't have much in the way of work unless you managed to talk your way past Aspen's walls. Cass wasn't built for housekeeping.

The trawler's winch whined something fierce. The rope was frayed to hell and back, but the overstuffed net just barely cleared the railing. An avalanche of flopping fish came spilling out across the deck. The crew of the Breadwinner fell atop it, puffing from exertion. Cass looked over, did a double take when she saw me.

Hell's bells, Escondido, she said. Where on earth'd you come from?

It's like the ocean spat him out on deck, said a crewman.

You're lucky I was in the neighborhood, I said. You nearly lost the whole damn thing.

Cass threw back her head and laughed. It sounded taut. Like a guitar string tightened near to snapping. The only kind of laugh we had, those days. One of her crewmen started picking through the fish. He clicked his tongue.

Got another one, Captain, he said.

Another what, I asked.

Look for yourself, said Cass.

It was the biggest marlin I'd ever seen. Pacific blue, near thirteen feet, glassy eyeballs down its length. Bioluminescent algae seeped out from its gills.

Damn things are popping up all over the northern coast, said Cass. Hell of a thing.

Up near Marble Canyon?

That's the place, she said. Something hinky up there.

Guess I'll see it for myself, I said.

Cass stopped me before I could dive back in. She gripped my shoulder tight. Listen, Pedro, she said. I know that's where Matt—

The water met me like my oldest friend.

LORELEI DIDN'T ASK too many questions when I climbed back on the *Treasure*. She stayed quiet for a while as the sun kept on its climbing. For a minute, I really did forget she was there. Too focused on heading north toward Marble Canyon. Hoped to make it before noon. Otherwise, the shimmer'd get too close to see the shore. Couldn't sail like that.

Around eleven, Lorelei spoke up again. Asked if I'd heard those rumors. That things fell from the sky sometimes, full of toxic chemicals and cosmic radiation. That they leaked where they lay. Made the land around them fallow.

I told her sure. I'd even come across a few. Those low-Earth-orbit habitats couldn't fling their runoff into space. Couldn't slip our gravity. So, they dumped it onto us.

She asked me if it bothered me. If I was scared of getting sick.

I thought of Matt. Staring out into the haze. Stepping off the bow.

I told her we were sick already.

WE GOT TO Marble Canyon just a hair before noon. The shimmer had long slipped the horizon to come and dance up close. It felt like you could reach over the rail and touch it with your hand. I did my best to look away.

The water sizzled as the sun hit its apex. I unfolded the *Treasure's* reflective tarp and raised it from the masthead. It didn't quell the heat, but at least it blocked that angry gaze. At that hour, the sun's reflection on the waves was nearly blinding. We used strips of plastic with little slits cut in as goggles, like the Inuits did before the ice caps went. The *Treasure's* deck was a tiny dot of shadow in an endless sea of haze.

I dropped anchor. Threw a handful of magnets and hooks over the side. Got to work. From there the time just stretched. It was like fishing, in a way. Toss it out. Wait for a bite. Reel it in. Check your catch. If you're lucky, hit a big one.

Most of what I dredge is junk. Old car bumpers. Waterlogged appliances. The occasional safe. Once in a blue moon, I'll get shuttle parts. Parting gifts from those who saw the writing on the wall and could afford a ticket into orbit. But mostly, I get junk.

Holy shit, said Lorelei. Is that an honest-to-god washing machine?

It was one of those fancy ones they made before it all went poof. The logo had been a decal. That was long gone. No buttons—must have been a touch screen. Against all odds, the door was still latched. A load of laundry stewed inside. I checked the pockets for change.

A lot of personal effects in all this junk, said Lorelei. I asked her what she expected. She didn't have any expectations, she replied. She was just surprised.

It wasn't that surprising, if you thought about it. My ma had told me that back then no matter the channel you turned to, the message stayed basically the same: the coasts' erosion was a hoax. That They were selling fear, and true patriots would never buy it. That the status quo was God. When the real storms hit—the category sevens, mind—the floods they brought killed millions. Maybe the pundits had thought they'd have longer to milk it.

Lorelei hummed an old, familiar tune, turning over a disintegrating T-shirt in her hands. She asked me if I'd heard another rumor. Well, more like a conspiracy.

They say, she told me, that those folks who killed the ice caps, those folk whose money paid the pundits, who gutted public transit and pumped the heavens full of smog, that they'd gotten asked to do it. That they'd been paid with keys to the stars in exchange for ceding the Earth. There were things that lived beneath the sea, that had lived down there since before humanity's early, shaky steps, and they wanted their oceans back.

You sound crazy, I said. Lorelei just laughed.

And the saddest part, she said, well no, not saddest, call it most ironic, is those pundits who made it happen, who kept the public from rioting and told them it would be okay? They weren't actually important enough to get onto the shuttles. They're still down here, stuck with us. Stuck with knowing what they did.

She paced as she talked. Fetched her egg-yolk briefcase. Snapped it open on the deck. Inside, there was some kind of boot-strapped amplifier. Like a bullhorn welded to a radio. She unspooled a length of cable and hooked it into her guitar.

Wait, I told her. Wait. 'Things under the sea?' Are you really blaming *mermaids* for the mess that we're all in?

She stopped, fingers on her fretboard, and looked me in the eye. Her eyes were ocean green. I hadn't noticed earlier.

It's not their fault, she told me. They shared the knowledge freely. They had no problem with everybody getting out, with humanity finding a new home among the stars. But the brokers had a different plan. That was what the sea-folk didn't count on. The capacity for cruelty. That the few, so practiced in their bleeding of the many, would abandon us all as they fled to the stars.

It was a motherfucking travesty.

Lorelei, I said. Who the hell are you? Why are you here? What is going on?

You know why, she said. Matt asked me to check up on you.

Matt is *dead*, I said.

She didn't seem to hear me. She cranked the dials on her amp. Strummed a chord that shook my chest. Even still, it didn't drown out her voice. And here we are! she cried. People carve out lives on picked-clean bones! You've gone from thriving to living to surviving to eking, and none of it's your fault! The world was sold from under you, and none of you deserve it!

Every piece of metal on the *Treasure* buzzed along to her guitar. The mirage on the horizon seemed to pulse and shake in time. Tears streamed down her face.

Nobody deserves this. You should lie in restful plenty. The sea-folk want to help you. You just need to learn to listen. To hear the call, and follow. Matt could hear. Can you?

Her question hung in the air just as heavy as her chord. At some point, she'd walked over to the railing. She stood straight and tall, a leg on each side, eyes locked onto mine.

Can you, Pedro?

And she was gone.

MY EARS RANG. The *Treasure* shook. Once again, I was alone.

I watched the shimmer where she'd been. Like she would pop back up. Like the world would get better if I just hoped and waited. Like hope alone was all I needed.

But she didn't. And it didn't.

'Cause it wasn't.

Behind the guitar's echoes, I thought I heard another song. A song that Matt had taught me. A song of better times.

The shimmer danced just past the rail. It grew 'til I saw nothing else.

If you really thought about it, I was only catching up.

The water met me like his arms.

⚓

SO FULL OF THE SHINING FLESH

Tiffany Morris

SUMMER'S JAWS TORE into them with rows of sharp teeth. When it arrived, the heat rose and did not dissipate, the sweltering air indifferent to the arrival of rain or thunderstorm. Dull light tinged everything silver. In this new gloom, the islanders shucked oysters and sucked at dried seaweed while they tried to brainstorm a way out of the land's death sentence. There were rumors of toxins, pollution, parasites named in a gnarled Latin tongue that no one understood. Nothing had been confirmed. The air quickly became too humid for anyone to breathe in full, deep breaths: mouth-to-mouth asphyxiation.

Just after midnight the shore was the black of a smoker's lung. Isobel was a shadow out walking among shadows, swimming in the distant dying stars of flashlights and the shocking blue-white beams of phone screens. Insomniacs lured to the lullaby of waves on rock, seeking the womb water of their ancestral mother, defying the sliver of the bad moon slavering up in the sky, dribbling light like a pearl melting out of an oyster's mouth. Deep into the night the silver hue was still present, a sharp, thin blade of serrated air.

"Isobel?" a deep voice to her right interrogated the dark.

She stepped back involuntarily. The voice was familiar; she tried to place the slight accent. He might have been in the shop earlier that day, hemming and hawing over the price of the jewelry as Isobel shucked oysters and strung the pearls together, savoring the quiet geometry of her work. Perhaps the voice belonged to the man who didn't know why he'd wandered onto the island. She didn't know why anyone did—the town was stained with a palliative pallor, all of the islanders hermit crabs crushed together in a plastic bottle, signaling doom to the new crabs who scuttled in thinking the detritus was home. She'd rather be a fish, some glinting thing, even if it meant eventually washing up on the sand, eaten by the light lacing through exposed bones.

"I don't remember your name," she confessed.

"Karl. The sound is different down here on the beach, isn't it?"

They let the silence swim over them, struggling to breathe in the gentle crash of waves.

"I don't know about that. Maybe you got water in your ear."

Isobel sat with Karl while he smoked a cigarette. He handed her his flask, and she sipped the glowing warmth of the whiskey contained within. Their conversation drifted into life in the time before. He'd been a construction worker out west, making his way across the country, his car exhaust dissolving state lines. The collapse was the same everywhere, from what he'd witnessed; the land in each place was different, but people tended to react in the same ways. The outline of his face was beautiful, even in shadow.

She didn't know how much of the night had passed before Karl kissed her and they ended up back at her cottage. Once she shut out the memories of Alfie—his eyes as blue and sad as the shadows of snow; the pile of negative pregnancy tests; his drowned body up north devoured by creatures with sharp tusks—her body crashed together with Karl's in transcendent distraction. They became a mythic multi-headed form, signaling desire through the deep black water of her bedroom. Just being and breath. Sweat and muscles and skin. She didn't usually do this sort of thing, but it didn't matter. Nothing that anyone did made sense anymore.

Karl was fully dressed when her eyes opened, and he kissed her again, lips paperdry but still yielding. Before he went out the door, he said that he would come back.

He didn't—a few days later his barnacle-blighted body washed up on the shore, his once lovely face bloated and purple and pustuled. He'd been with a group of tourists who'd gone out on the rough hot water in a canoe. The boat had tipped. No one had bothered with a life jacket. They hadn't seen much point in trying not to die.

So they died.

SOMETIME AFTER THE food stores ran out—even the dusty, expired, dented cans that threatened botulism were eaten, tin after tin scraped clean—this was when Isobel snapped briefly into focus. When was the last time that she'd slept a full night? She kept every fan in the house pointed at her, humming stale air into her sweating face. A futile exchange of precious generator power for their weak relief. The few people left roamed the streets, mumbling, pupils wandering, not fixed on any single point. Everything in the small poisoned town had closed indefinitely. Each house a cracked, faded exoskeleton. Each door a shell barnacled shut.

The hunger was familiar at first. She'd once been a pageant queen—small time, sure, but she'd perfected her tan, her skincare routine, her restrictive diet. Her hair would gleam under the church hall lights, glossy from expensive shampoo that smelled like designer perfume. This had been her proud work, her hunger; it earned her the praise and money that nourished her more. She loved to be onstage, adorned in her jewel-toned dresses, feeling like some sort of priestess while wrapped in the flowing fabric, her skin shining. She would flash a Vaseline-toothed smile white as the pearls that dangled their noose-knot around her neck and usually end up at least as a runner-up. The sashes were now packed away somewhere—probably in the attic; her parents had been too sentimental to throw out anything. Proud of her even though none of it had meant anything in the wider scheme of things, in the shape her life ended up taking.

The hunger clung to her as Isobel became transfixed by her father's trophy. He'd mounted the fish—she thought it was an Atlantic salmon but wasn't too sure—on wood and stuck it on the wall, and it had hung there for as long as she could remember. First, she started rubbing the stiff taxidermy, an odd sort of genie's lamp, empty of life and void of wishes, her fingers rolling over the bumps of scale, varnished and sharp and smooth all at once. When she finally tore into its scales, she cut her fingertips. She pushed through the pain and dug deep into the unliving body, sharp scales stabbing into the skin under her fingernails. She finally pulled a scale from the fish with careful precision, like prying out a splinter. It was slick with her blood and sweat. This piece of her history was preserved forever, her shared history of this place that was collapsing in on itself. All from some old catch her father proudly brought back from one of his trips offshore. In his fishing stories he'd caught many creatures. She'd loved hearing about the enormous monsters with strange bodies adapted for that alien world that coexisted with their own but was deep, deep below the surface of everything she knew and could name.

She looked at it closely: a silver shard like mother-of-pearl, abalone-pretty, glimmering in the light. She stabbed the scale into her forearm. Her skin broke easily, radiating with hurt that trickled from her in a thin drip of blood. A hot rush of shame made her flush, and she ripped the piece of the dead fish out of her.

She breathed heavily as the wound spat out in a stronger current. Isobel found a tea towel and held it down to stop the bleeding while she stared at the salmon's iridescence, fascinated by how it shone even under the low lamplight. She blinked longer and longer, the heat and hunger mixing into a strong and suffocating sedative.

When she awakened the next morning, the couch pillow was damp with sweat, her hair plastered to her face as if she had been underwater. The fans were silent, the power off. Isobel sat up. She'd soaked through a bandage she didn't recall putting on. She lifted her arm. The limb was covered in the rust of dried blood. Rorschach patterns formed on her skin. They were fish, belly-up and gasping.

WHEN SHE FINALLY left the house, stomach swollen empty with curdling pain, each muscle of her body was gnawing at itself and weak with want. There had to be something still living in the water, something she could catch and eat, some delicious tender meat stuck to shell that tasted of the silver water that housed it. As she walked, she surveyed the transformed landscape of the shoreline, its aborted rebirth. In the time that she'd been shut inside, indistinguishable bodies had beached onto the oceanfront: mollusks buzzed rot next to the unidentifiable bones and bloated bodies of humans and small furred creatures, flies and maggots and ants crawling over the heaped carrion in imitation of muscle movement. No one was left on the beach or boardwalk. The mermaid mural her mother had painted one summer grinned into the emptiness. Garbage was strewn across the parking lot, rifled through, picked at by gulls before they too had died, their wings outstretched in limp angelic poses.

Even there in that mess of boiling rot and baking sand, Isobel found oysters, plucked them out of the water, and carried them in her dented metal bucket. She sat on the first boardwalk bench she could find and pulled up her treasure. She rifled in her pocket. The steel blade on her small knife glinted in the dull afternoon light.

Isobel pried an oyster open, her chest heaving with the effort of each breath, struggling through every movement. She held the shell closer to her. Its silver meat shone with chemical beauty. Her tool slid under the wet skin, now exposed; the salted decay and sweet seawater smell stabbed into the thick air. She pulled the palate-soft nacre up from the shell and plunged her puckered fingers into the slimy creature. A hard sphere. Isobel pulled it out and rolled it between her hands before opening her palm to the sky.

It was the perfect pearl—the blue eye of her lover, blood vessels cracked pink over white meat. The eye rolled its gaze over and over the sky. Too precious to make into jewelry. She held it to her chest. Her beautiful Alfie. No, Karl. Whose eye was it? It didn't matter. Their precious gaze was hers. This beautiful seeing sphere from the sea.

Her fingers pried her mouth open. She sucked the eye between her teeth, crunching hard, wanting to shatter her teeth into perfect porcelain shards, into driftwood, into little seashells.

The eye had a sweet taste. Saltsweet. So salty that it stung and puckered her tongue, swollen and stuck like a barnacle to her soft palate. What blade could break her open and steal this precious treasure?

She swallowed it in a dry gulp that burned her throat as it fought its way down. For a moment she thought the treasure would catch there forever, roll and roll, searching for light like it was stuck at the bottom of the well of her throat, keeping her from taking breath. But she swallowed hard and then swallowed harder, and the thing made its slow descent.

Isobel sucked the salt from her fingers and chewed the rotted meat left in the shell. She summoned a deep breath. It was time.

WAVES POUNDED IN time with her sewing as the thread looped into the fish carcasses. Their rotted animal smell punctured into her as blood ran metallic from her pores. Her skin meshed against the fish, bluepale herringskin, sharpsilver salmonskin, her hand running over the sequined jewels of its many scales, wet with the mucus membranes drying into thick residues. Pain pulsed at each incision, but it was worth it to make herself anew, to adorn her legs with scales until they grew into her, transplant transference transcendence of the boundaries of woman and fish, until the fishes' bodies became her body, until she was so full of the shining flesh that she'd become a mysterious aquatic creature, mermaid beautiful, steel hair dancing in the silver light.

She stepped one foot into the bubbling bioluminescent sea: white scum glowed in the darkdeep. The waves rushed about her mutilated feet as she shed skins and scales; her fin dragged long tangles of thread, crimson with clots and empty shells. She would shine out there among the remaining creatures, all of them signaling their promises under the waves.

Isobel took a deep gulp of the hot salt water. The waxing moon of her belly cradled the baby in precious womb water. The baby, the baby she was sure was growing in her, would love this water. The baby, a perfect pearl growing from the shell of her father's eye. Isobel was a priestess spinning blood into flesh. Isobel was the moon. An oyster building beauty from her very bones.

LAST RESORT

Sloane Leong

THE ISLELUSH AROMATIZER stings Ikaika's nostrils as he opens the hotel room door. It's the same fragrance all the hotel's interior membranes discharge through their musk-secreting capillaries, a heady floral mix of ethanol and formaldehyde without a single drop of the flower extract. Sometimes, when Ikaika is anxious enough, the scent will push his body into a high-stress state, turning him from male to female, one of the many 'benefits' of mandatory gene acquisition all employees are required to undergo.

The Grand Royal Petal suite takes up the entirety of the west wing of the Refulgent Labellum Resort, but the guests—a family of three, including the guest he's attending—stay swaddled in a cradle of soothing anxiolytic membrane in the very corner of the room. Ikaika extracts his designated guest from the damp hotel room, disconnecting the wet payment system tendrils and feeding umbilicus from their various orifices.

"Time already?" the woman says, slopping down onto the soft silicon tile floor. Her metallic gold hair looks bronze with how wet it is with amnia, and her sunless white skin shines unnaturally. Judging by the neat seams bisecting various fusions of flesh, Ikaika can tell it's been microdermabraded and grafted with fresh donor dermis multiple times. The rest of the family are in similar states of custom upkeep. Ikaika tamps down on the growing sour wad of envy in his throat. What was it like not to have to reconfigure your genes just to survive?

"You're booked for a Crystal Beach™ excursion at 1 p.m., mistress," Ikaika says, putting her carefully in a soft-structured adult carrier at his front. She weighs very little, but it's still a strain on Ikaika's body. He wishes briefly he had his roommate's custom physique; six muscular arms boiling with anabolic steroids would make easy work of this client. Muscle removal, an expensive but ultimately aesthetically appealing procedure, had been a popular trend last year among the wealthy. This year the trend was mass skeletal microperforation, but so far Ikaika hadn't been lucky enough to get any bird-boned guests. In his HUD, his Customer Satisfaction stat bar begins to glow menacingly. "Would you like me to cancel the outing?"

NO I'LL GO THE CONCEPT IS INTERESTING, she says with a synthetic voice via his HUD. She allows him to dress her in a bathing-suit top and a skin-tight diaper before maneuvering her into the carrier. I THINK I KNOW THE ANGLE I'LL USE WHEN I START CAMMING. SIGN THIS RELEASE FORM IN CASE YOU STEP INTO FRAME.

He does. The guest continues to ramble on, and Ikaika soon realizes she is talking not to him but at him, musing over how she is going to stream her trip and present it to her social circle. After letting the guest peck her comatose father and maternoid goodbye, Ikaika carries her out to the restaurant in the lobby for lunch. She's been on a steady stream of nutrients all night but having something solid before they get to the water will keep her from leaking liquid shit into the ocean. Not that it was her problem; as her current attendant, he was required to oversee all her bodily functions while on the Labellum's premises. Though he thought it strange she wouldn't just use her own home attendant. Maybe this family wasn't as rich as they looked. Regardless, he wasn't in the mood to have shit smeared down his legs for the duration of the tour.

When he presents her with a nutrient fondant shaped into Labellem's signature violet orchid, she happily eats it. A hopeful sign; maybe she wouldn't be a difficult client. He dabs her face clean and trudges down to the beach, bending once to scoop up a handful of sand for breakfast. While mildly unpalatable, his teredinid genes and the little teeth ringing his throat crunch down the sand with ease until it fills his cecum with a satisfying muddy slurry. He could wait and plug into the nutrient umbilicus later but he's saving his Labellum scrip for a new gene acquisition.

CAN YOU NOT CHEW IN MY EAR PLEASE. I CAN HEAR DOWN TO .05 Hz. I CAN HEAR YOUR EGGS SPLITTING.

"Sorry, mistress," he says, closing his mouth even though his esophageal teeth are still working a shell in his throat.

In his ocular HUD, his scrip bar begins to lower. To distract her, he launches into the developmental history of the Refulgent Labellum Resort, how the resort ovum was planted in 2938 by real estate developers Jun Volta15 and Billie tha Chamaeleon and then cultivated by local hospitality farmers. In 2941, new features like the Lucent Sepal Tower completed maturation, a private section of the resort where high-end clients could go for luxury services such as gene casinos, sexual wellness facilities and culinary cannibalism experiences. The culinary cannibalism experience was a new feature on the hotel's entertainment program. It had been only recently decriminalized but only those whose ancestral culture practiced the custom were allowed to participate in it; the Refulgent Labelleum was very conscious of not perpetuating cultural appropriation and was 'all about authenticity.' Many native people, like Ikaika, had taken up the practice by selling cuts of themselves to tourists. It was so nice to see people reconnecting with their history.

But today they would be foregoing the culinary experience and instead be exploring the Crystal Beach ™ as envisioned by the

Refulgent Labellum founders. The entirety of the Beach Protection Palisade is patrolled by the United Resort Security, and getting clearance for the beaches was now something totally out of Ikaika's, or any of the locals', reach. Massive fifty-foot-high LED walls cut off the beaches from the interior of all the islands, projecting imagery of the beach behind them. In some neighborhoods, like Ikaika's, the LED wall has been defaced and destroyed, leaving a towering partition of constant glittering white noise that often triggers brief bouts of hysteria, which in turn contributes to higher homicide rates in the local population. The entries are limited to hotel premises and double as checkpoints; without a resort band or chip, entry is denied.

Ikaika's guest makes an excited squeaking noise and he tries to force a smile. Even though he hates what the beach has become, it's still a privilege to see it.

The security scanner buzzes over them, pinging the guest's wrist band and the employee chip in Ikaika's bicep and flashing green in approval.

HUH. THIS PLACE IS CUTE. IT WILL ONLY NEED A LITTLE EDITING IN POST TO MAKE IT PERFECT.

The beach is pristine, as advertised. After every human disruption, the resort's AI shifts the seashells and sand dollars and stones via the nanobots mixed into the artificial sand, into aesthetically pleasing compositions after every human disruption. The water off the shore is cleaned through filters hidden in the fake coral and occasionally squirted with dye to achieve the famous cerulean hue. White cabanas with gently billowing curtains sparsely line the shore, surrounded by potted plants.

START FILMING PLEASE. SET ME UP RIGHT AT THE WATERLINE, I'LL START CAMMING THERE.

Ikaika obeys, unpocketing his guest's camdrone and popping it into the air where it immediately floats and buzzes around his guest like an obedient horse fly. She starts ordering it around, commanding it to capture her at different angles while she poses and laughs and twists in the sand, showing off her muscleless arms and legs.

I AM HUNGRY, she says after a time, and Ikaika stiffens. HUNT ME SOMETHING NOURISHING. I'VE HEARD YOUR KIND ARE CAPABLE, HISTORICALLY-SPEAKING.

There are no animals to hunt here in the islands. In the world. Sweat pops on his forehead. "Would you prefer going back to the restaurant?"

HUNT ME SOMETHING, she says and shoos him away, angling herself so the ocean is caught in the background of her call. She starts a painful, boneless writhing in the sand, a performance Ikaika is momentarily distracted by; it's the hottest thing he's ever seen.

It's too far to the hotel restaurant to get her a snack. The AI would notice his deviation from the preferred guest schedule and severely dock his scrip. So, he looks around and sighs in relief at the sight of an attendant nearby. Pohaku works both as an attendant and as an entrée in the private culinary experiences, a position he got thanks to a rare starfish gene splice. His guests, a couple, are cavorting in the water, leaving him alone. Ikaika feels bad about disturbing him.

"Pohaku! Can I have a cut off you? My guest is hungry but she doesn't wanna head back yet."

Pohaku squints at him. "Sure, cuz. For one-hundred and fifty scrip."

"Bro, that's half my fucking pay today!"

When Pohaku only shrugs and looks back at his guests, Ikaika curses. Pohaku has the upper hand and there'll be no negotiating. "Fuck, fine."

Smugly, Pohaku lifts his uniform's shirt and extracts a pocketknife from his shorts. He feels around the parts of his fatty belly that aren't in the process of growing back. The flesh there grows in tight compacted bubbles of yellow fat and shiny red meat that makes Ikaika's mouth water. Once Pohaku finds a good spot, he begins expertly cutting a square out without even a flinch; pain receptors are a hindrance to good customer service and, as such, are removed in all employees. While he extracts the meat, Ikaika grabs a ti leaf from one of the plants near the cabana and comes back just in time to catch the meat as it falls. A timer starts in his HUD: he's not within the suggested three-foot radius of his guest, and his Employee Initiative and Customer Satisfaction stats begin to flicker caution.

"Thanks, cuz, you're a lifesaver," Ikaika says over his shoulder, meat in hand, while Pohaku stuffs the weeping wound with sand. His scrip bar lowers again, but his initiative bar sparkles up from Satisfactory to Good.

The guest is camming with her friend when he returns. The rectangle of meat is now carefully gift-wrapped by the leaf, and she accepts it with a suspicious squint. She bites and swallows half of it before clutching her gut and proclaiming herself full and tossing the rest. Her companion, projected from a small camdrone, squeals in gleeful envy, and the conversation continues for several minutes longer in a language Ikaika doesn't understand.

Finally, the guest ends the call and gives Ikaika a look he's familiar with: boredom couched within threatening expectation. It's time to move on. After brushing the sand off her immobile limbs, he situates her in the carrier and heads for the aquarium, which is partially submerged on the north side of the beach.

They're scanned at the checkpoint once more before descending via escalator through a tunnel of massive tanks. The aqua tunnel, situated as it is offshore, is meant to convey the sense that the viewer is looking out into the ocean itself. However, unlike in the ocean, artificial aquatic life darts and eddies all around them in the tanks. Most animals, including sealife, was discontinued decades ago, and now, to experience what it was like to see animal-like life in the wild, one had to visit these zoos and aquatic centers.

Ikaika pays close attention to the guest as she glances around at the marine life. A great white shark made up of almost fifty people attempts to float by with some modicum of grace. Besides some strategic gene editing, their bodies have been carefully stitched together to give the impression of their animal character, skin bleached and tattooed the exact shade of gravely gray and sleek white. Some actors have foregone retaining their eyes, surgically sealed them shut, or have had permanent white lenses installed so as not to detract from the overall illusion of shark.

Another actor swims by as a school of goatfish, his body carved up into fleshy yellowgold cutouts, a living collage in motion giving the impression of a shoaling pod. The spinner dolphin pod is played by more sophisticated actors—a family!—who've undergone more extensive adaptive gene and surgical body modification. They began their career journey early, taking on more comprehensive genetic evolution. In Ikaika's opinion, they look the most like the real thing. They're slender, shiny, and the only hint they're human is in their too-tapered tail and the slightly bulbous head. But besides that, Ikaika considers them a near-perfect replica.

The escalator ends and they exit into the touch zone which functions as the aquarium's tidal pool. Above them, the LED ceiling portrays a sunnier blue sky complete with flying, squawking gulls. Ikaika's guest makes a little whining sound, gesturing with her chin towards a pool of anemones. The anemones are grown off an actor's back, but the rest of his body is submerged in sand, giving the illusion that the anemones are simply attached to a rock. Other actors fill the pools with starfish and stingrays, even a sea turtle, though Ikaika finds the sea turtle somewhat uncomfortable to look at. Despite cosmetic surgery, the face, as it emerges from the shell, comes off looking skeletal rather than reptilian.

By the time Ikaika leads the guest to the last tide pool—the sea cucumber pool to be exact, the visitor favorite—and she'd been given time to fuck her pick of the actor, they are both exhausted. She asks if she can buy one of the actor's swim bladders as a souvenir before she leaves and Ikaika tells her, yes, of course, and that it will be delivered the following morning.

It's dusk when he finally re-inserts her into her hotel room membrane, pinching the barbs closed so she's sealed in tight. She tips him in a digital currency specifically meant for hospitality workers like himself that he can use to improve his Worker Quality stat. With that, he uses his HUD to sign out and the hotel's flooring instantly opens up, sucking him down a transport canal and expelling him in the employee parking lot.

He takes his company hoverbike home, even though walking is faster, because he has to use up a certain amount of miles or risk having it repossessed. As he passes through the invisible barrier surrounding the Labellum premises, the sweet ionized air shifts to something thick and sour. The streets stream with prematurely kyphotic workers, the area above their skulls wavy with heat. His genitals instantly shift back to male as his body relaxes, budding out against the bike seat.

The Sunset Gardens complex, on the east side of the island, is about thirty minutes from the Refulgent Labellum. Ikaika and his roommate for the week share a residential pod. It fits two sleeping sacs, an array of connective tendrils, and an omnidirectional treadmill. The essentials. When he walks in, his roommate is naked on the omni-treadmill feeling up someone in virtual space. As a professional masseuse at the Labellum, she specializes in clients with custom anatomy. It was a profession, she said, that she'd known she wanted to enter since she was a child, and she'd begun to take permanent steps to become the Ultimate Masseuse, like adding three genetically fortified arms on each side of her body, several oil-dispensing invaginations between her breasts, and a host of various genitals for client use. VR workers like to use her body for virtual gigs since customizing their own VR avatar is too expensive and they would be forced to use the dimensions of their meatbodies; her altered anatomy is of great practical use in the Multiworker Online Battle Arenas as she is able to wield six weapons or six mining tools at once.

Ikaika sheds his uniform and lets the floor membrane absorb them for cleaning. When his roommate—*what is her name again?*—doesn't answer, he pulls a nutrient tendril from the wall and plugs it into one of his ports. Then, sullenly, he connects the tenant umbilicus that will collect rent while he sleeps. Sometimes it takes semen, but more often than not the community welfare AI prefers hemoglobin and plasma. He rips a seam in his sleeping sac and crawls in before pinching it shut.

When he turns off his external visuals and opens his virtual eyes in their home interface, he sees his roommate's cartoony avatar curled up, floating in the air, asleep. Above her head floats an icon that means her body is currently being occupied by a gig worker who's mining Web Access Points for her in the neuranet. Without a constant stream of WAPs, he and his roommate would lose access permanently, rendering them virtual and social exiles. Ikaika had 'forgotten' it was his turn to mine tonight. Carefully, so as not to wake her, he shuts off his higher cognition functions and cuts off all thought and sensory input.

He dreams of a deep and beautiful numb nothing.

Then a red warning blazes into existence, interrupting his stupor with all the strength of an adrenaline impact.

Tomorrow already. Except it's not his work alarm; it's a hazard alarm. Ikaika wakes up to find long skinny black spines poking out from various spots on his body, jabbing through his sleep sac. His roommate, too, is littered with the spines but hasn't yet woken up to assess the damage. Her sleep sac weeps amnia, and her tenant umbilicus is fully severed. *Fuck.*

When he checks their complex's update stream, he sees a virus has infected the building in the night, transmitting the infection to all residents. Even if they patch the umbilicus, they won't be able to vacuum out their rent fast enough. And what's worse, he can't go to work like *this*. Low-poison spines are not regulation! When Ikaika admits this to himself in his head, that he'll have to call out, lose a whole day of work, and thus have to visit the job center clinic, his genitals begin to recede in a panic. His employee stats will plummet, and he'll have to rebuild his position *again*.

He curses as he attempts to disentangle his sleep sac from his new, violent anatomy. He drops onto the floor, and his feet hit a thin crust that crumbles into a stickier layer, a slurry of blood and cum that has leaked from his punctured tenant umbilicus. No no *no*. He can feel the eviction timer begin to tick in his HUD, like a warming rash beginning to throb in irritation. At the job center clinic, he'll be forced to edit his genes again, to customize his anatomy to fit a new shitty job role like waste-monger or community hole or actor.

He paces on the omni-treadmill thinking, cursing under his breath, feeling an egg drop into his pinhole uterus. Fuck this, fuck his new pussy, fuck this virus, fuck the clinc, *fuck–*

His roommate is still asleep. Her bulk bulges from her sleep
sac, thick black needles delicate against her muscle mass. She
has weight to spare.

In a fugue on fast forward, Ikaika pulls down all his extraction
tendrils and umbilicals at once. He rips open her sleeping sac
and shoves them up between her legs for egg collection, chews
into her wrist with his shipworm teeth, and plugs a tendril into
the fountaining red wound. He can drain her dry like this, pay
rent, not just for today but all fucking month.

When she wakes, she thrashes in her cocoon, but he's already
predicted this, tied her down with their dirty uniforms, knotting
all her wrists, her thick ankles. The tenant stat bar fills to maximum
and then his community fluid-donation follows suit. He's never
seen the stat bars turn green before; he almost orgasms with relief.
When his roommate starts turning blue around the face, her head
lolling as her brain shuts down, he unplugs all the tendrils and IMs
the community welfare AI.

"I saw her talking last night," he says, the lie easy as breathing,
"about something she was going to do to the tenants here. She's
always come off kinda shady. I think it was her."

We did not hear her speak to you last night, Tenant472892, the
community welfare AI echoes in his head.

This makes sense because, like the room's utility membranes
and the intranet, the surveillance unit is also busted and not
likely to be repaired. No radical acts have taken place on the
island since 2740, long enough ago that the landlord has, after
running extensive analytics, focused its attention elsewhere.

"She was...subvocalizing," Ikaika lies. "You wouldn't have
heard her. But I could see. Quoting a lot of radical anti-worker
aphorisms."

There is a silent moment of processing before the community
welfare AI speaks again. *I understand. Tenant99373 has no
history on record of extremist leanings, but it is better to be safe
than sorry. Thank you, Tenant472892. We would like to reward
you for your diligence and candor.*

Ikaika is granted the day off work, with no warning marks
on his record.

The wall—graygreen-swelling, odorous, and violet—opens up like a leech cavity and swallows his roommate whole then slits shut. With only him in the room, Ikaika takes a breath and feels the whole world open up inside him.

When he walks down to the Beach Protection Palisade and stares up into the static of the looming LED, a black-and-white froth flies in frenzy. Lunch is sand, regurgitated from his cecum. He chews and stares, picturing his own squirming white-sand shores, a spume of silver sky and ink black water swarming all around him, pixelated into a perfectly diffused balance. The grating sound of sand crunching in his throat fills his skull from the inside, and for a moment it almost sounds like shorebreak.

WE ARE NOT YET HEALED

Avra Margariti

THE GIRLS ARE told the pain sparking their nerve endings isn't real. Psychosomatic. A delusion originating in the head, the womb. The girls are paraded before family doctors, prescribed iodine-rich air and an indefinite vacation by the sea. Sent to a cove-concealed, crumbling sanatorium, its walls so thick with salinity they might as well have been built out of salt in place of mortar.

Their families have given the girls a summer to get better, a season of dour-faced nurses force-feeding them bitter medicine and fatty fish flavored only with natural brine. Back home await the hungry mouths of unweaned babies and aging parents expecting the same care afforded to their wayward daughters. Fiancés to wed and fortunes to secure. Academies or nunneries to join, fields to tend, younger siblings to help raise. This summer is a chance to get better. An ultimatum, too. And if they fail, if they show themselves to be lost causes, this summer is a segue to a much worse fate.

The girls trace splinters down their bare bodies—driftwood dermatographia in a runic dialect they only half understand. They carve fingernail spells on each other's skin, already alight with neurogenic agony. When they sleep, they dream of each other's fingers, and of the fathoms stretching vast under sea and sand. Vast enough to reach the other side: no longer sea but sky, no longer sand but stardust. Sometimes, they awaken in their dormitory and think they are sedimented into slime at the ocean's floor. Sitting anchor-heavy until someone finds them, plucks them free.

It's not long before the nurses realize the girls like to flee their dormitory at night. To push their toes into the wet sand of a starless beach, before nerve-numbness pricks their fatigued extremities and the sand particles writhe with creatures wanting to pinch and bite. To bury their fingers into the tobacco-jaundiced beards of local fishermen, the only ones in this deserted coastal town who can provide contraband snuff and penny dreadfuls—for a price.

The nurses claim these odysseys of pain are due to a condition known as a wandering womb. So, tonight, the nurses lock thrice the wide front gates as well as the narrower dormitory door. They tie the girls to their bed frames with clean bandages across wrists and ankles, *for your own good,* they say, and feed them spoonfuls of brandy like they are unruly, fussy babies to be soothed to sleep.

The girls bare their teeth in pretend-struggle. But the truth is, their work on the beach is already done. Nothing left to do as the moon waxes in the sky but wait. Breaths held as the sea and sand perform their susurrating magic.

The early summer night crawls on, and the girls are not yet healed. But they have a secret. What they buried in the sand. And what will soon unearth itself.

ON THE NIGHT after the storm, the sea having cast its benthic gifts upon the shore, the girls last sneaked out and found the blobfish mass on the darkened beach. Mishappen, barely breathing, but calling out to them with each viscous rasp of gills. The creature was unformed or deformed, its flabby pink flesh spanning the length of the girls' own bodies. Veined silver under moonlight, it resembled meat left to rot at the mercy of the elements and the tapeworms. Instinct-deep, they knew to bury this blobfish girl in dry sand. Let her bake in the sun throughout the day like clay in its kiln. The girls didn't ignore the pain starbursting through their wrists as they did the burying—they reveled in it.

The next night, the blobfish girl enters the sanatorium like a thief or a ghost. When her salty slime oozes in through the cracks of doors locked tight, the girls know to make space for her in their bunks. To help her wrap her wrists and ankles in bandages as if the nurses had bound them to keep her from running off into the sea.

When she comes downstairs for breakfast, the sanatorium girls pretend this new girl, this blobfish girl, has always been there in their midst.

This girl is Thalassa, named after the sea. She is full formed again, as full formed as a girl dredged up from pelagic depths can be. As full formed as any girl can be, really.

She eats and talks with her mouth hanging open, and the nurses scold her, *Thalassa, your food is falling out,* but they do not question her presence. When Thalassa grins, she shows off such sharp teeth. Nacre-gleaming, they catch the light like wind chimes made of seashells. Thalassa winks at the girls who buried her and baked her into shape, while the nurses busy themselves with poultices and opium drafts, smelling salts, and implements of shock-therapy.

When the nurses scurry from the dining room, Thalassa spits out a pellet of bread and blood-red jam she only pretended to chew in their presence.

The girls are not yet healed. Yet the summer has just gotten interesting.

DURING QUIET TIME reserved for rest and reflection, the nurses leave the girls alone in the library. There, tasseled floor pillows and chaise lounges of frayed damask patterns have been provided for young women afflicted with maladies of the womb.

"Maladies," the girls giggle one to another. "My ladies."

They sit in a cove-crescent around an open encyclopedia, ignoring the pain pulsating from their knee joints and thigh muscles, the numbness seeping through their fingers as they turn page after brittle page. In between, they tongue sugary confections smuggled in under the nurses' noses earlier that morning.

Before the girls found their misshapen messiah on the beach, trade with the fishermen had gone quite differently. *Smile for us,* the fishermen would leer, *Smile prettier, smile bigger if you want your precious contraband.* Yet, ever since Thalassa, the fishermen give without taking. They still remember when they asked her to smile, and she opened her mouth wide and full of needled teeth. Now, the fishermen hide behind their bushy mustaches, handing out sugary humbugs and spicy dime novels, cowed by the girls' new leader. The new predator masquerading among them.

Frissons of excitement traverse the girls' spines when it occurs to them that they do not know what Thalassa eats. It's not the sugar they scoop onto their sweetness-starved tongues, nor the nurse's unseasoned gruel. Sometimes, Thalassa slinks into the sanatorium with blood rusting her teeth.

"Epipelagic zone," the girls read dutifully from the massive tome, the pages now crusted with the sugar and salt of their fingertips, "where most known species of marine life swim."

Thalassa stands above the girls like a maestra, the borrowed dress she wears billowing around her as if clandestine riptides are caught in its froth-white folds. "Go on."

"Mesopelagic zone," the girls continue, "where no photosynthetic organism is known to survive."

"More!" Thalassa calls out, her waist-length hair now joining the eddies of her dress. *Like tendrils,* the girls think. *Like tentacles.*

She had been bald when they first found her. Her scalp looser than the skin of post-partum bellies, the girls who had gone through pregnancy back home had mused. Her skin soft as a newborn's, reminiscent of the babies waiting for the girls to harness their so-called hallucinations, relieve their families of child-rearing burdens.

"Bathypelagic zone," the girls obediently read on. "Where—"

"No, deeper!" she commands. "Darker! Down under!"

The encyclopedia—previously opened on the letter *P*, for *pelagic zones*—snaps shut.

"Abyssopelagic," the girls intone as one, staring straight into Thalassa's fathomless eyes. "A zone whose tenebrous depths are penetrated only by the bioluminescence of its grotesque denizens."

"*There*," Thalassa says with a satiated tilt of her head, familiarly predacious. "That's where I lived. But let me tell you a secret." The girls lean close, their sternums aching with eagerness. Sweeter than the sugar they compulsively consume. "It's not where I come from."

The summer is not yet ended. The girls wish to cling to the meat of it, like rot to a wound, long enough to learn Thalassa's truth.

THE SKY GROWS overcast, clouds matted as if by dirty brush-strokes of expired watercolors. When the girls are asked to draw outdoors—*art therapy*, the nurses call it—they paint blobs, amorphous and gnarled and sloughing. The nurses think this is because the girls are hagridden things, plagued by female afflictions. The visiting doctor believes their muscle atrophy stems from the girls being too nerveless to make a family, please a husband. The fire of their nerve endings nothing but mass hysteria. What else is there to expect from the females of the species?

Thalassa's canvas is tar-black corner to corner, like a ship spewing its poisonous guts into the sea. The oily residue sediments upon the beach to drown starveling seagulls and shallows-swimming fish in chemical corruption.

While the nurses stare out to sea, as if they, too, wonder how their lives could have turned out were they not wardens to a group of sick girls, flights-of-fancy girls, Thalassa steps out of her lustrous shoes. She buries her pale feet into the paler sand, and soon, the rest of her body follows. Sinking, slowly, sinking. The sand specks are so fine and white, they might as well have been ground bone.

The girls mimic her. The girls are always mimicking her, the way they never did with the nurses. Together, Thalassa and her entourage dive under the sand, to find the tunnels of surly crab kings, tunnels paved in dinosaur bones and dead stars-turned-starfish. The particles of sand become molecules of air. The girls' lungs remain unobstructed despite the rough scrape of granular sand.

"Show us," the girls beg of Thalassa in her coastal cradleland. "Your secret, please. We're ready."

"Tonight," she says—a mystic, whetted smile. "Tonight, when the sky weeps its errant children like so many tears."

The summer is crawling to completion with rheumatic-slow steps. The girls never want to heal if it means going back to the real world, abyssal wonders relinquished to the tide.

THE NURSES ARE onto their comings and goings. But ever since Thalassa joined the sanatorium, the nurses dare not lock the doors or tie the girls to their beds at night. Their jaws lock whenever Thalassa glances in their direction. Their throats bob as if fishbones are lodged in their linings. Even the visiting doctor's shock therapies have been put on hold, the treatment room gone unused for weeks, metal implements gathering cobwebs and dust. When the pain-thrumming girls chug laudanum now, it's not to cure the bright ideas in their heads—the ideas they were told to shed before their families summoned them back after summer is dead and gone.

Night falls—a blackened breath over the seaside sanatorium. Thalassa beckons for the girls to follow her. Like a Pied Piper, she leads a barefoot, white-gowned procession toward the corpse-pale stretch of sand.

On the beach, a reverent Thalassa kneels and turns her silver-veined, semi-translucent face skyward. The girls follow her lead, all of them craning aching necks to peer up at the muddy dark of the sky. Stars pierce the welkin, writhing.

"There," Thalassa says and points an elongated finger toward the first falling star.

It's the night of the Perseids, at the height of August.

"Did you know stars are an invasive species?" Thalassa asks with abject glee as the star shower commences in primordial choreography, saturating the sky with a light that streaks kaleidoscopic and vertiginous.

The first star falls like a flaming ball of plasma straight into the veil-dark sea. It sizzles as it hits the moon-mirror surface, stardust replaced by sea foam. The star doesn't bob to the surface, but sinks.

"It's what I did," Thalassa says, at once serene and starving—the paradox of sea and sky. "A shooting star fallen like a rebel angel into the sea, just as my people do before your eyes. Slumbering on the bottom—until I was summoned."

Did we summon you? is a thing the girls do not need to ask.

They think about the library's encyclopedia: P, for pelagic; pagefuls of painted illustrations. How oceanic pressure is known to deform all living creatures in profound enough depths. The ineffable becoming grotesque upon emergence, then molded beautiful again under the girls' fistfuls of sand. Fallen star to blobfish to Thalassa, the girl mistakenly named after the sea rather than the sky.

The girls' fingers have never been called clever, agile, graceful. Embroidery and other approved pastimes send pain shooting up their ulnae; nerve endings had gone aflame when tending home and hearth before being sent to the sanatorium by the sea. Yet to have their aching, deformed fingers remake something alien and celestial…oh, what an honor the nurses would never comprehend.

"We will help you," the girls fall one over the other to assure her, before Thalassa has even asked. "We will awaken your people. Bury them brand new."

"Did you know the moon is made of rib bones?" Thalassa asks, smug and stewing in approval and an ancient, tidal need.

"Ribbons?" the girls ask, and Thalassa laughs, laughs up a tempest.

More stars fall, plummeting into the sea. The deforming bodies of her constellary kin laugh in reply as the sea ripples and perforates like the skin of sour milk boiled twice over.

"Yes," Thalassa says at last. "You will help. When it's time."

The girls touch their own tender ribs and each other's. They tighten the ribbons of their corsets until they steal each other's breath like a kiss. They want to be ready when the time comes to be useful, to be used.

The summer thrums in the throes of ending. The girls, not yet fixed, thrum too.

"IS IT SOON?" the susurrus spreads through the sanatorium, the girls bursting with need at their weathered seams. Dreaming of dredging more beautiful, eerie girl-things from the deep. "Oh, please, can we perform the ritual?"

"Soon," Thalassa promises. "When the moon is full enough to burst into a shower of viscera. Moon, soon, soon, my lovelies."

Her smile is so cryptic, the girls want to lick it off her face. They wish to split their lips on her sharpness. Their longing has a taste, and it's ferrous and thick with salinity.

In the meantime, they practice the ritual on the beach. *Somnambulism*, the nurses whisper to one another to excuse the girls' wanderings and their own fearful inaction.

The girls steal into the deserted beach, where even the fishermen are too apprehensive to approach now. *How do we call the sea to recede, to reveal the stars cocooned in deconstructed slime?* the girls wonder. *Do we walk into the water and part it?* But these are girls deemed sick in the head, when in truth it's their bodies that are suffering. They are not messiahs, nor are they the martyrs of families tiring of this waiting game back home. The girls have been given a summer ultimatum to get better, before they are locked away somewhere far worse than this seaside sanatorium. Somewhere not even stars can invade.

Do we drink the sea? they ask each other next. Under Thalassa's watchful gaze, they try. The girls have been hungry for so long, it doesn't seem impossible their ravening is vast enough to engulf the sea and leave the sandy floor bare for Thalassa to reawaken her people.

"Did you know," Thalassa says, "the sands of time from which I was fashioned are older than the sand of this beach, and finer than the sand that suffuses your dreams? Did you know that even stardust is made of sand?"

The girls cup their hands together, fingers tucked cordiform, seawater raised to parched mouths. Yet no matter how much they drink of the burning saltwater that triggers their own tear ducts, the sea level does not diminish. Overhead, the moon sighs its disappointment, bulging full as an overstuffed throw pillow. The girls are running out of time. Already, August is dregs in a stained teacup. The summer threatens to heave its last breath, and soon.

The girls vomit saltwater and seaweed across the beach. They try to bury their shame for failing to swallow the water's entire body, even with their voracious hunger. Thalassa is there to push the hair back from their sweat-slick faces, to wipe their tears mingling with sea foam. Her touch, fish-guts-slimy, is the only solace to have touched these girls' skin.

"This is not how we unearth my kin. How we unsea them."

The girls gather round her, their long gowns sticking to their ailing bodies, their minds fever-burning with need. The girls are so tired, so slow, so numb, and no one will tell them why. Because it's all in their wombs, all in their heads. Or so the girls are told.

"We do not swallow the sea, but steal it. Soon, my lovelies. Moon-soon, my broken rib bones, my raveled ribbons."

The summer is dying. The girls think they might be, too. But later is later and now is now—and they will call the sea home.

THE MOON RISES. The sea, too. A moon-shaped sphere of luminous water hovers in the sky, orchestrated by the girls and overlooked by Thalassa, their celestial ringleader. Soon, the undulating mass of water lifts from the beach to traverse the night air, dripping saline droplets yet miraculously intact. A microcosmos swirls, captured in the sphere: jellyfish and driftwood, seaweed and shipwreck detritus.

The girls are dancing. It is a dance disjointed, clumsy, erratic. It lacks limb coordination and the propriety expected of young women. Yet Thalassa does not chastise them like their families or nurses would have done. She dances, too, and for the first time, a bioluminescence glows from within her core. Once more, her skin becomes near-diaphanous, like the first time the girls found her washed up on the shore—an amorphous, spilled blob. Her lower jaw juts out, teeth elongated like an anglerfish's extracted from abyssopelagic depths. Newly gouged gills flare in feral exhilaration.

The girls stand on the stripped seafloor, their bare feet slashed open by jagged mussels and sea-glass. Where shore was once kissed by sea, now a tongue of uninterrupted beach unravels as far as the eye can see. The cove where the sanatorium once perched is now a cauldron, a cradle of fallen pieces of firmament.

And it is toward the former sanatorium that the girls lead the levitating ocean. The water is summoned with their minds, not their muscles, and at this, euphoria rises ebullient within them, and they stretch a noetic limb they hadn't realized had long gone to sleep. The water slips inside the crumbling, salt-encrusted structure, through each tiny crack of window and doorway, mouse hole and bug burrow. Yet once inside, it dares not leak—not a drop. The gaps between window drapes become oubliette slits of shackled saltwater, sea creatures swimming languid from within.

The sand is laid bare, the stars ripe for the plucking.

A mouth, the sanatorium holds a draft of saltwater in its rotten cavity. The nurses drown. The sharp medical implements float like fishhooks. The encyclopedias on pelagic zones and female hysteria grow waterlogged, then turn to sugar-stained pulp under the ocean's pulverizing pressure. The girls' bedclothes, the gauzes that bound them docile, their letters from families and fiancés asking with ever-thinning patience when the girls will be healed, when the girls are coming home... Soon, it all vanishes into the murk.

The girls converge on the sea-orphaned beach. They gather pretty pearls and nacreous seashells to decorate their hair, silvered by moonlight. The coast is scattered with blobs like drowned sailors or jetsam, but the girls do not approach them. Thalassa shrieks like a feral thing, whirling from kin to kin, greeting each flabby mound with wet kisses and handfuls of sand. She waits for the rising sun to bake her constellary people into shape—simulacrums of humanity.

The tar-blighted bodies will need no help digging themselves up. In time, the stars will do their own unburying.

Stars are an invasive species, comes the unbidden thought through the girls' minds. An abyssopelagic army banishing the seas, felling the sky until the whole world turns celestial and grotesque. In the meantime, conjuring up a human façade while blood rusts their sharpened teeth.

The girls don't know what will happen next, after the star-kin heal and prowl the earth. But they know it must be better than this cove-concealed beach and its sanatorium where their pain had gone ignored.

The girls know anything must be better than this cruel summer finally coming to an end.

THE LOVE OF ALL SEEING FLESH

Hazel Zorn

THE BONELESS THING swam down her throat after the dark waves lapped over her head. It forced itself down, slimy as an oyster, with tendrils that pushed against the inside of her cheek. Slightly nauseous and lightheaded, she bobbed up above the waves and walked to the shore. *Where the hell were you?* her mother demanded. Her cousins had been crying. Their pale flesh was shadowed with gray sand, their eyes were swollen, and between them they'd collected her rainbow goggles and boogie board.

Just playing, she said.

She didn't care that she got in trouble. She knew—after half an hour of pretending she didn't—that nobody could do anything to her now.

IT THROBBED WITHIN her, a second heart. Sometimes it unfurled like a flower, other times it clenched like a fist.

Days later, as late summer finally blanketed Gloucester in a thick soup of heat, her father gave her a beating. It wasn't a matter of deserving or undeserving. It was like a storm. The reasons were backfilled. This one was his last hurrah before the school year. Before too many people would see her. Her tooth scratched her throat on the way down. The swelling of her lip impaired her speech.

An ice pack appeared on her dresser. That was, she understood, the only sympathy her mother would afford her.

She wasn't bad. She wasn't special, either.

She was no longer the same person.

In fact, she was not sure that she was a person at all, anymore.

THEY FOUND HER on the beach. They lifted her up, half asleep, and carried her back home. *I was comfortable*, she explained to her raging, inconsolable parents. *I burrowed into the sand and enjoyed it.*

WHEN SHE AWOKE, there was a chair crammed into the space between the bed and the door. Her mother was in it, her hands clenched in her lap. *Is it too hot? It's really hot out there. People are collapsing. Is that what happened to you?*

Eyes half-mast, she didn't answer her mother.

Take your medicine. Won't you please? It will help.

She finally determined, after all these years, that her mother was slow-witted.

SHE KNEW THAT her parents fought, in the way that most kids knew the cadence of an argument. Afterward, what remained was like the smell of ozone, the tense silence charging the air, something felt instead of witnessed or touched. But now it was as if a blanket had been thrown over her corner of the world and nothing could puncture it.

Two doors down from her own, a glass shattered. Their voices boomed.

She crawled under the bed and counted the slats above her, her body making a dark road through the dust. She traced shapes onto the floor: "W" shapes to make waves, hundreds of them, until she was surrounded. Water didn't have boundaries. Water went where it liked. She wanted to ooze through the cracks of the world.

SHE WAS IN the same bed a few days later. Or maybe a few weeks later. The room was empty. Through the open window she heard no sounds and felt no wind. Her chest was warm, humming. She went back to sleep.

HER FATHER WAS in the room. She felt it before she opened her eyes. *You won't take your medicine?*

The floorboards creaked, his breath in her nose. His grip on her small arm so tight it would leave a purple ring. *What's the matter with you? Huh?*

She snared him with her eyes.

He stilled, face like chipped flint. He was big in ways that didn't matter and small in ways that did. So small that she found him pathetic.

The *plip plip* of rainfall in a bucket reached her ears. The sky outside was clear. When the acrid smell of piss reached her, she closed her eyes, releasing him.

He let out a wobbling, raspy moan before he stumbled across the creaking floor. The door swung into the wall with an explosive bang.

THERE WAS A man in the room. His hands were gloved. *Don't worry, I'm here to help*, he said.

She closed her eyes. This seemed to irritate him. He shone a light into her face. *Don't you want to get better?*

There was no better. There was only this. She stared at him with the incuriosity he deserved. Finally, exasperated, he left.

THE ROOM WAS empty, as was the house.

A BOIL ON her inner arm looked at her. Then, it blinked.

The red evening light caught the metallic picture frame on her bedside table, which displayed a picture she'd cut out of a teen magazine. An attractive surfer in San Diego, his white-blond hair ablaze in the sun, his tan body glistening and wet. Next to that, her seashell collection from third grade. Dusty lip gloss. A pink and glittery rabbit-foot key chain.

She pulled the covers over her head.

OUTSIDE, THE WORLD was different. She walked down the street, and the sound of the waves on the coast filled her head. A roar that seemed to whisper her name against the salt-stained rocks.

She passed an overturned car with a body in it and did not stop but kept on, kept walking. Yellow tape that read "DO NOT CRO—" blew across the silent road, opulent sidewinders.

SUMMER WAS HOT and wrathful in her mind, like so many before it, especially without the respite of school. An overturned cooler on the sidewalk oozed a puddle of vanilla. The same flavor of ice cream she'd stolen from the freezer at the age of seven. It had not, in her mind, constituted hatred or disrespect of her father. But she remembered squirming in the lawn chair while he bellowed afterward, the roar of the shore accentuating his voice. And then his knuckles dropped a shudder over the light of the world. Her left eye had swelled shut, and the skin turned purple-black.

Why did you have me if you hate me?

I never wanted you in the first place.

THERE WAS A crowd of people now, all walking with her. Concrete gave way to sand, and the sky broadened. One boy about her age stopped, buried his legs in the sand, and lay back. Passers-by patted him on the head. *That's right. Rest. Rest.*

A keening sound to her left made her shoulders hunch. A woman. Not her mother, but someone just like her. The woman screamed, red in the face, and pulled on the arm of a teen girl. *Stop this, come here. Come with me.* She kept saying it over and over.

"This won't do." The boy to her right looked at her with all of his eyes.

She agreed.

They wrestled the woman away from the girl, who walked into the water until it covered her head.

When the woman continued to scream, she forced her fist into the gaping maw. Her hand bones shifted like rubber inside the wet cavity, the woman's teeth dimpling her skin but never penetrating. The woman thrashed, wide-eyed, scream muffled.

Her organs fused into one long and glistening tendril affixed to the hand down her throat. The woman was made to vomit up her insides, her skin reduced to a helpless and deflated wet-suit on the beach. *Please stop,* she begged them as the children interrogated her for days after.

Do you really want to eat this much? Practice walking in your heels. Are you watching your weight?

Her eyes, forced to stare at the sun, baked like poached eggs in the days that followed. The children eventually severed her insides from their body. The globular mass lay abandoned, undeserving of new life. Seagulls feasted. The children scattered her remains. No one came looking for her.

Finally, the woman was made to be silent.

I'LL RUN AWAY, she'd told him once, on a cool day by the shore as egrets circled above.

His brown teeth bared at her. *It won't do you any good. You'd never survive on your own.*

He was right. Her chest and legs burned as the wind off the sea filled her lungs. She ran and ran until her jeans were soaked, toward the horizon line of the never-ending water. The water rebuffed her, foamy waves slapping her like she was any other rock. Sullen, sodden, she relented and went home.

She noticed that her footprints remained in the sand for days after, as the gray sky kept the shore from drying out. She followed them back to the water where, finally, they disappeared. She wrote *help me* in the sand. The water crawled up and took the message away.

It was then when she realized, after some reflection, that the people who looked skyward for help, who begged the *divine* or the *universe* for answers—these people were not looking in the right direction. The sky receded to a lonely and black nothing. They were speaking to *nothing*.

But the water's depths were potent and teeming. It had many eyes and ears.

The real universe was there. It was not *void*, but *plenum*.

HER BODY BECAME like stretched taffy in the water, eyes bubbling up to the surface of her transformed skin, each hand joining hers merging and growing and stretching.

There was no *her*. There was no *them* or *it*.

Us.

OUR FLESHY MASS turned over and over in the water as the waves called out to the shore. Our snakelike tendrils dipped in and out of the water, lurching and writhing as we grew larger than a whale, and even larger still. We had thousands of eyes. The wet orbs reflected the blue-yellow vault above.

There were screams and shouts of rage along the coast. They choked. Gurgled.

Silenced.

AFTER A WHILE the sirens stopped. Her mother left.

At first, her mother hopped the barricade and returned to the house once, and then again. There, she turned over the beds, opened the closets, and screamed—*Come back! Come back!* But it was no use. She wanted to feel justified in letting go, in laying blame on things beside herself.

Birds nested in the kitchen sink. Frogs and flies inhabited the bathroom.

Her mother was escorted out by a patrol. *Nothing you can do,* they said. *Get to safety.*

LATE AT NIGHT, the beach cold and dark, she waded into the water and emptied out her father's bottles. The glass splashed and then dipped under the dark water. She was not littering but operating with knowledge and purpose, because she knew exactly what to do. What fueled her father's irascible rage would become a libation instead.

With her arms outstretched, she waited. She stood there until the cold curled around her like a fist. After a short time, she could not feel her submerged legs. It was as if they'd been cauterized from the rest of her shivering body.

The night seemed to be listening to her, the presence of the sea close and attentive. Her eyes flicked over moonlit water, the strange feeling growing. The light inverted, turning the black water a blazing white. She couldn't hear anything. Even the air was as silent as a held breath.

In that quiet, the water went as still as a glass sheet. The thing floated up to meet her. Dark, solitary, a flicker of night. It hovered by her kneecap and unfurled. It was like and unlike a starfish in shape and movement. More like a star made organic, energy cast in flesh the way lightning could forge glass from sand. A star of the opposite sky underneath the sea. A creature of the vast and deep plenum. It had risen to her, shooting up with uncommon speed and purpose from the seafloor, a comet with a long and dark tail.

SHE STOOD THERE until morning, until her cousins joined her on the beach for a day of play. She had lived through enough. Now she understood that it was her turn to make demands. Only the people who had nothing would be welcome. Her body vibrated with joy. *Watch me*, she ordered them. *Watch me go.*

The world would listen to her now, or it would be silenced.

⚓

SOMEWHERE BETWEEN TOMIS AND CALLATIS

Adriana C. Grigore

OLIMP, JUNE 11TH

WE START IN Olympus, because we always do.

Carmen is with us, although she doesn't know it yet; so
is Luca. From the top of the Majestic Hotel, we watch them
drift into town, dragging their not-yet-sun-bleached suitcases
along the perfectly empty road. They notice each other and
exchange a few words. They notice neither the emptiness
nor us watching from the highest balcony of this odiously
yellow building.

The good thing about Olimp is that it's almost secluded from
the other resort towns. You can see all five of them from up
here, but there is a stretch of road before you get to Neptun

that, at night, turns opaque with darkness. Alex likes it. They say it makes them remember sleeping.

They join me on the balcony as, thirteen stories below us, Carmen and Luca reach the lobby. Alex bends nearly double over the railing, and I wonder when I stopped being afraid either for or of them. In the unmoving summer sun, the freckles on their shoulders are ever unchanged.

When they catch me looking, they smile. No teeth yet.

OLIMP, JUNE 12TH

I WATCH CARMEN and Luca drift in and out of the water and take turns watching each other's bags without seeming to notice there's nobody else on this plastic-strewn beach aside from the four of us. Not that they've noticed us yet. They laugh at each other's jokes as they buy greasy plates from the fried fish vendor at the edge of the road, and don't seem to notice that the fish vendor is not really there either.

"Are you hungry?" I ask Alex, watching the waves splash into a bed of drying seaweed. The water is murky, and I am not afraid.

Alex sighs, dragging their fingers in and out of the scorching sand.

"We'll eat tomorrow," I say.

They trickle sand onto my palm, and it almost, almost hurts.

NEPTUN, JUNE 13TH

IN NEPTUN, WE decide to join them.

Rather, I decide, and Alex drags their feet until the smell of frying oil wafting out the Springtime across the road makes them beeline for the most secluded table. They kick up their legs on a plastic chair as I drift inside to the tune of an old summer song.

Inside, the restaurant is so brightly lit that the beige tiles on the floors and walls glisten like scales. The music is louder here, but the tray still echoes as I drag it from one counter to the next. As I return outside, tray full, I pass by Carmen and Luca, who are sitting together, dishes half full.

It takes four and a half minutes for Carmen to turn to our table and ask, "Excuse me, but is it just me or is this whole place *really* empty? Was there a warning? Is there another lockdown?"

They don't usually notice it this early.

Across from me, Alex raises their eyebrows expectantly and bites off the bitter head of a fish—also expectantly. Their way of saying, *See, un-fuck this situation by yourself now.*

"These places are larger than they look. You might've just missed the others."

"Have *you* seen anyone?"

I struggle to think amid the sounds of Alex's chewing. "Not really."

"No one on the beach either," Luca says. "Towels, yes, but no people."

He doesn't seem to have noticed there was no one to serve their food either. I reach across and pull the plate of fries out of Alex's reach. "Could've missed some lifeguard warning."

Luca considers it. "Yeah, maybe they all went to Mamaia."

Carmen snorts. "Not in the state that place is in. They tried to charge me and my friends in euros last time I went to a resort there. Who the fuck has euros?"

"Lots of people," he counters.

"Those people don't bother coming here."

Luca turns to us with an awkward, pleading smile. "Where are you two staying?"

"The Istria," I say.

"Huh!" says Carmen, forgetting her rant.

"Us too!"

NEPTUN, JUNE 14TH

THERE'S A LAKE in Neptun, right between the resorts and the beach, cut in two by a bridge down the middle. One side is filled with water lilies; the other, even now, with swans.

We get there after sundown, after Luca went to sleep and Carmen went for a smoke by the pool, and I peel a beer bottle off the bottom of a frozen-over cooler.

There are lights peppered along the lake shores, but they're quickly overshadowed by the encroaching dark. As the evening deepens, so does the lake. Until there is nothing but the slight reflection of stars on its black surface, and the faint ripples our steps send into the cloying water.

I raise the bottle to my mouth and taste blood, then ash, then at last something acrid as I sit down, feet dangling over the water, sea at my back. When the wind picks up, it turns deafening.

"Do you remember that first time," I say, "when we thought this was the sea?"

A breath away, the actual sea beckons. If we'd known ages ago what we know now, we might never have gone to see it at all, just stayed here, with the lilies.

Alex catches a fish, then another. Then another. Then a bird. I finish my beer amid the sounds of cracking bones.

NEPTUN, JUNE 15TH

WE GET DELAYED, if any such thing is still possible, by Carmen catching a stomach bug. Luca blames the food stalls. I don't counter.

"You don't have to stay in with us," Luca says. "I've got it covered. Go, it's a nice day!"

He's holding Carmen's hair as she heaves, wiping her brow every now and again. I wonder if either of them remembers that mere days ago they were strangers to each other.

We spend the day drifting through every remaining stall in the amusement park, then crank up every ride. Our cabin on the Ferris wheel creaks and creaks, like a branch about to fall off, but it doesn't.

On the way back, Alex gathers half a dozen glow-in-the-dark bracelets for each hand. That night, I see them flickering on the seashore.

JUPITER, JUNE 16TH

JUPITER GREETS US with smoother sands, clearer waters, and the odious green sight of the Capitol jutting out of the cliff side. It's tall enough that its shadow follows us down to the shore, where we spread our towels in the crook of a small breakwater and spend the morning skipping stones and gathering shells.

In the evening, we walk between the stalls along the narrow, empty road, filling our arms with corn on the cob and crepes, and our bags with bottles of liqueur that won't fit in the hotel's mini fridges.

At night, in our odious green rooms with their odious cement balconies and odious beige curtains, we listen to the mosquitoes sing in the air above our faces and watch the lights of the Tomis port gleam awake in the distance.

JUPITER, JUNE 17TH

CARMEN LOOKS BETTER, but not by much. Her fingers tremble on the lighter, and she eyes the sea distrustfully for a good long while before turning to Luca.

"Were we always—"

"Anyone up for a soak?" I ask almost too quickly, jumping up. Anything to break their focus.

"God, yes, I'm boiling," Luca groans and gets up too. "Cami, you coming?"

"Uh, no, I think I'm…"

"*Come ooon!* It's good for you!"

"Okay, fine!"

She laughs and lets herself be pulled up.

I look to Alex, and we stay two paces behind them until the sea water reaches up past our shins, autumn-cold against sun- and sand-burnt skin. It was too close. It was maybe nothing.

Alex kicks their left leg in a high arch, and it splashes me, plasters the hair to my face, lights yellow sparks in my vision. And they laugh, and laugh, and laugh, noiseless in the summer wind.

The water is clearer, and I am not afraid.

JUPITER, JUNE 18TH

IT WASN'T NOTHING. It's never nothing.

"No, I'm telling you, *this* is our hotel," Carmen says, pointing at the Capitol.

"Are you sure?" Luca scrunches up his nose. "These old communist hotels all look the same. I'm pretty sure we're a few turns that way."

"Yes, I'm sure," Carmen bristles and starts digging in her bag, at which point I know it's futile to intervene.

She pulls out her room key and dangles it in Luca's face, so he can see the seahorse engraving that's the same as the one hanging high over the Capitol's south side. He blinks, and just like that, we've lost another day.

"Oh, yeah… Huh, I could've sworn—"

"I need a fucking drink." Carmen swerves around and walks up to the hotel lobby without looking back.

When I glance Alex's way, their expression is indifferent. But their fingernails dig into my wrist while we're waiting for the elevator back to the room we should've vacated two days ago now.

CAP AURORA, JUNE 19TH

THIS TIME, I change our keys while everyone is otherwise occupied on the beach. I take out the green circlets of the Capitol and leave in their stead the blue and white squares of the Opal, and that does it. When we retreat for the afternoon, we do so in Cap Aurora.

CAP AURORA, JUNE 20TH

CAP AURORA IS a small enough place that it's easy to miss on the way from Jupiter to Venus. A string of jewel-christened hotels strewn along fewer than a thousand meters of land, squeezed between the Black Sea and the Comorova Forest.

To get to the water, an amalgamation of shared paths and stairs lead from each hotel to every other hotel in a strange impression of an abandoned tilted garden. At high noon, the air smells of scorched greenery and little else. In the evening, the paths get dark enough to make one fall while standing still.

It used to be one of my favorite places.

I lose track of Alex sometime in the afternoon of our second day on the shores of Cap Aurora. I was too focused on chaperoning Carmen and Luca's conversations, lest one's doubts pass on to the other. *Bit late for that*, I imagine Alex saying while I pretend not to see the glances Carmen and Luca throw each other when I've got my head bent down over a crossword.

Damage control, I think back at Alex, jotting down a five across.

Overcompensating, they retort.

Alex doesn't reappear when we meander back up to dinner, nor afterward while I keep Carmen and Luca insistent company—until the wine makes one of them doze off in the lobby. When I retire, our room, dark and loud as the sea, is empty.

I'm three-quarters through the last of the wine bottles when the door creaks open and a line of yellow light cuts the room in two before dimming back to moonlight. Alex gives me a look. Even in the darkness, I see it.

Their hair is matted and their clothes cling to their skin, like they've been diving, and their bare feet tread wetly on the carpet—and there's something more than water dripping off them. When they turn to lock the door behind them, their eyes momentarily glint black from corner to corner.

And I am not afraid, but I do worry.

"Are you feeling all right?" I ask, getting up to meet them. "We haven't been this late in a while."

Instead of answering, they push me back down onto the bed and crawl on top of me until whatever soaked them soaks me too. They part my lips like something starving, fingers sinking in like fishhooks, breath a leaden weight pulling me under. A ruinous kiss, a ritual drowning, a rising tide until I give them what they want. The promise of a whimper, the flutter of a prey caught. When their teeth find my tongue, I taste brine and blood alike, and I remember I'm starving too.

VENUS, JUNE 21ST

IT'S THE LAST good night, for a very stretched definition of *good.*

In Venus, we carry our luggage to the Calipso, and nobody, not even Carmen, acts as if anything is out of the ordinary.

I draw all the curtains closed and leave Alex cocooned in the hotel room, bedsheets slowly turning cold and damp around them, then I join Carmen and Luca on the beach. It's an overcast day, which is already unfamiliar. Usually, we are already in Saturn by the time the clouds come.

The lack of sun coaxes Carmen out of the shade at least, and she announces loudly that she's going to go hunt for sea glass. I watch her move along the rocky shore, from one breakwater to another, until she's obscured by the ever-unchanging mass of plastic and straw umbrellas cluttering the sand.

Luca sidles up to me. "I much prefer this weather, to be honest. Look, I've already started to shed!"

He holds his arm out to show me a patch of dead white skin bubbled over and torn in some places.

"We told you to use more sunscreen."

"Yeah, but I didn't know I was a *baby*," he huffs. "Plus, there was nobody at the counter when I tried to buy more. It's like a ghost town out here, isn't it?" A laugh titters out of him like grains from a ripped sack. "Everything okay with your...?"

"Partner?"

"Yeah."

"They're under the weather."

"Ah. Sunstroke?"

"Very possibly."

He shifts his weight from one foot to the other, tugs on the bloody skin around a fingernail. I watch the ships peppering the horizon, waiting to be let in to the Tomis port.

He follows my gaze. "Strange that none of those ships have moved since we arrived here, right?"

"Haven't they? I didn't notice."

"I don't know, maybe I'm imagining it..."

"Maybe."

I don't react, but he doesn't either, which is more telling than he probably wants it to be. When he reaches a hand to push the hair out of his eyes, it's trembling.

"I can't wait to get home," he says. "I know that's exactly what a workaholic would say, but I also really miss mountain mornings. All this fishy air is wreaking havoc on my sinuses." He kicks a bit at the sand. "What are you gonna do after this?"

I shrug. "Much of the same."

I FIND ALEX in the bathroom. They're in the tub, eyes squeezed shut underwater, only their knees breaking the surface. When I crouch beside them, they crack an eye open, and I see the moment they breathe in wrong. I see the first spasm that pushes the air out of their lungs. And when they make to rise, I place a hand over their chest and hold them down.

Instantly, their body jerks once more, then again. Their hands clench around the edges of the bathtub and their legs kick out against it until I'm soaked through, but I don't pull back. I hold them down until their hands leave the rim and reach for their throat, until they dig their fingers into the sides of their neck and tear the skin away in ragged strips.

What pours out is not blood but something much darker, and so cold that my skin goes numb within seconds. I hold them down until I feel them breathing again, and then I pull my arm out of the black water. Already, there's salt crusted around my fingers, ash-gray and abrasive.

This time, when Alex pulls themself up, their arms clink against the bathtub, and I run my fingers over the pallid barnacles now swirling over their skin, pressing on the tender spots where some have fallen. The gashes on their neck look old and weather-worn, smoothened like sea glass. Their eyes are murky, almost stained. Alex looks at me and spits black water in my face.

I laugh. "Feeling better?"

They run their hands over their face and groan.

"We might be speeding the pace soon."

They sigh. "Thank fuck."

VENUS, JUNE 22ND

IT'S A COUPLE minutes past midnight when Luca raps frantically at our door, and a quarter past when we make our way toward the barren strip of land that separates Venus from Saturn.

The road is dark on every side, the moon barely peeking through the clouds. On our left, there are ash-gray sands and the roiling sea. On our right, deafening black reeds and the Mangalia marshes.

"I don't know what happened," Luca says as we leave the sidewalk for the sand. "I saw she'd left her phone in my room, and when I went over to return it, she wasn't there."

He doesn't realize the moment we cross the line from Venus to Saturn, but we do.

Alex, half-swallowed by a sweatshirt large enough to hide their arms and torn neck from view, leans into my side, and I don't think their eyes are open as they let me drag them along.

"And you're sure she came this way?" I ask Luca for the second time.

"Well, yeah... I mean, I... Look!"

There is a light on the shore some way ahead of us, illuminating one of the many straw umbrellas.

When we reach it, we see that it was, indeed, Carmen's phone light used a beacon. However, Carmen is nowhere to be seen.

"I thought you said she left her phone in your room." I turn back to Luca, only to be greeted by empty air.

Next to me, Alex sighs. Then I hear Luca say, "I'm sorry about this." And I fall to the ground.

SATURN, JUNE 22ND

IT'S NEAR DAWN when I wake up. My limbs are sore, and my clothes are full of sand. I look up blearily and find Carmen crouched in front of me, a kitchen knife dangling from her fingers. The sea is only a few paces away.

"Who are you?" Carmen asks.

I look away to the side and see Luca fretting, wringing his hands over Alex, who lies unconscious on a plastic lounge chair, their wrists and ankles tied in similar fashion to mine. "Carmen, they really don't look well…"

"I said *leave them*," Carmen snarls, then kicks my leg. "Hey! Look at me!"

Luca chokes back a whine. "Carmen, please, there's something seriously wrong with them…"

"Shut up," she says and looks back at me. "Where are we? Where is everybody? Who the fuck are you?"

I grimace and incline my head to the right. "That over there's Saturn, and then Mangalia…"

This time, she angles the knife at my throat. "Bullshit! Why can't I leave?"

"Carmen," Luca warns, distracted by the knife.

"Shut. Up. Tell me!"

I sigh. "Because there's nowhere for you to go."

"What the fuck does that mean?"

Behind her, the sea draws a little closer. "This isn't a place."

"What is it then?"

"A cage."

The knife digs into my throat, and she makes a choked-off sound—and I realize: she's not angry. She's terrified. "Why are you doing this?" she asks.

The sea is now close enough that it touches her feet, but she doesn't notice.

"Oh, god…" Luca says.

As if glad of the excuse, Carmen whirls around. "What?"

Luca is staring at the empty lunge chair beside him. "Where… where did they go?"

For several moments they don't have, the pair hesitate. Then the sea is all around us, swirling like wine in a glass, so dark its colors seem to seep into the sky above, to bring the stars back into view. My arms and legs are still tied, and, as the waves reach past my chest, I remember the feeling of sacrifice, of rams brought to the altar.

I see a pair of barnacle-covered hands wrap themselves around Carmen's legs, and then she's gone. I turn to Luca, who is petrified, holding onto a tilting umbrella. The sea roils. He looks at me and begs without any words to spare.

"This isn't personal," I say, and close my eyes as the sea eats us alive.

SATURN, JUNE 23RD

WE END UP in the Siren Hotel, because we always do, and though I cannot move, I know we are alone. *I* am alone, in this blue room overlooking the sea, balcony door open and blue-white drapes moving in the breeze.

It smells the way it always does, like crisp sheets and scrubbed carpet, sea salt and something so old that no layers of paint have managed to hide it. It smells like childhood summers. It smells like a memory.

There are faces on the ceiling. Faint, bare indents in the chipping paint. In this moment, I see them looking back at me, countless in their expressions of grief and horror.

Except they're not countless. I know exactly how many there are.

The door opens, the breeze pushes the drapes above my eyes for a moment, and the faces disappear, and I can move. I sit up.

Alex walks in, fiddling with a set of keys. They glance my way, nod, and drop the keys into the hotel's wastebasket, where they clink against the others.

"It's done?" I ask, as they pick up a pen.

"It's done," they say, jotting down two more names on the wall, and I see, along their forearm, the reddened marks where two more barnacles have fallen.

"Are you okay?"

They give me a peace sign without turning around. "Wanna see who's next?"

"I suppose we must."

From our room on the top floor, we take the stairs down halfway. Half the doors on either side are open, making the wind inside so strong it's like walking through water. Through the last open doorway, I see the sun-bleached suitcases that had belonged Carmen and Luca. Then Alex turns the key in the next door over, and we step inside.

The room is as empty as all the others, but there is a black and pink suitcase on one side of the bed and a patterned backpack sitting in the armchair opposite. It doesn't take long to dig through them, to learn names and occupations and hobbies, to plan the exact trajectory of this deathly pilgrimage and to imagine just where exactly their faces will fit on the ceiling.

I walk out onto the balcony and consider screaming, but by now even that seems like overkill. When Alex joins me a few moments later, they say nothing. Just lean on the banister beside me, watching the sea.

We are still on the balcony when the air shifts, as if coming down from a great height. When, for a few moments, the gate of this cage cracks open, and the pressing silence is replaced by bustle, by traffic and shrieks and laughs and every other sign of life that is always missing here. Yet neither of us turns away from the sea.

The water is shining, and I am afraid, because any moment now they'll say it.

"Maybe you should go," Alex says.

"I won't," I say.

"You could make a run for it."

I stare at them until they look back at me. "I'm not going anywhere."

A bitter smile tugs at their lips. "There are so many rooms left to go."

"I'm not in a hurry."

They shake their head. "You're so full of shit."

"I know," I say, and I'm smiling too. "But we're halfway there."

"And then?"

"And then, we're free."

A hotel's worth of lives might seem many to barter out just two, but, then again, I'd gamble even more just to see Alex under different stars.

Around us, the sounds are already fading again, and I practically feel time seeping out of the room, the building, the town, the world. Until we're back where we started. Almost.

"Let's pick a north-facing room this time," I say.

"Let's not fucking talk to them this time," Alex says.

I laugh. "Okay."

⚓

NEIDHARDT

James Pollard

DRAPER

WE HAVE TO *stick together.* Draper shook her head at the repeated thought. The doors into the lobby of Neidhardt Resort had remained stubbornly shut when she'd pulled at their handles. She thought the *emotion* of their experience seemed to have come into her, not a voice that she heard from the handles but an impression that *there is no inside to come into* and *it's ridiculous to even consider the fire escape. Follow the others to the Water, to the Hand, to the Cage.*

Draper turned toward the south building and walked along the endless line of silent people until she came to a stop to watch them. It wasn't their faces she watched but the feet that shuffled to the door, mostly bare feet, some with hints of dried blood peeking from between the toes, some with nails overtaken by waves of hard yellow and pink, all of them pale from lack of sun, arches flat, skin wrinkled. The procession of feet kept coming, moving, standing still, until they became meaningless creatures separate and of themselves, like words repeated to the point of nonsense. She looked at her own feet and then in the direction of the north building but refused to make eye contact with it before she walked on.

DRAPER ENTERED THE conference room of the south building, its four blank walls lined with empty pedestals. Three of her group were gathered around a large, disquietingly pristine and anachronistic fax machine posted in a corner. They reanimated at the sight of her and rejoined the other three already seated at the table in the center of the room.

"The line keeps coming," Draper said. "We have to stick together." She knew it was a statement any of them could have made and anticipated the disgust in Chowdhury's voice before it even left her mouth.

"Like we did before?"

Draper pushed away Chowdhury's angry sarcasm, unwilling to process the loss of Grady and Jones again, and directed her question to the others. "Any communication?"

"Well," said Baruch, "there's this." She handed a single sheet of paper to Draper.

It felt too heavy, too thick. "A fax?" She scanned the page. "An ad for a weight loss pill. Very funny." She looked accusingly at the fax machine. *How old is the toner cartridge?*

"Don't show us that shit," Keller said protectively.

Baruch insisted: "It's *information.*"

"It's fucked is what it is," Portman said.

Draper directed her pragmatism into a question for Baruch. "What information does it give us?"

"It tells us that, yes, they're fucking with us, but also that they *can.*"

"Then we'll fuck back. We'll get at the Heads, *make* them give us answers. And the Humboldt Group, we have to assume they're still coming up the coast."

"Maybe they do come," Chowdhury shot back, "maybe they can help us, but they can't make the Heads give anything, and we can't either. They only take. The stairs aren't an option." She wouldn't let the fleshy image the stairs invoked take hold, open its way into her emotion.

Draper met her eyes coldly. "We need the Heads."

"They're responsible! Why would we need them?"

"We don't know that, Chowdhury," Brauch said, "but you've highlighted exactly why it would be valuable to know what they know, don't you think?"

Chowdhury turned to look out the window toward the jagged columns of refracted silvery yellow light over the coastal reservoirs. "They're laughing at us. They ruined us, and we still rely on them."

Draper, wearing her resolve tightly, addressed the others. "We keep with the plan. Is there anything new with the Cage? The houses?"

Holder partially lifted his head, as if his thick neck could barely hold it up. "There's nothing new with the Cage."

Draper, untrusting, wanted more.

"It's the same," Holder said defensively. "Those people go into the water, and they don't come out."

Her imagined picture of the seabed provoked a shudder. "They still don't say anything?"

"Nothing."

"What about the Hands?"

"We haven't seen any evidence of them," Holder replied, detached.

"I don't think they exist," Keller said. "Nobody can live like that, even if the ocean didn't kill them."

Holder straightened up. "The Heads don't accomplish anything without them. They exist—or existed."

Portman wiped perspiration from her upper lip. "We haven't been out to the houses in a while. Hard to see the point."

They had no name for what they'd witnessed and endured. Whatever the collection of preternatural devastation and reordering could be called, the group wasn't equipped to understand any of it.

Draper looked again at the fax machine, and another impression came to her: the bald, white Heads at rest in the central building office of their decades-old resort, their entry point into luxury real estate, the place they had often gathered in the past while they plotted the future their ever-expanding consortium would shape.

The first Head grunts. The second shifts its eyes between the first and the third. And the third, unhelpful as usual, focuses on a disquietingly exuberant and excessive application of lotion.

It occurred to her that *the Heads don't know what the Hands are doing.*

Holder, interrupting her reverie, said, "I'm ready to go back into the water."

Draper understood it was not a question. Holder would enter the ocean in defiance of the loss of his partner Hendricks.

Holder looked straight ahead at nothing.

Draper's thought that the houses should be checked was accompanied by a feeling of nauseated helplessness as she considered the task and the powerful indifference the houses held.

She looked to Portman. "I can check the houses."

Portman hesitated. "No, I'll go. I said I would."

Draper didn't pretend to protest.

Keller said, "I'll go with her."

"Okay then. Chowdhury and Baruch, you come with me," Draper said.

Draper had brought them to the same arrangement: same two pairs, same trio, same tasks. She followed the others out of the meeting room, watching the back of Chowdhury's head, the floor dripping from her shoes as she pulled them up from its sucking carpet.

DRAPER AND HER group headed to the north side of the central building. Neidhardt Resort seemed intent to hold onto its lost charms in the sunset, its perversion obscured in the shade. The sea air, sand, sun—and the ageless things they contained—had done their assault on its edifices, scraped the once brilliant white to cracked bone, scared askew the coppery terracotta roof tiles, attached themselves to past guests who'd become carriers of degradation into the interior. The resort, set a quarter mile from the ocean, was not creatively named or built. It consisted of three rectangular three-story buildings, two of which revolted from a straight line and sat at angles next to the central building.

Draper gazed up the fire escape and said to the resort, "See you when we get there."

She looked down at her bare feet as she climbed. *No stairs, just sand.* There was no in-between. Her feet settled on a thin layer of sand resting on the depressed carpet of the lobby. She gave no time to disbelief, to disorientation—she sensed the two behind her, saw the elevator directly in front of her, and punched its "up" button. The floor indicator stubbornly did nothing to dispel their tension but increased it by blinking, not numbers but letters. The indicator continued this defiance of the elevator which ignored it and finally arrived and opened its door to the group.

Draper peered inside at the dull reflection of the stainless steel, which felt too sterile against the resort's faded blues, greens, and yellows. The serious demeanor of the elevator provided no relief, engendered no trust, and belied its immature behavior. Nothing happened.

The three stepped inside. Draper opened her jaw wide to stretch it, a habit to release the seemingly ever-persistent ache in her activated masseter muscles, and pushed "3." As anticipated, the doors closed and the elevator traveled up, not to the third but to the second floor. Chowdhury and Baruch stepped off onto the second floor, while Draper continued back down to the first, then up to the third, over and again. When the elevator returned empty, Baruch boarded, traveled eventually to the third floor, and sent the elevator back to the second. Chowdhury followed and, after three hours, all were reunited. None of them could predict it but all understood that the elevator thought three was two until it arrived at three, and thought one was two, and therefore three was one, until all arrived at the ground floor. The elevator posed no opposition to their reasoning.

The group scoured each floor as they puzzled out the odd logic, the nonsense arrangement of rooms that held no consistency. Draper's hours-long thoughts were supposed to be speech but lost their way. Twenty-one hours passed between their entry into the elevator and the conclusion of their fruitless search of the three floors.

THE DEW

THE CLOUD OF Dew moved slowly and sinuously around the right whale, undisturbed by the lonely strands of sunlight filtered by the shallow salt water. If the Dew could think it might have thought, *The milk might come today, might spray from the fat cage,* even though the thing that was once a whale didn't release its milk anymore. The cetacean had seen its pod, and its calf, lose their ability to swim, come to rest on the seabed, break apart and then come together again in a frightening explosion, and eventually lift out of the water and out of its sight. It lost its mind before it stopped swimming and feeding and was now lashed to moorings on the seabed to keep it grounded—no longer a whale but an aquaculture cage, a shrine in a garden tended by a Hand.

PORTMAN

PORTMAN AND KELLER walked toward the houses languidly, listening to the birds and insects. Portman was grateful for them.

After minutes of no exchange, she broke the silence with resentment: "I'm ready to go."

Keller replied, "Yeah," perhaps maddened at the return of the impotent feeling always etched onto any effort they made.

Neither spoke, and they paused as they considered the door of 3224, its paint faded, worried away by the thin shafts of dull light that moved up the mottled wood.

Portman opened the door, and they graduated to the entry-way, looked up the stairs through the floating dust caught by gray light. She'd lived in Neidhardt nearly her entire life. She'd known Mrs. Henry, Mr. Henry, their son Charles. The Henrys had known her.

They began the ascent of the stairs, which felt like a descent, and came to the bedroom Mrs. Henry had given to her cat. The white door stood ajar. They peered inside and saw nothing but the furniture of Mrs. Henry's cat. It had been a spoiled cat to any observer, and Mrs. Henry's first love before and after her husband's death. Its regal portrait stared back at Portman, but the cat herself was not there.

They exited, turned left down the short, silent hallway, turned again, and entered Charles's bedroom. Mrs. Henry had begun sleeping there among her son's old things following Mr. Henry's death, the master bedroom made even more lonely after her husband's passing.

She must have been lying with her cat in that bed when it happened.

During their pensive pacing toward the house, Portman had wondered if they would become anesthetized to the sights, the sounds, smells. *Impossible.*

The scene of Mrs. Henry traversed through neuronal and synaptic pathways to access the memory of Portman's mother in the same state, and to recall the devastation of her body that preceded it.

Portman had come to deliver the tea—*two sugar cubes, please, honey please*—that her mother enjoyed while she sewed. But in the instant that Portman entered the room, her mother was rent apart by some unseen impetus, flesh, muscle, bone, blood, bile expanded out in an unfathomable burst. Her once-body became wet dust, gravel of bone and organ. Its own universe and the galaxies within expanded infinitely fast and then gradually slowed, ephemera spreading out, forming its own orbits, until it hovered there in front of her daughter's helpless eyes. Then, just as quickly, her mother's own personal universe collapsed back into itself, gathered, and reformed into a facsimile of the body it had been, her consciousness removed, her self undone. There she had hovered, floating up until she gently met the ceiling of her sewing room, naked of clothes and hair, motionless, eyes open, every emotion gone but all at once there, plastered crudely onto her face.

It was in this state that Mrs. Henry and her cat were now stuck on the ceiling over her son's childhood bed, never to know its comfort again.

Keller glanced at Portman, as if he knew what she was thinking.

In the hours that followed, in their overwhelmed despair, Portman and Keller released Mrs. Henry and her neighbors from the impediment of their homes, watching the rising bodies dot the sky.

Three figures walked into the neighborhood and into Portman's periphery. Portman and Keller immediately sensed a shared understanding and a knowing regret as the three joined them and looked again to the air.

HOLDER

HOLDER APPROACHED THE procession of people crossing the sand as it inched forward into the ocean.

The woman at the end of the line didn't acknowledge him. Her face broadcast a sad sublimity, an ecstasy he could know as well as he could know the depths of the ocean: the realization of enormity, of abstraction, of submission.

The idea of one half of her mouth moved, the other half lazy. "Don't ask me that, I couldn't say." The words fell out. "I only know that I have my role." She dropped the breathing mask she held onto the sand.

Holder shook off his disassociated shock and picked up the mask.

It didn't take him long to prepare himself to face what was in the ocean, what had taken his friend. He sat in the sand watching the last of the line advancing into the ocean. Then he rose and entered the water next to the procession of people, parting the oily layer of motionless fish on the surface.

THE HAND

THE HAND SWAM through the dim water around the restrained whale, his fingers gliding over the gashes of propeller scars along its back and the knobs of callosities on its head. He moved to its mouth and advanced between the baleen plates of its jaw, entering the cetacean, pushing himself into its gigantic head, along its immense pink tongue, into its guts, until he came to the flesh-rooted plants splayed out there. He observed the pearls of Dew around the kelp-like plants, admired their movement, their odd gravitational relationship to the plants, their agency. He hyperventilated, scooped up his limit of air, and removed the converter from his mask. Then he collected the beads, which were somehow colored and without color, and pressed them to the absorbing converter. He replaced it and breathed through it deeply, and again, many times over, inhaling the Dew it processed. He took a moment to feel the embrace of flesh around him, and the comfort of each inhalation, before he backed out, breaching the mouth of the cetacean legs first.

He swam a lap around its sixty-two-foot length, admiring the murky impression of the garden of bodies beneath him. He settled among them and arranged his totems—model representations of consortium businesses that his former research team had contributed to, and which he'd taken from the conference room—an oil derrick, a semi-truck, a package of shrink-wrapped ground beef, a stalk of corn, a model of the resort, a CPU motherboard, and a whale. He was possessive of his garden, had fought hard to wrest it from the greedy Heads and ignorant Hands.

HOLDER

HOLDER WALKED UNDERWATER in the old sand, among the dead. His eyes followed a thick cord that wrapped around the whale and lashed it down to a mooring. He then saw the woman who'd spoken in the procession, the last of her air escaping an open mouth as she fell toward the form of the Hand. The masked, naked man was placing a plant into the body he'd hunched over. The Hand looked up, cocked his head at the sight of Holder, and inhaled deeply. He removed his mask and exhaled green swirls of particulate luminescence and sprang forward, the water shifting with him, the dew orbiting him as he dove for the cord. Holder instinctively dove for it as well, imagining he could use the threat of loosening the cetacean from its seabed as leverage for negotiation.

DRAPER

DRAPER, CHOWDHURY, AND Baruch gathered on the roof, defeated again in their effort to locate the Heads. They rested momentarily, preparing for the journey back to the first floor. Draper sensed Chowdhury was barely suppressing her contempt for another failure.

She followed Chowdhury's gaze out to the reservoirs and down the beach, where she saw a figure made vague by distance. She stretched her jaw, squinted. The figure was walking toward the resort, two other figures trailing it, their faces in the sand, being dragged forward haltingly. A large floating shape rose behind them: the giant right whale let loose from its moorings. It floated one hundred feet in the air over the reservoirs, and rising skyward. The cords which had held it were now attached to the two face-down figures, who the walker was pulling to some unknown purpose.

THE HEADS SEND A FAX

Our work has come to this, the detritus piling together, mammalian masses cleansed with Dew. You are an accident. We are chosen. We are advancement, pulled apart and reordered. The universes of knowledge and purpose gifted to us in their infinite iterations. We hold the truth. We are progress, and you can't stop progress. We don't need you, and it feels so good.

Sincerely,

The Heads

DRAPER

DRAPER STARTED AS Chowdhury turned from the figures on the beach and jostled past her with no acknowledgment. Draper hesitated, looked to the beach again, and then quickly pulled Baruch into step to leave the roof. Fledgling guilt sprang from within, forming from what she now worried was her complacency.

Draper couldn't determine which way Chowdhury had left the rooftop, but she knew it was ridiculous to consider the fire escape, so she hurried to the elevator with Baruch and silently pleaded with it to forgo its usual petulance.

The elevator arrived and then brought them quickly to the second floor, which was now the first floor after somehow having moved sideways, as sideways was now down.

As Baruch rushed toward the resort's back door, Draper slowed, and her mind reeled at the possibility that this was the lobby, then again at the half-registered sight of a door with a plate that read "Administrative Office."

Draper had never seen the Heads, had never seemed *allowed* to, no matter the combination of efforts she'd made, practical, intuitive, imagined, painful, simple. Now, there they were—behind that door. Her rage blossomed in an instant and was excruciatingly subjugated by will as she resisted the office and instead snatched stationary off a nearby table. She folded the paper many times over and plugged it into the jamb of the back door, hoping the resort would allow her easy re-entry.

THE HEADS DON'T KNOW

HAD SHE WALKED into the office, she would have seen the three Heads there—one grunting, partially subsumed by the wall, its legs suspended above the floor and calmly kicking; one stealing suspicious glances at the other two as a vein of the floor throbbed against its back, lifting him rhythmically; and one compulsively pacing, smearing himself with obscene amounts of lotion—their agency all but lost, unable to overcome their endless and insignificant rituals, locked into obsolescence and delusions of cosmic purpose, no longer capable of contact with the Hand or the management of their consortium's last and most comprehensive concern.

DRAPER

DRAPER AND BARUCH joined Chowdhury on the beach, where Holder lay on the sand. Draper looked *into* Holder, whose skin was incised, abdomen torn open, breastbone and ribs pulled apart. His half-closed eyes were empty. The sight brought back to her the crushing memories of strangers, acquaintances, friends, family, in their moments of being gathered. She looked away from the violation of Holder and across the gathered party's faces, saw the same pain, the same collective experience she felt.

Holder's large body shifted lifelessly, disturbed by the invasion of a foreign body, as the emaciated Hand and its hideously incongruous protruding round belly frantically attempted to curl itself into him, fetal arms and legs suddenly darting outward as the slippery viscera revolted against it. Frustrated, it gave up its attempt to nuzzle into Holder, whined, and lay itself over him. They were two pathetic shapes, one stacked on the other.

The Hand breathed heavily and trained its vision on the cetacean still rising in the distance. In that moment, all that witnessed this intuited the motivation of the Hand: it was striving to make a new home of Holder, as its previous home had now been lost.

Portman and Keller arrived with the Humboldt group following close behind them. They stopped, their bodies immobilized, minds numbed with shock at the sight on the sand.

Draper knew she had failed in her leadership, had allowed the loss of Holder.

The Hand peered back toward the group and hiccuped violently.

They needed it to be anything but a man, but the evidence of their eyes betrayed their wish.

The Hand suddenly bounded up and turned to run, and just as quickly, Draper sprang out of her stupor to tackle it with Chowdhury following suit. They struggled, but its coat of human effluence cast them off. With a breathless whine, it scuttled toward the sea.

Draper ran after it, caught it again, and this time managed to subdue it with Chowdhury's help. Portman removed the cord from Holder and fastened its limbs.

All stood silent in their trauma and looked down into Holder, and at the exposed slick plants unfolding from within him.

Draper felt Chowdhury's glare, met it, and understood it. She sprinted from the group and back to the resort.

She entered through the invalidated door she'd propped open, still streaked with Holder, resolute in her purpose to burn the resort and the Heads to the ground. *It's simple enough. Find a maintenance closet. Must be chemicals.* She was followed, but that didn't deter her. *Let them come.*

Draper dashed across the lobby, found the maintenance room, and rummaged through the shelves and cupboards, gathering up any bottle that had flammable contents. She returned to drop them onto the submissive carpet of the lobby. She kept aside the gallon bottle of varnish and splashed it over the bottles. Then she reached for her lighter as she backed toward the door.

Before the flint was sparked, a hand grasped her wrist.

The woman who held her was calm. "There will be other things you'll want to burn," she told Draper, "and some of them you'll wish you hadn't."

"What interest do you have in keeping them going?"

"I don't have any interest in that. Just give me a minute."

The woman freed her wrist, and Draper watched as she walked through the lobby and into the administrative office.

Eventually, the woman returned and gave her a nod. They both retreated to a safe distance, where Draper lit the trail of fuel.

The fire erupted, the fume of the varnish and the heat of the flames shocking her senses as a malnourished old man ran into the lobby, pale and naked, his loose skin flapping. He began frantically squirting a never-ending stream of lotion onto the raging fire.

The woman by her side was stoic. She said, "My name is Pryor."

"Good for you."

The woman offered an open palm, showing Draper pearls of Dew. "It's the same across the coast. We may be able to make a difference with your help."

Draper nodded but understood nothing.

NEIDHARDT

THE GROUP SPENT the week gathering necessities in preparation to leave the resort. As they set out to leave the tree-lined neighborhoods, the Hand bound and lashed to Chowdhury, a shadow fell across them. The Hand fell to its knees and looked up, suddenly supplicant, and all were stopped by an artificial night which stretched over them, created by a miles-wide oblong conglomeration of animal and human bodies in the air, a mass that rotated on its side imperceptibly, eventually blocking all hints of sun, hundreds of thousands of limp limbs involuntarily gesturing.

Everyone froze, huddled together, unable to free their eyes.

Portman imagined her mother and Mrs. Henry joined together above her, and in that moment her body sat down, and her mind retreated back, now hidden away and useless.

Baruch looked to Chowdhury and thought, *This is only some of them.*

Keller stayed behind with Portman as the others reanimated and began to trail the slow mass as it followed the commute from the houses to the resort and beyond.

Draper led the group to the coast, where they could only watch as the cloud slowed and hovered over the outer limit of the reservoirs.

They stayed on the beach for days, watching as the mass gradually dissembled, dropping bodies into the ocean, until, on the third day, the last of them came down in a final great fall that brought waves to them.

The Hand imagined the Dew wandering, exploring, seeking, and the plants flourishing, completing their cycle and fulfilling their purpose, and he was content.

The group walked out of Neidhardt, unsure what would come next, where their procession would lead them, but certain they would never be grateful for the shade.

⚓

WHERE EVERYTHING STAYS

K. A. Honeywell

MY MOTHER'S GRAVE marker was cut from the log that had fallen on her father and brother as she watched. If it had meant to kill her too, she'd said, then it could rise over her in the end. She had saved a plank from it, carved her name into it, and kept it in her attic. I had always known it was there, glancing at it while searching for something else and thinking, *She wants a burial.*

Most of the graves in the cemetery were empty, unlike my mother's. I had been left with her body after illness had eaten away at her for two years. It had smoothed her like water over stone, and I had told her she never looked lovelier as she sat in bed with her bald, earless head and dark, dark eyes like a seal. It had been only a half-joke, for both of us. The best bedtime story she had ever told me had been about a seal, and she'd always said her mother was half-seal.

"This is her," I said.

My partner stepped away from an empty grave marked by a stone for a man who had gone to the sea years before my birth. She stood at my side and said, "It's lovely."

"It's just a plank," I said, but it was lovely to me.

We stood in silence, and I hoped my mother could see that her worries had been for nothing—I'd been able to leave home, and I'd found someone outside our village.

Back at the road, the fine mist had dotted our vehicle with clear globules that made it appear to have the skin of something I could have found in the tide pools. When I took hold of the door handle, I remembered plunging my hand into the water, over and over, with years and years of practice, to snatch the things that would feed us. I got into the vehicle but my entire being ached to be elsewhere.

"Can we go into the village?"

I paused from buckling my seatbelt to look at my partner. We hadn't agreed on going any further. I had hoped the cemetery would be enough, but it wasn't, not for either of us.

IT WAS THE tallest pine by the black rock shaped like a seal, the one mothers like mine told bedtime stories about, where the dirt road peaked and then dipped down. After, the trees thinned to nothing, and the village lay ahead. The houses were dappled with rot and nestled into the sand like a clutch of white chickens. Behind them, the sea stretched out wide and eternal. The homesickness I didn't know had been gripping me so tightly evaporated. Everything was here. I slipped into this place, and something missing was returned to me.

The first house we entered belonged to my uncle, the one who'd died beneath a log with his father. The place had been emptied and closed up since I was six, and it provided little more than an incomplete glimpse into the past. The door had been loose in its frame when I left, and while I was gone, someone had easily forced it open. Whoever came in had left their initials carved into the kitchen counter.

We wandered in and out of the other houses. My partner inspected each one carefully, touching windows and light fixtures as gently as she would a kitten. When I opened up my best friend's house, she laughed at the old tech: a scratched touchscreen in the wall, and phones and handheld consoles left behind in drawers, all of it out of date even when he got it. I'd helped him collect it, promising him until the end that we could stay home and also that we could find connections elsewhere. He had tried, oh, he'd tried.

I took us onto the beach, down a rocky path I knew by feel, every angle of the mist-slicked rocks like wrinkles in the hands of earth.

My partner surveyed the houses behind us.

"Which one is yours?" she asked. "Let's go there next."

"We'll have to be quick if we want to make the ferry," I said.

My house was still as I had lived in it: the shelf of scrounged textbooks, the sofa draped with the quilt my mother and I had made, the ice box and knives trustier than the frozen sea, clothes in the trunk, and the bed made and dry as desert bone. I had been careful to check the seals around the windows and doors before leaving. All of our houses could be returned to one way or another, but mine was mine, and this was how I wanted it.

My partner lay on the dry bed and licked her lips. Before today, no one's weight but mine had pressed against the slender mattress, but we sank into it together now.

TWO YEARS AGO

I BOUGHT THE bare minimum. Whether it was furnishings for my apartment, or groceries, or clothing, I took only what I could use today or let go of without trouble. I did not realize how spartan my habits were until my partner came over the first time. She looked at the eggs in the refrigerator and remarked that they must be lonely.

"They have each other," I told her.

And in the morning she sang over the pan as she fried the eggs. She told them they were doing a good job just as they were.

There was always a song at breakfast. There was always a way for her to tell us we were doing our best and it was good enough. How many times had I frozen and not known the way through life outside my seaside home? Just as many times as she, even with her own troubles, had taken my hand and led me through the throngs of people who already had it figured out, who had been born into it. I'd been born in saltwater with the sand at my fingertips and water-logged midwives who gurgled and cooed over me once I let loose my first kraken's wail.

I survived the world beyond every day. Always keeping my head above the water, only sometimes wondering if up was the right direction.

I WOKE FROM sleep in my old bed, borne across silken upwellings and surfacing into consciousness to breathe perfect salty air.

Dusk had come, and we had missed our ferry. So, with the hunger of newborns in a new world, we set off with my fishing gear.

My partner and I sat on the pier where I had once watched my friend's ship, on fire, sink in the night. Vessel and pilot had dipped so slowly into the sea it was like watching the sunset a second time. Nobody knew why it happened, and yet we'd all known that it would. Wondering over the answerless *why* would have been as eternal as the abyss.

Now my partner wanted to know, "Why did you leave?"

"I heard a song."

Her brow furrowed. "Where?"

"Coming from somewhere out there," I said, looking inland over my shoulder. "Maybe it was you singing over your eggs in the morning."

She laughed and shook her head, blushing because I knew something so deeply *her*.

"I never heard it again after I met you," I said.

She looked back at the houses, bright against the dark sand. "But you thought you were going to come back."

I smiled at the memories of what had once been. "Nobody really leaves."

Shadows slipped through the waters underfoot. The fish came as though they had longed for someone to be here again. Just as eager, I drew one of them up to me. We fried our fish in lamplight and ate with our fingers, pinching flakes of pearlescent flesh. Content, abandoned caverns filled once more by the sea, I fell back onto the bed and slept easy.

IN THE MORNING my partner had a fever. I opened the window and propped the bedroom door to keep it from slamming in the breeze.

"Is that a foot?"

She squinted past the corner of the bed to what I had used as a doorstop. The prosthetic was crude, ages behind modernity even when it had been brought into the village.

"My mother's," I said. "It's what she gave up to have me."

"Tell me."

"Something bit her in the shallows." I set a glass of water fresh from the desalinator on the bedside table. "Her foot swelled and blistered, and she knew was carrying me. She made my father cut off her foot. It was her down payment, she said, to not be taken by the sea just yet."

My partner looked at the glass of water. "But she's in the ground, not the sea."

"True," I said. Maybe a foot had been enough that time.

My partner took my hand. "You're happy here, aren't you?"

"Yes."

She smiled.

Then, when I began to leave the room, she rushed to the toilet. We had been sick together before, gently rubbing a heaving back, passing a clean towel, preparing medicine, but something kept me back this time. The sound of her vomiting conjured memories of storms, where sea and rain collapsed into one, and after the crashing and thrashing the world could not be precisely as it was before.

When it was over, I put a hand on her shoulder and looked into the toilet. Wet sand filled the bowl.

With a deep breath, she got to her feet and wiped her hair away from her forehead.

"I feel better now."

NO ONE FISHED anymore. Before yesterday, my partner had only eaten protein mashed together from things grown indoors. I never knew if they were living things, but they certainly didn't taste like it. What I ate in the city had befuddled me with its mysterious origins, and it left me sad for the lack of flavor I knew the sea and earth and air could provide. Today, we fished again for our food from the pier. Then I brought my partner to the tide pool, where I pulled out a creature with a shell so brilliantly red it was as though I held a beating heart in my hand. Everything I knew was in these waters. Truths in the deep, comforts in the shallows.

"Let's stay," my partner sang as we cooked our lunch. "Let's stay some more."

She ate as much as she had yesterday, if not more, and I watched her all afternoon and into the evening for any sign that she may be sick. Whatever it had been seemed to have passed.

At night, we lit the lantern, wrapped the quilt from the sofa around our shoulders, and listened to the lapping water and the creaking houses. It came long after sunset, the sound I thought only I would hear. A breathing as soft as the tide, in the same rhythm.

My partner sat up straight. "There's something out there."

Before I could say anything, she was on her feet and at the window. I joined her. I watched her turn her head this way and that, all the while knowing precisely where the shadow was coming up the beach, heading for the houses.

It walked on four legs with the memory of two. Sand sloughed from creases beneath ribbons of flesh the color of hope drowned in the midnight sea. The moonlight slipped over it in glancing blows that illuminated things that could not be seen: jealousy that groaned in the heart, the want and fear of knowing, and regret. The figure took the first step up to the neighboring house, my mother's, with such solemn effort that it could have been the last step it ever took, and then paused, breathing its tide-rhythm breath. When it regained itself, it took the last two steps, sidled over the porch, and let its heft spread across the bench there.

I looked away from it to my partner. She was smiling.

"You're not afraid?" I asked.

She watched the figure on my mother's porch with the same fascination I'd once seen her watch a plain brown bird on her balcony one morning. They came so seldom that they were good omens against the hazy sky. Now, with the same cautious interest lest she scare it off, she pressed her face to the window. The creature stayed for as long as it could remember why it had come, and then, with a sigh that echoed the breaking waves, it sidled down from the porch.

Until its last step into the sea, until it disappeared into the brine, my partner watched every movement of its glistening, sloshing existence.

TWO WEEKS AGO

THREE TIMES IN one year, my partner had the bad luck of being let go from three different jobs. Once had been enough to shatter her, twice had rattled loose the pieces we'd glued back together, and on the third I was terrified.

She moved as though underwater, slowly, as though she had forgotten the joy of breathing. Several times, I found her standing at the glass door to the balcony, waiting for fickle feathered hope.

"How do I get back into the world?" she asked me on a day she let me taste the tears on her lips.

"Same as before," I said. The salt on my tongue made me hungry for the sun-warmed, sour air over a seaweed-strewn beach.

"But I'm useless," she cried. "How do I become useful?"

"Find the right place," I said. "It's out there."

"I'm sorry," she said. "I don't want to be like this."

I passed my hands over her skin, flowing over her like water, caressing and smoothing the turmoil inside her until she was asleep in my arms. I held onto her without thinking of home but feeling it in my hands. There was something in her that kept me from caving to the despair of homesickness. I didn't know how to tell her how much she meant to me without telling her how much I wanted something else—something that already had me more than she ever would.

WE LOUNGED ON the beach and let the cool sand flow up our pants legs when the tide came to test our firmness.

"It *is* lonely," my partner said out of the silence, as though we were mid-discussion. "But it's just the sort where you're alone." Then she snorted. "That doesn't make sense, does it? I think I mean, it isn't sad. Everybody talks about loneliness as if it's the worst thing in the world, but this is something else. I didn't know this existed."

"What?"

"This feeling," she said. "That I am alone and I don't want anyone else. Except you."

"Except you," I echoed teasingly, as though it were a quick save on her part.

"Have you heard any songs since coming back?" she asked.

I looked out at the sea and listened. "No."

She kissed my cheek and stood. "I'm hungry."

I joined her to return to my house for the fishing gear. Along the way, she caught her breath and snapped her foot upward. Red smeared her fingertips when she touched it.

I searched the sand for what had gotten her and found nothing. When I looked at the wound, I feared there would be teeth marks like the ones described to me by my mother. Was there venom working its way into her now? Blood streaked down the side of her foot and across her heel from a line. A cut. I already felt as though I were gripping my hatchet, ready to take off the foot, but then the feeling washed away slowly.

My partner hopped alongside me, arm around my shoulders, taking the rocky path to the house on her toes.

Inside, I lowered her to the sofa and inspected the cut more closely. I brushed away the caked on, red-tinged sand and saw that what flowed from her now was not blood. The liquid dripping over my fingers and pooling on the floor was almost clear.

"Get a jar." She pointed to the row of glass glinting in the window above the kitchen sink.

I grabbed one and handed it to her. She unscrewed the lid in one twist and placed the jar beneath her foot. The liquid filling the glass was the color of cornsilk, dripping steadily until it reached an inch below the mouth and stopped.

"Can you use it?" my partner asked.

"What?"

"In the lantern."

She looked at me the way she had when asking to move in with me, trying not to show how much the answer meant to her.

With the filled jar in hand, I went to the lantern in the kitchen and took the funnel from where it hung over the sink. I poured in a slosh, and the brackish smell of fish oil rose to my nose. The side of the jar was coated by the substance, which leggily slipped back down. I could have drunk it down in gulps; it smelled as lovely as anything I had ever put in my mouth.

"Is it wrong?" my partner asked from the sofa.

"It has to soak," I explained, replacing the cap. When I turned back to her on the sofa, her eyes had a teary sheen over them. "I think it'll work," I said, and it seemed to soothe her.

We looked at the cut on her foot. While it had not closed, nothing more seeped from it.

"We'll see tomorrow," she said, and I had the feeling that she was hopeful for the same thing I was.

I LIT THE lantern in the evening and hung it overhead while we ate our supper. My partner never looked directly up at it, but she wore a little smile as its light fell upon us. And then when we went to bed, the lantern came with us, illuminating us as we removed our clothes. I placed my mother's prosthetic foot under the door so that the window could be opened to the breeze.

We nestled into the dark. Outside I could hear the creaking of wood all the way from the pier. It was the monotone melody that had put even the fussiest baby to sleep.

"I have to tell you something," my partner said, her voice as soft as hope. "I've always wanted something else. When my friends and I used to talk about who we wanted to marry and where we wanted to live, I had to pretend. I pretended to have been thinking about those things so much that I had them all planned out like they did. But I thought about nothing."

She paused.

"Those kinds of plans are hard to keep," I said.

"I kept wondering if I should have them, though. I tried to, but every time I thought of what I wanted, there weren't any cakes or parties or houses. There was *someone*, though. A person who I was going to die with because I loved them more than anything."

She paused again, and I was silent.

"I'm not saying I want to die," she said.

"I know."

"But I may as well be happy when it happens. Me and my partner." She turned her face toward mine. "I don't think you were happy before."

"I was happy with you."
"Still?"
"Of course."

ONE WEEK AGO

I WAS WAITING for what I didn't know to become familiar.

I found a fish swimming in a store's tank with others. It was like no other fish I'd ever seen before, brightly colored with a frilly tail, and I bought it and carried it home wrapped in the strange plastic they gave me. While my partner napped in front of a television she had not turned off in four days during her post-layoff depression, I laid out the weird fish on the kitchen counter. It was not dead, nor did it gasp. I took a knife and sliced off the fish's head—or I attempted to. Metal sawed against metal, and I saw that the fish was not meant for me, not to eat but only to look at. I wept then for what I missed and what I could not share.

My partner found me with the fake creature and took the knife from my hand.

"Let me help," she said, and collected the intricate pieces of metal skeleton and machinery I had shattered.

"I thought it was real," I told her, aflame with embarrassment.

"It was real," she said. "For a moment. Remember that part."

But I was all memories. All the buoys the outside world threw into the waters of my being, all those moments of potential to understand or to even one day belong, they all split open and sank. I had only my partner, who was no buoy but beside me in the water. When one of us began to fall beneath the surface, the other held onto them and kicked harder. I believed I had found someone I could not bear to lose.

LATER

WHEN THE PIER collapsed, the fish came to me at the rocks where I perched as a grizzled siren. My line was the true unbreakable strands of hair I had swept up from the floor many years ago. After catching what I needed, I carried the gasping fish back home. I took care on the rocks I knew by feel as much as I knew how my legs now strained against them.

The lantern was on in the kitchen, and I wasn't sure if I had forgotten to turn it off before heading out at first light. But it could burn all day if I wanted. It hadn't been filled in a long, long time, and I didn't expect to need to do it again.

I took care of the fish as the quiet of the house loomed at my back.

Sound curved wide around me as if keeping its distance. The breeze, the tide, the creaking of the houses. It was all so far away when I wanted to hear something so close. It was the quiet I'd heard after my mother died.

I left the house.

There were footprints in the sand, but they could have been mine, or they could have been from the day before. I don't know why I went where I did. Neither the tide pools nor the shallows gave me any answers. Nor the other houses or even the cemetery. But the sand murmured at my feet.

It wasn't until the evening that I returned to the house and stepped into the bedroom. The bed was empty and on the dresser were two glassy orbs with blood-red tassels bunched on one side. When I picked one up, I found a curve of sharp-pointed metal within the tassel, and when I turned it in the light, an iris and pupil rolled toward me beneath a soft, clear coating. I added these to my tackle box with the other lures, and then I went outside and wept.

I was alone. I was not lonely, but I was sad.

I went to where the sand was soft enough to lie down and disappear into it, the way all things did eventually, but it wasn't quite my time yet. I would only stay until daylight, and then the sand would be swept from the house of my body, creaking as it was. I would breathe in the rhythm of the tide until there was the day the coast fell still and the sand whispered in my ear when I crawled into it. I wouldn't know what it said, only that I would stay here and listen to every grain.

⚓

THE TEETH GAME

Alex Keikiakapueo Brewster

DADDY CALLED IT the Teeth Game, but the teeth were only part of it. They filled the mason jars that lined every wall of the dilapidated mansion we called home. They were balanced on shelves and tucked under couches and seeping out of closets and could be found anywhere else that space might otherwise be wasted. Daddy brought new teeth home when he came back from sea—not just the teeth of sharks but of squid and whales and fish so clever that not even Daddy knew their names. Together, we would fill new jars with the teeth while he told me tales of his fight with the beasts: the hours he spent trying to reel them in, the times he was nearly dragged into the salty depths, their valiant struggles to defy their fate even after they were on the deck becoming corpses fast, and he told me of the rain and the lightning in these moments that would so often try to bring him to his reckoning. Not all the teeth came from the sea, but we never spoke of those.

The first rule of The Teeth Game was that Mama could never see the game begin. Every night after dinner, Daddy would wait for her to start cleaning up in the kitchen, then he would wink at me and that was my signal to slip away and hide the secret jar again. The secret jar looked no different than any other tooth jar in the house, but I was my father's child, and I knew how to close my eyes to feel the damp and taste the salt that wrapped around the secret jar like a cloak. I always wanted to hide it in one of the old rooms of our house—the safe, dry ones with a firm floor and swathes of ceiling. The ones with solid walls that still stood strong against the perpetual torrent assaulting our sea-bluff home. Those rooms were warm and well-worn and down the narrow hallways whose creaks I knew by name. Daddy always warned me she would find it if I hid it in the old rooms, but some nights I would take the chance so I could hurry back and be seated at the table before Mama returned from cleaning. On those nights, we'd have an hour or sometimes even two to spend together as a family before she began to wail.

Most nights, though, I wouldn't risk my father's disappointment. I would run to where I'd hidden the secret jar the night before. I would take it from its pile or high shelf or leaking cupboard, tuck it under my raincoat to keep it secret from the peeping sky, and walk down corridors until the carpet was damp and mucid beneath my feet. The sun would start setting and Mama would start screaming in a pitch that transcended the wind and the rain. On those nights, once I was sure my charge was hidden safe and sound, I had to make it back to my room without her seeing me. I would lay bed as quiet as I could with my dolls and jars of teeth listening to Mama's screams turn to wails as she searched and searched for the secret jar. The wails would give way to sobs, and the sobs would fade to a desperate keen until the weight of her sorrow could sink her into the depths of sleep.

I ASKED DADDY why he made the jars, but he only ruffled my hair. "She was beautiful, my heart, beautiful and strong."

THE SECOND RULE of The Teeth Game was that Mama needed to be kept busy during the day. Daddy would wake me up before the pitch-black misery that was night gave way to the dark gray misery that was morning, and I'd get to work. Every safe room and every almost safe room had platters and cups and silverware and knickknacks from Daddy's travels that were so clean they sparkled at the slightest hint of light. It was my job to make everything dirty again, bringing in mud and grass and bugs from outside to smear on all the bits and baubles in the house. My morning shoes would drag and smear the filth onto the floor, leaving a record of every step I took in them. Sometimes I would make two or even three trips back outside if there wasn't enough sludge to streak throughout the house. Mama would wake up in bed, where Daddy always carried her after she fell asleep among the teeth jars of whatever room she made it to, and then she'd get up and make us a breakfast of oatmeal and mashed bananas before she started to clean.

Mama couldn't be talked to while she cleaned; her large black eyes could see only the grime I had infected her house and her wares with. That didn't stop me from trying, though. As long as Daddy was home, I was allowed to talk at her to my heart's content. I told her about my day and my nightmares, and which of my dollies was angry at the other one for slights I had concocted out of nothing. She never replied, and I don't think she ever listened—Daddy said our tongue wasn't one she knew how to hear—but sometimes, as she set a trinket down, she would briefly pat my cheek with her coarse, rough hand before picking up the next filthy bauble to scrub and scrub and scrub until it shined red with her knuckle blood.

I ASKED DADDY how he met Mama, but he only kissed my forehead.

"I was clever, my heart, clever and cruel."

THE THIRD RULE of The Teeth Game was that I could never, ever let the sea know me. If it touched so much as my toe, Daddy warned, it would grow so hungry for my flesh that it would try to swallow me whole, and if it did, it would never let me go. He had stolen too much from the brine, he explained, and the water wanted its pound of flesh for all the pounds he had torn bloody from its grasp.

But on days that Mama's wails could not be mollified and on days that Mama's starless-night eyes would fill with clouds, Daddy asked me to be strong and brave as we three made our way down the rocks to the sullen, sparsely grassed shore. We two would wrap ourselves in the thick, checkered blankets, which Daddy promised we'd someday use as a table for a picnic, and Mama would dance slow circles in the rain, her face tilted back and her mouth open to let the cold rain sooth her gums. In these moments, so rarely gathered, I would stop watching the dark fins that waited for me should I ever let the waves lap at my skin, and I would join her dancing. In these moments so rarely offered, with my mother's outstretched hand and her red-gummed smile, I would beg Daddy to join us in song. But he always refused, never taking his eyes from those dark fins waiting, and the chill of his rejection felt like frost upon my cheeks.

I ASKED DADDY why Mama would sing to the waves, but he only hugged me close.

"We were young, my heart, young and proud."

THE FOURTH RULE of The Teeth Game was that Mama must not find me while Daddy was out at sea.

The safe rooms were no longer safe; they were too easy for Mama to find me in when Daddy wasn't there to distract her. The broken rooms, too, were no place for a child so wanted by the sea and the sun and my mother's songs. On those days I hid among the rocks as Mama danced by the sea, and on those nights I crept into the leaking rooms, as far from Mama's seeking wails as I could bring myself to be. I wrapped my raincoat around my body and my body around the secret jar and prayed and prayed.

Every morning I would bring my mud inside before Mama woke up, and every evening I would brave the shore as the waves withdrew their reach, and I would gather clams and mussels to fill my stomach until Daddy returned. When Daddy was gone, her cries shaped themselves into the form of words I wanted to understand. When Daddy was gone, the dark fins drew closer to shore. When Daddy was gone, Mama stood with her toes pressed so close to the tide that they could all but kiss the foam, and she'd sing so loud and so long that even the rain would stop just to hear her for a while more.

I ASKED DADDY what would happen if Mama found me, but he just took my hands in his.

"You are soft, my heart, soft and sweet."

THE LAST DAY of The Teeth Game, in a broken room too far away to hear the crash of the sea, I woke up to my mother's smile. Rain fell through the tattered ceiling and caressed her silver hair, making it shine in the dull moonlight. It ran over her unblinking eyes and dripped from her curled lips and onto her always bleeding gums. She lifted her frail, ashen arm slowly and pointed a long withered finger at my frantically heaving chest. I hugged the secret jar tighter as she came closer. Her bare feet struck against the wooden floor with wet messy slaps. Underneath the sound of the eager rain and the reaching waves, I could almost hear her laughter. I found you, I imagined her saying with every step. I found you, you lost the game.

I pressed my back tighter against the wall and willed the rot and the mold to give way to my desperation. I pleaded with the sweetly decaying wood to provide me with a way to escape. I prayed for Daddy to come home from his days out at sea and to gather Mama in his arms and whisk her away to the shore or the kitchen or anywhere but here, filling the space between me and the smugly watching sky. The wood held firm. Daddy wasn't there. Mama came closer still, and I saw the labor of her heavy breaths in the way her chest swelled and shrank. Her lips closed and hid her black-hole maw. She opened them again with a moist, smacking sound. She said,

"Please."

I heard it under the sound of the crashing rain and the roaring waves.

"Please."

Louder this time. The first word Mama ever spoke to me. It was a whisper, nearly a dream forced through a throat unaccustomed to anything but song. She knelt before me and patted my cheek. She tapped my chest and said one last time,

"Please."

I NODDED. THE Teeth Game was over.

Mama reached into the secret jar without looking. She didn't need to. Her fingers moved deftly, shifting fangs and molars and incisors aside, until she had what she wanted. She pulled out the tiger-shark teeth slowly, almost reverently. She let me look at her prizes piled in the palm of her hand before she widened her jaw and sucked them into her mouth. I thought, for just a moment, that she had swallowed them. But when she smiled at me it wasn't the empty red smile I had woken up to but one that was brilliant and white. Her teeth shone brighter than the moon. She held the jar out to me, inviting me to reach inside. I pulled out my teeth and let them bite into my mouth.

Mama and I stand on the shore. The surf laps at my feet, greets me and invites me to come home. Mama sings, and this time I join in her song. The dark fins that have waited so patiently for so long come closer as we sink deeper into the salt. Mama wants me to meet her family, our family, and together we will find Daddy before he returns to the shore. We will embrace him and take him into the loving arms of the sea. And my family will be together, forever.

⚓

TWILIGHT TIDE

Samir Sirk Morató

THE REDFISH IS remarkable because despite the fact it's dead, it is still moving. Opal, straw flip-flops in hand, watches it arrive. The dimmed, bloated body (once golden, once maroon) pushes itself onto the beach. With one tail sweep after another, it lurches past mangrove roots and driftwood. It stops once it's struggled above the tideline and flops over.

Opal approaches. The redfish's milky eyes bulge at her. Seaweed snarls its fins. Its missing scales resemble gray, naked nail beds. The wind casts salt into Opal's face, and she clutches her sunhat and covers her nose.

She is about to ask the redfish what it wants, since nothing dead needs anything, when it clenches its distended stomach. Its powerful, hook-punched lips give way to dark matter. It retches silt onto the white sand. Sediment from the bottom of the bay fans from its mouth. It's a horrible mixture, rich with distilled death, softer than slime. Opal screams when she spots the wedding ring half-buried in it. She bolts to the fish, kneels in its putrid wake, and snatches the wedding ring from the slime. Sundress forgotten, she smashes the ring against her chest to clean it. Umber rot stains the linen. She turns the ring in her hands until she almost drops it, then slides it onto a shaking finger. The silver band fits as it always has.

On hands and knees, she looms over the fish. Her hair dangles around her face like an unraveling net. Above, egrets soar.

"Where is he?" she says.

The redfish doesn't respond.

Opal seizes its fin, her fingers sinking into the soft bloat, and rolls it onto its side. She leans in until its soon-to-stink body tangles in her curtain of hair, close enough that her lips almost snag on its spiny teeth. Garbled, unfinished noises burst from Opal. The redfish's gills threaten to slice her cheek.

"*Where is he?*" she says. "Tell me. Tell me."

No answer comes. The messenger, having delivered its message, disintegrates into rotten chunks. Opal shakes the fish carcass several more times before apologizing. Then she sits in her pooled sundress, the lacy froth of incoming tide eating at her legs, fingers clenched in a white-hot grip around her ring, and stares at Bon Secour Bay.

The sunset she came to see washes over the water in smears of Dreamsicle and blood. The sun, a blinding dot, lowers itself into the gulf. Wind tassels the cypresses. Crabs emerge to clean the dead. Pelican-shapes slash the fading sky. Opal, rocking, hands juddering, mouth spitting fragmented words, doesn't care about any of it. What she longs to see are the depths.

She stays on the beach even as mosquitoes puncture her skin and darkness swallows the shore.

IT'S DIFFICULT FOR Opal to explain anything to anyone. She is too forward. Too clear. It's impossible for her to explain that her husband, who walked into the sea a decade ago, who she loves (and loathed) more than anyone in the world, has reached out to her.

She still tries. Despite what others think of Opal, she isn't immune to elation, or the urge to share good news.

"My estranged husband spoke to me," she says, while fishing for cash in her wallet at the bait shop. "We're trying to reconcile. It's all I can think about."

The clerk, a grizzled butch, stares. She frowns when Opal flashes her wedding ring. They're surrounded by a claustrophobic labyrinth of tubes, tanks, and marine creatures, but the butch looks at Opal as if she's the most offensive entity present. Opal (forced to wear earplugs so the crosstalk of tank filters and people doesn't render her rabid) takes offense to that.

"Opal, honey, ain't he dead?"

The butch makes 'honey' into a seawall. A pseudo-friendly way of keeping Opal at a distance. It took Opal years to clock this. She no longer cares. At least the butch is honest. Opal shakes her head. For the hundredth time, she rotates the ring to bloodlet her jitters.

"No," she says. "Itai isn't dead."

Drowning isn't consensual. Opal knows that her husband let the seawater into his lungs in an entirely different way. And technicalities are important. She isn't sure what's become of him, but she's never doubted that he's alive.

The butch makes an unconvinced noise. She takes the ten from Opal's fingers to make change. The bag of shrimp Opal bought slumps on the counter. The shrimp glide around their prison, legs curling, their blue cores pulsing in their own translucent cages.

"Even if he wasn't dead," the butch says, "I'd be afraid to ask why you're excited to see a man who ain't done shit for you in a decade."

"He's a good partner," Opal says. "He supports me."

"How?"

Despite the openness of 'how?' it isn't an open question. People never want an exhaustive explanation. At worst, when given one, they assume aggression. At best, they feign interest while projecting martyrization to everyone else. Opal never sensed that they didn't want an explanation. Someone told her that while attacking her. It was a valuable lesson.

She's never forgotten the humiliation.

Opal says, "Itai always pays his part of utilities."

"Ain't you been paying that with his life insurance payout?" the butch says.

"As I said, he pays his part of the utilities." Opal thrusts the bait bag into her tote.

The butch retreats behind the counter. The tourists in the bait shop, clustered around the tanks and the cork board full of 'missing' posters, murmur to each other. Maybe some are local. Opal cares so little that she recognizes none of them. They are beneath shrimp. She at least understands shrimp.

"Enjoy your day, Miss Opal," the butch says.

"It's Mrs."

The butch retreats further at her loud, flat correction. Someone clears their throat. Everyone makes way for Opal as she exits, though they aren't near her.

She's seen schools of fish do the same for sharks.

"I HOPE SHRIMP is still your favorite," Opal tells the black waves. "I hope they get to you. I hope you weren't sending the ring to divorce me. I still want you. I've never hated you. There's a difference between your presence and you. I can explain that now."

The boat ramp concrete gnaws at her soles. Algae slicks her skin, fish hook and fish bones prick her toes. A shroud of Spanish moss whispers behind her. All the picnic tables in the park are empty. Opal only came here after the new summer renters called the police on her (she's always groundskeeping or trespassing on her own property), but she's grateful for the privacy.

"It's hard to exist." She fiddles with the shrimp bag. "You understand that, don't you, Itai? Sometimes I'd feel you in bed next to me, not even touching me, and it was like hearing the electric in the walls or feeling grocery store lights. It was unbearable. I hated it so much I couldn't sleep. You were like some boiling black hole put next to me to torture me.

"But I couldn't ask for space. I didn't know how to. We didn't *have* it, not in our house. We still don't. And I was terrified that if I left, or asked you to leave, you'd think I didn't love you. So I lay there wishing you'd just fucking die."

Far out in the bay, beneath the singular moonbeam spot-lighting the water, something razor-shaped breaks the surface. Maybe it's a wave. Maybe. Opal restrains herself from crying out. From trying to swim to it.

"But I never wanted that. I never meant anything I said while being alive made me insane. It still does that, but I deal with it now. Mostly." She speaks faster when she senses her voice failing. "You're the only person I've ever missed. Everyone was right about me being a monster. But I do love you."

The razor crest in the waves is gone. Opal's voice vanishes. Her sob thrashes inside her body. She releases the shrimp.

They vanish into the gloom.

IT'S UNFAIR, OPAL knows, that she's counting the seconds since she released the shrimp. That she's counting the minutes. The days. It's unfair that her words are bad. It's unfair that for years, she blamed Itai for their separation, then blamed herself. It was both of them. It's always been the both of them. Neither of them have ever stepped foot in a store, a school, or a doctor's office (or a family gathering, before their families finished dying) without being unwelcome. They're together in everything, even separate.

Did you hear? Another boat sank.

"You weren't easy to live with," she tells her reflection. "I want to try again anyway." She repeats it into Itai's wool sweater she sleeps with, then to his sparsely decorated corner of the room. There isn't much else to repeat it to. Her husband didn't leave much behind. He possessed little besides himself.

The one constant besides that was Itai's unease with his own body. Even after the injections, after the filet scars that reshaped his pectorals and pelvis, he remained lost. Opal had resented the way he'd floated in their lives, as if he was a jellyfish overflowing from a tiny tide pool while the water ebbed away.

Nah. No one died. A shrimp boat picked them up. But they said...

Every few months, Itai would shrink. He'd beg Opal for her clothes, then cling to them, to her, before ranting about how hideous he was. He never recognized their shared bay of a body. The idea that his words poisoned them both was unfathomable. Then, when he was done gutting himself, when he was done injuring Opal, he'd swell.

Opal misses her husband now, not just the concept of him. She doesn't miss the pounds of seafood that cycled through their refrigerator. The parade of baggy clothes that washed through the house before Itai starved himself down, trashed them, then started anew.

I dunno. There's something strange.

Perhaps he's found peace in the gulf. He must have. When their marriage became a slipped disc, when agony displaced something soft, they had agreed to separate until they both changed. Opal, afraid of her edges, chose land. Itai, afraid of his softness, walked himself and their wedding rings into the oncoming surf.

Hopefully, his metamorphosis has been good. Hopefully, they'll speak soon. Hopefully, their changes haven't made them hostile to each other.

With the renters gone, Opal walks circles around their house's stilts to avoid considering the worst. Her gray streak doesn't need to widen. She needs no more personal or historical loss.

Something's in the water.

She spends every night dreaming of bioluminescent stars in a bleak, wet sky.

SIX DAYS, EIGHT hours, and thirty minutes after Opal sends her gift, a surprise arrives alongside the news of two sunken sailboats and one missing person: a crevalle jack.

Opal almost trips on the fish when she steps out to water her banana tree. It's massive. Four feet of silver, emerald, and ocher. Seventy pounds of forked-fin generosity. It has rolled itself up to her stairs. Flies clump around the bite taken from its stomach. The hook that dragged it to an exhausted death shines in its nostril. Its shredded intestines haven't yet lost their color.

When she gasps, its eye rolls to look at her.

Opal keeps her ring on while she butchers the jack. She periodically stops to link her fingers and clap in excitement, even when she's slick with gore. The knell of her palms is a chime of gratitude. It floats over the hissing waves.

She buries the bones at the foot of her banana tree. After dinner, she releases a tiny paper plate of fish onto the water.

It floats out of sight.

FOR EVERY TORN trawling net, capsized boat, and uneasy story from an oilman, there is a gift from Itai: an endangered slaughtered sawfish, an eviscerated ocher-and-silver pompano, a fistful of ballyhoo dropped into the wrong waters, a young bull shark heavy with lead, a delicate, deep sea blobfish destroyed by a change in pressure. All the refugees killed for an indulgent surface-world feast crawl, slither, and flop their way to Opal's feet.

A hand washed up on the beach.

Time means nothing outside of deadlines or paychecks. After a stillborn dolphin gets caught on a crab trap line for days, unable to reach Opal until it's eaten to the bone (something she broods about even now), she ceases waiting on the beach. She waits in the shallows.

An abandoned trawler drifted ashore.

As a guilty pleasure, as a precaution, she begins going to the park. For a week, she sits breast-deep in boat-ramp water every night, salt licking her chin, stingrays gliding around her, undead vow renewals swimming into her lap. (And litter. She pushes that away).

The crew escaped in lifeboats.

"Do you finally feel comfortable?" Opal strokes the underbelly of the flounder blanketing her lap. Gigging punctures speckle its gut. "Can I trust you not to hurt me? Be honest."

Bon Secour Bay is shallow. She could walk for miles without swimming. Opal fears how she'd look by the time she reached Itai. Her brilliant, ripping terror is gone, but trepidation remains.

We can't divulge the details…

The flounder gently mouths her fingers. Its serrated teeth don't scratch her. Opal's reverie shatters when some drunk teenagers, fearing for her safety and sanity, begin yelling at her. Then, when they recognize her, the bottle hurling starts.

She walks home full of glass and apprehension.

OPAL ISN'T SURE who's giving in return to what.

Her banana tree's leaves swell into veiny, carnivorous hearts larger than her head. Hope tears at Opal as much as fear. It's rawer than honeymoon love; it's more ragged than gull-torn entrails. In her extended isolation, she forgot the feeling of company. To be tempted with it awakens her from hibernation. It sets her insides churning.

Opal starves. She can't go out without either loathing the faceless shunners around her or grasping for them. An atrophied need for community clashes with her exile. How did she last so long without Itai? How can she ensure this hunger doesn't rush her decision? All of her attempts at conversation get regarded as rude; her 'hellos' receive discomfort. Her scabbing wounds provoke unease.

Something's living under the rigs.

The safest landlocked entity in her life is the bait-shop butch. Another outcast. Opal claws her way into check-out conversations whenever possible. She can tell the butch is uneasy, but she's too desperate to care. One Saturday, she laughs at the news that a trophy fisherman fell onto his own propeller and died. The butch drops Opal's uncounted cash.

"What the hell is wrong with you?" she says. "Someone got hurt! Someone died! How is that funny?"

Opal thinks: Why isn't it funny that tourists are scared? Their grandparents hunted mine. They're trying to price me out of my inherited home. They're trying to hurt my husband. They scream into the sea. They slice manatees. They drag fish to death for sport. They spread disease. Isn't this funny because it's deserved? Isn't it nice to see someone else be the raw nerve?

Opal says: "It just is."

I reckon it's a monster.

The butch asks her to leave.

"DO YOU STILL think I'm tender? Do you think I'd stay that way if I joined you?"

Opal speaks to her reflection in the glassy water. Miles away, on the bay's otherworldly rim, oil rigs smoke. Dawn hasn't broken. The oncoming storm hasn't arrived. Copper stings Opal's gums.

She would rake her palm across sharpened barnacles for someone in need. She shoos cottonmouths across the road. She is capable of joy, of pleasure. Does it matter that she (apparently) has the eyes of a shark? Why is she inhuman for hating people that harassed her and her husband? Why must she smile for outsiders destroying a bay they don't think she deserves?

Must she bleed and cry in public to show she feels?

That wouldn't move the shambling shoals that live here. They would see it as an illusion. While apart from Itai, Opal has learned there is no proving herself. This world is simple: if enough people deem something true, it is. Belief trumps reality. Her peacefulness means nothing. Itai's softness meant nothing. The idea of their violent potential equals action.

The majority has spoken: her husband was wrong about her humanity.

So Opal is a predator. She is a cold, clockwork beast made for evil. Her bones are cartilage, her skin sandpaper, her teeth ever-replenishing. If regret or guilt ever dragged her backwards, they'd flood her gills and kill her. She is thus incapable of these emotions. Might also be incapable of pain.

What do sharks feel when sliced open? Probably little.

Probably nothing.

Only one person believes in Opal's vulnerability (has laughed with her, consoled her, and pleased her, when she could stand touch), and he's been underwater for a decade. Who knows what discoveries Itai's made in the murk. In the labyrinth of oil rig legs or sunless open sea.

It's hard to tell exactly what he wants when he isn't here. He may not believe in her anymore. He may not even be a person anymore. Opal only claps in anxiety when she considers the former. The latter might bring them closer. She probes her tongue at the back of her teeth, unsure if she's tasting resignation or hope. She fears the difference.

"Itai," she says, before her voice flees, "I need a sign you trust me."

She spits into the shallows.

Minnows eat her saliva away.

AN EVENING LATER, the next gift comes from deep water wrecks.

The snapper is nothing but scaly muscle rolled in a red-to-coral flush. Its eyes are scarlet. It's small, this gift slain out of season, but it crawls its way up the shore on tattered fins and tenacity. When she takes it into her hands, it opens.

In the prickly keepsake vault of its mouth sits an isopod.

It stares at Opal. She stares at it. The isopod, as if to greet her, begins waving its legs. It's a terrible, flesh-fed gem. It glitters. So does the object in its grip. Opal reaches for the object, her heart overflowing in its presence. With legs crafted for killing tongue, the isopod offers her a rusty heart-shaped locket.

Inside is a molar and a patch of shining, slimy skin.

OPAL DRIVES TWENTY minutes to Gulf Shores, a paradise of palms and bulldozed dunes, to test her taste for humanity. She enters a tourist trap across from gated beachfront property: a cornucopia of towels, neon inflatables, and bottled fetal sharks. Earplug-less, she faces the vacationing crowd. A century ago, Opal's people tended to this shore. That knowledge sits in her stomach with the swallowed locket.

With every wave of noise, the throngs blend into doughy, gaping tides: storm surges carrying pounds of plastic, wealth, and desecrated dead. This is no graveyard of gifts. It's an abattoir of cleaned, price-tagged victims. Is this worth staying landlocked for? A woman side-eyes her.

They remove Opal when she starts screaming.

THE STORM IS meant for them.

Not intentionally. Opal and Itai have always accommodated forces meant to destroy them. While everyone else ties down their catamarans then flees for condos on calmer shores, Opal sits in front of her rotting bulkhead. She stays put as rain stings her face. It soaks Itai's sweater, then her otherwise naked body. Seabirds flee the yellow sky. Opal, eyes closed, lets saltwater lick its way up her calves.

The gifts arrive with the darkening sky: anglerfish with lovers fused to their sides, decapitated sailcats heavy with roe, pebbles from ruined fish nests. A celebration of change. Carnal grotesqueness. Opal's fingers dip inside her. Her moans lodge in every coil of shell and empty segment of crab claw, ready to empty themselves into the depths when they wash out.

Opal keeps fucking herself even as pieces of ruined homes wash ashore. Even as driftwood hurls against her shins, bruising her. Milky froth washes in on the waves. It spikes in and out with the tide. It sprays between her curled fingers, eager to enter her. She feels the gifts, soft and skin-like, crowd her thighs. A roaring wave builds in Opal's ears as the tide recedes. She digs her teeth into her lip and arcs her body towards the oncoming storm. Her nerves scream, begging for destruction.

The wave makes land.

Seawater shoots into her nose, into her eyes, into her. A stray paddle turned javelin collides with her jaw. Her teeth slam shut on her lip then through it. Opal's nerves explode. When the wave withdraws, Opal—all of her ringing, elbows on the sand—holds blood and creamy milt in her mouth. Her neighbor's skiff, tether broken, floats nearby. Her lungs burn: not for the lack of air, but the excess of it.

The gift begins dripping out of the hole below her lip. It burns. Did Itai's first gulp of bay feel like this? Opal swallows. Her old fears vanish. Sandy hair and palm fronds catch in her wounds. Itai's sweater squeezes her. She is ice water, hot current, and agony. She is alive.

She understands what her husband saw in the bay.

"Alright, Itai," she rasps into the surf. "I'm ready to try again."

OPAL SETS OUT for the oil rigs. The skiff bounces across waves so steep she fears they'll break her in half. Her bones throb. The bay fumes. By the time she reaches the first oil rig, stormdark engulfs her. Only flare stacks and the scarlet pulse of rig lights pierce it. Curtains of lost bobbers and fishing line debris drape from their pilings. A hanged tern rots in one. She cannot see past the wind or pelting rain.

All quiets.

The engine dies.

Opal, nerves still aflame, hears herself panting. The water is dead. Black. There is no difference between the sky and the depths. The storm circles her, raging, pacing. Opal glides between oil-sucking monoliths on the last of her momentum.

"Itai?"

It's been so long. Staring into the unknown is worse when she used to know it. Opal isn't here to wound; she's too old to survive wounding. She aches. She waits, turning her ring.

A constellation lights beneath the boat.

Itai rises from the deep at a glacial pace. Even then, his ascent rocks the boat. He's longer than the vessel by several feet. Sparkling lateral lines trace his sides. A long, maroon fin trims his serpentine form. He is quicksilver married to molten glass. A man blown into an oarfish. As his plumed head breaks the surface, Opal recognizes the remains of a human skull under his skin. When his vestigial limbs grip the edge of the boat, metacarpals glitter inside them, outshone only by a band of silver.

Extra bones streak Itai's body alongside bioluminescence. A wavy rib there. A thread of radius here. The debris of humanity. He's been smeared into a deep-sea comet.

The boat groans. Opal rushes to the other side so Itai can heave himself in without tipping it. His coils land in the bottom with a crash. The boat begins to sink, its rim almost even with the surface, as all of Itai piles in. His eyes are quicksilver discs the size of her fists. Nothing reflects in them but iridescence.

Opal unfreezes when she realizes Itai is uncertain as to whether she can bear being touched.

She opens her arms. A whole sea's worth of coils piles into them. The boat overflows. Sinks. That doesn't matter: her teeth are against teeth, her sticky flesh against sticky flesh, her hopes against hopes. Opal's desire for sand and sunlight extinguishes when her husband's depth-distorted voice speaks her name.

She imagines quiet twilight waters. She imagines a place meant for monsters, and for gliding alongside company forever.

She imagines being able to bite.

i've missed you, Itai says, the taste of the drowned on his breath. every day.

Opal opens her mouth for him and the gulf.

KEEL

Santiago Eximeno
Translated to English by Alicia L. Alonso

A ship in harbor is safe,
but that is not what ships are built for.

—*John Augustus Shedd*

HIS MOTHER WAS his mother.

His father was a drunkard.

As a boy, he would sit on the water's edge next to the rocks. In silence. He would walk barefoot through the most rugged areas of the coast, oblivious to the occasional pricking and slipping, to anything that wasn't his father's barge. He would watch the small boat slide along the horizon, a false perception of distance that, to a child's eyes, made his father's feat so much greater: he was sailing the seas. He watched him raise the fishing rod, sink the fishhook into the water, and tighten the line on the spool. Then came the pause, the calm, the waiting.

He suspected that this was when his father drank, intoxicated by the placidity of the sea while the sun devoured the shadows. He drank to face his fear of the water and what hid underneath.

Sometimes he returned home with his nets full of fish. Other times only a small handful of fish waited in his basket. But he always came full of alcohol. And rage.

Every night after dinner his father would beat them. Sometimes he beat them with apathy and other times he beat them in earnest. Every morning before breakfast he would apologize and crumble into pathetic, remorseful weeping. The boy always forgave him; he was his father.

One morning his father took him to the sea with him. His mother didn't object; she said nothing. She simply let him go without a hug or a kiss, without a word of advice. He would never forget that. All she gave him was a small cloth bag with a couple of salted biscuits inside.

Sometimes, even now when time is no longer time and the boats whisper atrocities in his ear, he sees the bag floating on the water next to the hull, inviting him to try to catch it. That is his memory.

The rest of his memories are fragmented and corrupted. They reek like a net full of fish abandoned on the sand. The images are cold and alien; they don't feel like lived experiences to him. He thinks it's better like that.

A hand raises a flask to the lips, a quick gulp again and again, overly shrill laughter, a badly timed joke, a blow. Freezing water bites the skin. Bubbles, disorientation. A mute scream scratches at the eyes, a scream that reeks of salt. The hook sinking into the cheek, the blood blotting out the story. The ripping pull, the fear, the urine staining the water.

Afterward there is the calm that comes when the barge's keel kisses his back, when it tears his clothes and skin and caresses him, giving him the peace that the hook, in a last desperate pull, rips away from him.

He pictures himself on the barge in the arms of a terrified fisherman, but he can't remember.

He pictures himself in bed in the care of a selfless mother, but he can't remember.

He remembers only the caress of the keel, the kiss of the hook. The whispers, the voices.

The bag of cookies floating on the water like the remains of a sunken ship.

IN THE MORNINGS he wakes up screaming, but the cold sweat, the toothache, and the bloodshot eyes no longer bother him. He's used to all that now. He's the blessed one. In his current life there is no more room for selfless mothers and drunk fishermen. Now, when he stares into the mirror, he sees only an impossible smile on a mutilated face, a face crisscrossed by wounds that never fully heal. It comes with the job.

He takes a quick shower. He doesn't put much energy into it; he's going to be soaked the rest of the day. He´s also a bit wary of touching the scars on his back. Most of them are closed, and the skin surrounding them is callused. If you looked at his skin, you would get the impression that his spine has decided to exit his body while the skin refuses to allow it. The open tears ooze cold liquids that the water from the shower cannot wash out. The blessed one is used to it. It's nothing to him; his body is just his working tool, and he is content with making sure it stays in the best possible condition. Aesthetic issues are beyond his expectations.

He dries himself off with a pink towel. Over the years he learned that pink is the perfect color: he doesn't need to wash it every other day. He receives very few visitors, and those who do come never enter his bathroom, but it's also true that avoiding unpleasantness has become a habit in a life so full of unpleasantness. He leaves the towel on the rack and returns to his face in the mirror. The mirror is misty with steam, and that lets him see his sketch, a shadow of what he is. It makes it easier to accept himself and forget about the marks that work leaves on his face. It allows him to talk to the bothersome middlemen before diving into his work. Today he needs to concentrate. Today is a big day. It's the ferry's inauguration.

He has freezing-cold juice for breakfast. He drinks slowly, sitting at the kitchen table with the computer. The diving goggles are on one side. He doesn't feel like going online when he has an important job. He's already received all the messages he needed to get: the time, the place, the information on the people, and what he must and mustn't do. Work, just work. He'll have fun when he gets back home. Maybe, when he comes back and goes online, he can make a new avatar, as his psychologist advised; be someone different, be someone unrelated to the sea. The sea has damaged him too much. According to his psychologist, it will damage him even more if he's not able to unravel himself, to separate his work from his real life. As if work wasn't real life. As if he really wanted to become unraveled.

His bag with all his equipment is ready by the door. The blessed one finishes getting dressed, picks up the bag, and goes out on the street. From his house to the harbor, it is just two kilometers, which he usually covers on foot. He has a slight limp, and his somewhat rigid posture, the result of all the hours spent underneath the ships, is not ideal for walking. But walking relaxes him and mentally prepares him for work. He looks back once again, as always. It's a custom that reconciles him with the squat, whitewashed structure that is his house. His home. The only thing he has left from his family. The only thing, at least, that is not inside him, gnawing at his soul.

The house is on a small hill, and the whole walk is downhill. Down toward the shore. He watches the sea with every step he takes. So calm, so peaceful. He is well aware of how treacherous it can be, how evil. They are companions in misfortune; they have worked together so often that he thinks of it as his new father—a father with a thousand hooks, a thousand keels, and a thousand hungry giant creatures inside.

He whistles. He likes to whistle old tunes as he walks down to the harbor. At the houses along the way, curious people—mostly tourists who have come from other countries—watch him pass by. Over the years, the residents have stopped staring. Now they are used to his mutilated face and his body. After all, anyone who does his job would look similar. At least he's polite to the island's residents and visitors, and he has never behaved unpleasantly with anyone. The blessed one is aware that the island dwellers suspect that, like all of his kind, he has many reasons to be the way he is.

The ferry is a huge ship that will be sailing daily from the island to the peninsula. It will transport staples, but most importantly it will help the island reestablish a vital connection to attract more tourists and make the residents want to stay. It will help regain that certain luster and prosperity that seems so fitting and appropriate when you look at the dock. The fishing boats support the island's economy, but prosperity requires large yachts and small recreational vessels. In his job there are always new boats coming—new keels to tear his soul, mutilate his face, and perpetuate the odd angles of his smile. That is his story, a story where there is no longer room for hooks. For fishermen. For mothers.

"The blessed one," says the man, and offers him his hand.

He tries to remember who this man is, accepts his hand and shakes it. The man is wearing a hat with badges, a navy-blue blazer, white trousers. He could pass both for a tourist with an expensive yacht and for a bouncer in one of those nightclubs on the peninsula. His bearing and composure indicate that he must be the ferry captain.

A small crowd of onlookers and island personalities pulsates around their handshake. Over there is the mayor, and over there is the owner of the island's biggest fleet. He also sees fishermen who once hired his services in exchange for a day's catch or a hot dinner in good company. The fee is determined according to the customer's solvency; all jobs are accepted and performed with the same devotion. That is the law of the sea, and in these turbulent times he feels lucky to have a job and a way of life. To be useful.

"There's my baby," says the captain.

He points at the ferry standing out in the harbor like an orca surrounded by sharks. It's over forty meters in length and seems to have been designed to crawl along the desert on caterpillar wheels rather than to sail. Still, there is something impressive about it, something that shows off its power. Maybe it's the painting on the bow that looks like a hyena's smile. Maybe it's the disproportionate gray ramps offering access for vehicles. Or the bridges for the crew and travelers, stretching out to the dock like the tentacles of a freak octopus. Be it as it may, the moment he sees the boat, an amalgam of wood, metal, and fiberglass, he knows it has no soul. And if anyone can give it a soul, it is him. A soul for the ferry, so it can become a vessel that makes trails on the water without the creatures that live in the deep feeling a desire to trap it in their tentacles and jaws, to drag it down to the abyssal pits and devour it with all its contents. That would not be good for business. It has taken the world a long time to accept that all vessels, even the smallest ones, must be blessed; now there's no turning back. No one wants to suffer the agony of being digested by the Kraken for centuries.

"Do you think you can do it?" asks the captain.

An unnecessary and rhetorical question. Still, the blessed one feels tempted to answer it. But he doesn't; he won't speak more than necessary, at least not to men. But the boats, those with a soul…that is different. With them he can share his passions, feelings, pain. After all, everything is pain.

"What's its name?" he asks.

"Fortune Maker," answers the captain, almost instantly.

And then the captain smiles, a nervous smile born from his insecurity, because he knows that the name won't stick, that he will need to ask the printing company to erase the name off the canvasses, and that the posters and stationery items will need to be redone. He knows this because he can read it in the blessed one's eyes. The blessed one has very few prerogatives, but renaming boats is one of them. And the vacant look on his face tells the captain he won't give it a second thought.

"Fine," says the blessed one. "I will remember when your baby whispers its name to me."

The captain's smile breaks. He keeps his poise and invites the blessed one on board. As always, the blessed one accepts. Part of the ritual is the visit to the false entrails of the vessel, the mechanical viscera that are nothing more than a mockup of what he will discover later when they embrace, when they kiss below the water. The polychrome seats, the windows, even the engine room are nothing but fake props to the blessed one's eyes. He is used to the jargon, the words he is expected to pronounce, and he does so with no fear or embarrassment.

"Ah, it's beautiful. What an elegant design. It's an impressive ship. Congratulations."

He caresses the fabrics, the plastic, the metal. He lets himself be seduced by the artificial smells, the beating and murmur of the water against the hull. Twice he stops, crouches down and places his palms on the carpeted floor. The captain, in the company of the cabin manager and two or three other persons of authority, offers his hand when the blessed one stands up, but he rejects it. No offense, no apology. To them this is only work, routine. To him this is life.

He goes down the gangway back to land. He sits cross-legged on the dock and closes his eyes. He prepares. The others move away, giving him the space he needs. Some of them have seen this ritual before. Even though it's always different, it is essentially the same. The meditation, the immersion, the blessing. Afterward... well, the authorities are usually not there, just the medical team.

The blessed one meditates, but he can still hear the character-istic sounds of message notifications on cell phones, the click of cameras, the friction of the boats' hulls against the berth. And the flapping of the seagulls' wings, the murmur of the waves, the whisper of the breeze sliding down the sea. And the voices.

"Is he...? You know what I mean. There are so many, and one doesn't know if he really..."

"His own father blessed him."

"Oh, I see. I didn't know."

"He's the best."

"Soon you'll be sailing without fear. Don't worry, trust him."

So, he trusts him. The blessed one knows; he can hear him breathe, he can hear the beating of his heart. He can hear his trust. That is enough to start with, so he opens his eyes and slowly stands up. The old hook-scars burn on his face, the kisses from so many other keels sting on his back and his body.

"It is time," says the blessed one, and the small crowd gathered there nods in unison.

The next steps are simple, but most people find the process disturbing. The blessed one climbs back aboard the ferry and removes his clothes. He smears his body with oil, and then the men, two volunteers who can barely look at him, roll the thick rope around his body and tighten it. The rope mercilessly bites into his skin. The first drops of blood are already spouting, although most can't witness it.

"Go ahead," says the blessed one.

There is the sound of panting and sighing. The smell of the sea soaks up the deck. The two men pull the blessed one to starboard; a flexible methacrylate plank has been set up. It is bright pink, as if the tradition had no significance. The blessed one closes his eyes. He imagines that, in these minutes before the jump, his serene face and his closed eyes will invite the onlookers to believe he's praying to the gods to help him with his job. That's incorrect. He prays that this time he will not survive, that this will be the last boat, the last keel. He prays that he won't have to go back underwater, even though he knows he must; he cannot escape his responsibility. The responsibility that the man who claimed to be his father, the boozing fisherman, imposed on him with his drunken clumsiness. The same responsibility he has imposed on himself as punishment, as his destiny.

Beneath the soles of his feet, the blessed one feels the murmur of the ferry. It's a muffled murmur, begging him to let it be devoured. Boats harbor a secret desire to run aground, especially those carrying living beings. Sometimes he finds the knowledge he gains from the ritual very perturbing. In spite of its modern design, the ferry is no different from a five-century-old ship. Its spirit holds the idea of immortality, the kind that only comes when you are wreckage on the ocean floor. That is the job of the blessed one: to break its nature. What others understand as protection is nothing other than domestication. Control. Abuse. A vessel's soul is nothing more than submission to his will.

The blessed one opens his eyes, takes a few steps forward, and falls into the sea. He sinks into a swirl of bubbles, algae, and flowing black hair in the cold water of the harbor. He is in his natural habitat now, but to everyone else he will proceed as if this environment was foreign to him. The way his strangeness makes people reject him is already enough. He doesn't want to add any more condemning details to the rumors. He must live among men, since boats fear him and push him away. He must live on land, since the sea despises him for not feeding his hunger. It would not be smart to let his body mutate and adapt to the water, displaying the changes to his neighbors. Stakes and fires are a thing of the past, but these are confusing times where technology coexists with superstition, and his presence could easily shift from essential to abhorred.

A school of fish opens up as the blessed one sinks. He feels the graze of the rope unwinding, the kiss of the fish that stupidly have no fear of him. Then he feels the rope pull and, for the first time, sees the full magnitude of the keel. Soon it will be covered in dog teeth, but now they are just a marginal presence. The pull of the rope drags him toward it, and even though he's not concerned about freediving—people would be terrified if he told them he can breathe underwater—he knows he has limited time under the boat and he must do a lot of things on the way. The first thing, as soon as his body hits the ship and the blood starts to flow, is to know the ferry's true name.

So, he asks the question.

The same question he asked when his father threw him to the sea.

THE BLESSED ONE opens his eyes. He's lying down on the ferry's deck. They have covered his body with a blanket, and the medical team is working on him.

"Oh, God…welcome back," says a paramedic when he sees his eyes. "I thought you were gone."

"So did I," says the blessed one. But he isn't.

"No, no, all is okay now. You are stable, don't worry. The hemorrhages are under control, and we are taking you to the hospital. You'll be fine."

Yes, I'm fine, thinks the blessed one. I am. Knowing that in the future he will have to go through that again relaxes him. He had dreamt of failing, of not being able to speak to the boat during those endless minutes when his body and mind inhabited the water and were beaten, caressed, and kissed by the keel; but that didn't happen. He asked, and he was answered. Afterward, as the wounds opened up and the blood blinded him, he spoke to the ferry; he understood its motivations, its needs. Like an amateur psychologist, he listened and spoke, and then he convinced it. It's not yet time to sink. It's not yet time to go home. Patience. Like it or not, you have a soul now, and it's mine.

He knows all the blessed ones share his vision. Patience. They don't want to keep boats from sinking. What they want is for the boats to sink when the time and place are right. To sink in an orderly, controlled manner that lets them all return to the sea, the place that is now their home, the place where they belong. No, he will not allow the ferry's nature to follow its desire to call on the abyssal creatures and ask them to devour it. Not now. Perhaps in a few years, when the time comes. When it understands how this world works and when it can make sure that the sacrifice, the perfectly orchestrated offering from all the blessed ones, is worth something. When the sinking of all the ships traversing the sea promises them all a life of glory in the abyssal pits.

In the meantime, he will continue to bless ships, working for these men who look after him as if their life depended on it. And they are probably right. Sooner or later, they will all sail aboard a ship. They will all risk their lives crossing the sea. Only the blessing assures them a safe return to their homes. At least for now.

"What's its name?"

The captain is crouching down next to him. He's already been laid down on the stretcher and is being carried to the ambulance. But the captain grabs his bloody hand in his and repeats the question.

"What's its name?"

The blessed one blinks, turns his head to the side, and spits out the salty spittle building up inside his throat. The paramedics load the stretcher onto the ambulance, and the captain stays on the ground. The blessed one sits up and looks at the captain for a second before the ambulance doors are shut.

"Its name is Impatient," he says.

And he knows that's what they will call the ship, although its true name is impossible to pronounce or represent with any of the human alphabets. A perfect name, should it turn out to be the first ship that decides to sacrifice itself. The blessed one knows that when he goes into the water, be it in this harbor or another, he'll be able to speak to it. He can speak to all the ships he has blessed. And when he speaks to it, he will tell it to go ahead and accept its destiny, to call the abyssal creatures and let them devour it.

To be the bait.

⚓

ESTHER OF PRETTY BOY

Kay Vaindal

ON NIGHTS LIKE this, the Peat Cutters rumble down from the Fall Line and troll flooded highways, looking for ships to strip and people to steal. Esther was raised by a Peat King. It's good, she knows, to tuck yourself away on nights like these.

Instead, her boat pirouettes on its keel in a marsh channel draining away. To the west, the sun sets behind the faded roof of a half-sunk Shell station. To the east, a faded green sign reads *Riva Road*, taunting her with how close they got to the edge of Salmo, the Salt Marsh, the safety of the subtidal. She and Gio were out looking for the Manatee. Now, like the station, they're out of gas and out of time.

Gio's morning Xanax, it turns out, was not Xanax. He lies curled around himself under the gunnel on hour three of a bad trip, useless, moaning. Soon, the tide will recede fully. When there was still a chance to escape, she'd pushed and pushed the little outboard motor until fumes filled the air. The smell lingers.

She waits, watching the peach-toned sky, the ruins, and the steam settled low over Salmo, whipped into strange shapes by a ticklish breeze. Behind the Shell, a house still stands, its windows all broken, old curtains flying out like pale green tongues. Something else moves beyond it. Deer, coyotes. She sees a person dressed in black, faceless, wild-armed, staring at her. The fog shifts and it's the skeleton of a tree, dead branches swaying in the wind.

Gio sits up. He watches something far away.

"You better?" she asks him.

He shakes his head. "I see ghosts."

"You don't see ghosts," she says. "You see wind."

"I can see the families who used to live here," he tells her, watching the gas station, and the house behind it, and Salmo cradling it all. "I can see all the ghosts."

"No, you can't."

"Yes, I can. They're everywhere."

"Probably didn't even die here," she says. "Probably just moved to, like, Frederick County."

"Their souls didn't." He scrunches his face up like an elastic band.

Esther ignores him and checks the space under the decking for a gun. She finds three greasy bags of jellyfish jerky (Gio's), a shrimping net (hers), and a digital camera, in case they saw the Manatee. The Manatee hasn't been spotted all year, which means no one can marry, and no babies have names, and no dead have passed into the next world. She thought today might be the day it would raise its head from black water and exhale through wide nostrils, blessing their union in the eyes of Salmo, and they would offer it watercress and sea beans. That was before Gio's pupils uncoiled and he said, "Oh my god, Esther. I'm on fucking acid." It was funny at first. She'd told him there were fish in the sky. Then he threw a rock at a Maryland police boat patrolling the shipping lanes, forcing their retreat into Salmo, and it wasn't so funny anymore.

The sun goes down, and Esther's vision becomes staticky. Grasses and sedges mingle in the wind. The channel recedes fully toward the *Riva Road* sign, and black snails and grass shrimp retreat into the Mud, salmomat, which opens to receive them. She imagines familiar rumbles and pictures her brothers pulling semi-automatic rifles off the walls of castles built from salmomat, loading into the cutters, riding abandoned highways to where veins of land mush into the Chesapeake. Every low-low tide, desperate people get stranded in Salmo. It's Salmo's gift to the Bog, her father would say. A Bog needs bodies. Who are we to deny the Bog what it needs?

Maybe it won't be her brothers. Maybe it'll be people from the other Peat kingdoms, Loch Raven, or Liberty. Maybe—

"Esther?" says Gio, glancing her direction.

She raises her eyebrows.

"Are you mad at me?"

She watches grasses sway, caressing the pillars under the Shell station, and she knows their Leaders would say this is Salmo's doing, not his. "Why would you think your Xanax came in tab form?" she says.

He scratches his hairline. "They're always changing stuff, you know?"

She tosses him his bag of his jellyfish jerky, and he pops a dehydrated ctenophore into his mouth. She watches him chew and chew, veins in his temples made visible by every gnash of his jaw.

Hours go by, and they arrive. Bare salmomat under them bounces like gelatin. Shallow murky pools of water reverberate like there's something big inside, about to burst out. Then, the sound: groaning motors from the highlands. Gio comes down. Esther watches the gravity of the situation dawn on him. He was born behind the seawall, but that world crunched him up and spit him out. Here, Salmo favors him. It shows him patterns in the channels that it keeps from Esther, gives him gifts he finds hidden in the reeds. But the feelings of Salmo don't matter in the Bog. If she can't protect him, they'll chain him and make him cut Peat by hand, day and night, until he shrinks to nothing. Corporations behind the seawall will buy the Peat and sink it in the deep ocean for carbon credits, while the Bog sucks moisture from Gio's sunken corpse.

The cutters loom in the darkness. They move forward like trains, slow and heavy and unstoppable, rusted treads whining loudly over the wind. Esther and Gio could try to run to the crumbling house with the green-tongued windows, but there would be no point to that. Salmomat is centuries deep. It shouldn't be. Esther knows Salmo's origin. When the waters came, they took the cities apart piece by piece and moved the important bits upslope to the western counties. But there was still so much left for Salmo to eat, to crumble and crunch and turn to wet dust. It had lost time to make up for and a big appetite, thanks to green lawns and fields of wheat.

Esther stands up. "I am Esther of Prettyboy!" she shouts.

The cutters move forward regardless. Esther's voice is nothing against the squeals of their rusty vehicles, the whir of the giant chainsaws attached to their noses.

Gio checks the space under the decking for a gun.

The man driving the first cutter stands up. Esther doesn't recognize him, but she can't be sure of her eyes in the darkness. He throws a chain and hooks the gunnel, and then the long, long drag begins. Esther and Gio sit huddled near the stern as their boat tears like a plow through Salmo, ripping up grasses flattened by the cutter's treads, peeling salmomat in great curls at the bow.

"So, this isn't good," says Gio, eventually.

"No," says Esther.

"These guys'll know your dad, right?"

"They'll know him."

He scratches his scalp.

"We could jump?" she offers.

Gio looks over the gunnel, through the grass, down at the deep, black salmomat under the boat. "Salmo doesn't want us to," he says.

She rolls her eyes.

Hours go by, or minutes. The Peat cutters ahead of them drone noisily enough that time folds. They pass toward the pot-holed landward edge of Salmo. Esther sees a sunken old soccer field, a few inches of glassy water poured upon it like brown resin, rusty paint-chipped goal posts lit by the moon. A heron nests in the netting. They pass through a low-lying suburban neighborhood, and the boat floats again for a while, passing houses that jut from the water with faces missing, doors missing, siding missing, foundations like empty stages. Ghost trees wave goodbye to them. The white bellies of dead fish litter patches of high ground. A fat coyote watches them from atop a muddy island, unmoving. Esther thinks it's smiling.

Salmo mourns Gio when the cutters drag their boat up the unvegetated red-clay slope of the Fall Line. A coyote chorus yaps, and birds scream even though it's night. Esther knows where they're going: Triadelphia, the smallest of the four great Peat kingdoms perched between the sinking and the settled worlds.

When they arrive, it must be near five a.m. Esther and Gio hold hands at the stern. In the twilight is a world that looks to Esther like home. She sees the stumps of dead forests, some half-submerged by a shallow lens of water, islands floating upon it in slow circles, bare and orange-brown. Moss grows on the shores. Monstrous machines with chainsaw mouths and cranes pointed at the sky sit rusting in the water. Behind it all, rising like a castle from the earth: a palace made of corrugated metal and salmomat. Gio chews on his lip.

As soon as the last cutter ahead of them shuts off, Esther stands up and shouts, "I'm Esther of Prettyboy, and you'll release us immediately!"

The drivers—pale, redheaded—turn their heads as one. They look at each other, and then descend from their cutters. There are four of them, wearing bedazzled brown coats over hazel waders. "This is the rogue Prettyboy child?" says one.

"They say she's a Manatee Devotee now," says another.

"Are you a Manatee Devotee?" asks the third, loud so that she can hear.

Esther looks at Gio. He looks back at her and scratches the corner of his mouth. Then she climbs from the boat into the dirt and says, "Of course not."

They laugh. "What good grace Salmo has sacrificed for us today," says one of them. "The Prettyboy child, here. Imagine a union between our kingdoms."

"A great union," says the second.

"Would you marry me?" says the third, to Esther.

Gio hops out of the boat, adjusting his oversized pinstripe pants, and stands beside her. "We're *engaged*," he says.

The Triadelphian Peat lordlings laugh. Then they say, "Come, Esther of Prettyboy."

Esther whispers to Gio, "Follow my lead." She goes off after the redheaded Peat lordlings toward their salmomat-and-steel palace, looming over the Bog. It's a slippery path, compacted and plantless, and the ground is marked like the patches on a cow, alternating between weeping red clay and black-brown Peat crumbs. Halfway there, Gio grabs Esther by the arm and hisses something incomprehensible in her ear.

"What?" she says.

"The Manatee," he says again.

She turns to look at the Bog, and sees nothing. "Probably a cormorant," she says.

"I saw it!" he says, loud enough that a Peat lordling looks back at them.

She could say a few things: 1) The Manatee could not survive in a Bog. 2) You were seeing fish in the sky and ghosts in the wind a few hours ago. 3) The things that happened in the world behind the seawall left you disturbed. I love you and Salmo loves you but reality twists around you sometimes, frantic and rotten like you've smelled too much sulfur. Our Leaders think you're Salmo's favorite son. They place broad hats on your head in the ceremonies, but I know why you see faces where there aren't any. Instead, she whispers, "Okay. Keep an eye out."

They enter the shadow of the palace, where the earth feels cold. Goosebumps rise on her bare, sunburnt arms. The door creaks open. Behind it stands another redheaded white woman, too thin, sunken eyes with purple bags under them, bundled in a heavy brown coat like her siblings. "Miranda!" says Esther. "So good to see you! Congratulations on your coronation, and so sorry about your father."

Miranda stares at Esther for a moment, eyes half-lidded, then hacks into the crook of her arm. She waves them inside.

They enter a long hallway. It's dark and dusty and stinks like mushrooms. Black mold climbs corners in fractal patterns, and battery-powered lights flicker, screwed into the walls like portholes. Moths flutter alongside tiny biting flies. Miranda brings them to a sunnier room in the back of the structure. High ceilings loom over tall windows, and dark curtains droop like wet hair. A runway of moss leads to an impromptu throne: a folding chair with a coyote pelt laid across it. The floor is black and shiny, made with salmomat from downslope.

Miranda takes a seat on the coyote's flattened head. The spores and gnats and moths in the air, floating in beams of sunlight, make Esther feel like she's underwater.

Miranda's siblings stand at attention beside their tiny sister.

"Which of my siblings will you marry?" says Miranda in a voice like a whisper. Her closest sibling, beside her, repeats the question louder so Esther and Gio can hear.

"Esther," hisses Gio in her ear.

"I'm engaged," says Esther to the Peat lords of Triadelphia.

"*Esther*," hisses Gio again.

She looks at him. He points upward. Above their heads hangs a chandelier made from candles and pinkish bones.

"Should my siblings present themselves?" says Miranda, and her sibling repeats.

"What?" whispers Esther to Gio.

"That's the Manatee," he hisses back, pointing again.

"My eldest younger sibling is Murdoc," says Miranda, and another sibling repeats. "Murdoc, please step forward and remove your coat to show Esther of Prettyboy your unfreckled arms."

"That's not the Manatee," whispers Esther.

"That's the Manatee," says Gio. "Look at the chevron bones." Then he shouts to the Peat nobles, "Is that the Manatee? Is that chandelier made out of the Manatee, you fuckers? Did you kill the Manatee?"

Murdoc, holding his coat in his unfreckled arms, says, "The Manatee was a gift from Salmo to the Bog."

"Did you kill the Manatee?" shouts Gio, surging forward toward the stage.

From inside his coat, Murdoc takes a shiny silver revolver and points it lazily at Gio. "What's it to you?" says Murdoc. "I thought you weren't Manatee worshipers."

"It's trapped here!" shouts Gio. He jabs a finger at the ceiling, then at Esther, then at the Peat royals lined up by the wall. "It's trapped! Give me Its bones!"

Esther steps between Gio and Murdoc's gun, hands raised in the air. "Miranda," she says to the tiny Peat King, trying to exude calm and peace and understanding. "Look, this is crazy. You don't want war with Prettyboy, yeah? It's okay. You didn't know who I was, so you took our boat. But now you do, so you can let us go. Okay? Okay. Let us go, and we'll forget all about this."

"Let It go!" shouts Gio, squeezing a fist so tight that Esther can see the tendons stretched across his knuckles.

"The Bog needs bodies," wheezes Miranda, and Murdoc repeats for her, "The Bog needs bodies."

Gio stomps past Esther toward the Peat prince.

Murdoc fires his weapon. Just as he does, the salmomat floor—dry for decades—twists out from under his feet, hurtling him backward. The bullet strikes the rusty chain holding the chandelier to the ceiling. With a magnificent creak, it falls and crashes down upon little Miranda in her throne. Shards of chandelier bone fly like shrapnel. The force of the crash throws the others to the ground. The skull of the Manatee—a smooth, yellowed thing with bits of rancid meat still in its sockets—skids across the floor and lands between Gio's feet.

Thank you, Salmo, thinks Esther.

"Thank you, Salmo," says Gio.

ONE OF THE Peat lordlings checks on Miranda, and then releases a terrible, theatrical wail. "My sister!" he shouts. "My poor, tiny sister!"

Gio grabs the skull, and Esther grabs him, dragging him back out to the door and toward the Bog, toward the boat. Gio tries to twist away, crying out for the rest of the bones. "Chessie," he mourns, cradling the skull. "Chessie, Chessie, Chessie. No other manatee will come here but you, Chessie."

They run down the slippery trail, where sunrise has dyed the world a prehistoric sort of yellow. Sickly people with lightless eyes move across the Bog like automated skeletons, cutting squares of Peat from the floating islands. Under Gio and Esther's boots, the red clay oozes carelessly, inert. The Peat, though, will not let them leave without swallowing something. It climbs their ankles and tries to pull them downward, tiny bits of undigested twig and leaf and rock clinging to their pants like scraps of metal to a magnet. It slurps down Gio's shoe, throwing him forward to his hands and knees. The Manatee's skull clatters to the earth in front of him, skidding to a stop in a patch of red clay. A tendril of Peat moves like a staticky arm to retrieve it, but Esther gets there first. She grabs the skull with one hand and Gio's arm with the other, yanking both toward her chest. With a *schlock*, the Peat swallows Gio's shoe.

Gasping breaths of sticky air, Esther and Gio sprint to Salmo, which stretches below, glowing yellow-green in trapezoids of sunrise filtered through fluffy clouds. Great ripples of Peat race behind them. Somewhere behind them, guns fire. They tumble toward the Fall Line, where their boat sits teetering on the edge of the world. The tide is high now. Esther and Gio shove the boat to the slope, ribcages tightening around their lungs.

The boat slides down the red clay of the Fall Line and splashes into the water below, surrounded by the tips of half-drowned grasses that poke through the water like shaved hair. They hop in. Esther pulls the cord on the motor, but the propeller doesn't start. She didn't expect it to. Not with an empty gas tank, after dragging through salmomat and reeds and the ruins of neighborhoods all night.

"The paddle's gone," she says. "Gio, where's the paddle?"

Gio cradles the Manatee's skull, cooing at it.

"Gio!"

"I don't know! Why would I know?"

"Help me look!" she says.

The grasses hold them in place, close to the base of the slippery hill where Salmo meets the uplands: the bogs, the forests, the world behind the walls. Salmo looks fragile. But it's a machine, Esther knows, every day eating a little more muddy slope, red clay, and Peat, eating a few more ruined houses and gas stations and soccer goals and trees and fish and humans, digesting everything into salmomat. Everything, their Leaders say, will someday be Salmo.

Gio pulls the cord on the motor, and it turns on, coughing algae from the cooling system.

Thank you, Marsh, thinks Esther.

Gio holds the skull to his chest and keeps the prop high, tooling slowly into the shade of a dead forest, floor like a mirror. Hundreds of birds sing on skeleton branches draped in Spanish moss. A cownose ray leaps from the water, landing on its belly with a splash.

Then, without ceremony, Gio tosses the Manatee skull into Salmo, where it will become salmomat.

"Do you see it?" he says, grinning at nothing.

She wishes she could.

SOME HAVE NO SHIELD AT ALL

Karter Mycroft

JULIANA SAT IN the boat while the fisherman snuck through the mangroves with his net. Remnants of a rain shower dripped onto his bare back. The summer had been brutally wet, and the tidal channels that cut through the swamp were high and turbid. She couldn't see anything in the water, but she could tell from his slow, determined movements that he'd found a Cousin.

He crept into the shadowy underside of the mangrove, moving so slowly no ripples came to the water. Then he raised his arms over his head and became absolutely motionless, as still as the crooked roots. If he was breathing, Juliana couldn't tell. A humid breeze tumbled through the channel and leaves fell from the mangroves, their canopies unnaturally high after decades of genetic tampering. She clutched at her paperwork so it didn't blow into the stream.

The fisherman plunged into the water. Seconds later he arose, gasping for air, with something dark pulsing in the mesh of his net.

Juliana prepared her documents.

The fisherman made his way back through the stream with a grin, muddy water trickling down his broad shoulders. He tossed his catch onto the boat and pulled himself aboard.

He opened the net and the Cousin splayed out on the deck. It appeared at first like a large puddle of oil, though on closer examination its form was that of a sea slug or sea hare, with drooping tentacles on either side of its mouth and two more rising like rabbit ears on top, and a flat muscular foot spanning its underside.

Juliana approached the specimen. As the licensing agent on duty, her job was to determine whether it could be legally harvested. The Cousin's antennae seemed to focus on her as she approached. Not a good sign. She brought her face close to the inky black skin, which was covered in mucus and secreting a murky, purplish pigment. She began a physical examination, pressing into its flesh with her hands. It felt about the same as it looked, cold and wet and squishy.

Then something pressed back.

She dropped her ream of paper records all over the deck. The Cousin quivered as if upset that she'd pulled away. Inside its skin, just behind its propodial tentacles, a human hand reached out.

The fisherman watched intently from the stern. "What is it?" he asked.

"Put it back in the water," she said. "This one's not legal."

"You're joking. Do you have any idea how much it's worth?"

She started scribbling notes in her logbook. "Its anatomy is differentiated. You have to release it."

The Cousin expanded its body, tightening its skin around the appendage within. She could make out the individual fingers spreading open in the blackness. Like it was begging for something.

"Release it," she repeated.

The fisherman cursed loud enough for her to hear. He bent over the Cousin, bear-hugged it from behind, and lifted it up. With its tail off the deck and tentacles to the sky, it was nearly as tall as he was. Scowling, he lugged it over the side of the boat, then found a towel and wiped its various slimes off his chest.

She could have sworn it made a face at her as it sank.

THE MANGROVES STRETCHED in all directions, swarming the waterways like some great world-millipede of wood and greenery. They were created in an underfunded eco-engineering project intended to make the swamps more resilient to higher temperatures, which ended up modifying the mangroves to nearly three times the size of their natural counterparts. They were indeed resilient—too resilient by far—and they smothered and contorted the coastline, making it taller, darker, stranger by the day. Prop roots spiderlegged the water in a mad sprawl, their shadowy nooks home to nebulous communities of fish, bugs, birds, and large predators. Animals which had evolved to live here over millions of years, along with some recent arrivals.

Juliana had lived in the delta her entire life, but each passing season it felt less and less like home. When the rains came the waterways swelled until their village all but washed away, and in the dry season the tides crept further and further inland, ravaging their agricultural areas with sea salt. Garbage, human waste, and polluted silt trickled down from the cities far upriver, accumulating in eddies and lagoons until even the stalwart mangroves were sickened. And then there was the biotech, discarded from distant laboratories whose methods and research goals no one understood. Scientists suspected that illegal discharge of modified human nucleic acids, combined with the natural ability of sea slugs to uptake complex molecules from the ambient environment, led to the appearance of those creatures that locals called Cousins.

Juliana was not naïve—she understood that all things in this world must change. But she had a notion that recently even the force of change itself had started to change, operating in fits of unpredictable accelerations and reversals, such that by the time she managed to get used to anything, it was already something else.

Now, as the fisherman drove them up some obscure channel where the mangroves gave way to thickets of sharp green palms, she felt more untethered than ever. Here the tidal channels drank in fresh water from the river, forming a brackish churn even more opaque than downstream. On the banks the palms competed with mangroves for territory, and their tangled branches cast jagged shadows onto the water. Not even the plants were sure who was supposed to live here.

"Those are good spots." The fisherman pointed out a chain of stagnant ponds that broke off from the channel. "But mostly juveniles. Don't worry, I'll be careful." He seemed to have recovered his composure since she'd forced him to discard the large Cousin earlier. He steered the boat toward a nearby bank. The biofuel motor sputtered in the active water. Birds fled from the noise in multiple directions, some flying toward the river and some toward the sea.

He tied the boat to a mangrove root and raised the motor, its sharp propeller gleaming in the afternoon sun. Then he went to work stalking the perimeter of the shallow pools.

Juliana felt conflicted about making him try again. That Cousin might have fed his family for months—the luxury markets were paying exorbitant prices now that the harvest was so limited. But her job was to uphold the regulations, and the regulations said the take of individuals with "pronounced humanlike characteristics, including differentiated anatomy" was strictly prohibited. Her department took the issue of sentience very seriously. So did she.

A loud splash snapped her to attention. The fisherman had snagged a Cousin about three feet long from one of the pools. This time, though, he shook his head and replaced it. "Teeth," he said, disappointed.

The next one he found was larger—a good sign, since the morphology tended toward that of a "pure" sea hare in older specimens. He brought it to the boat and sat across from her, waiting patiently while she examined it.

She prodded several key zones on its body, pressing through ink and slime, squeezing its tentacles and rhinophores in her hand and updating her logbook as she went. The animal was very sluglike. The only hints of human DNA were tiny lateral projections on its underside—vestigial toes, maybe—nothing fully differentiated.

Though she was reluctant to admit it, this Cousin could legally be harvested under the provisions of the Convention on Potentially Sentient Neo-Organisms.

As she backed away to tell the fisherman—relieved to give him good news, though unsettled about the fate of the creature—something stopped the words in her throat. The Cousin's rhinophores had followed her movement. Those two long stalks at the top of its head were trained on her, and when she moved her head side to side, they moved accordingly. In sea slugs these were chemoreceptive organs—only able to perceive smell and taste. They should have no reaction to visual stimuli. But here they were, undeniably *watching* her.

"Come on," he said. "There's no people parts on this thing anywhere. It's exactly the kind we're supposed to catch."

She was barely listening. She imagined being a Cousin, her mind merged with the mind of an invertebrate, her human emotions filtered through chemical sensors and alien instincts. She wondered what this Cousin was experiencing in this moment, whether it was terrified or despondent or simply confused. She was pretty sure she saw it cock its head while the fisherman argued, as if it understood their speech, as if it wanted to know more about what they had to say. It made her sick to imagine something like a human being in there, under that oozing face, its future in her hands.

"You hear me? This is a legal catch. I'm going to drive you back to the village now, and then I'll take it upriver to the processors."

"No." She dropped her gaze to the deck, unable to face him or the Cousin. "It's demonstrating this, what is it, a mammalian visual acuity. That's a disqualifying trait. It would violate the Convention's decision criteria. We have to return it." She was making this up as she went, trying to phrase her personal revulsion in the most regulatory terms she could think of.

The fisherman stood upright. A dense grove of palms swayed behind him, needles sharp and green. For a moment she thought he might become violent. And he did—but only to the Cousin. He gripped it tight and hurled it into the churning waterway.

He sat near the motor and buried his face in his filthy hands.

In her logbook she noted a second specimen had been caught and released alive. Part of her felt sure that she'd done the right thing, that she'd "saved" something. The other part was down there with the slug, peering through the murk with eyes that couldn't see a thing. It was difficult to tell how aware the Cousins were, but on some level that one must have known what had happened. She felt dirty for almost letting it be harvested.

They sat in the boat and rocked on the bubbling stream. Small crustaceans darted out of mangrove chambers and into other ones.

She looked up at the fisherman. "So what do you think about them?"

"What do you mean?"

"I mean, how do you feel about the Cousins exactly, when you go to catch them?"

He rummaged through his drybag for a half-smoked cigarette. "I know you think I'm just some dumb fisherman."

It wasn't true—in fact, she was thoroughly impressed at the skill and patience he employed, his tenacity in hunting down fishing spots, his simple yet precise manner of speaking. In another context she might actually have been quite attracted to him, not that she would ever admit it.

"I'm interested in your perspective."

"My perspective, okay." He blew smoke up at the sky. "Well, they're animals. Animals kill each other, if you hadn't noticed. All the new rules about 'sentience' and 'harvest criteria' are bullshit in my opinion. You know what happens when we toss them back?"

"What's that?"

He started to flick his cigarette into the water, then put it out in the boat under his shoe instead. "The poachers get them. If people like me who follow the rules can't catch any, the guys who come through at night with shock prods can. They'll take the ones who have eyes and tongues, the ones with little pink brains in there. I've heard of guys who kill them just for fun. People don't give a shit."

Juliana's jaw popped from clenching her teeth. She had been imagining herself as a Cousin while he talked. Now it was impossible to get the image out of her mind. When she moved her arms she felt detritus in the air, and when she looked up at the sky it was like the surface of a tide pool. A sheen of sunlight fell around her, and she searched the currents for some impossible clarity.. Did cool water pass through gills in her neck? Did the smells of predators appear like static on old film? She imagined a poacher standing over her, flipping a coin to decide her fate. Did she wish she had a shell to shield her, like her ancestors the snails or her ancestors the medieval knights?

"Did you want to say anything, or is this all for your report?" said the fisherman.

"Yeah, no, thank you, sorry. I need to pee."

She stepped off the boat onto a damp bank, barely noticing the mud soaking into her socks as she slipped behind a thicket and threw up.

When she returned the fisherman was starting the motor.

"The tide's heading out," he said. "We can try near the spits before dark."

THEY REACHED THE coast in under an hour, the journey sped by the fisherman's impatience and the rapid seaward flow of the estuary. Here the mangroves dissolved into wide, shimmering mudflats, a vast temporary beach which appeared for only a few hours a day. The sea breeze brought a welcome chill to the humid evening, along with the reek of brine from the newly exposed flats. Crabs and seabirds made strange advances across the mud and in the distance a crocodile was either resting or dead.

The fisherman took them all the way to open water. He reduced speed to circle a small mangrove island not far offshore. There were many such islands out here, oases of green among the dull gradient of mud and ocean. Below, the orange beams of setting sun danced on a bed of seagrass, tendrils spasming in the current.

They puttered around the mangroves, one saltbitten cay after another. The sun was seeping into the horizon when he finally raised the motor and tied off the boat. He pointed a few yards off the starboard side. Then he gathered his net and plunged into the water.

Alone in the boat, she watched the waves break in the distance, where the wetland was finally devoured by the ocean. She wondered if the Cousins ever ventured out that far, sliding down the continental shelf into the cold abyss. She knew that some sea slugs—at least those which hadn't been altered by genetic runoff—could live at fairly extreme depths. But maybe the Cousins felt it was too dark down there, too unsafe and unpredictable. Or maybe there was something else that kept them in the mangroves, close to the rivers, close to the towns.

The fisherman burst out of the sea. He tried lifting his net from below but could only raise the mesh a few inches above the surface. He'd caught something very heavy.

"Give me a hand." He struggled against the weight, barely keeping his mouth above water to speak.

She reached over the side of the boat and grabbed the net. The Cousin inside was so massive it almost dragged her overboard before she steadied herself.

The fisherman climbed aboard, and together they hauled in the net, careful to avoid the blades of the upturned motor.

It was the largest she had ever seen. Its facial tentacles hung like deflated tusks as long as her arm. Its skin oozed so much navy-blue ink it covered the deck completely. It likely could have capsized the boat simply by shifting its weight to one side, but it remained still.

She reached into her bag for her logbook, then froze. There was a noise. A low, wet gurgle, barely distinguishable from the slosh of the waves against mangrove roots. *Aaacch-aaaacch-aaaaach.* It sounded like the boat had sprung a leak under the Cousin's weight.

No, the sound wasn't coming from the boat—it was coming from the Cousin.

Aaacch-aaaacch-aaaaach, came the voice from the Cousin's throat. When it made the sounds, its mouth moved and the stalks on its head shuddered in time.

It was talking.

Aaacch-aaaacch-aaaaach.

The fisherman was still catching his breath. "That's not—"

"Listen," said Juliana. "It has vocal cords."

The fisherman slouched backward against the motor. He screamed, a long and desperate howl of frustration that echoed up the tidal channel they'd taken to get here. The Cousin wagged its tentacles when he started screaming, and again when he stopped.

"Guessing that's it then," he said. "I go home with nothing. That's what you want, right? You want me to tell my family we're back to eating rice once a day. You think that slug is more important than me."

"It's not that, it's just—hold on."

Aaacch-aaaacch-aaaaach.

Juliana couldn't begin to guess what the Cousin was saying. There was no real pattern to its speech, just the same liquid syllable repeated at different lengths. It was attempting to communicate something, but its ability was restricted by something in its bastard physiology. Were they all trying to communicate with humans? People were treating these things like fish, like big dumb clueless animals, and the whole time they were trying to speak. She peered into its tentacles and listened and tried to understand.

The slug inched toward her, extending its neck and gurgling, *aaaacch-aaaaaach-aach.* Judging from its size it must be old, possibly one of the earliest hybrids to spawn. The Cousins were first documented seven years ago. Seven years spent slithering the mangroves, alone and unprotected, with all those words stuck in its throat.

Its head was very close now. *Aaaaaach-aaach-aach.* She wanted more than anything to know what it was telling her. It must be asking for safety, for someplace to hide, for a friend. Someone to keep it safe from harm—and hadn't that been her mission all along? She wondered if she could convince the fisherman to bring it back to the village. Maybe at her department office, it could be cared for properly. Maybe they could even start to communicate with it.

The slug's tentacles were inches away, and for a moment she was sure it was going to touch its face to hers. Instead, it moved past her.

She realized it hadn't been approaching her at all. It pressed on to the stern of the boat, where the corkscrew blade of the motor glinted in the sunset.

The Cousin stretched itself over the sharp edge. It raised its head and lowered it onto the propeller. It was trying to cut itself. It flopped pathetically on the blade and croaked, *aaacch-aaaacch-aaaaach.*

Now she understood.

She scurried across the boat to the fisherman's side. She would have thrown up again if there was anything left in her.

"What is it?" he said. "What's it doing?"

She didn't answer. Panic rose in her like a typhoon. She stared at the Cousin, still trying to slice itself on the propeller. There was a consciousness somewhere in that shapeless anatomy, a real sentience—she was more certain than ever. And now she knew how it felt.

"Come on, help me toss it back," said the fisherman.

"Take it," she said quickly.

He started to curse, then stopped himself. "What'd you say?"

"Take it upriver and kill it and sell it. I won't report you, don't worry. Just—don't let it suffer."

"Is this a test?" said the fisherman. "This is a test. You're trying to trick me."

"Here." She reached in her satchel and hurled her report into the sea. The ink smeared over the papers, and they caught on the roots of the mangroves like old advertisements.

The fisherman stood still in the boat.

Juliana watched her reports dissolve and sink.

The Cousin slouched on the propeller and said, *aaacch-aaaacch-aaaaach.*

The fisherman stepped past the creature and lowered the motor.

Juliana leaped out of the boat into the water.

"What the hell?" he shouted. "Where are you going?"

She swam away from the boat until she could stand on the bottom, then continued walking onto the mudflat. There was nothing more to say. There was nothing more to do here at all.

"Are you crazy?" he called out behind her. "It's two hours back to the village and that's with a boat. The tide will be in before you can make it halfway."

She said nothing. She fell down on the mud and let it soak her legs.

"I'm serious, get back in here," he said.

She said nothing.

The Cousin said, *aaacch-aaaacch-aaaaach*.

She lay on the mud next to a pile of dead wood covered in flies. Seawater bubbled up around her. The sky turned brackish, all mud-brown sunset and sea-foam clouds. She imagined black skin enveloping her, blue-black ink in her veins. Her words all fizzled into foam, she reached out with her hands and could touch nothing. Humanity had built entire new forms of suffering. Souls doomed from birth with nothing in the world to save them. And they would keep breeding and growing and living, trapped every day in bodies that even Nature wasn't cruel enough to design.

The fisherman fired the motor and then the boat was moving, and the Cousin was croaking, and Juliana was lying on the mudflat alone. He started the boat up the channel, and she closed her eyes and sank back into the mud and waited for the tide to come in. And she heard the motor grind through the water and she heard the Cousin say, *aacch-aacch-aaaach*, and then those sounds all faded away.

⚓

A DATE ON BERBEROKA ISLAND

Mars Abian

"HUNGRY." LUZ CARESSES my hand with her pincers, drawing blood. We're all hungry here, our bellies empty as her hollow fish mouth.

But salvation comes.

He rides Ka Isko's boat, pointing a metal stick over the water as he poses, flashing, smiling. He's a handsome man. Tall. Bright. Lively. The gray skies and seas roar in protest. An intruder. *Another* one.

No, he's our savior. The Children take him in with silent reverence, with lidless, bulging sights, with W-shaped cuttlefish eyes and bulbous-eyed fins on temples.

"Go now. Hide," I tell them.

Tentacles slither, pleopods scurry, and crab-like legs lurch sideways, and they leave me alone by the shore.

I color my cheeks with blood and sprinkle seawater along my hair for luster. He'll see the untarnished beauty of the island, not what remained after the oil spills. He'll feed us out of love, not sympathy.

As I approach the newcomer, mud blossoms between my toes, emitting a foul gas smell. My lungs burn with anticipation. Fear. Hope.

He hops off the boat, giving Ka Isko a good pat on the back. The emaciated old man with his sunken ribs and cheeks attempts to pick up the luggage, but he gives him a handful of notes and hauls them himself, laughing like a seabird that has found its mate.

He wades through muddy water with black rain boots.

He grabs my hand gently.

Pulls me in for a hug in false familiarity.

Smile...and *snap!* A blinding flash comes like a lightning strike. I find myself back on a pier in China, blue-and-red lights and cameras flashing at my naked body.

I stiffen at his touch. A reflex. Don't push. I need him. We're hungry.

Damien had been one among many journalists, would-be journalists, and "content creators" who flocked to the mainland to interview me back then. He stood out with his clean scent, a welcome change from oil, sweat, come, or gas. There had been others who promised to help the island, but they hid behind musk of sandalwood and roses. Damien still smells like nothing.

Pleasantries are exchanged. I smile throughout, laughing when needed. My name is Perla—how did you forget? Welcome to our island. I'm sorry about the mud. Yes, we have a church with electricity. Oh...yes, I'm seven months pregnant now. Wait, no—

He leans in with his phone, the camera a box framing my stiff expression. "Hey, broskis! Damien Andrews here with Perla. Yes, *the* Perla. The girl found in the suitcase on a ship to Beijing. I'm here at Berberoka Island to begin the Aplaya Project, which will help clean up the oil spill and raise funds for people like Perla and her baby! The donation link is in the description below. Say hi, Perla!"

He touches my belly without warning. I flinch, mindlessly grabbing onto the termite-infested railing to catch my balance. A jolt like an invisible whip replaces the vertigo, but then I see his noble smile, far from the hyena-like smiles I've known from many men.

He pans his phone camera around, the eye of an unknown world, and signs off with a "Like, subscribe, and hit that notification button!" and then pockets his phone. His nose scrunches against the rotten-egg smell, but he fakes a sneeze to hide it. He's a man peeled from a dream, an image projected by my heart.

It hurts to ask, but I must: "What about the food?"

The mudflats stretch before the church, a bed of impotence caressed by a trailing veil of mist. Far in the distance, the Cimmerian bride stands still, waiting, watching.

"Gosh, I'm sorry," he says. "It was too much to bring all at once. I told the old man I'd row it across myself, but he wouldn't let me." The island can be stubborn.

He tries to take my hand, and I recoil in disgust. My hands are mine alone.

"I will get the food here somehow," he says. "I promise you that." Another promise.

I subtly scratch my arm, digging the implication of his words out, clawing at invisible tentacles creeping under my skin, suckers kissing their way up my throat. Squirming. No, no, no, *no*... the word is without power no matter how many times I say it.

No. He's not like them.

He's good.

I guide him to the dilapidated church. Its boarded windows have seen better days. Now it's blindfolded. Ashamed. Shunned. Faith did nothing to help the people of this island.

He disappears inside the church, coughing. He doesn't see the malformed starfish-human splitting itself in half beneath the stairs, regenerating into two separate creatures with five oily eyes. A Child.

I follow him inside, the dust he disturbed swirling in his wake. It fusses in the light of the gas lamp on the cross-bearing podium. One decaying wall of the church features a large hole that frames a view of the all-seeing mudflats. An oystercatcher with three red eyes pokes its head through, a yellow beak with a thousand tiny teeth opens cravingly.

Damien sets up his laptop and camera equipment, wheezing a little, and guides me into a pew.

Before the camera whirs into life, he confides, "I used to be a lazy gamer until I got dumped by my girlfriend and needed money for my elderly grandpa. That's my story. Can you tell my subscribers yours?"

I take a breath, the nitrous soul of the island seeping into my lungs.

1996. The island housed humans who were not her Children. They were predators. And like every predator, the not-Children had to taste blood. Oh, and they were cunning. They hid their claws behind reassuring handshakes and their fangs behind hospitable promises. "Your island will be the center of commerce!" they said. "More ships and boats will dock for your hauls; you won't need to row for miles to the mainland anymore. We promise."

Then the foreign men came with their roaring, metal-toothed machines. They tore pieces off the land like shreds of sheer clothing. Penetrated the earth to place their leaky pipes. Spilled their oil and fuel indiscriminately across land and sea. Raped our island and left us to perish in a living gas chamber.

But Berberoka Island refused to die.

Instead, it bred more of its Children. This last part, however, I had to keep to myself.

"Then the vultures came for the carcasses," I continue for the camera. "Descended for me."

They had come promising a new life to the dead. And I had believed. Because I was desperate to save the island. One by one, the vultures plucked at my flesh, exposing my bones for the salivating hyenas. They owned every part of me. Night after night, man after man.

I was drugged for seasoning. Bruised. Whipped. And they kept promising. They said, "We'll get you work as a waitress at five-star restaurants." They said, "You'll be rich." Promises, seasoning, punishment, more promises.

For two years and six months, I waited to become a waitress. I shared a banig of dried leaves to sleep on and a bucket with fifteen other girls. Girls like me, baited with the promise of a better life. We got to shower when clients wanted flesh. Sometimes a girl never rejoined our stable, her fate unknown. Most days, I worked, handweaving banig for futures like mine soaked in blood and tears. Most nights, I was dutifully in bed with a stranger, satisfying the salivating hyena in them. During those harrowing nights, I hear ocean waves.

"I ended up pregnant," I tell Damien. "So they punished me and sent me away."

In the dark suitcase, I smelled the salty sea mingling with the boat's fuel. I felt every dry crust and clotted mess that caked my thighs, ribs, fingers, and lips. For days, I hydrated myself by sucking on a button. My saliva tasted like brine and iron. I rocked like I was inside the ocean's womb, hoping we would dock in Beijing—the promised freedom.

I pause in my telling. I don't dare mention the dreams—those moments when I sank into the depths, shadowed by a boneless sac of variegated effluent. Those slow descents, almost like being cradled as the water sang its lullaby, penetrating my flesh and bones. Here and there were soft, glutinous scales outlining an inchoate body, the skin, or lack thereof gleaming with oil. Her mouth was a golden disc as if she'd swallowed the sun…getting closer and closer, brighter and brighter, mesmerizing me as her mouth opened wide to devour.

I look directly at the camera. Damien's silhouette is blood red behind it. "Then the next thing I knew," I say, "the suitcase was being opened, and a bright flashlight was beaming in at me. I later learned that someone placed a tip about the human trafficking operation, and so the Coast Guard raided the ship, rescuing me and some other girls."

Damien looks away and wipes his eyes. "I'm sorry. I didn't know. I mean, I didn't realize it was *that* bad."

He types out his frustration on the laptop, as though it'll spare me some pain. If only I knew him sooner.

"We can only go forward." I absentmindedly stroked my protruding belly, a child of an unknown monster.

"I'm going to give your video the best clickbait thumbnail possible."

"Bait? Is that legal?"

He smiles at me, a patronizing smile. I'm not stupid. I'm not some stupid island whore just because I don't know everything about online content.

But…no, it's a glowing smile, an admiring smile, a forgiving smile. "Perfectly legal." he says, and he turns his laptop to me, talks me through it. "People tend to judge by the first thing they see, so we have to bait them. It's only bad if you fall short of what you promised."

I know he's the one. He's the angel that'll save us.

I put him up in the attic of the church building, dusting the bed before he gently moves me aside. He won't let us fall.

Tonight, I hear ocean waves.

"HE WILL SAVE us," I tell the old albularyo, Nay Fe.

Luz uses her pincers to chip at the blocks of crystal alum that Nay Fe uses for healing. Her eyes *squelch* as her focus moves from plate to plate. Uncut to cut. She proudly shows me a crystal she has shaped like a doll. I give her moss hair a gentle rub.

The albularyo pinches herbs and places them into a blackened pan that hisses hungrily for more oregano and luya. Everything and everyone on Berberoka Island is hungry for *something*. Nay Fe circles the pan over my head, muttering incantations. I keep silent, familiar with the witch doctor's healing method. The loose skin on her arm moves like water waves, ebbing at each incantation, hypnotizing me with foreign enchantments like a siren's call.

When she's done, she puts down the pan and picks out the tawas from the pulsating coal. The white, melted crystal stands out among the char. Her cloudy, gray eyes look directly at me as she crushes the crystal between her fingers, turning them into powder.

Nay Fe smears the burning powder on my green scab, making it simmer and reek of acid. Luz inhales sharply, fan-shaped gills throb on her scaly neck. I give her a reassuring smile. The Children always think pain is misery and suffering, never that pain can be good.

"We have starved for too long," says Nay Fe.

"Damien will bring money and food soon," I say, protectively caressing my belly. "Then we'll leave and start again somewhere."

The hundred-year-old woman roots herself to the bamboo floor and looks up at me. "I will die on this island."

I purse my lips. "Luz will come with me."

Nay Fe holds my gaze. Under her lips are hard troughs of skin. "Do you remember what happened to you when you were away?"

The whips and lashes from my traffickers were ant bites compared to the poison of being away from the island. The longer I went without the island's breath, the worse I became. Bioluminescent sores had clustered on my skin, blooming round and red. Tendrils of thorny pain shot around my legs at night, torturing away my sleep. Then, three of my toes started turning black, decaying. The moss-cloud darkness had grown threateningly.

"Then, my baby will leave. With Damien."

Nay Fe shakes her head, sighing. Her graveolent seaweed crown briefly overpowers the poison smell. "When you two finish sinking the island, maybe then you can leave. But remember, the island will always seek out its Children and bring them back." She glances at my belly. "Always."

Luz presses her cheek against my cooling wound, crying slimy tears.

I HAVE TO let him see the Children.

I lead him past the village where the huts on stilts stand on decaying, blackened bones, each of them crowned by defeated, sagging nipa roofs. There are no walls to protect anyone from the forces of nature. But the huts didn't need walls. Tall rocks stand sentry on the horizon. They are fingers engulfing the island in the ocean's palm.

Damien's camera hovers on a stick, a little metallic bird on a leash. The mud wraps around his boots, rooting him in place like a fly on a spider's web. But he frees himself with a grunt and moves forward, trying to hide a limp. So strong, so determined. He will prove her wrong—he must.

"The cave is just ahead." I feel a kick and soothe my belly. If the baby stays here, it'll be one of the Children. Poison and blackened mud will be its breath and blood.

I slow my pace and let Damien catch his breath.

"What's wrong?" he asks.

I can't tell him, so instead I show him. I swallow the disgust and offer him my hand, the wound now nearly healed. Of all those disgusting men, all the things they made me do, none had touched my hands.

My hands were mine, I tell him, always mine.

"And if we keep going, I'll be…"

Yours.

I study him for a seismic shift in demeanor and find his expression dawning with understanding, his breathing labored. He reaches for my hand, his eyes asking permission, then grips with the sureness of a savior. Nay Fe, dear old woman, you are wrong.

At the mouth of the cave, hymns welcome us along with the lingering smell of Nay Fe. The inside is dark save for some luminescent curtains of teal liquid oozing on the walls.

Damien calls out for a break and chugs a bottle of water.

It's the air. It looms heavily with a sandy texture. A metallic miasma fills my lungs.

Damien wheezes.

He's our savior. He'll endure. This is just a cross he must bear.

I wipe the sweat off his forehead with my sleeve. "We won't be long."

Damien is almost walking on his knees. He perseveres.

We stop before a precious coral that glows and throbs like a hearth. The old albularyo is there kneeling on the ground, hands hovering over the starfish Child. The Child retracts a piece of calcified skin, and Nay Fe places a cloth-wrapped coin on one of her five limbs. A piece of the white cloth sticks upright like a candle wick. Nay Fe lights a match, an extension of the fury in her eyes.

The ritual is something I've known and loved since I came back to the island. The fire attempted to suck away the predators' musk inside me. Many times, many times.

The flame never hurt me.

Damien gasps as Nay Fe lights the cloth wick, and the fire turns every fiber ablaze, going down, caressing, threatening to burn the starfish Child with its passion. He's innocent as a Child, thinking pain is always misery and never good.

It feels like being inside a giant conch shell. A cleansing sound, briefly making me forget of the drought that is my past.

As the fire calms, its intensity briefly satisfied, Nay Fe covers it with a glass cup.

The flesh on the Child's back swells up, the fire bending the water inside her to rise like a giant wave.

Damien wobbles forward, swiping at the glass to put the fire out, but Nay Fe grabs his wrist, adding her full weight behind it. Her twig-like fingers scratch his face, turning him away like an alley cat.

He reaches out for the Child's fingerless hand as Nay Fe studies him with unyielding gray eyes. She stares down his flickering promise. Until it crumbles.

Damien falls and drives one foot into thirsty sand. His coughs multiply, bringing blood to slake the earth. A sour and sweet delicacy Berberoka Island has tasted many times.

Nay Fe holds my attention with her truth. The truth.

Together, we watch as Damien gathers himself and stumbles away, back outside where all the frail and broken promises go.

THE OYSTERCATCHER PERCHES on the church's landing, glowing red eyes watching me. Lava-like mollusks cling to its wings, anchoring it to the island. It drops something by my feet, a gift.

An anglerfish. Lifeless white eyes gawk at me in accusation. Icicle-like teeth bare at me in cold sincerity. The dorsal spine above its mouth has lost its light. A female one.

A tawny streak of light spotlights the dead fish as if it is in ascension. Damien leans feebly against the threshold, his red shirt hanging from his suddenly thinning frame.

"Perla…"

I nudge the blackened flesh hanging on the underbelly of the fish with my toe. "The male latches onto the female because they know they can't survive. Then the female absorbs the male into her body."

Damien pales, the kind where his skin almost looks blue. He grabs on to the railing, balancing himself.

"Ka Isko will come soon." Inside, I see his luggage is packed. "He can get those for you."

But Damien hauls the luggage himself, sweat tracing his popping veins, before he wheezes out whatever strength he has left. The luggage slips from his hands, tumbling down the church steps. He limps down and retrieves it, a spark of his old fire. "I can still take you and the baby away from here."

My child must have a different life far away from Berberoka Island. I will go. Leave with him. Every mile will be an inch of my body decaying.

Where my toes were, phantom pains tug at my decision. I place both hands on my belly as if it were a crystal ball that could give answers.

A kick.

"Don't worry, Perla." Damien's chapped lips quiver; white flakes like fish's scales peel off as he speaks shakily: "I'll give you and the baby everything. I *promise*." His wiry fingers wrap around my hands, prickling me awake with an all-too-familiar feeling that laps at my feet like ocean waves, a tide slowly rising until it completely envelopes my being in cold realization.

I nod. "We can wait for the boat at the mudflats."

A smile. It's weak, but it's Damien's smile.

I lead the way to the side of the church, where the entrance to the mudflats lies between two dead precious corals.

Damien steps in next to me like a specter. The seabed-gray sky, silken with clouds, cradles a pearlescent moon. His inhales are frail, his exhales ragged as if breathing takes too much effort.

"Damien," I say, gently grabbing both his hands. I look deep into his eyes. They're sunken now but still clear and blue like oceans seen from far away. I reel in his promises and secrets.

But they're all muddy gray.

Like the seas of Berberoka Island.

We should do it now, right here where my heart cried out for him.

Gently, I lead one of his hands to my breast. This startles him, but he's too weak to pull away.

I push him down on the mudflats so he's on his back and I am on top of him.

Damien looks nowhere but my eyes. His warm hand is sunlight cupping my cold cheek.

I ride Damien as slowly as the waters crawling toward us. I feel the cool relief of the sea first on my feet, then on my knees. Damien stays underneath me, pleasure taking over his face. His grunts sound like enchantments calling out to the island. Our flesh violently meeting becomes a drum circle for what's to come.

The water rises, faster now, and Damien tries to sit up. But I keep him down, straddled by the weight of me and my baby.

Then, the riptide drowns out his scream.

A FEW WEEKS later, Damien's body washes ashore on the other side of the island. A fat, tumor-like entity grows out of his stupefied, screaming mouth like a parasitic copepod, *squelching* and sucking everything from the bloated body. His once white skin shares the island's gray, his bright blue eyes are now wan like the mist. I loved his eyes.

Luz, along with the other Children, circle around the creature as it grows eight-feet tall within seconds. Damien's body becomes nothing more than dry brittle paper as crab legs and lobster legs stampede over him, scaled tails thrashing. I nod at Luz who slithers in close, pincers tearing apart the white tumor that bleeds more fat.

The Children feed, eyes glowing with nutrients, stringed gills singing gratitude.

I hand my baby to Nay Fe. My baby coos at me, ten fingers reaching out, white eyes with brown irises blinking sleepily.

I tiptoe around the Children, their upturned mouths and proboscises busy exploring, sucking, gnawing. At the back of the creature are four pinkish bulging roe. Inside the translucent sacs, pincers and fins reach out to me, lively golden and green eyes blinking. The new Children coo.

INSIDE THE CHURCH, Damien's equipment remains. I open his laptop and delete the last few days of files, all except a short video with a smiling Damien on Ka Isko's boat for a thumbnail.

Then, I upload to his channel. In the description part, I type:

"Hey, broskis! I need a clean-up crew to help set this island straight! You'll meet me, the #1 broski, and get paid from the funding we raised. And you'll have a great time, I promise! Like! Subscribe! Choose that notification button!"

Bait is only bad if you fall short of what you promised. Perfectly legal.

Luz calls me out to the water and carefully holds my hand with her pincers. My blood feeds the blackened mud of the island.

The Children and my Child wait with me by the shore. Waiting for Ka Isko's boat. Waiting for salvation.

THE BENCH

Jacy Morris

SO FAR, LONG Beach, Washington had underwhelmed them. The motel they'd checked into, which had looked so charming on the internet, had turned out to be a bit of a dump. It hadn't looked that way to Paula and her husband as they sat in their apartment studying the cute pictures on their shared laptop. From the comfort of their couch, it had looked quaint and cute. The quaint pictures on the Internet did not match up with the reality of the Dolphin Inn.

Built in the '60s when summers had been milder, the motel baked in the daytime, forcing Paula and Kane to sit there with the window open, a window which looked out onto the parking lot. All sorts of pollution infiltrated their motel room: cigarette smoke from the RV park, the noise of the highway, the unpleasant laughter of impish children from the room next door.

On top of that, the restaurants and eateries were expensive but cheap. Cheap in that the food was not what one would expect for the exorbitant price. Paula and Kane had bought two burgers and two orders of fries for a grand total of forty-four dollars from a food cart. A food cart! And the food was average at best!

Their idyllic getaway was quickly turning into a disappointment. But no one comes to Long Beach for the food, and after exploring the town's small row of kitschy stores, they had set out for the main attraction: the beach itself. The beach was the reason they'd traveled from Portland on the one vacation they could afford per year.

They parked at the edge of a parking lot, leaving their car behind them. In the distance, the ocean roared it's greeting, the wind whipping against their eardrums as they plodded across the baking blacktop, past rows of vehicles with out-of-town license plates. They stopped to take photos in front of the amazing sandcastles left over from the previous week's sandcastle competition. Paula mimicked the pose of a mermaid sculpture in front of an intricately detailed castle, and Kane roared like a dragon in front of one with a dragon curled around it.

They continued up a boardwalk, lengthening their strides to pass a family of rounded Americans calling for their dog. She hoped they found it, though they didn't seem to be trying too hard; the mother walking and calling out "Astro!" every few feet while glancing at her phone. Once they'd passed the family, Kane called out a mocking "Astro!" and Paula playfully slapped him on the shoulder.

The boardwalk wasn't like the ones she'd seen in typical tourist towns. It was merely an elevated path nailed together with treated wood and railings, not lined with the kitschy T-shirt shops and taffy stands of the other towns on the coast. It kept the sand out of your shoes and kept you away from bounding dogs on the beach and roving vehicles driving across the sand.

The sight of the vehicles disturbed Paula, then annoyed her, and finally enraged her. *Here you are on the edge of the world, all this glory around you, and you just want to cruise along the sand like an asshole, blasting country music and spewing exhaust into the air.* It didn't seem right. But nothing in the world seemed right these days, as if it was all going to come to an end soon.

"You okay?" Kane asked.

Well, if it came to an end, she would be glad to be with Kane. At least there was one thing right in the world. "Yeah, just… taking it all in, I guess."

"Look at those pieces of shit," he said, pointing to a group of people racing up the beach in a massive, gas-guzzling Ford truck, a giant American flag unspooling from a pole affixed to the back of the vehicle.

Paula grabbed his hand, and, as they did so often, they tried to tune out the world, to make it all disappear until it was only them. The sun was sinking, and they hurried, looking for a place away from the squeal of children, the roar of engines, the calls of annoying women looking for a dog they probably shouldn't have taken off its leash in the first place.

The boardwalk gave way to another street for beach access, and then they passed a foul-smelling public restroom and found themselves walking on a paved path that wound along the coastline. All around them, coastal grasses grew tall, the prevailing winds making them dance as if they heard a song no one else could hear. Farther and farther they walked, the sun sinking lower and lower by the minute.

The sounds of the busy, selfish world melted away, until the only signs of humanity were the large, opulent beach houses towering into the sky to their left. But those were easy to ignore if she kept her eyes on the beach and the waves.

Hand in hand they strolled, heading south as the sun hovered over the sea, preparing for its daily kiss of the sea to the west. They walked for miles, passing small benches offering great views, though none of them seemed quite right to Paula. She wanted the perfect view of the sunset.

Onward they strode. A man on a bike zinged past them, breaking their solitude.

Paula was still trying to get over the annoyance of encountering another human this far along the beach when Kane said, "What about that one?"

She looked where he pointed and spotted a bench sitting on the crest of a dune. Next to it, a large pole jutted up into the sky, an eagle's nest perched on top. Behind them, opposite the sea, sat a massive two-story mansion, its wraparound porch festooned with patriotic bunting. Something about the bunting disturbed her. First off, where did you get it? She'd never seen it for sale anywhere. Secondly, even if you had it, why would you put it all around your house?

The mansion's lawn was trimmed, a harsh contrast to the waving beach grasses. The lawn looked well-trodden, not too perfect, as if the people in the house weren't afraid to walk across it to get to the beach. Hell, maybe it was them who had put up the bench in the first place.

The bunting bothered her, made her think of murderous beach people who didn't like people whose skin was darker than the sands of the beach. She and Kane were far from help if someone should come for them. She shook her head, tried to kick the fears of the white world out of her head. "Looks good to me," she said, grinning and actually meaning it.

They left the paved path, stepping upon flattened grass clods set in the sandy soil. They struggled up a shifting rise and, at the crest of the hill, beheld the ocean in all its glory. The Pacific Ocean shimmered with diamond reflections of the sun. Seagulls trundled along the beach, poking their beaks into the sand for tasty treats. Not a soul marred the sand, and she sighed with relief.

The bench sat off to their left, a perfect place to watch the sun dip behind the swell of the ocean.

"Oh, man, this is perfect!" Kane said, echoing her thoughts.

The air was fresh out here, the temperature a comfortable seventy degrees. Pretty good for the middle of July. Back home, amid the constant roar of air-conditioning, the city of Portland baked like a potato in an oven. But here, the body could breathe the way it was supposed to.

The bench was a wooden thing, bleached to a salty gray, riveted to a steel frame. Paula took a seat on the left side and found her feet didn't touch the ground.

Kane sat beside her. "Damn, this is a tall bench!"

"I know. I feel like a little kid." Paula swung her feet back and forth.

They settled in, wrapping their arms around each other, and they let the fireworks begin—not those sulfurous contraptions that always went off in the middle of the night but actual honest-to-goodness, miracle-of-nature type fireworks, the ones God had made for them. What good were sparklers and fountains when you had something like this to look at?

Paula stared at the haloing sun as it dipped down through the faint haze of clouds. She pulled her sunglasses down off her head, slipped them over her eyes, and basked in the sun, watching its shifting rays as they ripened from gold to orange.

Kane did the same, and they squeezed each other's hands. Long Beach had been a disappointment so far, but not even a town like that could fuck up a sight like this.

Down and down the sun went, inching ever so slowly to the water. Evey time she watched the sunset, she hoped to see the water sizzle as the sun dipped into the ocean. Wouldn't that be something?

As she soaked in the radiant glow of the setting sun, she marveled at the enormity of the ocean. And then the waters seemed to swell, as if a great tsunami was on the horizon. Her heart double-pumped in her chest, and she felt the need to run, to flee as fast as she could from the impending doom. But when she looked at Kane, he showed no signs of panic, and she realized it must be a trick of perspective. Still, though she knew it was an illusion, she couldn't stop seeing the ocean rising upward, and then she wondered how she could see so much of the ocean at all. If the world is curved, how can I see so much water?

These questions went through her head as the sun turned a bright pink, painting the sky and the clouds in coral tones.

"Oooh," she said, the sound escaping her throat without her permission.

Kane squeezed her hand.

They sat rapt and in awe. No phones, no cars, no squawking children: the world the way it was meant to be.

The life-giving orb dipped lower and lower, the winds picking up as the air cooled, seagulls seemingly hanging in mid-air on the shifting winds. In captivated silence, Paula and Kane watched the sun sink lower, and then finally it was gone, leaving a pink haze in the sky as its final gift.

Only then did Kane speak. "That was beautiful."

"Mm-hm."

"Man, my legs are killing me."

The glory of the sunset had masked the pain, but now that Kane mentioned it, she realized her legs ached from hanging off the edge of the tall bench. The seat was wide enough for her bottom, but Kane hung a bit off it, his legs dangling like brown twigs.

"Yeah, let's get the blood flowing."

"Not yet," Kane said. Then he leaned over and gave her a kiss, which she returned. They smiled at each other, with plans of intimacy dancing in their heads, and then Kane rose from the bench—or attempted to.

"What the fuck?" Kane said as he thumped back against the bench.

When Paula tried to rise, her world shook as she found herself stuck to the wood.

She tried to reach her hand under her butt to see if she was caught on something, but she couldn't physically slide her fingers between the bench and her shorts.

They looked at each other, eyebrows raised.

"I'm stuck," she said.

"What is going on here?" Kane tried to push himself off the wooden surface using his arms.

Around them, the pinks turned to dark blues. The only lights were in the distance. Stars began to appear in the sky, forcing their luminescence through the atmosphere.

Paula tried to force her hand under her thighs where her shorts ended, but it was as if her body and the bench were one, as if her skin had bonded to its weather-beaten wood. Panic welled in her chest, and she looked to her husband in fear. "This doesn't make any sense."

They pushed and struggled. Kane even tried to slide out of his shorts, but the fabric clung as tightly to his skin as it did to the bench.

He pulled his phone from his pocket and dialed 911.

Paula leaned in close to hear the conversation.

"911. What is the location of your emergency?" a male voice said.

"Hello? My name is Kane Vasquez, and me and my wife are stuck on a bench on the shore at Long Beach."

"Don't worry," the voice on the other end said. "It'll all be over soon."

Kane pulled the phone away from his face, looked at the screen in disbelief. "They hung up on me."

He dialed the number again. No answer this time.

Paula began striking the bench. Her palms filled with slivers, and her knuckles became bloodied.

"Babe," Kane called. "Babe."

More punching at the unyielding wood.

"Babe."

"What?" she screamed.

"It's not doing any good."

"So, what? We just sit here?"

Kane ran a hand through his black hair. "I'm gonna push you off. Then you go and get help. You hear me?"

She nodded. This isn't real. I'm dreaming the whole thing.

"Alright, you ready?"

She nodded again, afraid to speak for fear she would start screaming.

He began shoving her, pushing on her legs. Pain filled her, and she felt as if she were being torn apart, as if someone was peeling the skin off her legs and ass.

Hearing her cries, Kane backed off. "Whoa, whoa, whoa," he said. "Are you okay?"

"No, I'm not okay," she sobbed.

Even though he had stopped pushing, the pain hadn't diminished. In fact, it had intensified, as if their attempts to escape had angered the bench.

Paula searched around her for some explanation of how or why this was happening. She ran her hand along the edge of the bench—and her hand stuck to it, as if the bench was covered with invisible octopus suckers. She wrenched her hand free, losing a few layers of skin. Hissing, she studied the damage to her hand, the pink splotches of raw flesh amid the pale skin of her palm. Paula clenched her hand in a fist to prevent the salty air from setting the nerves singing.

As the evening blued, she studied their surroundings. What had once been a cheery and quiet spot had grown ominous in the failing light.

"What is that?" Kane asked, pointing at a pile of something in the sand.

Paula leaned forward, her legs aching as if they were being dissolved. The nondescript pile grew clearer: discarded fish, their guts ripped open, flies emerging from the rotting innards.

"It's dead fish."

She looked up at the pole jutting into the sky off to their left. A hand-painted wooden sign read, "Don't feed the birds." Something about the words made her skin crawl, and she shivered.

Kane torqued his torso so he could look back at the path they'd left. "Someone's gotta come along," he said, his voice full of hope.

Paula cranked her own torso around, a wave of pain shooting through her, making her grit her teeth and hiss inward.

They remained corkscrewed, watching the path for any sign of passersby. The ocean roared behind them, and the squawk of seagulls faded away. The moon climbed high in the sky—not a special moon but a plain old crescent, a little too thin to be considered a half-moon.

Now Kane tried battering the bench, but the wooden boards, though weather-beaten and bleached, were as strong as the steel frame they were riveted to.

"I can't feel my feet," Paula said.

A bicyclist sped by on the path, and they both called out to him, but the wind kicked up at that exact moment, snatching the words from their lips.

Above, a slight disturbance in the air, the flap of wings in the night.

As they looked up, their bodies returning to their natural positions facing the ocean, they saw two eagles, wingspans the size of a car, circling in the sky. Their white-feathered heads glowed in the moonlight, and they peered down at the two humans with razor-blade beaks and eyes hidden by the shadows of their brows.

"Great," Kane muttered. "Can you train an eagle to go get help?"

Paula, despite the situation, laughed. "Can you train it to get me a sandwich?"

The eagles screeched, a piercing, plaintive sound.

From the corner of her eye, Paula spotted a flicker of light. She twisted around once more, searching for the source, and found that the bunting-covered house had grown glowing eyes. "Someone's home."

"Oh, thank god," Kane said, echoing Paula's own thoughts.

Inside, a shadow moved about the home, flitting from one room to another. For a second, Paula considered yelling out, but the ocean breeze had a way of snatching away all but the closest noises.

"Please see us, please see us," Paula chanted.

More shadows passed the windows, and soon, the house seemed a-bustle with a dozen people.

Paula locked her eyes on them, sent up prayers she'd thought she had forgotten long ago. In the meantime, the pain intensified until her eyes were awash with tears. She wanted to cry and wail, but she still clung to the small hope that the people in the bunting house would see them at any moment—would help them.

Finally, she could take her torqued position no more, and she was forced to look away from the light and stare out at the bleak depths of the sea. She tried to focus on the waves, to send herself into a trance to whisk her away from the pain. The agony had become so intense that even Kane's presence had stopped mattering to her. Her love for him evaporated when confronted with the constant reality of her suffering.

"Someone's coming," Kane said, his voice cutting through the stinging of her thighs and ass.

She turned by placing her raw hands on her thighs and pushed her torso around again. She didn't want to touch the bench with any other part of her body.

In the distance, a man walked marched across the house's manicured lawn, heading in their direction, an old-timey lantern gripped in his hand. He strolled in a leisurely manner, the lantern held high to guide his steps, as if this was but a part of his daily routine.

Even in the darkness, she could make out the shock of white hair on his head. It bulged out from the sides of his head in an uneven manner. Onward he came, crossing the ribbon of the paved path and walking sure-footedly up the sandy incline.

He seemed to ignore their calls and attempts to get his attention. But it was no matter. He was here for them, after all.

As he neared, she beheld his old-fashioned clothing: a long velvet jacket, the shirt underneath white and bedecked with frills. The chain of a pocket-watch dangled from a pocket, glinting in the lantern light.

"Good evening," the man said with a rich voice like cigar smoke.

"Please," Kane said, "you've gotta help us. We're stuck to this—"

"There is no way to help you," the man said. As he held the lantern up, Paula spied his face, creased with a thousand wrinkles, as if his entire body were in the process of drying up and blowing away. His eyes, perhaps once blue, were pale things.

"Just call the cops," Paula begged.

"Oh. There's nothing they can do. I'm afraid once the process is begun, there is no way to stop it."

The man came closer, his thin arm shaking from the effort of holding up the lantern.

"What process?" Paula grunted. Her body was covered in sweat, and it took all her concentration to form words instead of screams.

"Did you know they call this area the Graveyard of the Pacific?" he asked.

"We don't need a history lesson," Kane said. "There's something wrong with this bench."

The odd fellow paid Kane no attention, just continued his strange spiel as if he were but a lighthouse tour guide. "This place...shouldn't even be. Everyone who lives here knows that. Why, out there in the unfathomed depths, there is a crack in the earth—a great fissure—where the seafloor holds on for dear life. Why is it cracked? Well, let's just say, something wants through. It was almost here, too. The natives who lived here knew about it. The tribe used to send people into the water as sacrifices. Their lives strengthened the land underneath the waves."

The man's words washed over them like waves—calming, cooling. Their complaints and fears remained locked in their chests, held down by the weighted blanket of the man's voice. Paula turned to Kane, waited for him to rage, to shout, but he sat as dumbfounded as herself.

The old man sighed and ran his hand through his hair. "Used to be we could rely on shipwrecks to feed the land beneath the sea, but what with technology getting better and better, we simply don't have as many wrecks these days. Or we could find volunteers, those who believed in the sacrifice or who were suicidal, but now that's frowned upon. So instead, we have the bench. I wish we didn't have to do it, but you are the future. You are the ones who will strengthen the land now. I wish to thank you for your sacrifice, and if there's any way I can make this more...tolerable, please, ask away."

When they said nothing, only sat gaping in shock, the old man pulled a harmonica from his pocket and began playing a sad tune.

Paula and Kane locked eyes as the haunting music washed over them. Somehow, it had a calming effect on them. "This is stupid," Paula said.

"I know."

They struggled some more as the moon crawled across the sky. Their bodies, exhausted from being on the bench all evening, gave way, and they sagged and leaned against it, their skin binding with the wood.

In their pain, as their bodies began to dissolve into the boards, they found themselves unable to speak. They interlocked their fingers, squeezed with all their might, as if they might fuse themselves with each other before they became one with the bench. Tears flowed from their eyes until they had no more left.

As the night progressed, they grew lesser and lesser, soaking into the wood, their bodies shriveling and drying up as if they had lived a thousand years. They lost the ability to speak, to cry, to feel, but still they held hands, still they clung to what had mattered in their lives.

The old man played his song for the entire evening. It was the least he could do for their sacrifice. When the first rays of orange appeared in the east, nothing was left on the bench, though the wood looked a little less bleached now.

The eagles above flapped their wings, pierced the morning air with a plaintive wail, and then shot off into the day to live their lives, taking comfort in knowing their nest was safe and the land would hold together for a little bit longer.

⚓

BLUEBELLS

Amanda Minkkinen

THE MAN AND his wife moved into a cabin on the beach. They were newly wed, prone to impulsive arguments and immediate reconciliation. She painted the house green, which he thought was silly considering they lived on the beach, and wouldn't brown or blue be more complementary to the landscape, to the view? If you think about color theory, he said, wouldn't that make more sense?

She remarked something about what it represented, green being the color of spring, of new starts, of this and that and a third thing. The wife arranged the worlds in symbols, and the floral design of their wedding was also organized by that logic. Bluebells for everlasting love, roses for romance, white lilies for fertility. The colors were awkward, cacophonous smears, but perfect for what they represented.

There was something remarkable about that beach, with its glinting sand, its howling, relentless seagulls, and the blue sky framing a modest cabin fit for only two. Perhaps it was the laundry, the white linens billowing in the breeze. Or maybe it was the lunch they took together, silently sharing an apple which the husband cut with a dull blade.

They went down to the water to dip their toes one afternoon. She kicked water at him and laughed as he wiped the droplets from his glasses with the corner of his shirt, which was crooked by one button. When she turned away, he kicked water at her, a great slap of cold water against her back. She swung around and told him off, saying she had only been teasing and he had retaliated too harshly, and now look at the state of her, cold and wet and unhappy.

"Don't you love your wife," she said. "Don't you want to give her the world?"

"What does the world have to do with a splash of water," he replied.

The wife's sundress rippled in the wind.

They quickly reconciled and returned to their cabin. They propped open the front door and opened all the windows. It was a hot day, and the air was heavy. They went to their bed and lay there silently, side by side. There were moving boxes all around, stacked on top of each other.

One morning, the husband woke up in their marriage bed and found that he and his wife were not alone. On his right side, his wife was lying there as she always did, turned away from him, knotty hair, underwear lopsided on her body. She was breathing softly, still asleep, and she smelled faintly like sweat. He turned to his left and found that there was another woman in their bed: naked, facing him, in perfect likeness to his wife. As soon as he noticed her, she opened her eyes and smiled at him.

"WHO ARE YOU? What do you want?" They tried at first asking her questions, as they were not unreasonable, but she said nothing. She only sat and looked at them, as if making a discovery of her own.

The wind whistled through the house. A window slammed itself shut. The waves were violent, persistent, groping the sand and sucking back, and then doing it all again. The doppelgänger fixed her eyes on the wife.

"What do you want?" the wife asked her again, louder, and felt the rising tide of bile coming up to her throat as she spoke. The base of her stomach tightened in anxiety. As expected, the doppelgänger said nothing.

"Wife," the husband whispered, "what do we do?"

"Get her something to wear," the wife said. "I can't stand seeing her naked."

THE HUSBAND WENT off to buy clothes for the doppelgänger that morning, and also to get away and clear his mind, leaving his wife with the mysterious woman. He couldn't ask his wife to share her clothes with her doppelgänger. He did not know why that would be so bad, he just knew that it would be, and that he couldn't ask his wife to extend herself as such.

"What do you want," the wife said after her husband left. "I know you can understand me. Why did you come here?"

The doppelgänger only looked up at her. She wore a serene, knowing expression. They were two women who were identical to each other, but one of them nude, her skin pale and unblemished as if new.

"I know you understand me," the doppelgänger replied slowly, mimicking the wife. The wife slapped her across the face.

"WHY WOULD YOU buy her a dress," the wife said to the husband once he had returned from his shopping trip. "What does she need a dress for—where could she possibly be going?"

The truth was that he had not really thought about it much and had just grabbed something from the store that he thought his wife might wear, or any woman for that matter. At his wife's implicit accusations, he got hot in his cheeks and indignant, because what was wrong with a dress? What could he possibly have done wrong? What other people have been in this position, going through this exact trial?

The wife took the white cotton dress in her hands and examined the blue flowers printed on it, which were actually very pretty and exactly like something she would wear, but she was only wearing her pajamas and was sweating under her armpits and between her legs. She felt very undone and ugly, and so told her husband that she was going to take a shower and left the room.

"Wife," he said, "I love you. We will figure this out. I am also scared."

To that she nodded and kept her face hidden from him, closing the bathroom door so that she could be alone.

She went to the mirror to examine herself and saw that the pores on her nose were overlarge, that a blemish had appeared on her chin, and another one on her forehead, right above her eyebrow. Her doppelgänger did not have those blemishes. No, she did not have a single imperfection. The wife brushed her teeth and took a shower, plucked the hairs on her eyebrows, shaved her legs, found a bottle of lavender-scented body lotion, and rubbed it all over.

Meanwhile the husband was finding a way to dress the doppelgänger, whose nudity embarrassed him. He kept his eyes away from her breasts and her bare ass as she turned around. But this was his wife's body, was it not? Why should he feel ashamed? And yet, the doppelgänger was novel in her nudity. He couldn't help but notice it.

THE WIFE WATCHED her husband teaching the doppelgänger new words in the kitchen as he ate his lunch. He pointed to different objects in the room and spoke their name, which the doppelgänger obediently repeated back at him.

For now, it was easy to tell the difference between the two women. But what if the doppelgänger advanced past its childlike state? What if it learned how to mimic the wife so that the two women were indistinguishable? Would the wife dissolve, breaking apart like sea foam?

The wife couldn't stand it. In protest, she took a towel and walked past the duo in the kitchen and out the door to the beach. She spread the towel out on the sand and undressed to sunbathe.

As she lay out on the beach, naked limbs spread out and the sun beating down, she thought about the doppelgänger. She could not be real. She was synthetic, a poor fake. If you cut her apart you would see wires, flashing lights, a slab of metal with strange markings. She drifted off to sleep, thinking about androids, wires, lights. The husband noticed his wife through the window, and it crossed his mind that she ought to wear sunscreen.

The doppelgänger was a brilliant student. It was as if she already knew the language but needed only a guiding hand to bring her into her full consciousness. She was now more animated, more expressive. She was able to speak very small and simple sentences, but still, there was meaning.

"How do you feel?" he asked.

She looked around for the words, hesitated, and said only one word: "Hot."

"Hot?" he asked.

"Yes," she said.

He put his fingertips on her arm for just a second. She was cold to the touch. He didn't understand her at all, but he didn't mind it so much. In fact, he liked her quite a bit.

The wife woke up hours later, still lying on the sand outside. Her body, her skin, it all hurt with every movement. She forgot everything but her pain. She struggled to her feet and, still nude, walked across the burning sand and into the cabin. Once her eyes adjusted to the light indoors, she saw her husband and the doppelgänger on the couch. The doppelgänger lifted her hands to cover her gaping, shocked hole of a mouth.

The bathroom mirror showed her a body made unrecognizable by equal parts sunlight and neglect. Her skin was glowing coal-hot red. She filled the bathtub up with cold water, but it wasn't enough. She hurt all over, and it took everything she had not to cry.

The husband heard the bathroom door lock shut, and he sighed. It was too much for him to deal with alone. The doppelgänger was almost like a child in how dependent she was on him, constantly requiring attention. He tried to entice her with the TV, but her attention always rubber-banded back to him. He went to the kitchen to cook and brought out ingredients.

"Onion, tomato, oil," he said, showing her each item.

"What is?" She pointed at a cucumber, and then an apple, and then a box of dry spaghetti.

THE DINNER TABLE was set for three, and the wife came in nude. Her skin was too tender to be clothed.

"What is she doing here at the table, seriously?" she said to her husband, ignoring the doppelgänger completely.

"I assume she has to eat," he said. "Would it kill you to be polite?"

The doppelgänger watched the tense discussion. The wife said nothing more and sat across from her husband, not acknowledging the doppelgänger, who sat at the head of the table.

The husband gave the doppelgänger small, thoughtful portions of food, and explained what each thing was: spaghetti, tomato sauce, cucumber salad, bread, fork, knife, plate.

"This is how you eat." And he demonstrated.

His wife looked at him like he was crazy.

The doppelgänger picked up the fork with unsteady hands and tried, and failed, to pick up spaghetti. The noodles kept sliding off the fork and landing back on the plate, sending little specks of red sauce onto the white tablecloth. Following the demonstration of the husband, the doppelgänger tried to twist the noodles with the fork, but she was horribly uncoordinated. The wife finished her meal and watched the agonizing performance.

"Did you have to make spaghetti?" she directed at the husband. "It's not exactly the easiest thing to eat."

He stopped smiling and looked at her.

"Well, I didn't know how to shop for a clone of my wife who inexplicably appears and doesn't know language," he said. "I didn't know that she couldn't use a fork. These are not the types of things I prepare for."

The doppelgänger picked up the knife and began to cut through the spaghetti, chopping it into small pieces. She then took her fork and scooped up the pieces of spaghetti.

"She is wonderfully innovative," he remarked.

As he said that, she missed her mouth, and the fork hit her chin so that the food dropped into her lap. The husband laughed at her, big gulps of laughter, and the doppelgänger also began to laugh along with him. One of the pieces of spaghetti had landed on her chest, on her pale white skin, and the husband removed it with a napkin, and the wife noticed how he looked at her. She could read each detail and frame of his feelings, as if seeing him in slow motion.

The wife felt like she could become a murderer that day. The feeling swept over her. It was a reaction made of pure disgust and the impulse to hurt the doppelgänger, to pull on her limbs until they popped off like a plastic doll. And then to throw those limbs into the sea and let them become heavy with sand and seawater, water bugs and seaweed, for the doppelgänger to drown and to be eaten by a big fish. And for that big fish to be caught by a sailor, and for the wife to go to the market and buy that fish, to take it home and slice into it and cut directly through the plastic limbs of the doppelgänger. She would throw that fish away in the trash, because of course it's now inedible.

ONCE DINNER PASSED and the table had been cleared, the wife was left alone in the dining room with a glass of wine. The sun was a blazing red eye. She downed another glass and slammed it onto the table. She wiped her lips and stood up.

He husband and the doppelgänger had returned to the kitchen to clean. They did not even turn to look at her as she walked past. She went into the bathroom and turned on the light. She saw that her skin was no longer just red, but red with hanging pockets of yellow liquid. Blisters covered all the burned parts of her in spots. There were little speckles of blisters down the sides of her arm. It was worse on her chest and belly.

She heard running water, cutlery and dishes clicking against each other as they were washed and put away, one of the plates breaking, and then her husband's simplified explanation of what soap is.

She found an old salve for damaged skin in one of the bottom drawers of the bathroom, looked for an expiration date, and gave up. She squirted a little white smear into her hands and rubbed it into the parts of skin which had not yet bubbled up. The wine was too much—it made her lightheaded.

She went to the bedroom and opened a window. A small and kind breeze wafted in, so she lay down in her bed and listened to the gentle tugging of waves on the shore until she fell asleep.

As the wife drifted off to sleep, the husband demonstrated how to dry the dishes and put them away. It was no use. The doppelgänger's memory was limited, and her hand-eye coordination was poor. She dropped another plate. He sighed. The day had worn on him, made him heavy. When he looked at the doppelgänger, he found that he could no longer find the resemblance to his wife. Physically, yes, they were identical. There was something else though, something which his wife lacked. It was a trait that, if his wife ever had it, had been snuffed out. This woman standing in front of him was entirely new. And he thought to himself: What is she made of? What is inside of her? Is she a woman? Is she human? Did it matter at all?

WHEN THE WIFE woke, the red sun had set, and she was alone in the dark bedroom. Time had passed without her, it seemed. She had no idea what the hour was or how things were meant to be arranged at that present moment. But then a sear of memory lashed her, and her bubbling, hot skin ensured that she could not fall asleep again. It was all wrong, everything. There was no sound from the kitchen, no sounds from the TV, and even the sound of the waves had stilled.

She discovered that the entire house was dark as she walked down the hall to the kitchen. The house was unrecognizable by night. Every long shadow, bump and curve was unfamiliar. She went past the bathroom, the dining room, and ended up in the kitchen, where she was drawn to a small slit of light coming from the pantry. She gently pushed open the door.

At first she saw the floor of the pantry, and the feet of a man, the feet of a woman, standing together. Then dust balls and tinned foods, all of it needing cleaning and organizing. Wrapped around the man's fee were pants, a belt.

She raised her eyes and saw thighs, a hand on the inside of the woman's thigh, caressing it from the inside. It was a male hand, and with an engagement ring on its left finger.

Her gaze continued to pan up, and saw a white cotton dress with blue flowers, which she now recognized to be bluebells.

She now saw that his other hand was cupping her breast. The strap on one side of the dress had fallen below her arm so that her chest was exposed. Her head was raised up and tilted back onto his shoulder, and his lips were on her neck.

He rocked back and forth inside of her, gently, as if trying not to hurt her, as if she were new. They did not notice the wife watching as they stood in the middle of oats, flour, canned fruit, pickled vegetables, pasta, touching it all without touching it.

She slammed the door shut and ran to the sink where she threw up all her dinner, and stomach acid ran from her nose.

THE NEXT MORNING, the husband woke up again in his bed fully clothed. On his right side was his real, sunburned wife, who now turned her back away from him and, even in her sleep, was tense and closed off. On his left, the doppelgänger.

He tried to sleep longer, but something was pressing into him from the left side, and it was not a hand or hip. He turned to look at the doppelgänger. As expected, she was already gazing at him, as if she had not slept at all. Looking down, he saw that she was fully pregnant, big as a moon, as if they had slept for nine months without waking.

The doppelgänger threw her arms around him and hugged him close, as close as she could get. Something had gone terribly wrong here, he thought, and it must end immediately. Something must be forcibly ended here. His heart beat fast, and he could hear his wife shifting in her sleep.

He got up quietly, careful not to wake his sleeping wife. He herded the doppelgänger, who looked at him lovingly all the while, out of the room. She still had her cotton dress on, which was now tightly stretched out around her protruding belly and riding up so that the tops of her thighs were exposed.

As quickly as the onset of the doppelgänger's pregnancy, so too came the birthing pains. She had been brought to the living room when it came all at once: a tightening, and a sharp pain. A look of confusion in the doppelgänger's face, and then fear. The husband, well, what could he do? He watched the winding path of this creature's pregnancy and saw her fall to the floor with a thump.

She landed on the carpet on all fours and started to gag. Her back curled up and then flattened as she heaved, and it went on like that until she vomited like a cat.

"What's the meaning of all this?" the wife said, entering the living room, disturbed by the noise.

There she saw her doppelgänger, who was moaning and hunched over. With each contraction, she howled like a wild animal, as if hit by a car and then run over again, and again, and again.

"What do we do?" the husband said.

"How should I know?" the wife replied, quick and sharp. She went over to the doppelgänger and moved her to the couch. She propped a pillow under her head. She had not prepared for something like this. She put her hands to the doppelgänger's belly, and immediately recoiled. She had felt a strange grinding sensation below the skin, as if there were an unsettled, venomous snake coiled into a ball.

The wife, feeling disturbed, tried to remove herself from the situation once again, but the doppelgänger reached out and grabbed both of her wrists. She held her with such force that it almost made the wife cry out, but she was silenced by the eyes of the doppelgänger, and, for the first time, she felt recognition beyond physical similarity.

It was not a recognition that came from the degradation of pregnancy, or from suffering itself, but from all the feelings that came along with that violent pain: fear, anxiety, uncertainty. The realization of the body, how limited it is, that death follows closely behind life. The eyes of the doppelgänger pleaded for explanation, but there was no time to explain it all. And the wife had no words inside of her anyway.

The doppelgänger's stomach ripped apart from its base up to the ribs in a clean line, as if a seam had been torn open. Her eyes rolled back, and she screamed. The husband looked away, the wife stared in horror.

The doppelgänger reached out, frantic, waving her arms around like an overturned beetle. Neither reached out, neither held the hand of the doppelgänger. They would both come to regret this failure for many years. Out of everything that had gone on, it was the only truly unforgivable moment.

Between the pieces of disassembled skin from a belly sliced open, past the layers of flesh, there was only sand. Neither could believe what they were seeing. The doppelgänger was dead, that much was certain. Her arm hung limp over the edge of the couch, her mouth gaping.

Her body began to shrivel, sucking itself inwards, dehydrating, and then it broke apart into chunks. Her hanging arm fell to the floor. The doppelgänger's body was in active decay. Still, neither the husband nor the wife dared reach out to touch her, to see what she was made of. The doppelgänger began to break into smaller and smaller pieces, until she was nothing more than a pile of sand–sand in the shape of an unfortunate and borderless woman.

For a moment, there was silence. And then a single violent gust of wind ripped through the house. The doppelgänger's body was dispersed in the wind, spiraling like smoke and flying out over the beach, and the wife and her husband stood and watched the swirling remnants of her corpse in the sky until they were out of view.

The husband and wife were left alone, just like before, without even the wind, without the sound of the waves or those incessant seagulls. Had it all been a cruel joke? Would she return? They were alone again, husband and wife, left with their memories of the past day, forgetting the other and simultaneously being too aware of the space between them. They didn't know what to hope for, both feeling violated and, more distantly, ashamed. The husband went to go turn the kettle on and asked his wife if she'd like a cup of tea.

NĀ HEʻE

Wailana Kalama

I GOT TO meet the cold thing living inside my dad that June I turned fifteen. I don't know how long it'd been hiding in him. Maybe always. Or maybe he'd caught it, the way you catch a cold, that night he dove to the oyster beds. All I know is, on that blanched coral beach all those years ago, my dad showed me what magic really was.

Back then I was still taking over the wheel for Dad, because he'd check out midway on our drive to the shore. The second school was out every June, he and the twins and I, we'd pile into the 4x4, turn sharp at that painful cliff striated with monstera. And because Dad couldn't focus, swerving dangerously at times, it was up to me to take us through that final dirt strip to Weka Bay.

"Home, sweat home," Dad said when we wheeled to the edge of the coral, and the twins rolled their eyes.

Was supposed to be a week. Time for Dad to recharge, unwind, rewind. Add a dash of snorkeling for us three girls, and it was textbook summer fun.

The twins wasted no time. Damn the tent, the cooler, the sandwiches I'd packed for dinner—they dove in at the first glimpse of ocean. Twelve-year-olds. Left Dad and I to lug tent poles out under the palm grove, sand eating our toes.

When I look back now, I think: my sisters didn't see it, how Dad was different from all the other dads in the world. From how dads are supposed to be. They weren't paying attention. It's why what happened, happened to them.

But I noticed. Because we were close, Dad and me. Once upon a time.

And what I noticed was the way those summers at Weka seemed to slide around him, like he didn't quite belong. The way they brought whatever was in him straight to the surface. I saw it in the wistful way he looked out over the bay, to the black sea stacks at the far-off tip of 'Awe cape, curling inward like a sickle.

It was why we were there in the first place. And why none of us ever really left.

ON AN ISLAND, Dad always said, there are a thousand rules, and a million ways to break them. It's a balanced ecosystem of prey and predator, ebb and flow, cause and effect. A cow dies in a mountain stream, and a swimmer picks up leptospirosis in an estuary two miles down.

The rules: Don't whistle at night. Don't fish out of season. Never remove a stone from the island. And if you break a rule, who knows what ancient law you've upset. Who knows what comes bubbling to the surface.

Was Dad who taught me most of that. It'd slip out, on long drives through cowboy country, twins dozing in the back. "Momi," he'd pipe up from the passenger seat. "Momi, you know what? Get a million ways to break tings. But, fixing them? Make pono? I dunno. Some things you just can't fix."

But dads are supposed to fix things. He used to be like that—fixing everything from leaky faucets to torn stuffed animals. We used to call him Gandalf. A real wizard.

I'm not sure when he started to slip, but that cape had some-thing to do with it. Every summer we'd go, he'd get a little smaller, thinner. Like Weka wrung out the best of him, left the rest to shrivel under the sun. The rest: earth-scoured knuckles, a bony knee that hadn't mended right after a roof-fall, eyes gauzy with the beginnings of glaucoma.

And I tried to be patient. Tried to understand why he kept himself out of reach, like not wanting to be known. Like I didn't deserve to know him. But—though it's been thirty years since that awful summer—I can say I still don't.

When we got that tent pitched, Dad and I plopped on grass, munching on crackseed. Sparrows darted in the sugarcane sky and the afternoon loam licked the coral bones, and I remember thinking, *This time, this time, he's going to stay.*

But he said: "You'll be alright, Momi?" Flicking his beer hand to the reef, where my sisters were shriek-laughing and skidding water into each other's faces.

"Ah. Yeah," I said, shrugging, because I knew this dance by heart.

"Just a few days, yeah? Like before."

You can count on me, yeah.

Then he brushed the sand from his calves, armed himself with a mini-cooler crammed with a six-pack and koozies, and walked out to 'Awe cape alone.

See, part of the *recharge, unwind, rewind* was that Dad would head out, all by himself, to the tip of that headland. Spend the whole day out there, come back only at sunset. What exactly he was doing, he'd never say.

The twins never asked, and part of me hated them for it. Hated that giggles came so easily to them. That it didn't seem to affect them, Dad being gone. They didn't seem to feel it, the way dads' absences can be heavier than the real thing, the way dead weight is heavier than a living person. But I could. Couldn't fathom *not* feeling it. Could even see it sometimes, bobbing in the surf like a bloated air sac.

When I'd asked him once, timing it post-couple-beers, he let slip that out there on the cape was his way of going back in time to the good ol' days. Back to old Hawaii. When you could sleep on the beach naked as the day you were born. When fish were more plentiful than now. When he knew who he was. When the world made sense, before things got muddled. Before us three kids.

Okay, he never said that last bit. But kids pick up things, all the same. Especially kids who read too many books and who, even at fifteen, look for small ways that maybe—just maybe—they could be magic. Magic was: Hearing the words, the real ones, in the undercurrent of what dads say out loud. Of what they want to say but can't. Of what's lurking below the surface.

And sometimes, if you hold your breath and count to four, you can hear those unspoken words gurgling around in their larynx. A strangling in the making.

SO WHENEVER DAD was gone, we three made the best of it.

Or, the twins did. They'd slide on their snorkel masks, shirk away to the labyrinthine reef. Dare each other to hoist those prickly, purple sea urchins from their tide pools, little pin cushions crumbling in their grips. They'd snatch fat sea cucumbers, squeeze them tight until their jetstreams squirted everywhere. Real charmers, those two.

I'd set myself on the beach. Shifting my butt because thin pineapple pareus are useless against bony coral. Hala hat pulled low on my forehead, and reading my book—or pretending to, anyway. Eyes trailing out to where Dad was. Wondering what he was up to. Skin-diving deep for oysters? Somersaulting into the water like Maui? I'd picture him toeing across the rocks, their eyelets glinting with saltwater. The lava was so prickly out there, your feet had to make a thousand minuscule shifts to get to the edge.

And whenever I spied a dark spot on that edge way out there, I'd imagine it was him. Picture him standing there for hours, milk eyes staring out from a hollowed face.

And at sunset I'd catch sight of a shadow detaching from the cape. Passing through a cluster of four-armed wave breakers that reminded me of stars crashed from outer space. And by the time the shadow became a silhouette, the planets were in full bloom.

I'd always ask, like clockwork: *How was it?* And, like clockwork, he'd flinch away, make like he was dirty, *Don't get it on you.*

He always made it in time for the green flash. We'd eat our sandwiches together in silence by the fire. Venus blinking in the sky, and Jupiter trawling along his arc. And in the tent that night, Dad tucked his legs under him, like a shrimp–makai, oceanside.

And the next morning, the inevitable sound of Dad's slippers against sand. A sound defined by its diminishing.

IT WAS THE third morning, maybe the fourth. That's when it started, that's when I set things in motion. It's why, on my worst days, I blame myself. You swim too close to that undertow, don't complain when you get pulled under.

The thing was splayed on the crumbling stone wall, arms shoelacing out like lichen. All moisture evaporated from its flesh. Tough and gritty, like rawhide. Shriveled tentacles puckered with traces of deep violet. Its translucent body unfurled over gray stones like a sacrifice gone wrong.

"What'd you find, Momi?" Leilani called out from the reef, her toes doing that *bob-bob* thing they do when you're not tall enough to keep the sea slinking into your throat.

"Dead octopus," I said.

And when I picked it up, it slid into my palm like it was home.

"Gross," Leilani yelled.

"You should bury it," Maile said.

There was a hint of a pulse. Somewhere deep in its papery folds, it shuddered.

A heartbeat.

That's not right.

It was dry as tissue paper at that point, so what was keeping it going?

Like running on empty.

And my fingers went searching for that empty, the source of that pulse. Pinched every inch of its underside until my nails came to rest on a tiny sac in the folds. The *ala'ala*.

Thrum, thrum.

"Show it to Dad when he's back," Leilani yelled. "He'll love it."

And that's when my fingers switched to autopilot, and I squeezed.

Hard.

A weak pop, a fizzle that erupted—shrill, like the last breath from a dying lung.

Then a wetness, silky and cold. Ink, so violet it was almost black, dribbled out over my fingers.

And now, nearly thirty years later, on those cloudy nights when I can't see any stars from my tent—just one me in all that empty—I still wonder, was that the moment? The moment I broke something? Because a rule needs a person to break it.

See, sometimes if you bury things, if you toss 'alaea salt in the four corners of your tent, sometimes the transgression curls back in itself, becomes nothing but a harmless mistake. An accident. You wake up the next day, give honi to your dad—never knowing how close you came to losing everything.

But if you squeeze the life-ink out of an octopus and string it up by its tentacles on the flap of your tent, like it's a trophy for all the celestial sphere to see, well, that's not an accident. That's an invitation.

AND THAT EVENING, Dad didn't come home in time for the green flash.

I'd fallen asleep with my hair jackstrawing through a tear in the tent door. The twins clung to each other like 'opihi, and the moon shone one night shy of full.

Dad crouched by the campfire, his cheeks sallow. And for a moment, I didn't recognize him. I don't know if it was the trick of the flames or something awful already at work, but for a minute he wasn't any dad I knew.

Dads have a way of shrinking when you're not looking. If you're not careful, they can age in a day. The ones who get unmoored. Who let disappointment chip away at them, little by little, until *I'll do it one day* loses all meaning. They shrivel into themselves, like kindling on fire. And Dad, who used to dash over tidepools nimble as a goat, his bare legs were now thin as stripped hala leaves discarded under the sun. His spine stooped, and his chest sagged, concave. It happens to everyone, I guess: one day you wake up and see how weak your dad really is, really was, all this time. Clear as aquamarine.

He murmured: "Something out there."

And we both gazed out to the cape, under the moon.

When I asked him what, he shook his head. "I saw...saw these two big eels. Came up right behind me. I caught one. Woo-hee, she was thrashing about. Wasn't sure where all that strength came from. I got this urge to...bite her. Tear right into her."

He bit his lip, like almost revealing a secret. And I found this so strange I nearly didn't catch the slow trickle of blood from his ear.

"Auwe, Dad, you're bleeding!"

But when my hand flew up to his ear, he brushed it away, muttering about burst eardrums and oyster beds in the murk and *Why don't you leave it alone.*

And an image flew into my mind then: his waterlogged lungs, ear-blood suspended in a cloud underwater. The weight of his bloated body dragged with the undertow out into the impenetrable Pacific. And I wondered, *Would I look for him?*

It was like I'd been tiptoeing on a bedrock for years, struggling to keep my head above water. And all that I had left to hold onto was this gray, dwindling father-thing sitting across me in the flickering dark, and the best reassurance it could offer was: "I'm tired, why are you doing this to me, Momi?"

I kicked out the fire. And that stain where my fingers had kissed his earlobe, it was silky smooth.

DAD AND ME, we always slept makai, closer to the ocean. Because on nights when the moon was full, if you were lucky, you might catch the surf in your hair. In summers before, he'd stay awake with me for hours, whispering things like how to find the Andromeda Galaxy with the naked eye, and why Venus is the most beautiful orb in the sky.

It doesn't matter anymore, I guess. Any of this.

Bad memories become prophecies, and good memories? Good ones are worse. Look at them long enough, and you see them for what they really are: pitiful buoys bobbing in a dark, limitless ocean.

Dad slunk into slumber on his hala mat, didn't stir when I lay down beside him. The twins together mauka side, like soaking the moisture from the mountains. Like "safe and sound" were more than just words.

And they were lucky—they were all luck that night. Because they never woke up. They'd sucked the fortune from the tide pools and hogged it for themselves, and I was the only one awake for it all.

And for a while there I was listening to his wet breathing, to the twins' soft giggles, to the waves crashing onto coral. Pretty soon, everything was quiet but for the steady inhale-exhale of the water.

I must have fallen asleep, because the next thing I knew the moon was glaring down through the top flap. But it wasn't the light that woke me; it was a cold tickle around my shins. I froze. For a minute it was Dad, here to whisper again, to finally spill all his secrets about why he was so shuttered inside himself, and what he dreamed about there on the cape. Because he owed me. Because we were close, once upon a time.

Because both of us, we were magic.

But when I sat up, Dad was still sleeping, curled in on himself, his skin glinting. When I set my fingers on his chest, it was damp, viscid. A mucous line stretched from his lips to his belly.

And then a thing detached itself from the darkness at my feet and shuffled up over my thighs, too agile. I gasped, shoved it off, drawing my knees in close.

Its skin was dark speckled with white, pale suckers and bumps on its head, all gleaming with a sick luster like it'd just emerged from the sea. But it wasn't the sea it'd come from; that wasn't saltwater coating its delicate limbs.

No bigger than a cat, its two wet tendrils reached upward toward me, like seeking, like it could pluck shapes, colors right out of the air. And maybe it could. Maybe it could see every surface of me, every pore. I had the creeping sense that it peered into my every cell, and the gaps in between them.

It slunk over to the sleeping form of my dad, unfurling its tentacles, resting on his cheek, like tasting him. Those tiny feelers slid over his moist lips, gently prying his teeth apart.

And I couldn't move, couldn't stop it.

And with one swift, awful spasm—awful because it was so graceful—it eased into my dad's mouth. I remember the bulge in his throat, the heave in his chest. I remember the sigh he made like it was home.

He choked and writhed, and bubbles foamed at his lips, and that's when I grabbed him, shaking his shoulder, sobbing, *Wake up, Dad, wake up!* again and again like mad froth on my lips.

Then my dad, he woke up.

DID YOU PICK up that thing on the cape, Dad?

Or was it inside you to begin with, something you grew up with, carried like a pregnancy?

He lurched up like half-dreaming, like possessed. Shuffled over sideways on his knees to where the twins slept.

Was it you, Dad, or something else that laid a hand softly on each mouth, like you were shushing them, going to tell them a secret?

Their chests rising, and falling, and I thought: *Don't.*

Then he thrust three fingers deep into each of their mouths and—in one irreversible act that has fixed all past, present, future in place—yanked out their tongues.

Their heads bucked in protest, clunked to the ground, and an awful shower of thick blood rained down their cheeks. I thought they would wake up then, but they didn't. Abnormal rivulets of blood coursed from their mouths, and they coughed, sputtering flecks of red to the ceiling. Air fighting to get out, get in, keep those small bodies going. Fighting, and failing.

Don't.

And their tongues in Dad's grip, all sleek in the moonlight, longer than I'd ever imagined tongues could be.

He really could do anything, change the very nature of things. Like a wizard. Make dead things live, and live things dead. Turn a tent into a slaughterhouse. Make even the moon complicit.

Daughters, too.

Don't wake up.

He ate them then, the tongues: first the left, then the right. He tore the flesh off in slow bites, easily, like they were carrots that'd gone bad and all soft. The slowness telling me he enjoyed every minute of it.

Was it you? Or was it me?

Maybe I could've stopped him, shoved him aside, screamed myself hoarse trying to wake them, broken the spell. But part of me figured this was it. This was the moment I'd been waiting for. The moment I'd see who he really was.

Real magic.

Don't ruin this.

Because the truth is, what happened, didn't happen *to them.* They hadn't even been paying attention.

No, it happened *for me.*

Right, Gandalf?

HE SCRAPED THE hala mat where he kneeled in between them. His shoulders deflated, like whatever had been propping him up had leaked onto the tent floor. Like the stars had pressed against the mosquito net and sucked out the meaning behind it all.

And it enraged me, how defeated he seemed then, in the moonlight. How any explanation of what he'd done slipped off his shoulders as easily as foam slips off wet sand.

His lips parted, saliva dribbling from them; words formed but with no breath to back them, pitch them forward. So what I heard in the shadow of the tent can't be called speech, can't be called sound:

The slime…which created…the earth

But dads, they're not supposed to be like that.

They're supposed to be the immovable rock in the surf. The stocky palm tree weathering February storms. They're supposed to fix anything.

But my dad, he was diminishing, right before my eyes.

His feeble murmur twisted into a low, faltering chant, like the words were splintering in his chest. In mine too, because something was here after all. Something unknowable was swimming in my dad, and I couldn't stop the tide from coming in.

The slime which created the earth

The source of deepest darkness

Dots mottled his skin, dripped like sweat from his pores, in droplets first, then in trickles. The ink snaked off his body, weaving tiny rivers across the mat, all the way to where I crouched in the corner. Like it wanted to share.

It tasted of brine. Of something found and forgotten.

DAWN BROUGHT A bruised sky and clarity of what the night had wrought. Violent splatters of ink on the polyester walls. My bare legs brindled with streaks. And him, the dry husk of a threat in between the twin figures of his murdered daughters.

His breathing dry and tattered, eyes closed and crusting over. He was drying…he was dying. And it came to me without question, what was needed.

I dragged him by his armpits out to the shoal. Sunk his legs in the saltwater. The morning waves nuzzled at them, plumped them with life. I cradled him in my arms while his strength slowly returned. While the sun rays crawled over the mountains and glittered in the blood on his chin and throat.

He lifted one finger, weakly, to my cheek.

And I bent close to his blue lips, ready to listen, to hear, to take it all inside. I was an eager sponge waiting.

But then his eyes glazed over, and his hand dropped to his chest, a hollow thud.

A smile tucked like li hing mui in his mouth.

Like that was all the explanation I needed.

All I deserved.

And I've hated sunrises ever since, and green flashes too. Because even the changing of the light grants no gifts.

And before I could gather enough strength to speak, my dad slipped beyond me.

His arm slid over the sand, pulling his body into the foam. The morning current welcomed him, bore him to where the spindrift ravaged the lava rocks, and he submerged, slunk below the foam into a crevice much narrower than himself, folding his body like he was made of silk, and I was left alone, shin-deep in the cold of whose fault it was.

IT'S BEEN THIRTY years, and I've never seen him since.

They took my sisters away in a jeep because the ambulance couldn't risk the road. Stripped the tent too: evidence. The papers dubbed it murder-suicide.

I got a new tent, a two-person. I have to drag it closer on the coral every year. Later and later summers means receding shorelines, dwindling schools. From the tent flap I can see the ocean and the stars.

No one gets it, why I'm still here. Anyone else would've left long ago.

I break open black-needled wana and crabs and leave them by the tide pools. He must be a kupuna by now; I don't know if he can still hunt by himself. I don't know what steals the carcasses either, but they're gone when I look out every morning.

Sometimes I wonder if I'll ever see him again. I'm a bit scared to; time and water deepening his changes like they're something to celebrate.

And every time my stomach rolls, my chest tightens, I wonder if that thing is inside me too. If it's hereditary, like all bad compulsions.

Time has brought new shacks and sinewy dogs to the shore, and baggy-shirted kids who chase sea roaches from palm to palm, who still squeeze sea cucumbers until they squirt. They snap photos of my silhouette, and it doesn't bother me anymore. I stamp my feet to scare them off, beat their legs with palm fronds when they're about to dive, but I don't have enough mouths to warn them all. And I know one day soon, I'll be gone from this shore.

And sometimes, when I dream of soft nibbles on my face, tugging at my tongue, my hands bolt up, like shielding me from it all, like if they were just quick enough, they could catch all the colossus of a celestial body.

It's never him.

And worse than the fear it might be him looming in the hole of my tent flap—his hourglass eyes finding mine—is the realization it never will be.

⚓

HELLS SHELLS

Raymonde Chira

THREE DAYS BEFORE the drowning of Erin Gundry, she rose before
dawn and met the suffocating air of mid-July. That summer
was humid like a yoke on the shoulders weighted down by barrels
of brackish water. The motel's AC had gone out overnight. Her
father was already gone, so she gently woke her mother and
told her to drink some water and complain to the motel staff.

"Honey, it doesn't bother me," her mother said. "They're letting
us stay here at half the rate."

"Humidity is supposed to be through the roof today. It's not
safe at your age."

"I'm still kicking. I'm stronger than I look."

Erin stepped into the ebbing darkness and set off to meet up
with her father. The Singing Sands Motel stood between the
beach and the main town of Scuttlers' Bay. She took the long
path to the bay so that she could pass the docks. There was her
father, his feet over the edge of the pier.

"We need to get out of here before everyone wakes up and the boat club arrives," Erin said.

"Half those boat-club fools are summer people."

"Besides, crew's waiting for us at the graveyard."

The morning wind cut through the muggy air and cooled the sweat on their sun-burned skin. She looked into the water as the sun broke the horizon. Before the storm, she'd felt there was nothing sweeter than the saline breeze blowing in her face on the hottest day of the summer. Now that scent reminded her of the advancing ocean that had carried away her childhood home last year, and she wondered if anyone in Scuttlers' Bay could escape these waters in time.

They walked down to the beach to meet the rest of the salvage crew. Seabirds called out over Erin as she stepped carefully to avoid any rhubarb jellyfish. The crew were drinking coffee from a shared thermos, and she chewed out their foreman, Harvey Douglas, for not rationing enough for her. He grumbled that kids shouldn't drink coffee, and Erin snapped that she would be twenty-one in a month.

The ship graveyard extended out deep into the bay, but retrieving those vessels required equipment the buyers never wanted to cover. Besides, the profit for the crew was bigger just scouring the beach. They could keep things going by salvaging vessels like the Whale Canoes, which had once carried tourists under the surface in the shallows; the crew had skinned those boats down to their frames and sold them all to an amusement park in Royal City. Erin's biggest payday had come when she pulled the steering wheel off the wreck of the *Sweet Tooth*, the first vessel to pull in sugar-snapping crabs in 1893.

Now it was mostly picked-clean skeletons. The crew needed every minute of low tide to rip apart the remaining wrecks.

"How much you think is left here, Dad?" asked Erin

"Another three years of work for this crew, I reckon," he said. "Of course, the wrecks aren't the crabs. Environmentalists aren't gonna swoop in like they know better."

"No. And wrecks don't replenish their numbers either."

"Not on their own, anyway," he laughed. "Don't go getting ideas."

They were supposed to continue salvaging what they could from a capsized ferry pontoon and remove vintage seats. But when the crew reached the wreck, Erin thought she was seeing a mirage: where once there had been only sand behind the dilapidated ferry, there appeared from the ocean a vessel from yesteryear—the *Venus Smiles*.

She looked at it, and then at the haunted expression on her father's face. It was a good ship in its heyday, and he'd told her how it brought in sugar-snapping crabs by crates that could feed the town and still have enough left over to process for buyers across the country. At sixty-one-feet and with a crew of powerful watermen under Captain Sidney Cobb, it had been the last offshore vessel in the town's fleet before it disappeared.

The sea had stripped away any outward majesty, but the crew descended upon her hungrily nonetheless.

As her father helped Erin scale the starboard hull, he wept with rapture.

Harvey Douglas ordered that not a thing be removed yet. They would mark up anything in good condition and report to Captain Cobb.

Erin found the stairs that led below deck, and she and her father descended to look for the captains' quarters. Soon they were waist deep in water.

They waded onward, listening to the sound of the ocean beyond the walls. As they wound through the corridors of the *Venus*, the air grew still and hot as a hell of dark water.

The captain's quarters were dim and mostly submerged. All of the furniture was fixed to the walls and encrusted with barnacles. Erin ran her hands over the barnacles and found a crook where she could slide her fingers. She took the spade from her backpack and began tearing them from the wall.

The two shoveled away at the barnacles, which plopped into the water to join the sound of the waves. Erin tried to relax and breathe in the humid air. As they worked, her hands became slick with something that wasn't water. She held one up in the faint light of a porthole and saw it was covered in black liquid.

"Blackstar barnacles," said the crabber. "The one kind that can spray ink. Don't worry about it—they're not poisonous and they can't spray out of the water."

It struck Erin then just how dark the waters were.

Above her father, bolted to the back wall with brackets, was the skeletal jaw of a greenfin beaming shark.

"Yep," he said, noticing where she was looking.. "I reckon he put it there so it'd be the first thing anyone noticed when they came in. Crew used to joke that since he seldom smiled, he mounted that thing to do the work. Only known shark species that don't frown. This was our claim to fame. Marine life like nowhere else on the coast."

"I know."

"No, you don't. I wish you could have seen it all, my girl. Not that I wanted you to have a waterman's life. Proud of my work, but I know when something's dead. Much as I'd love to see you on that ocean…just don't go on resenting it."

Erin felt something shift below the water. In an instant she was under, blinded by the pitch-black water. It was hot, even hotter than the air above. It rushed into her with ferocious speed.

Just as quickly, she was coughing again in the open air. She wiped the sea water from her eyes. Her father had pulled her up, but now he cried out in pain, gripping his back.

"Holy fuck." Erin retched another gulp of black water. "Dad?"

He leaned against the wall. Each time he went to straighten his back, he groaned. She took his arm before he could fall under too.

By the time they returned to the beach, water still clogged Erin's ears and she could still hear that resonant sound like a conch shell's echo. Her father went back to the motel to recover while Erin and the crew worked until the afternoon high tide.

She spent the rest of the day at Pitou's Penny, trying to reclaim her high score at pinball. Mr. Pitou plugged in a fan for her after a while.

After nightfall, when she opened the door to the motel, the AC's flow turned her sweat cold, making her squirm.

She had only started up the stairs when she heard it: a squelching noise like many feet scurrying over a wet surface, coming from just over her shoulder. She told herself it was just the sea water that still hadn't drained from her ear, but then, from the periphery of her vision, she caught sight of a tall, hunching figure shuffling down the hall toward the elevator. It disappeared around the corner. Even in that fleeting glimpse, she recognized Captain Sidney Cobb, with his gray cap, slouched shoulders, the long beard that lost none of its red with age.

In Suite 27, she found her parents in bed but wide awake. The AC was pumping, and color had returned to her mother's face, but Erin still saw too much exhaustion for someone who spent all day at a cash register.

"Dad...did Cobb just stop by?"

"What?" he asked, yawning. "I haven't seen him in weeks.."

That night, Erin dreamed of that bright sea she remembered as a child, until it heaved and crashed and she woke startled and panting in the motel, wondering if the water was closer now than it had been the day before.

TWO DAYS BEFORE the drowning of Erin Gundry, her ears still hadn't cleared of sea water. Her hearing was so muffled that Douglas had to repeat all of his orders for her. But worse was when things went quiet and that sound kept pulsating at her eardrums. She'd read somewhere that smell was the strongest trigger for memory, but sound—echoes—always struck her as worse. She remembered the damp noises of their home after the deluge, the one that had come too early for hurricane season. She'd found a hermit crab crawling out of her childhood collection of winding mollusk shells in the marsh that was now her room.

At the beach, the air was even hotter than the day before and her sweat would not evaporate. Douglas had left a message for Cobb, asking what he wanted salvaged from the *Venus*. The crew stuck to the older wrecks through two low-tides, but there still had been no word from Cobb when they broke for the day.

That night, Erin decided to get a bite at the Mermaid Cafe. She squeezed onto a stool at the end of the bar next to a group of vacationers about her age. The waiter took her usual order of country ham and cheese with BBQ corn and sweet tea. He asked after her family, and she told him the FEMA money was keeping them afloat but the insurance wasn't enough for long-term relocation.

The eatery stayed open despite the regular flooding of its floor, though it still closed for high-tide. Not that it clashed with the decor—life buoys and nets and a plastic marlin on the walls complemented the algae-tasting water on tap, which Erin had begrudgingly gotten used to. Eventually, the vacationers trick-led out through the tidal pool, leaving Erin with the sound of her waterlogged ears as company. Each bite and gulp became unpleasant drills of water into her head. She heard it again: the wet scurrying, clicking across wood.

She glanced out of the window just as a shadow barreled past through the darkness, beyond the diner's light. She couldn't discern its shape, only that it had many appendages that flashed in the moonlight. Before it vanished into the darkness, she heard a dog barking. Just as quickly, it ceased.

She turned back to her sandwich and for the first time noticed Cobb on the other side of the bar, sinking his teeth into fish and chips. He might have been sitting there all along. Erin took her plate and waded through the ankle-deep water over to him.

"Good evening, Captain."

"Miss Gundry," he grumbled, casting a vacant glance at her. "How's your father?"

"Threw out his back. Did you hear about what we found on the beach?"

"Aye. And I am telling you what I told them: I want you to retrieve nothing for me, and I will pay you nothing."

For a moment, Erin worried that the heat had finally made her delusional.

"I don't want the wheel of my *Venus* hanging in my house like something from a maritime museum," he said. "I want that ship back on the water."

"How are you going to do that? I've seen the thing. It ain't floating ever again."

Cobb looked at her dead on and pinched his face. "The ocean gave her back to me, and I just need to see her out. Scuttlers' Bay was always a waterman's town…" He stuffed his mouth with coleslaw. "We ain't fishing, we might as well be dead. Goddamn government set us up to go under with regulations. Town is a shell of its former self."

"People still fish around here, even if it's not in the big boats offshore. No shame in that."

"The ocean is on my side once again, but catch is pitiful. We may be a town of watermen, but Scuttlers' Bay needs its crabs."

He wolfed down the last piece of his fish. Even through her waterlogged ears, Erin could hear him chewing, and her patience ran out.

"Where the fuck would you even find a crew? The young folks are all leaving this town, and the men…my father can barely pull on his sweater when it's cold."

Cobb let out a click from behind his lips. Still facing Erin, he reached into his mouth and pulled out a thin, curved bone like a hook. "Young Miss Gundry, are you so blind to your future?"

He stood, placed some bills on the counter, and leaned in too close for comfort. He whispered, "The ocean will have us back. It's calling to me. Don't pretend you can't hear it too."

Erin smelled brine. The diner's lights rippled, and everything seemed to distort and slacken. She looked for the exit, but it was miles away, down a pathway that curved infinitely out into the humid night. The reverie broke. She looked around and Cobb had disappeared.

ONE DAY BEFORE the drowning of Erin Gundry, her father remained in the motel as she went to work. Throughout the day, the conversation with Cobb played on her mind. Contrary to what he thought, Erin was all too familiar with the fate of the

Venus. It had been a slow death, easy to deny as it happened. The massive boats from out of state had swept in across the deepest parts of the bay and spread trawlers that scooped up anything for miles. Season after season, sugar-snapping crabs would be hauled in and battered dead under the bycatch before the big operator crews tossed them back to skirt the environmental quotas, leaving the crabbers of Scuttlers' Bay with empty pots. With that, and the way they tore away at the nesting ground out in the bay, the *Venus Smiles* and her kin would return after days offshore with a tenth of their old catch.

Her father tried to remain optimistic. "We ain't crabbers nor fisherman; we're watermen. Any life we can pull from the water, we can make do." But halberd trout, cracker shrimp, polka-dot scallops, pepper clams would all collapse. "Every goddamn day it's another fish. The environmentalists say they need to replenish their numbers. By the time that happens, there won't be boats left."

Erin hated it when he blamed the environmentalists and not the out-of-state boats that hauled and then went to richer waters. But she wouldn't take their side either. They chastised Scuttlers' Bay, as though the town did not know the ocean with its own kind of reverence.

Erin was still a child on the night of the storm that took the *Venus Smiles*. No one knew why the ship hadn't been tied off, but the next morning when Cobb heard the news that somehow his beautiful ship had floated away in the night, all he'd said was, "Well, shit. Sea wanted her back."

ON THE DAY of the drowning of Erin Gundry, she returned to the beach without her father again and found the crew in disarray. She walked between the scattered crewmen in the muddy sand, and when she saw the bearded, slouching figure waving his hands at an exasperated Douglas, she felt a pit in her stomach. She couldn't discern what they were saying—the gulls overhead and the churning water in her ear canals drowned it out. She marched up to them.

"Erin," said Douglas, "I'm in the middle of something."

"No," said Cobb. "I can listen."

"Just you and me," Erin stammered.

They walked until they were out of earshot of the crew, and then Erin turned to face him.

"What the hell did you mean last night?" she asked. "And no cryptic bullshit."

"Don't deny this shell of an old man, Miss Gundry." Though his mouth was hidden behind his beard and the sound of the ocean had not disappeared, his voice somehow rang clear. "We're on the same side. You want the sea to love you back as much as I do."

Erin felt dried brine melt on her face as sweat ran down her forehead.

"All the young folks are getting ready to leave, except you," he said. "Your father was a good waterman, but his generation can't do it anymore. When I get the *Venus Smiles* back on the water, you're going to be part of my crew. Scuttlers' Bay's days aren't numbered. And the ocean gave you a gift. You can hear it anywhere you go."

"That isn't the ocean. That's the blood echoing in my ear like a seashell."

"No. It's the ocean. Just listen. The crabs have returned. I seen 'em. You must hear 'em. Scurrying around. They need a shepherd, and that'll be you. You say what you hear is your blood—well, crabbing's in your blood. Saltwater."

"Once I strip that wreck of yours," Erin said, "I'll pay for my family to move out of here. Get a place inland, escape before the sea rises."

"Don't run. We've nothing to fear. The ocean wants us back. They say it's dust to dust, but we come from the ocean, and it awaits our return." He turned and marched away.

Erin, even more frustrated than before, followed him.

"All right," Cobb told Douglas. "The *Venus* is all yours. But only Miss Gundry boards the ship for now." He turned to Erin, his eyes calculating and assured.

Erin's skin crawled as she realized that Cobb trusted her, kept faith that, as part of his crew, she would not harm the *Venus.*

"Mr. Douglas," she said. "I need the welding equipment."

ERIN WADED BACK through the inky waters of the captain's quarters, welding torch in hand. It was an insane notion, she knew it, but whether gripped by spite or hope, she was ready to reclaim this ship from the sea. She would pull the *Venus Smiles* out one piece at a time if she had to. As the water sloshed all around her and the waves crashed outside, they drowned out the deluged chamber of her ear canals.

She shone her flashlight across the rusted walls, cleaned of barnacles, and up to the smiling shark's jaw bolted to the wall. She lit the welding torch. The heat was so enervating that she thought she might faint, but she called on her adrenaline reserves. Once she cut this thing off the wall, she'd sell it to the Mermaid Cafe or the aquarium in Royal City or any collector. Just as long as she didn't have to look at it for long. Its hungry grin, now illuminated, stood as a taunting face from Cobb, from the sea itself, from all those pleased with their work in leading her here.

She cut through one of the bolts, pulling on the massive jaws and avoiding the teeth, when a frantic scratching rang out from behind her.

Erin whipped around and, trembling, held her flashlight out. In the hallway, where it curved into the ship, black outlines of stick-like legs scurried across the ceiling and out of sight.

Erin bolted out of the cabin and back the way she came. She hurried through the water, but never lost the sound of scurrying legs. After winding her way through the ship, she found the stairs to the deck. The scurrying was the only thing that broke through the sound of the ocean in her ears. It followed her as she broke the surface hatch and scrambled to the deck.

The bay waters swept over Erin's ankles. High tide wasn't for hours. Yet the sea taunted her certainty by stretching out in every direction.

The shoreline had vanished from sight, either long past the ocean's horizon or below the sea itself. She saw the red algae across the water, gathering around her feet, and fought back the urge to vomit. She slowed her breathing; in this heat and humidity, and now with a red tide, her lungs needed to be steady and relaxed.

Erin moved away from the algae to breathe clearer air. Alone with the seawater echoing in her ears, she wished for any other sound to penetrate. She wished her father were there with her; he would have some pollyannaish thing to say, folksy stuff about the sea, and Erin could have someone to talk to—anything to break this terrible drowning resonance that pumped through her ears like leeches engorged with blood.

A shape began to rise in the water, and Erin stared until it broke the surface. It was an eye, floating still and as big as a truck tire.

It might've been a squid's eye, but she couldn't rule out that it might be human. She relaxed when she saw it wasn't attached to anything.

For a while, they stared each other down. It didn't blink.

"I guess we wait it out," she said to it. "Cobb said we belong to the sea. That's what we're about in Scuttler's Bay. But you don't belong here anymore than I do."

The floating eye did not respond, only stared.

"Sugar-snapping crabs…did you ever get a chance to see one? Eat one?" Erin asked it. "Mom told me they weren't as sweet as you'd expect. They were a bit like Meyer lemons, but they flavored anything they were cooked with. The name came from how you could snap the arms off with your bare hands. Easiest crab to eat."

The tide splashed against Erin's knees, a wave carrying the eye upward before returning it to its spot.

"The best part about growing up near the sea is knowing there's no limit," she said. "When you see that horizon day in, day out as a little kid, you get this idea you can go anywhere the ocean will take you. But I got the whole thing flipped around. The ocean doesn't carry you, doesn't even care that you're around. It's not *you* that goes on and on; it's the ocean."

She remembered what Cobb had said and decided to listen.

Far off in the deepest part of the bay, she heard the ocean floor sinking into the earth.

The earth is swallowing the sea, she thought. No, she corrected herself, where there was once earth, there is now water. If the ocean could reach something, it was already underwater.

"That's it, isn't it? The water wins out in the end," she said. "Most of this planet is water. We think it all revolves around us, but that's bullshit. If we were really the masters of this planet, how come we only float when we're dead?"

It gave no answer, and Erin's throat hurt. The breeze on the water had gone still some time ago, and it seemed that the stifling air could take no more water into itself. Erin coughed and concentrated on staying on her feet, sweat now all across her body. It was so muggy that none of the moisture evaporated, as though the air itself was just a vessel for water. The briny sweat covered her pores.

She listened to the ocean sound, thinking of all the twisting pathways that had led her here, spiraling down like a mollusk's shell, and she inhaled with all her might, that vapor filling her lungs.

THE BEACH HOUSE WITH ITS BACK TO THE SEA

Íde Hennessy

ITS WINDOWS HAD been facing the Pacific the first time she saw the house—a two-story wall of glass like the rest, all glittering beacons on cliffs dark with trees. The gray water below frothed into white crests, dashing and drooling between teeth-like formations along the cove.

Marta Montejo closed her eyes and tightly gripped her armrest as the Cessna was rocked by coastal gusts. It's *just* the ocean, she told herself. People *love* the goddamn ocean. Can't get *enough* of it. She bounced in her seat as they lurched downward fitfully, and a memory intruded on her silent affirmations.

Salt stinging her eyes, knees scraping rocks and shells, head pushed down by the waves like some wrathful god she was too small to fight. Little lungs running out of breath—

"I hate to be that guy, Clint," Dane Prescott yelled from the seat beside her, "but when you said you had a private plane, I was picturing something a bit more lux. You're Hollywood *royalty*, after all—TMZ said so."

"You love being that guy," Clint Mezzasalma called back from the cockpit, "and I haven't won an Oscar—yet."

"You alright there, Marta?" Dane asked in his fake Italian accent, prodding her arm.

"Viola," she corrected him, hoping Clint would notice. Clint had insisted they call each other by their characters' names even when they weren't filming.

The plane was jostled by some invisible hand again, and feathers floated around the cabin as the parrot in the cage at their feet bobbed its head and shrieked.

"Viola, no!" the bird screamed.

"I see he's memorized my lines," Dane said. "What's up with him anyways—is he supposed to be my understudy?"

"No, he's clearly your stunt double." Marta made kissy sounds at the little green dinosaur, and it cocked its head at her.

"That's Oswald," Clint shouted back at them. "He knows all your lines because he practically wrote the screenplay."

"*The* Oswald?" Marta asked.

"The Oswald. He's older than both of you."

"And we're ancient in Hollywood years," Marta said, pouting. "I should have been born a bird, I knew it."

2. EXT. SEQUOIA POINT AIR STRIP – DAY

ON THE TARMAC, Marta lost her breakfast into an empty popcorn bag from the plane—such a cinematic touch, the barf bags—while Dane chatted up the minimal camera crew. They had traveled separately, in a slightly larger plane with their gear.

"Why the hell did we have to fly here?" Marta asked when she was able to.

"The winding three-hour drive from the nearest highway is even worse." Clint fished around in his pockets and offered her a cigarette. "And it's blocked half the time by mud slides, so I didn't want to chance it."

"I offered up my yacht," Dane said, joining them. "So, don't blame me."

Clint handed him two suitcases. "It'd be smashed to pieces. There's no safe harbor here; this is the heart of the Lost Coast."

Marta took a drag of the cigarette to calm her nerves. She could feel the little wrinkles above her lips deepen with the effort, reminding her why she was here.

"We could have filmed on any vaguely rugged beach," Dane grumbled, "and used a studio to recreate the house. You didn't have to get all Werner Herzog about it."

"It could only be here, and it could only be now," Clint said cryptically. "You'll see."

They were filming the end of the movie first, but they would only be here for three days, thankfully, before returning to L.A.

"But why no cell phones?" Marta wrestled with the wind while trying to tie a scarf around her hair. "If you don't post to TikTok every day, you fade into irrelevance."

"Too late for that, dear," Dane said, passing the suitcases off to her as if she was a valet.

3. INT. MEZZASALMA BEACH HOUSE – DAY

MARTA GASPED AS the bunker-like, windowless entrance to the house transformed into a 180-degree view of the ocean. She kept her distance from the glass while Dane rushed to press his face against it like a child.

"God, I miss having a view like this." He breathed in deeply as if he could inhale it. "Mine's been condemned, you know, after the cliff collapse in Newport Beach."

"*Everyone* knows," Marta said. She averted her eyes from the view, only to be startled by a wall of mirrors reflecting it behind her. No escaping that endless expanse of sickly-blue. She focused on Dane instead. "Anyways, that's what you get for owning a yacht—hardly a small carbon footprint."

"Well, you know what they say about the size of a man's footprint."

"Your sense of humor hasn't aged a day."

Marta turned her attention to the décor of the house. It was as if a glamour spread from a 1970s issue of *Architectural Digest* had been preserved in aspic. A time capsule of open concept, shag carpet, stone accent walls, and dance studio mirrors, with a pillowy conversation pit in the center to pull it all together like a black hole.

On the coffee table in the conversation pit was a driftwood sculpture that reminded her of tentacles. It had been knocked over onto its side, and a fist-sized glass sphere lay unceremoniously on the floor below it.

The more she explored, the more there was something *off* about this place, even for the seventies. In the hallway leading to the bedrooms, she turned on a light switch and jumped as a human form in black confronted her. The pale, featureless mannequin wore black robes with an upside-down red triangle on the chest. Crudely stitched into it were the letters *OTO*.

"Ordo Templi Orientis," Clint said from behind her, startling her again. "The Order of the Golden Dawn. My grandparents were always hopping from one occult interest to another, then growing bored of them. There's an original Thoth tarot deck around here somewhere."

Clint's grandparents were the esteemed Italian director Eduardo Mezzasalma and the less esteemed 1940s starlet Viola Vasco. Marta and Dane would be re-creating their final weekend together at their second home here in Northern California. Their final weekend, period.

"I want to show you something," Clint said, leading Marta behind the mirror wall in the living room, where a single painting hung. It was a portrait of a woman on a beach, standing inside a circle drawn in the sand. Her dark hair was twisted into the shape of horns, and a sheer blue veil hung from them, making her head look like a blurry, inverted triangle. A stark ray of light cut the painting in half, with her at the center. On either side were two moons in a starry sky, one waxing and one waning.

Marta was repulsed by it in a way she couldn't explain, but she said, "It's stunning."

"They liked to tell people it was a Leonora Carrington," Clint said, "but my grandmother just painted it in her style. She turned to painting when she stopped acting, but she burned most of her works as soon as she finished them."

Marta supposed this was a special insight into the character she'd be portraying, but it only confused her further about the woman.

She followed Clint back to the living room, where the assistant director was pulling a colorful rug over a faded stain between the wet bar and the sunken sofa.

"This is where it happened?" Marta asked, hairs prickling along her arms despite her knowing the end of the script already.

"I've never seen a haunted conversation pit before," Dane added, looking unsettled for a moment before cheering up with, "Can you *picture* the orgies they had here back in the day? I wonder if ghosts still pile in here for a go at it.

Clint stepped into the haunted orgy pit and righted the fallen driftwood sculpture. He gently placed the glass ball on top of it and turned to smile at them. "Tomorrow, we shoot. For now, this is the perfect place to watch the sunset. Champagne or scotch?"

"Champagne or scotch?" Oswald the parrot repeated from the ornate bamboo cage he had been transferred to. Marta had forgotten about him. He'd been Eduardo's parrot, supporting star of his only critically panned film, the 1967 trainwreck *The Beach That Death Forgot*. The creature must be in his sixties or seventies by now.

That night, Clint insisted that Marta and Dane sleep in the guest rooms—Marta chose the one furthest from the living room—while the crew slept at the only hotel in town. The sound of sea lions kept Marta awake for hours, like dogs warning of a trespasser, so she helped herself to more scotch to drown them out.

4. INT. MEZZASALMA BEACH HOUSE - LATER

IN THE MORNING, Marta dressed in the costume that had been laid out for her and then emerged to find the crew already gathered in the living room, drinking coffee. Dane was doing tai chi facing the ocean, which looked like it was in a different place than it had been yesterday. The horizon wasn't right, like the teeth formation in the cove had formed a smirk.

"Did I sleep through an earthquake?" Marta asked. "Why does it look like the house has moved?"

Clint laughed, and the crew joined him.

"I saw you helped yourself to the rest of the scotch," Clint said. "That'll do it."

"I look ridiculous," Marta complained to change the subject. Her costume was a shapeless white muumuu with an abstract embroidered design that drew too much attention to her crotch.

"*You* look ridiculous?" Dane turned around and opened his robe to reveal his own costume beneath: a white terrycloth leisure suit with bell bottoms. "I look like a giant towel for wiping up semen."

Marta snickered, picked up a zucchini muffin from the breakfast spread on the bar, and spat the first bite into a napkin. "Do these muffins have weed in them?"

"A local delicacy," Clint explained. "You have to understand, when my grandparents were here at the beach house, they were never *not* in an altered state."

Dane snorted a line of coke off a tea tray the crew were passing around. "It's called method acting, *Viola*—something you wouldn't know about."

"No, method acting is when young men effortlessly gain or lose thirty pounds for a role," Marta said. "But if you can pretend to be attracted to someone older than your daughter, I guess I can try new things too."

She needed to impress this up-and-coming director more than Dane did. He was still landing romantic lead roles, even if they were in made-for-TV movies. She finished the muffin and grabbed a second one for later.

5. EXT. SEQUOIA POINT BEACH – DAY

FROM HIGH UP on the wooden steps that led down the cliff side, it looked as if the receding tide had stained the black sands of the beach neon blue. Marta had never seen anything like it.

As she drew closer, it looked more like the ocean had deposited a layer of blue tinted condoms all over the sand.

"Velella velella," Clint said, waving his arm as if casting a spell. "Also known as By-The-Wind Sailors. They live on the surface of deep waters, but they're at the mercy of currents. Usually, they wash up in late spring and summer, so it's early for a mass stranding like this."

"Are they still *alive*?" Marta picked up one of the blue translucent disks by the rubbery "sail" protruding from it. There was a hint of movement in the tiny tentacles at its base, so she hurled it back into the waves.

Each movement she made caused a sort of shimmer in her vision, as if a giant piece of plastic wrap was a few feet in front of her, quivering in the wind. She picked up another of the jellyfish-like creatures and threw it through the shimmer into the water. And then another. Soon she was racing along the beach, grabbing them up by the handful and tossing them underhand as far as she could. They broke through the shimmering wall in front of her, but more washed to shore moments later.

"You can't fight Mother Nature," Dane called after her, his voice slowed down and distorted. "I'm sorry, Viola."

Marta spun around to see that the camera was rolling, and the assistant director was struggling to hold a boom mic steady in the wind.

"You're *filming*?" Marta demanded. "With ambient lighting? And no *bounce boards*? You can't do that to a woman in her fifties!"

"We can't even see your face in those shots," Clint assured her, "and you were *perfect*. You did exactly what my grandmother would have done—fight the higher powers, in the face of certain death. Dane, that was some nice improv as well."

"Did I improv?" Dane asked. "I fear I've had too much of the local cuisine."

"I think we're ready for you to get in the water." Clint put a hand on Marta's shoulder. "Before this fog rolls in any thicker."

"*In* the water?" Marta shrugged away from him. "That's not in the script. I would never have agreed to that."

"You're in the water now," Clint said, pointing at her feet.

Marta looked down to see foam curling around her sandals, lunging at her toes. She jumped back onto the dry sand, leaving one of the sandals behind in the muck.

"Oh, don't be dramatic," Dane said, primping his salt-and-pepper hair. "So, you drowned and died for a minute. That was over *forty years* ago. And this spray tan isn't going to survive in the fog much longer."

Marta reluctantly accepted the script from Clint's outstretched hand. He may be a bit of a weasel, but at least he cast someone the actual age of the woman they'd be playing, instead of having a thirty-something actress play fifty-something, the usual way. She had once been the young actress playing decades older in a film directed by Clint's father, so this opportunity wasn't even karmically deserved.

She had to concentrate all her attention on the script to make the letters form coherent words. "I shouldn't have had that second green muffin. I honestly *don't* remember this scene."

"Focus," Clint said. "What's your motivation?"

"I'm dying." Marta closed her eyes, listening to waves crash on the rocks farther out in the cove. "I'm dying, and I resent the path I chose. The path chosen for me." Viola was a mysterious woman who eschewed interviews, but Marta knew the basics. Viola had stopped being cast in leading roles after birthing her only child—Clint's father—then she had disappeared from the Hollywood scene entirely, except to smile in photos with her husband during awards season.

"Roll sound," Clint said softly.

Marta took off the second sandal, turned around, and walked towards the angry sea, carefully avoiding the swaths of beached velellas. She stepped into the water and let out a scream.

Clint rushed to her side. "What is it?"

"It's fucking *freezing!*"

"We've got the fireplace going back at the house, and another bottle of scotch on the bar," Clint said, lighting a joint he'd pulled from his coat pocket and handing it to her. "This'll be over in a flash."

Take two. Marta walked into the water up to her ankles and seductively pulled the white muumuu over her head. Normally, worried about cellulite and spider veins, she'd insist on having a body double, but by now it was so foggy there may as well be Vaseline smeared on the camera lens. She turned to smile at Dane on the beach and threw the muumuu in his direction. Then she trudged her way through the frigid water up to her chest, while Clint followed with the camera to the water's edge.

"What if you could live forever," she called to Dane over the sound of waves bursting against rock, "but you had to be someone else?"

She ducked her head under the numbing water, plugged her nose, and found that she was buoyant this time as salt sloshed against her. She had to fight the ocean from pushing her up onto the beach instead of pulling her down to deeper waters. Marta pictured herself as Godzilla, plotting to storm Tokyo from his watery abode. Heavy. Dangerous.

Out of breath, she emerged from the foam, dark hair dripping, while Dane ran to her. He held her, his back to the camera, while she looked past it into the distance.

"Do you hear it, Eddie? Do you hear it calling me?"

6. EXT. SEQUOIA POINT BEACH – LATER

WARMED AND DRY, a little tipsy, and wrapped in a black and red poncho with fringe, Marta was glad there would be no more outdoor nudity. The fog had drifted away up the coast as the day wore on, but the air had grown colder without its murky blanket.

A little further down the beach was an archway in one of the rock formations, which she hadn't noticed due to its west-facing direction. The hole in its center reminded her of the shape of a key—an almost rectangular opening with a larger, rounded top. This is where they would be filming that night.

As the sky grew darker, Marta saw why Clint had insisted they film *here* and *now*. The sun's descent into the sea lined up perfectly with the keyhole in the rock, so that a fiery red path appeared against the black sands, with her in the center. She turned to look at Dane and saw that her shadow had devoured him. It split the path of light in half, stretching all the way to the cliffs.

The dark windows of vacation homes suggested they were the only ones to witness this wonder of nature—what a shame and a thrill at the same time.

How ominous she must look to the camera, silhouetted in that feverish light. She was reminded of the painting that had repelled her the day before.

"Cut!" Clint called out.

As the glowing path withered into glints of orange on the water, Marta was strangely tempted to dive in. Just to see how that liquid sunlight felt on her skin. "Up for a night swim, Eddie?"

Dane recoiled from her as if she were a random fan who had interrupted his dinner. Someone he didn't recognize. "I'm not going to freeze my ass off if it's not in the script, darling."

7. INT. MEZZASALMA BEACH HOUSE - NIGHT

IN THE GUEST room's vintage waterbed, Marta dreamt of blue velellas washing up on the beach. Each wave brought thousands more, until they had piled up higher than the cliff side. The weight of them broke the beach-house windows, and they flopped into the conversation pit, as if they had been drawn there by some unseen force.

7. INT. MEZZASALMA BEACH HOUSE – DAY

"TO DIE AND be revived," Clint said after exhaling a mouthful of smoke, "is to become a conduit." He passed the glass pipe to Marta. "That's why you have such potential as an actress in the right role. Like a…medium channeling characters."

Marta stared at the milky blue swirls in the blown glass, and they coiled up like jellyfish tentacles. She took another sip of champagne and passed the pipe to Dane. "I've probably had enough of this."

Clint had claimed the weed grown here was different than what they were used to, and she was beginning to believe it was more than a cheesy cannatourism pitch.

"Grab me another, would you, Eddie?" Oswald the parrot said, dancing from foot to foot on his perch. He puffed up his feathers when he caught Marta watching him.

"The sun will be setting soon," Clint announced, rising from the sunken sofa, "and tonight is the Spring Equinox. We only have one chance to get this scene right."

"Oh, please." Dane stood to follow him. "There's this thing called CGI, Clint. You should google it."

Marta climbed out of the pit and tripped over her new costume, a maxi dress embroidered with moon phases. Clint caught her and patted her on the shoulder, saying, "Almost done here."

She braved a look past him, out the windows. In the middle of their view, where it hadn't been the day before, was the keyhole rock formation. But so much of what she had seen in the last couple days seemed like a place found only in dreams.

The clap of a film slate in front of her face made her wonder how long she had been standing there, staring. The long wisps of cloud in the sky were now salmon pink.

"Action!"

The salmon pink was now burnt orange, and Marta was lounging in the conversation pit.

"I know about you and your little Prop Master," she recited, swirling an ice cube in an empty rocks glass. "But it doesn't matter anymore. Grab me another, would you, Eddie?"

She held out the glass to Dane, who looked somewhere between embarrassed and tortured. He hesitated before taking it from her and busying himself at the bar.

The sun was kissing the top of the rock formation now. As it aligned with the archway, the blazing path appeared again on the water, stretching towards them. Marta was momentarily blinded as crew members on the dark beach reflected it up to them with mirrors.

The clink of ice in a glass. The scent of peat and smoke.

The sunset glowed upside-down in the glass sphere now, on its driftwood stand. Marta pulled the vintage revolver from under her cushion, hid it behind her back, and stood. Dane stepped away from the bar, into the path of light, and she aimed the gun at him, thinking it looked like something out of an old cowboy film. "*Per lunam et oceanum—*"

"Viola, no!" He held up a hand, and the glass fell with an unsatisfying thud on shag carpet.

"*Et omnia sidera celestia,*" Marta continued, and another voice joined her. Oswald was repeating her lines, the little green menace. She continued anyways and pulled the trigger.

She was thrown backwards onto the sunken couch. Her ears rang, and her vision blurred and wavered as if she were being pulled underwater. The gun was warm in her hand, and she flung it away, trying to focus.

Dane was face-down on the throw rug, and Clint and the crew had joined in Oswald's throaty chants. Before she could ask what the hell was going on, the ground beneath them all groaned and shifted.

The house was moving. The view in the windows shifted, like that skyscraper restaurant in San Francisco where she had once filmed a romantic dinner scene. But it kept going, until she couldn't see the ocean anymore. She tried to scramble out of the pit, but the pillows slid beneath her, dragging her down, while the room shook.

A high whine pierced through the rumbling, and Marta screamed over it as her vision faded out again: "What is *happening*?"

7. INT. MEZZASALMA BEACH HOUSE - LATER

VIOLA GAZED AT the stranger reflected in the mirror wall, touching her high cheek bones and running fingers through her dark, silken hair. "*Luna saeculorum*, I'm exquisite."

Clint ran to her, stopping at the edge of the conversation pit.

"You found my instructions," she said, turning to him. "Who are you?"

"Clint Mezzasalma, your grandson." He blushed and held out a hand to help her up. "I found what you left on the back of the painting, and I had some help from Oswald too."

"He never could keep his mouth shut," she said, and the parrot shrank away from her. "I see it's finally come in handy."

Viola stepped over Dane on her way to the bar and poured herself a drink. "What do you ask of me, Clint Mezzasalma?"

"Who better to play you, in the story of your life, than you?"

FADE OUT.

⚓

THE OCEAN VOMITS
WHAT WE DISCARD

J. A. W. McCarthy

SEVENTEEN TODAY.

On an untouched stretch of the central coast, under a fog-blotted sky, seventeen girls take long, graceless strides across the beach and into the ocean. Bare feet sinking into sparkling sand, ankles roped with seaweed, hands instinctively reaching out again and again as they brace themselves with every stumble. The water froths, salivating at the sight of all that vulnerable sun-scorned flesh. The girls proudly offer flushed cheeks and heat rash-speckled shoulders for the tide to lick clean.

It was sixteen last week. Sixteen identical girls—they're grown women, but locals and tourists alike fantasize innocence in those fawn limbs and salt-water–brittle locks, anointing them "girls"—trudged their way through sand and seaweed and driftwood obstacles, eyes focused on the endless blue lapping at the horizon, and walked into the Pacific Ocean with a purpose both alarming and admirable. They traversed centuries-smooth rocks and broken shells, the water swallowing their legs, their hips, their breasts, their stoic empty faces, until only their dark hair was left, coarse nests floating atop the waves.

That's the worst part, how the hair keeps washing up. Clusters of loose hair, anchored by tough, slimy kelp where a scalp should be, return to the beach after each migration, nipping at my feet, chasing me with the tide. Tangled with jetsam, the detritus of doomed girls formed around plastic water bottles and candy wrappers and used syringes, creating a new creature.

And now there are seventeen girls' worth of hair and tourist garbage. One more than last week. I'm standing here bleeding on the beach, and it's not a relief anymore. These girls with my dark hair and eyes and round cheeks keep coming, and I can't get them all out.

NONE OF THESE girls are missing. There are no families waiting at home for a call from the police, no flyers with photos of round-faced women with their melancholic smiles plastered on the windows of every fish-and-chip place and tacky gift shop. There are no grave markers, no park benches dedicated to another "gone too soon." The phenomenon of multiple identical girls voluntarily walking into the ocean is nothing more than a magical sight, a pop-up event inducing awe and wonder and the sense that you are special if you're lucky enough to witness it. Same as the annual fireworks show on the beach or the increasing number of whale carcasses washing up, desiccated and yoked to plastic sheeting, bones capped with party cups and six-pack rings. These girls have no names, no families, are never missed by anyone—because they never really existed.

Tourists turn up year-round, hoping to get video of this macabre parade. They gather on the beach, cell phones and professional camera equipment held aloft, but all they ever capture are rolling waves and footprints in the sand. The girls remain stoic, focused, even as the vultures hover close, pushing cameras into their faces, waving their arms and yelling for the girls' attention. News crews come, but they too leave empty-handed, expressing their disdain, accusing us locals of cheap trickery for tourist dollars. They all scratch their heads, slap their palms against equipment that "must be malfunctioning," compare girl-less photos, disappointed at what is just another postcard-perfect shot of a sunset against endless crystal blue. They speculate, assuming too many margaritas or some sort of heat-induced collective delusion, before returning to the vacation rentals that line the boardwalk a half mile away. Crushed that they didn't capture all those girls drowning themselves in the Pacific. Funny how not a single person has ever tried to save those vulnerable girls.

In the flurry of shutter snaps and pointing fingers, no one has ever noticed me on the beach, standing among the driftwood, blood running down my arms, either.

When I first cut myself open, I thought I'd be whisked off in an ambulance called by my neighbors. When the reporters appeared, I thought I might be a headline. But they never acknowledge me, not when there are girls marching to their demise. Even the locals, jaded to such a sight after all these years, have never bothered to snap a picture of me or any of the women who came before.

MY MOTHER WAS the one who called me back to this town. Like my grandmother and great-grandmother and all the women before them, she fled inland to the blush-brown mountains once she learned of the curse in our bloodline. That escape never lasts, though. Every woman in our lineage was forced to abandon every love found, every child made, every dream achieved, to return to San Clarice when it was her time. I guess I should consider myself lucky that I got to see a little bit of the world and the life I could've had before my mother's voice jolted me back to this place.

There is no ancient and unknowable god in the water, waiting to devour the earth if we fail at some ritual sacrifice. We don't seduce tourists with our long locks and lullabies, dragging them under the waves. There is no cycle beyond the moon's pull of the tide. Our curse—the thing that tethers every woman in my family to this land—is the weight of a vague responsibility to protect this beach, though the origin was lost long ago, washed away by decades of blue-gray waves and clockwork sunrises. Someone has to sit in the little house on the bluff, surveying the cyan water as it swells against gray sky, a pristine patch of sea bookended by encroaching luxury condos and a revamped boardwalk bloated with theme restaurants and lost flip-flops. Someone has to move and blend among the other locals, who will never know my family is the only reason that beer cans and plastic bags haven't devoured this tiny section of coastline.

Like anything left to the water, the girls I release never entirely dissolve. Their hair collects an armor of plastic cutlery and other debris to form the indestructible creatures that chase me back up the bluff to my front door. They arrive at all hours, sometimes right after the girls sink into the Pacific, sometimes in the middle of the night so I awaken to the odor of sulfur-edged seaweed, heavier and more accusing than the brine-kissed sage that has burrowed into my nostrils and pores since my first breath. Like wolf spiders, these hair creatures scurry along door frames and windows, creeping in through the smallest cracks, encircling the couch, the kitchen counter, the chair where I sit facing the window, watching the swirling water as it prepares to cough up more consequences.

All that hair, deep brown laced with auburn and dirty gold when the sun hits just right. There'd been a man who admired those same colors in my own hair, but I left him a thousand miles north, same as my mother left my father before I was even born.

She never spoke of her duty, not even when she was called back by her own mother. As she packed her bags, I asked all the questions that had been crashing against the back of my teeth since I learned of our family's curse, but all my mother would say was that she had to go—there was no choice, and this time I couldn't come.

I wallowed in my memories of building sandcastles and hunting for silver dollars while the women in my family watched from the saltwater-stippled house, their bodies covered and their faces drawn. Even as an adult, I couldn't understand why our visits were so rare when we lived so close to this paradise. My grandmother and I walked together along the water once every three years until I turned fifteen, her sun-vulnerable limbs draped in black crepe like a Victorian widow. She refused swimsuits and dips in the ocean, encouraging my mother and me to enjoy our youth, our unmarred bodies, the way the sun kissed us golden-brown. When I asked her if my mother would be called back here—if I would too one day—all she said was, "You can't break the cycle" before her words became thick and twisted in her mouth. I watched, stunned, as the Pacific raced long arms to us, its waves battering my grandmother's body, her face, stifling her. The ocean lapped up her tears as fast as they came. When she was finally dry, seaweed, leech-green and studded with condom wrappers, poured from her mouth.

My mother never returned to the mountains after my grandmother's death. Her calls and letters became more infrequent as the weeks turned to months then years. She stopped writing, and I moved north. I learned to bake bread and pull espresso. I didn't think about the seaweed or the little house on the bluff or how warm the sand felt between my toes. There were men, and birthdays, and Mothers Days where I avoided flower shops and drugstore card aisles. I eased into the shallow contentment of not thinking about her. Like every woman before me, I became a motherless daughter.

I didn't consider a reunion with my mother, not one that would feel more like a wake. Not until that inexplicable urge struck, that same pull that distracted my mother just before her call came. That nagging feeling like I'd forgotten something, neglected some ineffable task, interrupted days in the café and nights out. Men told me I smelled of salt-bloated breezes and summer-sweetened cypress, and I found myself dashing out of strange beds before I could gather my clothes.

When the call finally came, it was my mother's voice, far away, her words fat and wet and loose on her tongue. I listened, but didn't speak. I was afraid of my own mouth, afraid that my words would come out as seaweed.

MY MOTHER WAS dead when I arrived in San Clarice. A couple from Albuquerque found her face-down on that little stretch of beach a half-mile from the boardwalk, her bare arms outstretched like a snow angel carved in blood-soaked sand. They said they'd been hoping to see the girls drowning themselves in the Pacific, but back then there had only been a handful each year—it was not the phenomenon it is today.

When I went to claim my mother's body, the coroner handed me a condensation-fogged plastic bag containing her black crepe dress. The mortician returned her to me as a box of ashes the same color as the sand.

I gave her remains to the sea then cut myself open for the first time.

I thought I was so clever. None of the women in my family had chosen to be here, accepting a responsibility no one could articulate without their mouths filling with seaweed, their words smothered by ceaseless trash. I understood that nagging weight, how there is no use trying to resist the tide that pulled me back to this stretch of sand and hungry waves that made a home in my bloodline generations ago. The minute my plane had touched down, sage coated my tongue and sea air gritted between my teeth. The mountains my mother had fled to and the city I'd found up north fell away like dead skin before I even made it to the family home on the bluff. I'd sat in that chair by the window, resenting the elephant seals that postured for attention, the pulverized oyster shells that made the sand sparkle under the sun's golden arms. I cursed my mother's name, her acceptance, her mouth full of seaweed and secrets. Why keep birthing daughters into this same fate?

Why not try to end it? San Clarice is in my blood, so why not bleed until that bloodline is gone?

So, standing alone on this perfect stretch of beach, facing the ocean, I took a kitchen knife to my arm. My teeth clenched so tight I thought I might bite through my tongue, but then I found a path between veins and sunk that blade in, slicing in jagged bursts from wrist to elbow. It hurt more than anything I'd ever experienced. The sting of salt mist on the open wound burned and throbbed and reared toward the water as if it was its own animal, a live and galloping birth. Every stitch of clothing I wore was soaked red, but the sand remained silvery, unblemished. I understood then why my ancestors hadn't done this. Until the first girl appeared.

My vision swirled. Woozy with pain and blood loss, I struggled to focus on the girl standing in front of me. She was my height, had my shoulder-length dark hair, the same sloped shoulders and wide hips as all the women in my family. She walked toward the ocean with such purpose that it didn't even occur to me to call out as she stumbled her way into the water. I didn't move, didn't say a word, as she soldiered on, offering herself to the hungry Pacific until all that remained was a jellyfish of auburn-kissed brown hair undulating atop the water.

I didn't tell anyone about the girl or what I'd done. I went back up to the house and dressed my wound. I put on a long-sleeved black crepe blouse I found in the closet and exhaled sulfur and brine into my palm. Out the window, the waves sputtered loud and angry as they licked long swaths of the coast, spitting back broken shells, tiny crab carcasses, the occasional lost fishing line. The girl's hair—all that was left of her—rode every swell, a self-made nest gathering more tourist garbage from up the coast. The ocean was loud, but this new creature was nothing more than a whisper as it made its way up the bluff and back to me.

NINETEEN TODAY.

I stand on a barnacle-crusted log and slice both of my battled-scarred, no-longer-sun-vulnerable arms open and watch nineteen girls pour out of me like so much blood.

You can't break the cycle. My grandmother's warning weighs heavy in my mind every time I do this, but I still feel lightened by dumb hope as I take the blade to my flesh. Garbage and commercial sprawl crowd in, hovering like hungry diners waiting for a table, but this little length of coastline remains as clean and lovely as I remember it from my childhood. Sand crabs traverse tide pools and bleached-bone driftwood, not the ever-expanding peninsula of trash abutting the shore a half mile north. Seagulls alert each other to plump starfish and sandpiper eggs, not French fries and cigarette butts like on the boardwalk. Here, the waves bring back iridescent abalone shells, not whales corseted in derelict fishing nets, gasping on the sand for the relief of death.

Yes, it's selfish that I don't want to do this anymore, that I'm trying to break this cycle. I accepted the call, let that line in my blood draw me back, but a year has been enough to break me. This morning it's nineteen girls; next week it will be twenty.

I watch them make their way to the water and feel a new compulsion to fall in line with them. Let the water swallow me, hips to crown. Let the waves carry back my brine-chewed bones. Let all those nests of hair gather pieces of me as their armor, indestructible filters skating along the bluff and sweeping clean the sand.

But I have no daughters, so, no matter what, the cycle ends with me.

Back at the house, I bandage my new wounds and drape my arms in more black crepe. My body is a map of scars, a jagged topography, the valleys between growing too narrow for even a blade. The women before me were dutiful and kept their bodies as pristine as our beach. Perhaps my grandmother and my mother knew they were bleeding out their ancestry when they cut themselves open on the sand. Perhaps they knew I would succumb to the same futility. My mother left behind all those long sleeves and kitchen knives, either trusting me with this duty or knowing exactly what I would do.

When I crawl into bed, the hair creatures creep in, surrounding me on the floor below. Locks of long dark hair drift and swirl as if still in the water, auburn-studded tentacles splaying in all directions. Some grip bulbous lengths of kelp, pulsing and squeezing until the bulbs pop, sending a milky mist into the air. The scent of eucalyptus fills my room, weightless, as crisp and clean as the cool salt air outside. They are the products of my cycle, the filters that purify and preserve this one last stretch of San Clarice. This is what I protect.

The tourists with their selfish desires and the town council buoyed by myopic greed will never see, never know. Generations of women tried to warn the governing body, even as the seaweed threaded their teeth and jetsam choked their tongues. We vomit up tampon wrappers and hypodermic needles same as the waves do, and still, we are ignored.

All that the locals and the tourists see now is the endless parade of identical girls I make every week. Girls drown and people squeal with a terror that sounds more like delight. They point and snap photos they'll study later, brows knit in confusion and disappointment. That pristine strip of coastline—what should be paradise—is not the story they'll bring home.

I'M WAVING MY arms around, lightheaded, woozy from the pain. It's an exhausting task, cutting through endless ribbons of scar tissue, haphazard layers of collagen resisting before releasing to a bone-deep throbbing that almost eclipses the sear and sting of flesh violently cleaved. I'm sweating and shaking, sounds I don't recognize seeping out from between my teeth. A spectacle if I were anyone else. Blood splatters my face, but all those transfixed eyes and cameras are focused on the twenty girls staggering their way into the ocean.

Gasps of delight crowd the air as the girls sink into the Pacific. Any true terror, any sober moment of "somebody do something!" is smothered by oohs and ahhs and satisfied sighs as shutters click in harmony. Then the disappointed moans once everyone compares shots of sand, surf and sun with no girls in sight.

"Over here!" I shout, jumping up and down. I stumble on the slick rocks, tunnel-vision taking hold. "Look! Right here!"

They're slow to turn, but they do. One by one, crossing the beach, they form a wide arc around me. Palms open, arms turned outward and stigmata still bleeding, I'm the saint beckoning with her last request. It's mostly tourists, people who wandered from the boardwalk once word of the girls moved up the coast. But I recognize some locals: the woman from the post office the next town over, the man who owns the corner store where we overpay for day-old bread and nearly expired milk. Mouths drawing impatient lines, they cross their arms and wait for me to speak or dance or entertain them. Something even more spectacular than twenty girls marching to their deaths in the Pacific.

"It ends here," I announce. "I can't do this anymore, and there's no one after me. There's no one left. I can't hold back—" I gesture north toward the boardwalk, the vacation condos, the peninsula of garbage bobbing against the shore. Dozens of eyes follow as I swing my arm toward the south, where the same sprawl and jetsam creep in. My blood splatters the rocks below. "This is all that's left, and my—" Something thick and bulbous catches in the back of my throat. I cough, sending a wave of cold frothy brine across my tongue. "You have to stop—"

I'm coughing uncontrollably now, wet and salty but thinner than mucus. My tongue recoils from a flood of saltwater as seaweed crawls up my throat, filling my mouth with a mineral tang. Clenching my jaw, I'm crying ocean water—yet another thing I'm struggling to hold back. Then those bulbs surface, pressing against the roof of my mouth until my teeth are forced apart, my jaw popping as the bulbs pass one by one, anchored to their seaweed rope, over my lips and down the front of my shirt. My teeth catch on one, and it bursts, spraying a milky mist as a cascade of bottle caps and shards of plastic clamshell packaging tumble to the sand below.

A murmur ripples through the crowd. I have their attention now, but there are no shocked faces, no brows furrowed with concern; this is just another party trick to the people gathered around me. A woman raises her phone to snap a photo. Then another, and another. Again, I try to speak, but it's just more bottle caps and now the mealy copper—raw, animal, steaming with a heat so solid I could chew through it—of my torn gums. A man in an upside-down visor unwraps a neon-red Popsicle and drops the plastic sheath onto the sand.

More seaweed, plastic, a flotilla of used condoms spill onto the sand. My mouth stays full with the same garbage that chokes the Pacific on either side of this stretch of San Clarice.

I can't speak, so I point.

Behind the crowd, surfacing against the pull of the waves, hundreds of nests of hair crawl out of the water onto the beach. Threaded with auburn and dirty gold, I know they are mine, the girls I released. But there are new nests this time, ones I haven't seen before: sunburnt sable like my mother's hair, more gray than brown like my grandmother's, white patched with translucent strands like my great-grandmother's. They come together on the sand, an undulating army gathering plastic bottles and candy wrappers and the other endless garbage from the waters already ruined.

The crowd gasps, cameras flash. Under their hungry eyes, these new, impossible beings are yet another attraction to be shared for clicks and "likes."

Video rolls, even as these ravenous hair creatures sweep over people's feet, toppling them into the sand as they consume the rubber flip-flops and the bottle caps and other detritus that fell from my mouth.

Then the screaming, everyone screaming as so much exposed skin puckers, cracks, dries to leather, as the creatures filter people's blood into clean water for the ocean to reclaim. But the waves are louder, hungrily chewing the shoreline. Seagulls swirl above me, the Pacific endlessly slurps, the sand shifts as it thickens with my own blood. There should be a stampede as those left standing attempt escape, but all I feel is the warm sand absorbing me as I fall into it.

No more girls emerge from my wounds, but their remnants shuffle down from the house on the bluff. I can't see them, but I hear these hair creatures even above the waves, washing lamb-soft over my face, my sticky arms, my legs speckled milk-white and green.

I sigh, finally relieved, breathing in sulfur and breathing out sage and eucalyptus with the creatures' undulations. As they strip my body and clean my bones, I think about the generations of women who have given themselves to a shrinking San Clarice, all for this moment. For this summer-sweetened cypress carried by a tide so crystalline it brings back only polished stones, ancient shells, and thriving sea life.

What this place once was.

⚓

SUNK

Richard Thomas

...AND WHEN I turn the corner away from main street, barefoot
and naked, scratched and bruised, several miles east of the
compound and its wooden fence running the perimeter, thick
woods hiding the structure from prying eyes, and finally glimpse
the endless ocean with its oily patches shimmering in the distance, relief washes over me in waves of heat and cold, but I
know it's only a matter of time before they're aware that I've
run, that I've sent letters to major newspapers and law enforce-
ment documenting the rituals and brainwashing and abuse, the
love bombs that filled my emptiness for so long, the burial pit
inside the damp cave lined with bones, just one of many horrors,
memories of weeping in the darkness, of voices calling out for
help, for succor—never trusting what called to us from the
expanding gloom with its gibbering tongue and chortling gut—
and my eyes dart left and right looking for people, for threats,
for danger, the seaside shanties and shacks around me an empty

resort town in the off-season, bustling when the tourists come
to play but today filled with only shadows and a sour breeze, a
creeping claustrophobia more alive than dead as the sun sets
over the glistening waters, the golden orb that is my goal, the
glowing sphere I'm trying to beat to the surface of the ocean,
running as fast as I can, legs aching already, tightening up, a
stitch in my side, pain from the infected sutures, violated when
I removed the tiny blinking metal device in an alley not fifteen
minutes ago, screaming and tossing the bloody disc to the
ground as I covered the wound, trying to rub away the pain,
trying to understand the lengths they went to in order to track
and monitor me, the rotten stench of fish heads filling the air,
amorphous gelatinous blobs in every nook and cranny, every
surface coated with buzzing flies and twisting maggots, and a
heatwave of confusion, the last of the storefronts fading behind
me now, the outline of silhouetted dock workers posed like
mannequins ahead, some in yellow slickers and galoshes despite
the absence of rain, unmoving, caught in some deviant act, their
arms filled with boxes, some bent over, others stuttering as if
unsure how to move, as if waiting for the software update, the
buffering pixelating their appearance, wondering what to do
next, their long gazes turned to me, dull eyes filled with an
expanding void as I sprint for the ravaged beach, past the twisted
driftwood, piles of furry decay, and mossy undulations, past
black timbers burnt from some disaster, down the shore through
violet morning glories between the creeping vines and thorny
leaves that wind across the dunes, the boardwalk rattling under
my feet, lose nails and curved, faded boards all under the watchful gaze of the seaside mansion that crumbles on the hill—siding
splintered, spires rusting, windows broken—towering over the
salt marshes that line the decaying waterfront, the cordgrass
and needlerush swaying in the cooling breeze, the crooked
house looking down on it all—judging, laughing, sneering,
dying—its rooms lit up with a sickly yellow glow as behind it
gaudy luxury hotels are slowly reclaimed by the sea, the salt and
wind picking at the exterior of these fading relics, drifts of sand
pushing up against the tilting walls and under the doors, the

greed of capitalism dying in these abandoned husks, as sweat
coats my body like a fever, a second skin, a maddening itch
spreading across my flushed skin, something I am trying to
shed while in the distance there are gulls and herons at the edge
of the water, hopping and pecking at the rotting seaweed, pulling
out something pink and elastic, snapping it in two before gob-
bling down the slimy, twitching morsel, while not far away a
red-bellied woodpecker digs furiously at a downed tree trunk,
searching for beetles and grubs or anything that squirms, ignoring the sound of my footsteps, which send a mutiny of tiny
orange fiddler crabs scuttling over the land and into cracks and
holes, disappearing as if they were never there, and I close my
eyes for just a second, the inside of my eyelids quickly filled
with iridescent scales, slick white flesh, her sharp teeth overflowing a mouth with red lips turning up slowly into a smile,
and I hear her song, her call, something that has kept me up for
weeks now—promises and warnings, predictions and fears,
offerings and demands—and exhaustion weighs me down, the
growing clutch of tiny turquoise eggs in my bloated belly jostling
back and forth, filling me up, leaking out of the tear in my side
now as I murmur Not yet and limp and stumble and push my
way forward, knowing this has to end one way or another—a
sense of failure wrapped in a feeling of completion dipped in a
greasy layer of uncertainty—hearing the water smash against
the dock, sending foam and detritus into the air with every
violent movement, slamming into the shore and then retreating,
crystal blue water turning to indigo and then to pitch black as
the light fades, and then the shouting comes, torches and bodies
back by the arcades that are lit up now—filled with the ringing
bells of prizes won, beeps that repeat incessantly as buttons are
mashed and joysticks turned, gunshots that exhale silver bullets,
glowing lasers buzzing across space and time, alien ships that
disappear and then reappear with authority—the traps set,
moths to the flame, as the rest of the disciples swarm toward
the beach, the crack of heat lightning cleaving the sky, and then
they shift, as they often do—skeletons lit up like neon signs,
several tipping over and breaking into smaller pieces that scatter

across the dirt and sand, a few lowering onto all four limbs as they gallop forward, tongues lolling out of their fetid grins as they pant and growl and whine, webbed feet slapping against the wet sand—and ahead of me is a transitionary zone, red tide and pink foam frothing at the place where land meets water, the angry disciples trying to stop my advancement, to silence my filthy mouth, to make sure that what has infected me is spread across the land like a disease, it is their primary goal, their overflowing desire, but my intentions are something else entirely, a singular hope in the deep, dark, rippling waters, and out on the sand shoals by the rocky cliffs, whose ragged edges and missing chunks make them appear as if something has taken a bite out of them, chewed and spat-out rocks and boulders with an eternal indifference, the entrance to the harbor and bay opens up to me—and standing there is a solitary elderly woman hunched and broken, her long gray hair blowing in the wind, casting out her rod and pulling the line in, stopping every now and then to raise a conch shell to her chapped lips and weathered mouth before she pushes out a throaty call, the bucket at her feet filled with squirming, jumping flesh, her waders buried deep in the muck as the darkness expands and encroaches on the quiet town, only the lonely lighthouse standing in defiance, red stripes running around the pristine white pillar, watching it all unfold as its beacon splits the night, rolling this way and that, and blood rises up in my throat, spilling over and out in a cough of red mist, leaking from my ears, rivulets running down my face and out of my nose and into my gasping mouth, the hatching due any minute now, those tiny beaks and clawed fins already tearing at my organs and skin, and, fearful that I am too late, I sprint down the dock with heavy, plodding footsteps, a rusty nail sticking up sharp and defiant in the rising moonlight, piercing my sole, forcing a weak yelp paired with hot tears, their gaze on me now from the beach, burning with desire as they accelerate toward me with arms and legs akimbo, knocking each other over as they yell and pant and bark and cry, spilling over the shore and toward the water, multiplying as they go, and my stomach churns, every joint throbbing with pain, my head filled with sawdust and shards of broken glass, my soles leaving bloody footprints all the way to the end of the swaying dock, and they aren't going to get here in time, so I laugh—remembering a small farmhouse in the middle of Missouri, the faded red barn holding pitchforks and wheelbarrows, rakes and shovels, shameful acts and dark deeds; a small farmhouse where my mother stands on the front porch, drying her hands on her frilly apron and wishing me luck, a black Labrador sitting by her side, panting in the heat and thumping its tail on the wood over and over again, my father long dead and buried (good riddance to bad rubbish), her face flushed and full of worry as I leave the only mother I've ever had, her outdated views and closed mind abandoned at the end of that winding gravel road nestled back in the woods, tucked away like a secret never to be seen again—and my laughter changes into a wave of sweaty fear, and then I'm diving into the cold water, caught in the still night air for just a moment before penetrating the freezing liquid, the jarring sensation turning my skin numb, the only sound my erratic heart pounding drum- beats in my chest across copper tympani and rattling snares, a red trail of suffering drifting up behind me as I furiously swim down into the murky depths, a swarm of jellyfish in all of their translucent glory drifting overhead as if migrating across a never-ending blue sky, and beyond them there is a gathering of black, spiny sea urchins that slowly descend all around me like depth charges dropped by a passing ship, as well as schools of tiny yellow fish gathering together under the assumption that there is safety in numbers, and then the singular lantern light from the approaching depths dangling at the end of a long crooked appendage, the behemoth's shiny scales reflecting in the expanding gloom, its bluntly rounded head holding two black glimmering eyes, its terminal mouth filled with row after row of tiny teeth, and in the shadows behind it there is a flurry of movement—flowing hair and swishing tails, slicing fins and treading arms, blinking eyes and bubbled exhalations, and below that, the skeletal remains of sunken fishing trawlers, tugboats torn in half, square-rigged vessels and tall ships with their masts snapped in two, rusted cannons and bent anchors, splintered hulls pierced by long mottled tentacles with suckers on the underside of each limb, schools of long-necked barracudas swimming in and out and around the swaying structures as they grin in their swooning madness, a carpet of green algae covering the decks, barnacles and tubeworms scattered over the hulls—and I'm disappearing, letting it all go, the little glow that is left in this world fading to black as the leviathan opens its gaping maw, welcoming me into its eternal embrace, ending my infection with a violent snap—closing, swallowing, chewing, gnashing—ingesting the latest crop of warped offspring, the eggs snapping and popping as I'm torn limb from limb, this batch at least gone and eaten, filtered out into the ocean as nothing more than organic waste to fertilize the lesser species, feeding the food web that covers the sea floor, the seaweed and coral reef, my memory erased in a matter of moments as back on the shore the cult gathers, hidden in a thick, toxic, rolling fog that engulfs man and coastline in equal amounts, staring out into the night, out past the water and my humble offering, their eyes to the horizon and beyond, angry and unfulfilled: a relatively minor setback, but a setback nonetheless.

⚓

THUMBS UP

Anna Lewis

Lucy: hi guys

what do you think of this place

can book now and free cancellation

Lucy: [*shared a link*]

Rob: [*thumbs_up*]

Sarah: Looks lovely thanks for finding!

Nick: will check dates with work again

sunday to sunday?

Lucy: the sea's right at the end of the garden

can just hang out on the beach

go on walks

it'll be a nice break from everything

[water_wave]

Lucy

warmed Sarah up first, knows Sarah's the one people listen to
told everyone to get the 10.32 Sunday train but nobody
listened so,
is arriving first at the house, looking in the lockbox, checking
her phone for the code, keying it in once then twice, breathing
in through her teeth,
tries again and gets it right
experiences most of the holiday like this, a series of terse
attempts followed by brief happy success, like it's one of the
games on her phone where she matches colors together or draws
a line between two points

Sunday

Lucy: have set house key lock box to our 3rd year house number

Sarah: Why the code hahaha we're the only ones who can see this

Lucy: idk what if someone read over our shoulders!

and broke in!

I'd get a bad review

Sarah: ok well I never actually lived there so

Rob: 138b

Nick: guessing you left off the b though

Lucy: no I turned it into a 2

Sarah: ffs lol

Lucy: sorry Sarah

you were over so much

watches the others splash into the water and takes her phone out for pictures and for a moment forgets to be sad, just like that, how nice, then Nick runs up to chat and drips cold water everywhere and she's flinching away and she's back again

doesn't like how the boys speak to each other, how they use aggression as a joke, a form of bonding, thinks after everything maybe they would have learned to be nicer to each other,

Nick: menu for the pub

Nick: *[shared an image]*

Rob: this is blurred to shit

how did you make a photo misty

Sarah: loooool

Lucy: thanks nick!

used to sit next to (don't think it) in the pub with the insults flying past her and think, is this really how you show love to each other,

is trying not to think about that as she watches the supermarket exit for her friends, trying to push down her anger because she's lost her one person and she should be less alone here, but they arrived late and they made her wait outside with the beach stuff and they're taking ages with the shopping and they're pricks, they're all selfish pricks,

Monday

Nick: nearly done out soon Lucy hope that's ok

Got caught up

Lucy: no worries!!

Sarah: Rob not doing great

Monthiversary breakdown

Lucy: awww

Take as much time as you need

[red_heart] [red_heart] [red_heart]

feels in general a bit destabilized because everything is different here, at home she lies in bed texting Sarah most evenings, frowning at her screen in the dark and typing *on my fifth episode, I'm obvs not coming, enjoy*

but on this holiday has been staying up later and later with Rob and now he tells her about his childhood, about that funny scar on his leg, they talk and talk,

can see a name pooling in his mouth and that's when she stands and says they should sleep,

can't bear the salt lick of it

on that subject, can't believe anyone would need to realize it's a monthiversary, death-day mark five, Rob with his girlfriend who's still alive and doesn't know how lucky he is for that, doesn't even count the months

knows that lunar rhythm better than her actual period now—weird comparison—but thinks there's something in that, how women do that work of marking the tides, of holding the space for a repeated pain, how each time the blood comes and reminds her it's been another month she looks down at it blankly and thinks *how hasn't it stopped,* which is illogical

tries to remind herself that maybe it's different because he was just their friend, he wasn't their day-to-day like he was for her, it's their weekends that have shattered not their evenings and mornings,

thought this holiday would help them all forget for a bit, a change, but since Rob brought it up (on the first day! Get it together!) she's seen red ribbons in the sea-waves,

doesn't know how to fix her head once it's been said, it's not like they're in a new place anymore, it's like they're in the same place with different scenery and there's still one person gone,

and now wonders why the others can't see how weird Nick is getting, on holiday with them but disappearing for hours at a time, it's obviously a warning sign isn't it, and she can't watch another boy crack out of their lives but she also can't be the one smoothing him over,

was already waking up at night to a sound that can only be described as gargling, must be something in the pipes,

doesn't know any more how to make brunch as if no one died, how to wait for Nick to get back from his walk as if she doesn't spend every moment he's out of sight wondering if he's still alive,

steps away from the onion she's chopping, pretending that's what prickles her eyes,

is the first of them to sink, unprotestingly, into the sea.

Rob

finds the house funny, a kind of budget horror-movie aesthetic, which is so ironic considering the circumstances

does his best to record it all, the elaborately framed family photograph askance in the bathroom, the two driftwood antlers jutting from a cold glass-eyed deer head

is lying on the beach listlessly scrolling his phone for people to send the video to, but the person who'd have really got it is, well, permanently offline, so,

sends it to the group chat, next best thing, bless them,

Tuesday

Rob: *[shared a video]*

Rob: guys lol I took a shaky shot of the hall and it literally looks like pre-jumpscare

Sarah: whats going to come up there lol

Rob: Nick in his hand towel

Sarah: you wish you could see that again

You were praying for ballsack

Lucy: rather not think about nicks ballsack thanks

Nick: there is something weird about this place

Lucy: yeah

I keep finding seaweed in the drains

Rob: no that's just nicks pubes

Lucy: I will literally leave this chat pls stop!!!!

never really had friends before he met James, had mates instead, but with this lot it's different

keeps annoying Lucy and goading Nick and making Sarah laugh, because that's how it's always been, doesn't know what else to do

keeps staying up late with Lucy too, Nick gets up early for long seaside runs and Sarah gets snappy with Lucy when she's tired so it's just the two of them left getting creeped out by the creaks in the house that keep them awake, talking about anything, thinking about James but not saying his name,

is trying not to have another breakdown which by the way is not the word he'd use, just because he got too emotional, the girls are always telling him to be more emotional and then he does it and they call it a breakdown, fuck that, he's allowed to think about it sometimes

has loved Sarah for a longer than she knows, back in uni with
the smoke machine going and two VKs in each hand watching
her across the room,

now picks moist not-quite-clean fish bones out of her hair
in the mornings and lays them along the windowsill, doesn't
say this but he thinks they came from him somehow, because
at night it feels like there's something bad in his body but
when he wakes up in the mornings for a few breaths he feels
fresh, clean,

Lucy: seriously guys I found shells in my bed

if you're pranking me this is gross

they're really sharp I could have cut myself :(

Nick: genuinely no

Rob: yeah idk

Sarah: probably just tracked in from the beach

Lucy: this much???

Lucy: [*shared an image*]

Lucy: Wtf

agreed with her they couldn't tell anyone, even when Lucy
brings up the weird shit too—because how do you make sense
of something like that, how do you convince the others that
you're really not pranking, that when you took that video of
the stairs you were genuinely half-waiting for a corpse to flop
out of the ceiling,

could swear he can smell death rolling in from the ocean
right now, something dank and festering even on this bright
day, and some part of not-quite him wants to follow the smell
to its source,

wants to see the corpse

lies on the beach imagining if Sarah died, how he'd have to cry at the funeral even if he just felt numb, how he'd never be the same,

wonders how it would happen—something in his mind is catching on the idea of a head cracking open, like an egg, because they're so fragile, so gloopy inside, even though there was none of that when James died, he looked so intact, like he was barely even dead,

Wednesday

Lucy: [*shared an image*]

Lucy: Can I put these on insta?

Sarah: [*thumbs_up*]

Nic: [*thumbs_up*]

Rob: not the one of me and sar
others r fine

Lucy: what why, you look so cute

Sarah: Almost looks like we're in love lol
Got a secret girlfriend youre hiding me from?

Rob: lol
No my face just looks moody

feels sick when he thinks about if she knew he was imagining this, her head heavy and peaceful on his chest as they lie in the sun, but it's a way of making sure he cares, isn't it, you have to check how you'd feel if people died, it makes you appreciate them more,

has been doing this a lot as a way of making sure he doesn't miss anything, finds it exhausting but doesn't know how to ask anyone else if they're doing the same or if not how they stop themselves,

thought he'd feel less alone here but if anything it's worse, the house is small and cramped but they look at each other like they're far away,

thinks about bringing it up at the pub and at the waterpark and in the smoking area of the grotty seaside club but just can't,

has been here before, knows what it's like, you see someone getting worse and you want to tell them you're their mate but every time it comes out as another misstep, another piss-take

slips, too, shocked by the cold skin sting, into the sea.

Sarah

pretended to forget about booking the 10.32 train so she could read on the 11.15 instead, but somehow Rob and Nick follow her lead, fuck's sake

hates being in a group on trains, the fact is they're a five and a table seats four,

remembers, fuck, that they're not a five anymore, thinks, *woo! first group train journey without him! a new death milestone!*

thinks to herself it's selfish to top yourself in those circumstances really, depriving her of a good excuse for alone time, because now on the train they're—this is the entire problem—a three

spends the whole time feeling grudgingly responsible for the start-of-holiday vibe because Rob and Nick don't actually know how to speak to each other without someone else between them, they can do triangles, squares, pentagons, but not straight lines, boys only relate in 2D

wishes the others got dark humor, they're all so delicate, even Rob gets randomly set off these days, freaking out at the sell-by date on a packet of ham because it's the sad number,

really doesn't know how to process that if she can't laugh about it, certainly can't cry about it

doesn't miss uni, gets groped less now, is friends with fewer men who act like children,

is still friends with all the same men of course, but they've changed, these same men, they've grown up

thought this holiday would help them all figure out who they are now, like they're introducing themselves to each other anew, *hello my name is Sarah and one thing we have in common is a dead friend*, but there's no banter, if they met now like this they wouldn't be friends

has been launching herself into the water every time she gets a chance, at least when they're in the sea everything feels lighter, like their *what-if-I'd-stopped-him* memories are floating too, a string of missed opportunities like pool floats around them

thinks every time she can reason her way into the cold but it turns out the only way is to dive, while Rob shivers up to his neck and Nick takes slow thoughtful steps and Lucy, weirdo, worries about tidal currents and stays on the shore,

doesn't understand why the others don't need this, to swim hard until their gasps sound like sobs

isn't sure if James was really her friend so much as a group-friend, a friend-of-friends, which means actually it's very self-aggrandizing of her to care that he died, which means her fascination with the others' grief is actually macabre and sensationalist, because if she felt proper grief she would be going through it like them, whatever the fuck is going on with them,

has been trying to get Lucy to bring it up for months now, poking her like a pufferfish, but every time she hints Lucy dodges, and she remembers: she's the support, not the main character, so she doesn't get to bring it up outright

can't remember the last time she didn't feel brittle, dried out, like her life had been packed in salt,

Friday

Lucy: where u?

Sarah: smoking area
Rob a bit sick

Lucy: what on like 6 units?
on my own at bar

Sarah: units?? lmao

there used to be a moisture to nights out, a sparkling dewiness—of course, after all the slow beach days and messy dinners together she's ready to act young again, but that's all it ever is these days, an act watches Nick slip out the back of the smoking area and mostly just feels annoyed, they came here to spend time together and he's off on these dramatic sojourns alone, if he's got something on his mind why doesn't he fucking talk to her,

Rob: sorry yeah idk what happened
Sarahs looking for you
Thought Nick was with you

Lucy: What I thought he was with you?

Rob: lol is he getting off with someone

Lucy: No seriously though @Nick?

Lucy: [*missed voice call from Lucy*]

Nick: chill I'm just in smoking area

Rob: no youre not lolllll

Nick: Ill find you when im done dw

Rob: get IN

half-knows when she sees him later he'll have sand in his shoes, he came into the kitchen dead of night when she was getting water, made this weird susurrating howling noise, looked right through her,

doesn't tell the others because their worrying is annoying her, lightning doesn't strike the same place twice does it, it's not like they're cursed,

despite all that isn't surprised when, in a moment of lucidity, she opens her eyes to see water dragging at her sodden clothes,

does surprise herself by thinking, *of course it came for me too.*

Nic

thinks it's weird to go on holiday so soon after James's death

has been trying to come up with metaphors, like, your parents are divorcing and when the papers come through they take you to that childhood holiday spot to rehearse their best arguments,

tries to text it to a friend from home: *its like the this is fine meme but they're not even sat still they're toasting marshmallows on the fire*

checks his phone when it buzzes back but it's only saltwater trickling out of the gaps in the case

never liked haunted house stories, doesn't understand why a ghost would confine itself to a building when the whole point is they can go through walls,

starts to understand on this holiday though that a place can feel like a fulcrum of bad vibes,

imagines one of those charity donation buckets where the penny spirals enticingly downward before dropping except the penny is discomfort, unhappiness, the potential for madness and the dissolution of self

doesn't remember much of last night but knew Rob wasn't drunk enough to throw up, they all knew that, he hurled as if it was off the side of a ferry, as if his inner balance was confused by the roiling of the waves, and some time after that is when his memory goes weird felt a grim satisfaction watching it though, the guy's barely reacted to James dying, there's laddish and then there's heartless

Saturday

Nick: the sea is so loud

How is no one awake

Does everyone else have sudden onset quadraplegism

Lucy: not a word

also I think offensive?

Sarah: ??? Not a real word nick

Nick: so you are up

Rob: we are in BED because we are HUNGOVER

Sarah: *[replied to Lucy at 11.23 a.m.]* Snap lolllll

Sarah: yeh Im out of action

Sarah: *[shared an image]*

Sarah: this was Rob 10 min ago lol

Nick: its really loud though right???

like the waves but close

it's like

slosh

slosh

krkrkrrrsplosh

right in your ears

Sarah: no

Interpretative though thanks

Nick: ok well im going for a walk

was too young when most of his grandparents died to remember much except for Granny who in his head is a comforting mass of soft wrinkles and Dr Seuss books, not an actual fucking friend, a mind who is now missing, who made arch eye contact in seminars and ate supermarket pizza on his bedroom floor,

hasn't thought about that in a while, five of them in his room failing to agree on a film every Sunday, these days he suggests something and Lucy and Rob don't want to argue so Sarah gets overruled—the balance is all fucked but no one's acknowledged it yet,

hears the pebbles louder every night though so starts agreeing with Sarah about poppier films, the louder and brighter the better, and it turns out Lucy likes romcoms which is all the better because people rarely die in romcoms

Sarah: Can u let us know your eta @Nick. lucy and rob are doing brunch

Lucy: [shared an image]

Rob: nick u r making me cry

jokes its just the onions

Lucy: nick are you coming back??

Lucy: [missed voice call from Lucy]

Lucy: slosh

slosh

krkrkrrrsplosh

Rob: nick

Sarah: fuckj

come back

Rob: [*missed voice call from Rob*]

Sarah: [*missed voice call from Sarah*]

Sarah: [*missed voice call from Sarah*]

Sarah: [*missed voice call from Sarah*]

can't fathom it, how one moment James was a person and the next moment he wasn't, and what makes people people anyway, what is it that made James that isn't here anymore, it doesn't make sense,

offers his pondering as an invitation and the sea takes it, takes him over, drags him out of bed at night to sprint along the sand,

thinks about how many shores the sea laps at, all the beaches he's never seen and never will, and how it's deeper than he can know and dark with secrets,

says to the air *ok cool so haunt me do you think you can do worse,*

can't imagine worse than this: your friend is on the edge of something previously unspeakable, and you fail to pull them back

watches three other friends around him splinter like wet wood, and doesn't know where the danger is coming from any more

hears the calling of the sea like a long-lost friend

follows all of them, in the end.

Lucy

Yes

I mean is that Lucy

I mean I am Lucy

Sarah?

Yes and Nick, Rob,

what happened

got swallowed
swallowed yeah by the waves
where am I
can't breathe
don't panic
need to stay together
can't
we're all here
it's ok
Lucy, Rob, Sarah, Nick,
and oh god
You
You
You
You
Yes
You
I mean is that you
I mean I am you
Where am I
we?
You?
Where am we?
What is we?
You?
YOU!
why did you leave
where did you go

are we with you

are we

we?

are we you

are you

you?

I mean I am

yes

miss you

yes

miss we

miss you

why

are you

here

you're our

silence

swallowed

got swallowed

we

know

forgive you

want you back

all the time

in between us

and your laugh too

can't

we

know
can't
stay
no
you?
are you
are we with you
where did you go
I mean I am you
slosh
slosh
krkrkrkrrrsplosh

Lucy, Rob, Sarah, and Nick

wash up on the shore in a tumultuous rumbling of water and lie there for minutes that could be hours, saltwater clinging their clothes to their skin, cold and clammy and still, until they
start reaching out for each other, checking they're okay, calling names with throats too salt-dry or too full of the sea, rolling onto hands and knees and standing with a weak crunch on the pebble.
talk at first in stops and starts about what happened.
increasingly talk about it and much more besides, in a conversation that begins like the tentative patter of rain and continues like rivulets gathering into a river, into the sea.
don't know what sunken spirit thing they each—all—encountered, but between them
make the carrying of an impossibility go from wrong to right, look each other in the eyes and say *yes, I felt it too.*
take it not as a haunting but as a turning of the weather,
resolve to mark these strange tides for however long it takes, to float in grief together.

⚓

EACH-UISGE

Dave V. Riser

JAIME'S ADDING OIL to the lantern of the lighthouse when he sees the creature crawl out of the ocean. The light shines on the great, writhing dark thing upon the sand, visible even so far from the beach. It's gone before he's sure he saw anything. Late at night, you see a lot of things that aren't really there.

Jaime often wonders how it might feel to be surrounded by ether and chaos on the deck of a rocking ship, searching for any hint of the mainland. He wonders if Thomas stares into the darkness when he's on watch, if Thomas pictures the darkness looking back at him. If Thomas thinks of him.

Jamie sees the creature and then he blinks and sees the absence of the creature, a bright spot on the back of his eyelids.

He finishes feeding the light, walks down the spiral of stairs, and returns the oil canister to its place. Outside, there's nothing. Grass, rocks, the storage shed with the oil house behind it, and the edge of the headland. The lighthouse throws its steady beacon across the clear, dark sky.

The fixed light extends almost twenty miles out to sea, but behind him, Jaime can't spot even a single candle-lit window in the main Keeper's house, half a mile inland. The distant town is only a memory in the darkness. Still, he feels watched as he walks from the tower to the oil house and back.

It's not unwelcome.

FROM THE LANTERN at the top of the tower, Jaime watches for dawn. When the first rosy fingers extend, he goes to bed, falling into his cot in the empty room of the storage building.

He wakes mid-afternoon to the sound of the head keeper, George M. Wilson, returning from town. There are supposed to be three keepers to mind the light, but they've had trouble retaining a third man—one was lost to drink, another to a better paying and less isolated job. Now it's just him and George doing one and a half jobs each. They alternate nights off until the days blur into their own distinct patterns, time no longer measured in weeks or even months. On his nights off, George stays in the main house with his wife and children, two sons and a daughter. Jaime tries not to hate him for it.

Jaime takes a moment to shove on his boots—wearing thin—before he goes out to help George bring in the supplies.

"Mornin'," George says when Jaime emerges. He's leaning against their wagon, shirtsleeves rolled up.

Jaime keeps his eyes level, allows himself half a smile in return. It's well past morning.

"I've brought back your favorite; Anna sends her regards." George winks.

Jaime looks down, pretending to be flustered. Somehow George has got it in his head that Jaime has the time and the inclination to court the cashier at their dusty general store.

"As long as she gave us the flour without weevils in it this time," Jaime says. "Or are the weevils what you mean by 'her regards'?"

George laughs, which is kind of him. The words weren't smart or fast enough to warrant it. George M. Wilson is a large, warm man, quick to laugh and quicker to smile, with rough hands that Jaime feels the heat of even when George is half a mile away.

"Any trouble with the lantern?" George asks, handing him a parcel.

Jaime hefts it; it feels like a cut of salt pork. It's better than hardtack. "None to speak of," he says. "How's Mrs. Wilson? And Jera and the boys?"

"All fine. Jera's been bothering me to come see the lantern. She's been reading about the different lenses at the library, apparently. Wants to take a look." He shakes his head.

"Mmm." Jaime doesn't see what harm it would do to let the girl into the tower, but he doesn't say it. George has a look on his face like it should be self-evident, like he's sharing a joke with him. Jera is nearly fifteen, Jaime thinks. Old enough to stay out of trouble, but maybe George is worried she'll fall. "Any good gossip?"

George laughs again. "I'll tell you over dinner. Anna about talked my ear off, the things she'd heard this week."

Jaime shakes his head, rueful, and sets about unloading the wagon into the other half of the storage shed. The wind picks up, throwing his hair into his face.

"What's that smell?" George asks, suddenly.

Jaime breathes in deep; there's something too sweet on the air, like something rotten on the beach, all salt-tang decay.

Together, he and George circle the building, seeking the source.

On the side of the storage shed that faces the sea, Jaime discovers a crumpled shape. Flies buzz above the shiny viscera. He thinks that the thing used to be a dog, but it's now a pulped, fleshy thing.

"Must've been wolves," George says, shaking his head. "Better be careful this evening."

Jaime tries to believe him. He can still see the dark shape on the beach. It could have been a wolf. It could have been anything.

They bury the dog, then finish unloading the wagon. George is quieter now, the air gone tense. When Jaime starts hauling blocks of salt pork and flour into the storage house, George follows him in and closes the door hard behind them. The proximity makes Jaime's pulse flutter in his neck, which he ignores.

Jaime moves by rote. The flour goes on the middle shelf, pork on the top.

"I'll send Jera with the rifle," George says. "You should keep it with you tonight. Wolves will rip down the door to get in at you, you know." He bends to move a box to the lowest shelf.

"They must be getting bold," Jaime says.

"Or desperate."

JAIME USED TO follow Thomas around something awful. His mother called them thick as thieves, but it was more that where Thomas ended, Jaime began. They were neighbors growing up, with Thomas only a five-minute walk down the road. Accessible and inevitable.

These days, Jaime follows George around instead, learning the ins and outs of lighthouse keeping: signals for different weather disasters, how to gauge a ship's speed from afar, how long hardtack will keep if you need it to. Jaime tries not to mind the drudgery. He watches George. Can't help himself. The way George's shoulders strain against his flannel shirts, his rough sailor's hands, his full, dark beard.

When George's children are around, Jaime keeps his eyes to himself. Once, he'd turned to find the daughter, Jera, standing with them. Watching, quietly, so quietly that Jaime had started at the sight of her, believing her an apparition for an absurd moment.

Late nights, or days when the weather is foul, George tells him stories to pass the time. Sometimes ghost stories, but more often he repeats snatches of lives lived in town, of his wife's family, what it was like when he was a young Navy man.

"Honest work," he'd said one night early in Jaime's tenure at the light. Both of them were hauling oil to the top of the stairs while the wind screamed outside and the tower swayed. "Good men, for the most part. When you get tired of this mess, you could enlist." Then he'd glanced up, caught a glimpse of Jaime's face, and his expression had changed. For just a second.

Jaime unpracticed, had only enough breath to keep standing. He looked down at his hands on the canister, not yet callused. His and George's shadows were intertwined on the stairs, stark against the brilliant light at the top of the tower.

"The things you see," George had said. "The world's a bigger place than you can believe, Jaime. And it's good work, too. They take care of you."

It was more or less what Thomas had said, once upon a time. *You and the sea and the strength in your arms, and your brothers.* When Thomas had said *brothers*, he'd traced a finger over Jaime's pulse.

"I get seasick," is what Jaime said to George, after far too long a pause. A testament to his character, George had laughed.

LATER, JERA COMES by with the rifle. It's huge in her small hands, but there's something about the cold steel that matches the set of her mouth.

"Your mother let you carry this?" Jaime's too surprised to remember to be silent.

"Yes. And shoot it, sometimes." She must be at least fifteen, caught between the frank manner of childhood and the adult set of her shoulders. Jaime wonders for a moment if a passerby might think that they were related: two thin, dark-haired things staring awkwardly at each other.

"I see." Jaime doesn't. He takes the rifle and leans it against the wall beside the door, the muzzle pointed away from them both.

Jera peeks around him, taking in his cramped living quarters.

"Why do you live all the way out here?" she asks, her gaze meeting his own steadily. There are extra rooms for a third keeper back at the main Keeper's quarters, where George's family run a modest garden and tend goats.

Jaime nearly bites his own tongue.

"I prefer it," he says, after too long a moment. "The quiet."

"My father isn't a quiet man, but you seem to like him well enough." Her eyes are sharp, made sharper by the cold gray of her irises.

Jaime tries to reply, but he can feel himself flushing, his throat closing up.

As if he had answered, Jera nods to herself. "It must be lonely out here, is all," she says, not quite an apology.

Jaime watches her walk home down the dirt trail until it turns to dense evergreens, shadows swallowing her form. It's too bad that she wasn't born a boy. It would suit her better, he thinks.

IT TAKES HIM hours to calm himself after she leaves. He must get better at keeping his eyes down. He'd applied for a stag light, but the lighthouse commission had needed him here instead. Next season, they'd said, when we have more men. He still has the letter. He tries to reread it as the night darkens, but his eyes won't focus. This close to the lighthouse, the sound of the foghorn cuts right through Jaime's narrow frame.

All he can picture is the shadow of the thing crawling out from the ocean. It must have been big to be visible from as high up as the lantern. Big enough that a rifle would be a mere bee sting, only enough to make the thing angry. Big enough that it couldn't possibly exist.

"It wasn't there," Jaime says to himself, out loud. Nothing was there.

THE WEATHER TURNS. The first bad winter storm of the season, with raging winds and a shipping vessel wrecking a few miles offshore at the worst possible point. Jaime and George don't even get rest during the day. The rain keeps coming, and the fog rolls in. They badly need a third assistant keeper.

One night, hauling the oil canister with George, Jaime drops it on his foot before even mounting the steps. Abruptly, George jerks back, hefting the canister on his own.

"Get," George says, and Jaime flinches at his tone. "Take a night off."

"George—"

"I'll take tomorrow. It'll be fair. Don't worry your head about it."

Jaime's face burns. Don't worry your head about it, like he's a woman or a boy, to be so easily dismissed. Without another word, he turns and walks out of the tower.

The rain is worse outside, but without the screaming winds it's bearable. He means to walk to his room, to try for some sleep, but frustration bubbles inside him stronger than even the blackest coffee, and he walks right past his quarters. He can't sleep like this. He doesn't want to look at the little room he's made a life in. He doesn't want to think about how small it is. Instead, he plunges into the woods and curses every errant fisherman who decided to make his living on the thrice cursed abominable ocean.

After a few minutes, he realizes he might be lost. He stops. The wind howls through the tops of the trees. If he dies out here, ripped to pieces by wolves or who knows, George will probably think him a coward.

As if the devil heard his thoughts and decided to make it so, a branch snaps somewhere behind him. Jaime turns, hand going to his hip, his pocketknife—he should have taken the rifle, he shouldn't be in the woods at all.

A man is standing under the trees.

For a moment, Jaime thinks George came after him, and his heart clenches, but then the figure moves. He's slimmer than George, hair longer, moving with an easy grace toward him.

"Thomas?" Jaime says, even though he knows it's impossible, hasn't seen Thomas in years, doesn't even know if he's still living.

"If that's what you want to call me." The figure steps closer. It's so clearly not Thomas that shame creeps hot and stark up Jaime's throat.

"Who—?"

"Just passing through," the man says, and he's close enough now that Jaime can see the startling red of his hair, trailing in wet tangles down his neck. "I got a little turned around. Do you know where a man can get something to eat near here?" Another step closer.

Jaime steps back.

"Somewhere warm?" The man smiles, slow. His accent is thick, Scottish or Irish, maybe, although it's the wrong coast for Celtic sailors. Jaime can't see the color of the man's eyes, can't see anything but the red of his hair and the way his shirt is stuck to him with rain, almost translucent. It's indecent.

"I don't—" Jaime swallows. His back hits the trunk of a tree. The man is beautiful. Unreal.

"I think you do," he says, and he's close enough now that Jaime can feel the heat of the words on his cheek.

"I—"

"It's all right. Nothing wrong about sheltering a stranger in a storm," the man says, and he raises his hand as if to stroke Jaime's cheek.

Jaime jerks away, hitting his head on the trunk.

"I'm sorry," he gets out, staggering a few steps away, enough to catch his breath, to just get some breathing room.

The man watches him, uncannily still.

"I can't," Jaime says. Later, he will be ashamed of the misery in his voice.

This time, when the man smiles, it's almost sad.

"Town is—if you follow the road, it's a few miles south."

The man nods. He runs a hand through his hair, pushing it off his slender neck, and then he's gone.

Jaime stares at the space between the trees for a long moment. It's worse, in a way, than when Thomas left. The sense of loss eats away at his insides. He wants to follow the man, to catch his hand, apologize again, take him back to his bed.

Instead, he turns. The way to the lighthouse seems obvious now, its faint glow visible even beneath the trees. It calls him home.

JAIME HADN'T BEEN an easy child for others to like. A tall, thin, quiet child who became a tall, thin, quiet man. His mother had called him careful, but boys at the schoolhouse had called him worse things, names that still crawl around his head when he's alone, polishing the glass Fresnel lens of the lighthouse hour after hour. Like now.

The storm has more or less passed with only one ship lost. They'll get the list of dead and missing tomorrow morning, or the morning after that.

Jaime is the aching kind of tired that surpasses exhaustion and becomes only weight. He doesn't dare sleep. So often, his dreams betray him, and he wakes sticky and guilt-ridden. He paces outside the lighthouse just before sunrise and watches the storm-rough waves crash on the beach below.

When he was young, when the other boys started to notice girls, Jaime had started noticing the length of Thomas's legs, the curve of his mouth. Things he shouldn't notice. They spent more time together than apart, Thomas passing out on his floor or on the end of his bed on those late nights when they came back from running through the woods, or from begging smokes off the men outside the tavern. Jaime had always made Thomas do the talking.

One night, he'd woken to Thomas next to him, the two of them pressed together back to front. Thomas had been awake.

The warm pad of Thomas's thumb over Jaime's mouth was electric. Magic. When he breathed in, Jaime breathed out. His skin tasted like salt. When Jaime turned to look at him, his green eyes in the darkness, cheeks pale and illuminated, everything was different. His mouth was wet, soft against Jaime's, and then it was something else. Heat. More natural, easier than breathing.

The Navy recruiters came to town the next morning. People are your whole life, and then they leave.

Jaime clenches and unclenches his cramping figures, taking a brief break to stare out at the sea. In the distance, lightning strikes, and for a second the whole landscape is illuminated. A dark silhouette stands at the edge of the beach, where the trees meet the sand.

Jaime's pulse quickens. He leans against the side of the light-house tower. Another flash. Now he's sure: there's something tall and misshapen moving on the beach.

He can hear himself breathing, air tearing through his ragged throat. He waits for the next stroke.

This time, he can tell it's looking up at him. He can also see that it isn't alone. There is a shape on the creature's back. Her skin and its hide are welded together but uneasy, liquid, at the seams. Jaime thinks he can see blood on her face.

He covers his mouth with his hands. It was dark, he couldn't know, he doesn't know—

The girl on the back of the horse-thing, the girl that is becoming part of the beast, is familiar.

Darkness again. When the next bolt of lightning flashes, the thing is gone.

Jaime presses himself to the glass of the lantern, but he can't see anything. The rain has stopped. Even the distant lightning has faded. There's nothing, just the sky and the still forest. Nothing was there.

When dawn comes, Jaime crawls into his bed without so much as taking off his boots. He closes his eyes, and he sees the red-haired man, remembers how hot his breath felt on Jaime's face.

HE WAKES TO rapid knocking on the storage-house door. It's George, inconsolable. Jera is missing.

He has to go to town to amass a search party, but someone must man the light. Jaime tells him not to think of it. Of course Jaime is capable, is more than willing. He can't imagine how George must feel. No, George should take the rifle.

"She snuck out," George says. "We found the window open. She was always too damn curious. Too smart for her own good." The words seem to spill out of him, like he can't stop trying to explain something to himself.

"I'm so sorry," Jaime says. It's all he can say.

George nods. He thanks Jaime, who burns all over with shame, too much a coward to tell George about the thing he saw on the beach.

EVERY NIGHT AFTER Jera's disappearance, Jaime climbs the steps, trims the wick, feeds the light, and polishes the Fresnel lens. He can't sleep for longer than a few hours at a stretch, fear turning acid in his stomach and waking him, over and over.

On the seventh night, the shadows follow him, reaching out when he climbs the stairs. It's nice to be reached for.

There's some rain, but nothing he would have to signal through, nothing to make him send for George. It splashes against the glass panels of the lantern, and Jaime is so, so tired. He leans against the glass, closing his eyes, promising himself he'll stand in just a few moments. He will stand, walk down the spiral steps, and then walk back up, and repeat until the night is over. He owes George that. He owes Jera that.

The light helps. It's bright enough he probably couldn't sleep, even if he wanted to. He tries to love that, to embrace it, but the resentment builds up in his chest. He can still see that distant figure illuminated, the silhouette from over a week ago haunting his nightmares, the flash of lightning revealing the grotesque details of the places that should've been human but weren't.

He shouldn't have seen it. He shouldn't have kept it from George. He shouldn't have become a keeper. He shouldn't have—

Thomas had asked him to come with, had begged him, on their last night together. Thomas had wanted him. When Jaime had still refused, when he couldn't, Thomas had kissed him, in front of God and the world. But Jaime couldn't make himself kiss back.

Thomas left because Jaime was a coward.

When Jaime opens his eyes, they're wet. The rain's stopped, and the sea is almost eerily still. There's something small on shore, right where the black waves meet the black sand. It looks wrong, too fleshy, too soft to be another wave-swept rock.

Ninety feet down spiral steps, and then longer for him to half run, half fall down the rocky path from the top of the headland to the beach. Jaime knows what he's going to find, but he has to look, anyway. He has to. For George.

On the beach, his boots sink into the sand with every step, like it's trying to suck him under, but he slogs through, doesn't let himself stop until he can see.

The shape in the sand is a pair of human lungs. They're still glistening with blood and salt water, perfectly intact, and small. What someone with dark thoughts might expect to find inside a young girl.

Jaime's knees hit the sand, water instantly soaking through the fabric of his trousers, but he barely notices. He gags, forces himself to swallow, then gags again.

In his head, he can see the place where her hands stopped and the creature began, that bloody in-between space. It was ugly, but Jera had been smiling. She'd looked like a wild thing. Free at last.

Jaime wants to be brave like that—like her, like Thomas.

Out to sea, somewhere close to the end of the light's reach, a wave crashes out of sync. At the edge of his vision, a dark shape crests, breaking the surface of the water. It could be a whale. It could be a ship, half drowned, or a girl with blood on her teeth. A creature that no longer needs lungs.

The organs feel fragile in his hands. Jaime holds them up to his lips. The membrane is soft. The lungs smell wrong, not like decay, nor coated with the salt-slime of the ocean; their scent is almost sweet. Saliva pools on his tongue.

The outer layer is tough, so he bites down hard, tearing the flesh with his teeth. The taste of blood, of salt, is heavy on his tongue. He swallows anyway. The tips of his fingers are numb, the feeling spreading down his hands, his arms, as he takes another bite. He has never tasted anything so rich.

The taste coats the inside of his mouth, spreading to his sinuses. His eyelashes are wet. The ocean around him is silent, unnaturally still. Jaime crouches on the beach, bringing chunks of lung tissue to his mouth, swallowing, until there is nothing left to consume.

When Jaime looks up, the creature is standing only a few feet from him. The huge horse-thing, its long, red mane trailing seaweed and kelp, is familiar and not, all at once.

Jaime stands up and steps toward it. The horse steps back. Jaime feels his own mouth twist, a rictus of a smile. He takes another step. Water swirls around his calves. The creature takes another step backward, and together, they walk into the depths.

⚓

DUALHAVEN

C. H. Pearce

I LUG MY suitcase along the station platform in the night-dark afternoon. It's drizzling, and the air is salt and cold.

The wheels of my suitcase rattle on the concrete so loudly I wince, as if there were anyone for me to disturb. The puddles I splash through are dark oil slicks in the yellow light of a shop window.

There's a woman in silhouette—but I realize in an instant I'm mistaken. It's a streetlamp, thick, slightly curved. I feel ridiculous.

Every year, on January 2nd, my friend Alice and I meet in the old hotel by the sea at Dualhaven. Our respective families began the tradition. When we outgrew our family holidays and childhood homes, Al and I made the pilgrimage alone. Her brother joined us one year, but he never visited again. Each year the sea level rises a little higher. The dampness problem in the hotel worsens. The tourists thin. The long-faced locals thin, too.

I'm twenty-two, in uni, studying a major which makes people ask if I'm *absolutely sure* that's a good idea. I'm making enough from my part-time work for this annual holiday.

Al has missed the last two years.

Her drunk-texts sound like this, at 4 a.m., two months ago:

> **Al:** *you wish i was someone else, don't you?*
>
> **CeCe:** *No! Of course not. I just wish you were happier.*
>
> **Al:** *fuck you*
>
> **CeCe:** *I want you to be happy because I care about you. That's what I meant.*
>
> **Al:** *don't say that a third time unless you mean it.*

I'm worried about her. I message her as frequently as ever, but she rarely responds. When she does text me back, it's at odd hours, and she sounds…like that. Every question a test for me to fail. I'm not sure if she's having problems, or outgrowing our friendship. I'm not sure if she needs me here more than ever, or needs me gone.

Is she telling me to move on?

I reach the stairs leading down to the street—the elevator is out—and contemplate whether to carry my luggage or drag it.

If that's the case, perhaps she could just tell me, so I don't spend a week alone here every year, waiting for a friend who never shows.

A worse thought, worse than anything: *Is she dead?* She isn't. I check her social media regularly. Even her professional account, which I fear automatically notifies "Alice Leach" that "Cat 'CeCe' Chester" viewed her profile.

I make the pilgrimages anyway. I couldn't live with myself if I missed my chance to see her again. *Especially* if she isn't doing well and needs my help. I don't mind. I can study. I can decompress after a fraught family Christmas. I like being alone.

I see her walking toward me along the shop-lined street as I bump my bag down the steps. A curvy young woman with long, black hair, tousled over her face like she wants to hide behind it. Is she smiling? Al never smiles.

"Al," I call, grinning, waving both arms frantically above my head. My suitcase *bump-bump-bumps* the rest of the way down the stairs and splashes sadly into a puddle. I run down and prop it upright.

When I look up, she's—not her. It's a stranger staring at me, shaking her head fractionally. She laughs once, a puff of breath in the cold, almost a sigh. Perhaps she thinks I'm drunk. She walks on.

My face burns. Waving like that to a stranger and dropping my bag in front of them! I'd know my Al anywhere. The stranger looked a little like the Al I remember—but that only makes my mistake less forgivable, because she was the wrong age, and Al has diverged from that particular look with time. From her social media, Al is currently a cherub-faced, smirking twenty-two-year-old with an undercut who's flirting with being a goth but can't commit.

I use the maps app on my phone to find the hotel, even though I've been coming here every year since I was five, and I could in theory follow the faint roar of the sea. Directional sense isn't my strong suit. Drops of rain spot my phone and make me nervous I'll damage it. I return it to my raincoat pocket.

I FIND THE hotel after longer than I'd like to admit—at the abrupt end of a street on the shoreline, the short cliff and beach curving out below.

The waterline laps at the first houses in the street, and at the hotel veranda. The old beach and the rock pools are now several meters under black water. What would it be like to dive under there? On a clear day, obviously, not in this light. Somehow, I can't imagine there are clear days anymore. The ones I remember seem superimposed, a page out of someone else's scrapbook of a different childhood, a different beach, two different girls having a different fumbling first kiss, each pretending to close their eyes.

There are no lights on in any of the houses in the street. They used to be holiday rentals, leading up to the grand beachfront hotel that stands like an exclamation point on the shoreline, and they were almost always occupied.

There is a single light on in the hotel. I hurry on.

I PUSH THROUGH the heavy door to reception, dripping wet. My shoes squelch.

Inside, it's warm and yellow-bright, with a musty smell I recognize as mold.

I decide this will be my last year. I decide this every year. In a year or two, the rising sea levels will take my decision from me; perhaps it would be psychologically healthier if I give myself the illusion of control by making the decision first—

I ring the bell on the empty counter.

Blinking furiously, I push my sodden hair from my eyes.

The receptionist is here. He was here all along, behind the counter in the half-light. I feel silly.

He looks ten years older than when I saw him last year. His mustache has turned white. His face is thinner, saggier.

"Sorry, Bill. I didn't see you there. You're looking well," I lie.

Bill stares blankly. His eyes are clouded.

"It's me. CeCe? I booked under Cat Chester, but you might remember me as CeCe? Like the chips? I'm checking in, please."

Bill blinks. He shakes his head and hands me my key. It's number four. My usual room. A family room, the one my little brother and my parents and I always took. I only need a single, but I'm sentimental. That, and I worry Al won't be able to find me if I switch rooms.

"Any other guests?" I ask hopefully. Al would normally take room six, the adjoining room, but the last time I saw her—three years ago—she took a single at the other end of the hotel. She said the whole thing about the rooms was rot and sentiment, and she, for one, preferred *not* to be reminded of her fucking family. I wasn't sure what to do with her anger, not when she's more concerned with presenting a certain front to her family than I am.

Bill waves a pale hand. His eyes water—less like tears, more like he's leaking. I presume this is a sensitive topic. There are hundreds of rooms, empty. I'm worried he'll cry if I press him on the matter of the number of guests, and the town's decline, so I leave.

AT THE END of the first-floor hallway, there she is, and my heart gutters like a sputtering lamp. Plush carpet gives under my shoes, soft as new grass, a yellow lamp casts huge shadows, and a sour-faced woman stands facing me, dwarfed by her outsize jacket, hands thrust deep in her pockets. I'm so happy to see her I think I'm going to die. The force of it frightens me, like I'm drowning. I grin at Al from the other end of the hall.

Her white front teeth peek out in a small smile, the most Al ever does in the way of smiling. She's cut her hair short, one side buzzed in an undercut, the other tumbling loose to cover her left eye. I knew she'd changed her hair from when I stalked her on social media. How could I have imagined the laughing stranger was her?

"Hey," I say, and advance on her at a run, gather her in my arms, squeeze her tight and kiss her neck before I can stop myself. She's warm and heavy. She smells wonderful, even in the mustiness of this place. Like smoke and her cooking and coming home.

Al makes a wheezing sound. She pushes me away. "Hey," she says weakly, voice low and raspier than I remember. She pushes her fringe from her eyes, and it immediately flops back again.

"That must get annoying. It looks good, though. Your hair. Have you had dinner?" I babble. "Bill seemed—It doesn't matter. We'll rustle up something. God, it's so good to see you. Do you want to have a sleepover? We could see who's got the best room. Or we could open the adjoining door and join our rooms together, like we used to."

Al doesn't respond. I keep talking like a train rolling over a body. I can't stop myself. I'm so happy it feels wrong, like my heart is going to beat right out of my chest. I don't care.

Al's heavy brows knit together. She regards me intently, brown eyes bright. Her mouth is downturned, but it quirks slightly. She's difficult to read.

"It's miserable here," she says eventually, her affected low voice all coolness and vocal fry. I wonder what her real voice sounds like. I asked her once, and she took offense. *This is my real voice, loser.* "My room stinks like wet dog. I'll bring my things to yours. Yours has to be better."

"Maybe Bill will give you a refund," I suggest, but she purses her lips. Maybe he won't. Or maybe it's better if we maintain appearances, because we don't know what people are like here, even though there seem to be two souls left in the whole town, apart from us.

"I packed snacks," I add, which clinches it. My voice is tremulous. I couldn't affect half Al's coolness if I tried. I never want to leave.

WE SETTLE IN my room. I have a hot shower in a bathroom so scungy I regret not bringing flip flops, and dress warmly in my pajamas. I close the ensuite door behind me, the wood warped with damp under my fingers.

Al sits cross-legged on the carpet, toying with the contents of the minibar. She doesn't look up.

I sit on the carpet beside Al and grin at her. I spread out our snacks—Al has already raided the minibar and laid out the little bottles of assorted alcohol like tiny families. I ask if she wants to watch TV.

The rooms haven't changed—there's a television, a mini -fridge, two beds, a wardrobe, and an age-spotted full-length mirror. There is a window with the curtains open, which looks out to sea but by this light appears to look out to rain-spattered void.

I want to kiss her. I don't, because the last time I did that, I didn't see her again for three years. Though I'm wary of calling it cause and effect; surely, if she'd had a problem kissing me, she'd have left after the first time, when we were fifteen.

I've gone on dates since Al was in absentia, with three pushy boys and one shy girl—separately, obviously—but not one of them was a patch on my Al, not one. I can't remember their names or faces with any degree of certainty. The others were like kissing my own reflection in the mirror. Like sitting across the table from a shop-window dummy. None of them made my heart skip a beat or my breath quicken or even made an impression in my memory that wasn't washed away as easily as footprints in sand. The only way I could get through more than one date with any of them was by peeking through my half-lidded eyes and imagining I was with Al.

"You're such a loser," Al says, lips quirking with her ghost of a smile, and I wonder if she's reading my mind.

Al tears open a packet of skittles and offers me the pack. The rain pelts outside. The sea roars. The room shakes. I love the sound. With the other hand, she deftly uncaps a mini-bottle of Jack Daniels and proffers that to me, too.

I check her wrists, but it's difficult to glimpse the skin under her long sleeves. I think it's old scar tissue. I think she's doing okay. I'll push up her sleeves later, incidentally.

I take the bottle and pop a skittle in my mouth to stop myself saying something stupid. It's sour.

"IF YOU MET your double," Al slurs, her face flushed, setting down an emptied mini-bottle of vodka with wonderful elegance next to all the other mini-bottles, "what would you do? Would you kill it? Or would you, you know, do it?"

She smacks her wet lips. She's emptied the minibar while I'm still nursing the Jack Daniels, wrinkling up my face whenever I take a sip, then forgetting and doing it again.

"Neither." I'm perplexed. "I'd be friends with my double. We'd get on, obviously. We'd enjoy all the same things. We could have our introvert time together..."

I realize belatedly that Al asking me was nothing but a precursor to her own planned answer—that she was never interested in hearing my rambling response. My face burns. I ask politely: "Why, what would *you* do?"

"I'd do it, then kill it," she says instantly. "Doing it with your double is purely masturbation. Killing it is suicide, not murder. But if I was feeling risk-averse, I'd kill it straightaway, no messing about."

"*Alice.*" I giggle hysterically despite myself, leaning forward to squeeze her hand, knowing she's only saying this to shock me. For attention. Adults and peers who professed to love Al often said that about her. That she does these terrible things, says these terrible things, for attention. It would make me so angry I'd go bright red and couldn't speak. *If—if—she'll do these things for attention*, I'd imagine shouting back to the adults around me, but only once brave enough to do it, and then it came out a squeak, *then perhaps we should give her some goddamned attention?*

"Do you want a hug?" I ask.

She eyes the black-spotted mirror on the wall like a personal enemy. It's an old mirror. Our reflections are slightly warped.

"If you could have me, but better," she asks, "perfect, like me but *nicer*, smarter, happier, better adjusted, more reliable, and without the scars and the drama and fucking off for several years at a time, would you?"

"That's a trick question," I say quickly. Everything is screaming, *Shut it down.* "I just want you to be happy."

She frowns at me. Like I've failed. Goddamn it, she doesn't like it when I prescribe happiness; I should have remembered.

"Let's go to the beach tomorrow," I say, trying to change the subject.

Al yawns performatively and climbs into bed.

I slip in beside her under the covers and throw an arm and leg around her, but she pretends to be asleep.

304 • C. H. PEARCE

As I drift off to the roar of the storm and the waves, I remember the beach no longer exists. There is nowhere to go.

IN THE GRAY morning before sunrise, Al and I have breakfast on the veranda, which used to look out over the beach. I'd normally sleep in, but she's an early riser, and I want all the time I can get with her. The water laps at the edge of the wooden beams and occasionally slops over our shoes.

"There won't be a next year." Al stubs out her cigarette in the ashtray.

"Yeah, but you didn't have to say it." I don't like how my voice comes out a whine.

Bill brings us toast and butter and jam, fruit salad, eggs, orange juice and coffee. I wonder if we are getting all the food intended for other guests who never came. I taste a forkful of omelet, half-expecting it to taste of wet rot, like the hotel smells.

It's lovely, a burst of flavor in my mouth, even lovelier, perhaps, for my abysmally low expectations.

"Delicious," I tell Bill, failing to keep the surprise from my voice. "I'll leave a glowing review."

Not that it will matter. I want to ask Bill his plans for the hotel, but watching his haggard face and leaking eyes, I'm again too afraid he might cry. He shuffles away.

AFTER BREAKFAST, AL gets up and goes to the veranda railing. The breeze catches her T-shirt, puffing it up slightly. She slings a leg over and drops, splashing into the sea like a stone.

She's fully submerged. The water ripples. She doesn't come up. I can't see her—I can't see a thing in the murky water.

I kick off my boots, clamber over the railing, and jump in after her without thinking. It's ice cold. I cut my heel on something sharp as a tooth.

The water is dark. The salt and grit stings my eyes.

I thrash about, feeling for Al, but I can't find her.

My lungs burn. I surface and take greedy gulps of air, ready to dive again. My heart is pounding. Blood rushes in my ears.

Al is bobbing in the water beside me, quite calmly, her black hair plastered to her skull. She dog paddles.

I smile, awash with relief. I'm too breathless to speak. What would I say?

I overreacted.

It doesn't trouble me—that she made me think the worst, or that I thought the worst all on my own. I'm just happy everything is all right. The sun is rising red and watery, the splash of color embarrassingly half-hearted, like spilt soup spreading over the carpet and gathering dust. My heel burns.

She smiles back. I've never seen such a smile from Al.

Was she testing me to see if I'd immediately jump in after her? I know this time I passed.

WE CHANGE CLOTHES, then walk into town, hands interlinked, which shouldn't thrill me as much as it does, given there is no one here to observe us. Presumably this is why Al is holding my hand. Perhaps Dualhaven is our special place where we can be ourselves. I can be myself anywhere—I'm no good at not being myself when I *try*—but Al can't.

I try not to think about next year. I try not to think about a week from now, when our holiday is over. I squeeze her plump, cool hand. Mine is sweaty.

We pick our way through empty suburbia and abandoned shopfronts. My foot throbs awfully. I disguise my wince as a smile. I'm too happy she's holding my hand to risk her thinking I feel otherwise.

IN THE AFTERNOON, we return to our room. I shower and remember I need to dress the wound on my heel. There are yellowish bandages and nail scissors in the bathroom cabinet. Perhaps the salt water disinfected the wound—no, the water was clouded with grit and detritus, and it stank. I doubt salt would cancel that out.

It's a deeper cut than I initially thought. Tears sting my eyes, and I wish I'd packed a first aid kit. As I'm hopping on one foot on the slippery tiles and fumbling with the bandage, Al pushes the door open and walks into the bathroom, polite as you like, as if I'm not naked and bleeding and struggling to keep my balance.

She takes over bandaging my heel.

"Is that a mushroom?" asks Al absently.

"*Where?*" I peer at my injured foot in horror.

"In the gap under the door." Giggling, she cocks her head. There's a pale mushroom the size of my thumb sprouting in the rotten wood where the tiles fail to meet carpet. It seems obvious now, but I don't remember seeing any sign of it yesterday.

Her fingers are wet and cold when they brush my skin as she winds the bandage. She's being sweet, letting my silly assumption about the mushroom go. Why on earth was my first thought that it was growing out of *me*? Normally she'd milk that for days.

When she's done, she kisses the skin of my ankle, above the line of my bandage.

I begin to say something about how she ought to knock, next time, but the words die on my lips.

WE SPEND THE following days in bed together. Al likes to have the lights down and the covers over us. She smiles and laughs. We get room service. At several points, I wonder whether I have died. I hope I have, because if I haven't, this will end.

I have a sense of unreality. Is it because of the hotel? Or because I cannot accept a good thing is happening to me?

ON THE MORNING of the third day, I wake beside Al, hazy-happy. I trace her cheek. Her skin is soft and damp, her hair clinging to her pale skull, like when she emerged from the water. She smiles blearily.

"You haven't called me a loser in days," I observe.

Her smile drops.

"My mouth's been busy," she says flatly, and I laugh reflexively, but something is wrong. Al has these ups and downs to her moods—that's normal—but she's been *up* for unusually long.

I catch her wrists in my hands under the covers and trace the skin. I look into her eyes, so as not to draw attention.

There's no fresh scarring.

There's no *old* scarring either. Her skin feels perfectly smooth under my fingers.

I keep smiling. I kiss her.

I don't need to look. I know.

It's not my Al.

I WAIT UNTIL I am sure the thing in my bed is asleep.

I creep out into the hallway in my nightie. My bare feet fall softly on the waterlogged carpet. My heel throbs.

I go to the veranda. The water is calm. The sun will rise soon.

I slip quietly over the veranda railing, and drop down into the freezing water.

I want the old one back. My Al. I'd do anything to get the old one back.

I dive again, and again. I swim fruitless laps. I cut my other foot—the ankle, this time. I begin to shiver.

THE SUN RISES.

Not-Al pads out onto the veranda in her dressing gown. She yawns and stretches. She sits at the breakfast table and eyes me languidly. She smiles.

"Dip before breakfast?" she asks. "Looks cold as balls."

If I want the old one back, do I have to get rid of this one?

Do I have to get rid of her?

"Come join me," I say, teeth chattering, passing my nervousness off as cold. "It's—bracing, I guess. You work up an appetite. Then we'll have breakfast."

The other Al, the one who made me happy and never said an unkind word to me, tilts her head.

Not-Al smiles hugely. She sheds her robe, drapes it on the back of the chair, vaults the veranda railing, and slips down into the water like a stone.

When she is submerged, I follow, searching.

ACKNOWLEDGMENTS

⚓

AN ANTHOLOGY IS created by a team, and I was so honored to work with an incredible group of insightful and passionate first readers on this one. A special thank you to my trio of Weird-fiction aficionados, Zach Gillan, Ende Mac, and Rebecca Summerling, who spent so many long evenings reading, drinking tea, and discussing stories with me. I loved every minute, and I could not have made it through all the challenges of this project without you. And of course, a huge thank you to the whole first-reader team: Marie Croke, Alayna Frankenberry, Anna Madden, Bryce Meerhaeghe, and Marie Villa. Your insights all made this book what it is.

Thank you to the brilliant writers whose stories appear here and to all those who submitted. And to Dark Matter, for being so enthusiastic about this pitch and giving me the opportunity to make this vision a reality.

Last but not least, thank you to my parents Eddie and Christine, who took my sisters and I out to the coasts every chance they could. I wish I lived closer to you so we could take a walk around the rocks at Piha, watch the gannets dive at Muriwai, and get fish and chips at sunset. Those many wanders inspired my love for nature and the theme for this anthology. I carry those black-sand, windswept coastlines in my heart always, along with both of you.

—Marissa van Uden

ABOUT THE AUTHORS

Mars Abian is a Filipino speculative writer and digital artist known as Flairiart. She graduated cum laude in BA Literature from the University of Santo Tomas, Manila, Philippines. Her artwork often showcases the mythical and the fantastical and has appeared on the cover of *Factor Four Magazine*'s September 2023 issue.

Alex Keikiakapueo Brewster is a mixed Kanaka Maoli (Native Hawaiian) spreadsheet operator from California currently residing on Acjachemen lands. When not reading moʻolelo, they can often be found despairing at the cubicle or hiding from their emails in the stairwell.

Raymonde Chira is a writer-artist of dark short stories and comic zines from New York City. Her past publications can be found in *Djed Press, Ghost Parachute,* and *Let Her Be Evil: A Comics Anthology.*

Santiago Eximeno (Madrid, Spain) is a Spanish genre writer who has published several novellas and collections, mainly horror literature. His work has been translated to English, Japanese, French or Bulgarian. He is a HWA Active Member. His last collection published in English is *Umbria*, by Independent Legions Publishing.

Adriana C. Grigore is a writer from the windswept plains of Romania. They have a degree in language and literature, a penchant for folklore, and a tendency to overwater houseplants. You can find their fiction in *Clarkesworld*, *Beneath Ceaseless Skies*, *The Magazine of Fantasy & Science Fiction*, and others.

Íde Hennessy (she/they) haunts the shores of rural Northern California, where she lives with her partner and a blind cat who can see ghosts. Her writing has appeared in or is forthcoming in *Cosmic Horror Monthly*, Apex's *Strange Machines* anthology, *Reckoning*, *Fusion Fragment*, and more. She also writes lyrics for and performs with sci-fi-themed darkwave band Control Voltage.

K. A. Honeywell is a fiction writer who lives in the Pacific Northwest. Her work includes short stories, the novel *Damn Wilds*, and the novella *Veiled Scarlet*.

Wailana Kalama is a dark fiction writer from Hawaii, with credits in Weird Little World's *Mother: Tales of Love and Terror*, *Pseudopod*, *The Maul*, *Apparition Lit*, *Rock and a Hard Place*, *Dark Matter Presents: Monstrous Futures*, and *Dark Matter Presents: Monster Lairs*.

Sloane Leong is a cartoonist, illustrator, art director, narrative game designer, writer, and editor of mixed indigenous ancestry. Through her work, she engages with visceral futurities and fantasies through a radical, kaleidoscopic lens. She is currently living on Chinook land near what is known as Portland, Oregon with her family and two dogs.

Anna Lewis writes stories about yearning, power and magic. She has previously been published in *Clavmag, Speculative Cities* and *The Isis*, and is working on a novel about wealthy university students who use magic to manipulate and beguile. She lives in London and works as a climate justice campaigner.

Avra Margariti is a queer author and Pushcart-nominated poet with a fondness for the dark and the darling. Avra's work haunts publications such as *Vastarien, Asimov's, Liminality, Arsenika, The Future Fire, Space and Time, Lackington's,* and *Glittership.* Avra lives and studies in Athens, Greece. You can find Avra on X @avramargariti.

J. A. W. McCarthy is the Bram Stoker Award and Shirley Jackson Award nominated author of *Sometimes We're Cruel and Other Stories* (Cemetery Gates Media, 2021) and *Sleep Alone* (Off Limits Press, 2023). Her short fiction has appeared in numerous publications, including *Vastarien, PseudoPod, Split Scream Vol. 3, Apparition Lit, Tales to Terrify,* and *The Best Horror of the Year Vol 13* (ed. Ellen Datlow). She is Thai American and lives with her spouse and assistant cats in the Pacific Northwest. You can call her Jen on X @JAWMcCarthy, and find out more at jawmccarthy.com.

Amanda Minkkinen is a sociologist and writer from Copenhagen. She has work published in *Mycelia, Odd Magazine,* among others. You can find her on Instagram and X as @aljminkkinen.

Samir Sirk Morató is a scientist, artist, and flesh heap. Some of their published and forthcoming work can be found in *TOWER Magazine, ergot., Seize the Press,* and Neon Hemlock. Above all, Samir writes about meat.

Jacy Morris is an Indigenous author and a registered member of the Confederated Tribes of Siletz. At the age of ten he was transplanted to Portland, Oregon, where he developed a love for punk rock and horror movies, both of which tend to find their way into his writing. He has written several books, including the *This Rotten World* series, *The One Night Stand at the End of the World* series, The Drop, and *The Enemies of Our Ancestors* series. In his spare time, he enjoys helping writers build their writing careers as a writing coach.

Tiffany Morris is an L'nu'skw (Mi'kmaw) writer from Nova Scotia. She is the author of the Ignyte, Indigenous Voices, Shirley Jackson, and Aurora award-nominated *Green Fuse Burning* (Stelliform Press, 2023) and the Elgin Award-winning horror poetry collection *Elegies of Rotting Stars* (Nictitating Books, 2022). Her work has appeared in the Indigenous horror anthology *Never Whistle At Night,* as well as in *Nightmare Magazine, Uncanny Magazine,* and *Apex Magazine,* among others.

Karter Mycroft is an author, musician, and ocean scientist from Los Angeles. Their short fiction has appeared in *F&SF,* Flame Tree Press, *Apocalypse Confidential,* and elsewhere. In 2022, Karter co-released the "Los Suelos, CA" project, a multimedia anthology benefiting marginalized laborers in California. Karter is currently working on some songs and a book.

J. P. Oakes is a pseudonym for Jonathan Wood, who is the author of eight novels (*The Hero* series, *The Dragon Lords* series writing as Jon Hollins, and *City of Iron and Dust* as J.P. Oakes). When not writing he spends far too much time playing video games and sharing memes on Facebook while society collapses around him. He can be found online at jonathanwood.substack.com.

Zachary Olson is a writer and freelance composer based out of Phoenix, Arizona. After many years of telling stories with his friends through tabletop role-playing, he decided he hadn't inflicted his ideas on enough people. Now he's made it your problem.

C. H. Pearce is an artist and an Aurealis, Ditmar and Brave New Weird Award-nominated writer of horror-tinged speculative fiction from Canberra, Australia. Her short fiction has been published in *Body of Work* anthology, *Aurealis*, *Cosmic Horror Monthly*, and more. She's currently on submission with a novel set in the same world as "Dualhaven." Find her work and links to social media on chpearce.net.

James Pollard is making his publishing debut with Dark Matter INK. He lives, parents, and works in Oklahoma, where millions of competing realities may, or may not, exist.

Dave V. Riser is a gender ghoul currently pursuing an English PhD at University of Pittsburgh. His short fiction has appeared in *The Arkansas International* and in the *Brave Boy World* anthology by Pink Narcissus Press.

Richard Thomas Richard Thomas is the award-winning author of eight books: four novels—*Incarnate, Breaker, Disintegration,* and *Transubstantiate*; as well as four collections—*Spontaneous Human Combustion, Tribulations, Staring Into the Abyss,* and *Herniated Roots*. He has been nominated for the Bram Stoker (twice), Shirley Jackson, Thriller, and Audie awards. His over 175 stories in print include *The Best Horror of the Year* (Volume Eleven), *Cemetery Dance* (twice), *Behold!: Oddities, Curiosities and Undefinable Wonders* (Bram Stoker Award winner), *The Hideous Book of Hidden Horrors* (Shirley Jackson Award winner), *Weird Fiction Review, The Seven Deadliest, Gutted: Beautiful Horror Stories, Qualia Nous* (#1&2), *Chiral Mad* (#2-4), *PRISMS*, and *Shivers VI*. He has also edited five anthologies. Visit whatdoesnotkillme.com for more information.

Kay Vaindal is a coastal ecologist and fan of weird fiction, whose work has appeared or is forthcoming in *Dark Matter Magazine, Seize the Press,* and anthologies including *This World Belongs to Us, Thank You For Joining the Algorithm,* and *Dark Matter Presents: The Off-Season.* Kay's favorite biomes are sagebrush steppe and brackish wetland.

Hazel Zorn is an American SFF and horror author. Her non-fiction criticism, "No Excuses for AI Art" can be found in *Blood Knife*. Her debut novel is forthcoming from Tenebrous Press. She spends her days as a freelance oil painter and Fine Arts teacher. Website: hazelzorn.com.

ABOUT THE EDITOR

MARISSA VAN UDEN is from Aotearoa New Zealand, but made her second home in Germany. She now lives in northern Vermont, in a cabin in the woods. When she's not communing with wildlife or taking photos, you can find her writing, editing, or reading dark speculative fiction, especially of the Weird variety. She is the Editor-in-Chief for Violet Lichen (Apex Books), freelance manuscript editor, and an active member of the HWA. She posts on X @marissavu and Instagram @marissa.vu.

ABOUT THE COVER ARTIST

SYLVIA STRIJK is a Dutch fantasy artist who blends traditional and digital techniques to create enchanting artwork. Inspired by mythology, fantasy stories, and the beauty of nature, her ethereal female figures gracefully blend with the natural world to create a dialogue between beauty and the mysteries of nature. Her works often explore the delicate balance between beauty and horror, embracing the life and death cycle.

Sylvia's art has graced book covers, posters, and advertisements, and adorned the walls of galleries worldwide. Her impactful creations have found recognition in publications and art fairs, solidifying Sylvia Strijk as an artist whose work resonates globally.

⚓

PERMISSIONS

"The Beach House with Its Back to the Sea" by Íde Hennessy, copyright © 2024 Íde Hennessy. Used by permission of the author.

"The Ocean Vomits What We Discard" by J. A. W. McCarthy, copyright © 2024 J. A. W. McCarthy. Used by permission of the author.

"Sunk" by Richard Thomas, copyright © 2024 Richard Thomas. Used by permission of the author.

"Thumbs Up" by Anna Lewis, copyright © 2024 Anna Lewis. Used by permission of the author.

"EACH-UISGE" by Dave V. Riser, copyright © 2024 Dave V. Riser. Used by permission of the authors.

"Dualhaven" by C. H. Pearce, copyright © 2024 C. H. Pearce. Used by permission of the author.

Frost Bite by Angela Sylvaine
ISBN 978-1-958598-03-0

Free Burn by Drew Huff
ISBN 978-1-958598-26-9

The House at the End of Lacelean Street
by Catherine McCarthy
ISBN 978-1-958598-23-8

When the Gods Are Away by Robert E. Harpold
ISBN 978-1-958598-47-4

The Dead Spot: Stories of Lost Girls
by Angela Sylvaine
ISBN 978-1-958598-27-6

Grim Root by Bonnie Jo Stufflebeam
ISBN 978-1-958598-36-8

Voracious by Belicia Rhea
ISBN 978-1-958598-25-2

The Bleed by Stephen S. Schreffler
ISBN 978-1-958598-11-5

Chopping Spree by Angela Sylvaine
ISBN 978-1-958598-31-3

Saturday Fright at the Movies
by Amanda Cecelia Lang
ISBN 978-1-958598-75-7

The Threshing Floor by Steph Nelson
ISBN 978-1-958598-49-8

Club Contango by Eliane Boey
ISBN 978-1-958598-57-3

The Divine Flesh by Drew Huff
ISBN 978-1-958598-59-7

Psychopomp by Maria Dong
ISBN 978-1-958598-52-8

Disgraced Return of the Kap's Needle
by Renan Bernardo
ISBN 978-1-958598-74-0

Haunted Reels 2: More Stories from the Minds of Professional Filmmakers Curated by David Lawson
ISBN 978-1-958598-53-5

Dark Circuitry by Kirk Bueckert
ISBN 978-1-958598-48-1

Soul Couriers by Caleb Stephens
ISBN 978-1-958598-76-4

Abducted by Patrick Barb
ISBN 978-1-958598-37-5

Cyanide Constellations and Other Stories
by Sara Tantlinger
ISBN 978-1-958598-81-8

Little Red Flags: Stories of Cults, Cons, and Control
Edited by Noelle W. Ihli & Steph Nelson
ISBN 978-1-958598-54-2

Frost Bite 2 by Angela Sylvaine
ISBN 978-1-958598-55-9

The Starship, from a Distance by Robert E. Harpold
ISBN 978-1-958598-82-5

Dark Matter Presents: Fear City
ISBN 978-1-958598-90-0

Part of the Dark Hart Collection

Rootwork by Tracy Cross
ISBN 978-1-958598-01-6

Mosaic by Catherine McCarthy
ISBN 978-1-958598-06-1

Apparitions by Adam Pottle
ISBN 978-1-958598-18-4

I Can See Your Lies by Izzy Lee
ISBN 978-1-958598-28-3

A Gathering of Weapons by Tracy Cross
ISBN 978-1-958598-38-2